SOULSEEKER

Fall of the Enclave, Book II

A Seven Realms Universe book

Written by Emily Lankow

This is a work of fiction. Names, characters, business, events and incidents are the products of the author's imagination. Any resemblance to actual persons, living or dead, or actual events is purely coincidental.

Summary: After months of struggling to survive alone after her twin brother Monroe is murdered by a corrupt ruling group of magic wielders, Monica finds an unlikely friend in a human boy named Finn, whom she swears to protect when the two get unexpectedly stranded in the dangerous magic realm.

Content advisory: This series contains mentions of murder, slavery, child abuse, magically coerced suicide, death of a main character's family members, death of a childhood friend, and sexual themes. Please do not read if this content will cause you distress.

ISBN: 978-1-961958-02-9 (Amazon edition)
Imprint: Independently published

Written by Emily Lankow
Editing by Grace Augustine (A Touch of Grace Editing)
Amulet model for cover by Dawn Spears (dawnydawny.com)
Cover by Karen Dimmick (Arcane Covers)
Map drawn by Emily Lankow

First paperback edition, 2024

Books in this series:

Riftrider- FALL OF THE ENCLAVE, BOOK I
Soulseeker- FALL OF THE ENCLAVE, BOOK II
Deathbringer- FALL OF THE ENCLAVE, BOOK III
Fatechanger- FALL OF THE ENCLAVE, BOOK IIII

These books are part of the Seven Realms Universe

Pronunciation guide

Amadarus: Ah-mah-DAR-us
Arkynesta: Ar-KIN-es-tah
Crognak: Crog-nack (crog sounds like frog)
Dahvi: DAH-vee
Elandis: El-lan-dis
Enderfel: En-der-fell
Grunnar: Groo-nar
Haedahl: Hey-doll
Maal: Mahl or Mall
Maalavario: Mall-luh-vaR-ee-Oh
Scondera: SCON-dare-ah
Stenna: Sten-nah
Vhalta: Vault-ah
Vhenra: Ven-rah
Wurick: Whir-rick

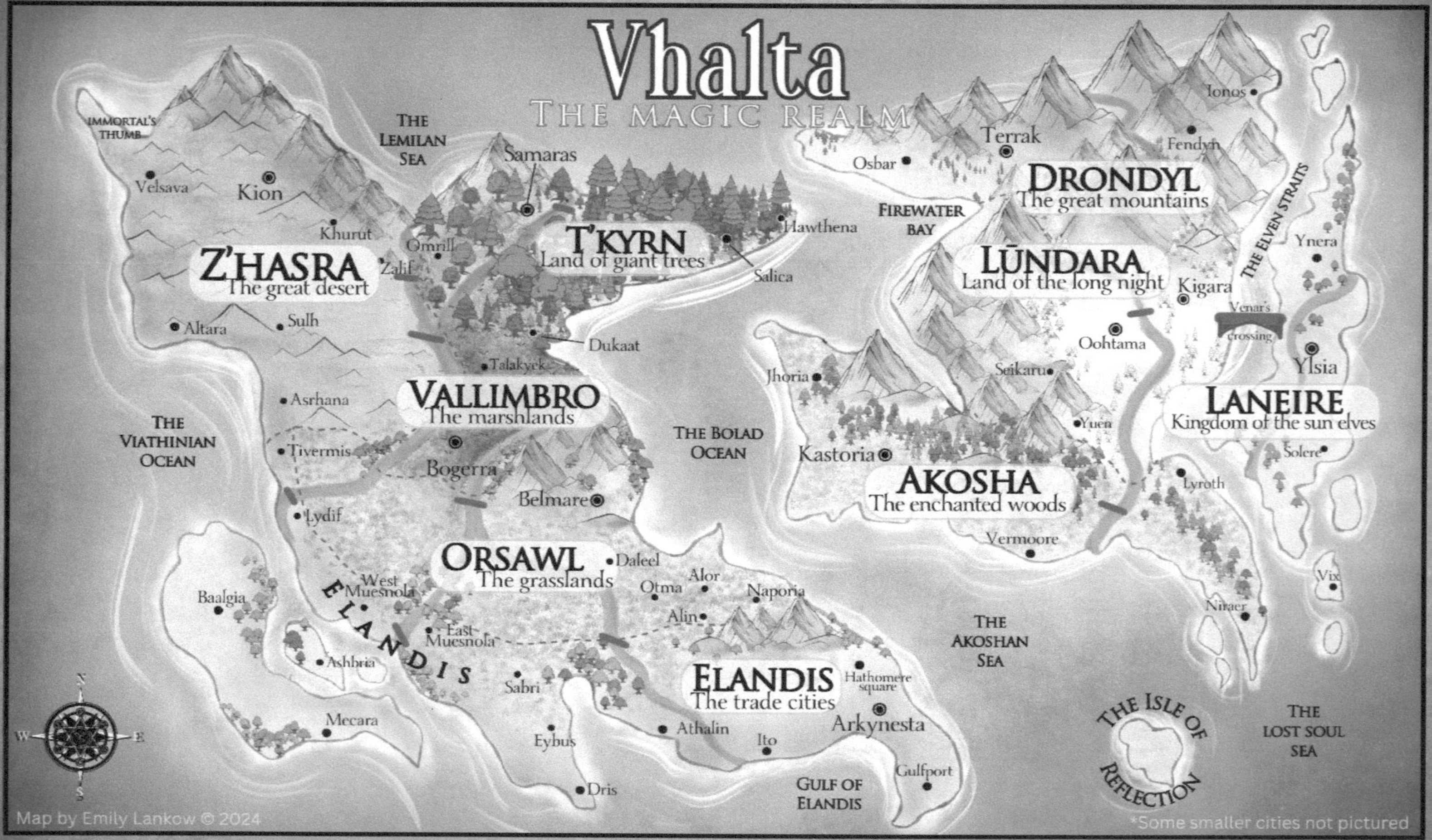

Vhalta

THE MAGIC REALM

IMMORTAL'S THUMB
THE LEMILAN SEA
Velsava
Kion
Khurut
Samaras
Omrill
Zalif
Hawthena
Salica
Osbar
Terrak
Fendyn
Ionos
FIREWATER BAY
THE ELVEN STRAITS
Ynera

Z'HASRA
The great desert

T'KYRN
Land of giant trees

DRONDYL
The great mountains

LŪNDARA
Land of the long night

Altara
Sulh
Dukaat
Talakyck
Kigara
Venar's crossing
Oohtama
Ylsia
Jhoria
Seikaru
Asrhana

VALLIMBRO
The marshlands

LANEIRE
Kingdom of the sun elves

THE VIATHINIAN OCEAN
THE BOLAD OCEAN
Yuen
Tivermis
Bogerra
Kastoria
Solere

AKOSHA
The enchanted woods

Belmare
Lyroth
Lydif
Vermoore

ORSAWL
The grasslands

Daleel
Alor
Otma
Naporia
West Muesnola
Baalgia
Alin
Vix
Niraer
East Muesnola
THE AKOSHAN SEA
Ashbria
ELANDIS

ELANDIS
The trade cities

Sabri
Hathomere square
Arkynesta
Mecara
Athalin
Eybus
Ito
THE ISLE OF REFLECTION
THE LOST SOUL SEA
Gulfport
Dris
GULF OF ELANDIS

N
W
E
S

*Some smaller cities not pictured

This series is for my family. You know who you are.

"Family isn't always blood, it's the people in your life who want you in theirs: the ones who accept you for who you are, the ones who would do anything to see you smile and who love you no matter what."
-Maya Angelou

Prologue

"Mom? Finn called out. The fear within his voice echoed within the stillness of the empty house as he entered. "I'm home."

The silence was unbearably tense as he waited for a response. Monica said nothing as she joined him, closing the door behind her as quietly as she could manage as they listened. Several seconds passed, but there was nothing. The lack of a response dismayed him. After all, Finn had been gone for almost three weeks. He hadn't anticipated being pulled through a rift and into the magical other realm of Vhalta, so he hadn't had the chance to warn his mother or justify his sudden disappearance. He knew she'd be worried. Worse, he knew she'd be furious.

And, having seen her car in the driveway and a glimmer of light from outside the curtains of the living room when he entered the house, he knew she was home.

"Mom?" He called again, this time louder.

This time, the response was immediate.

The silence shattered with the sharp, staccato pattern of urgent footsteps approaching across wooden floors. Their hollow tap-taps increased to what sounded like a sprint, but lasted only a matter of moments before their owner's presence was upon them.

Nothing more than a sharp gasp came from the other room as she entered. Both Finn and Monica spun to face her, but her dark eyes only fixed upon the face of her son. She froze the moment she saw him, her thin lips agape as her voice failed her.

Her face was ghostly white, marred by circles of purple unrest that lingered beneath her bloodshot eyes. Her sandy-blonde hair was pulled back into a low ponytail that was messier than her normal, sleek style, and her bare face displayed every line of worry and every detail of her recent distress.

The warm brown of Finn's irises trembled beneath the screen of tears that swelled across their surface as he grappled with the suspense preceding her next reaction. The fear that currently made his heart pound warned of her impending anger, but until then, he was a prisoner in the purgatory of her statuesque hesitation. After a long moment, he dared to approach her with a single step, his brow pulling together in a pleading arch of supplication as he awaited judgment.

A single word uttered from his trembling lips was all it took for her to break.

"Mom?"

In a fraction of a second, she rushed to him and wrapped him in a strangling hug, convulsing as she sobbed into his chest. He looked so tall next to her, Monica observed; but then again, so did most people from her own diminutive perspective. Finn's expression was overcome with shock, his own words stalling as he looked to Monica for guidance.

She saw no need to intervene. After all, this was far better than the outcome Finn had feared. But it only lasted for a second.

The second Finn's mom released him from the hug, her face had completely changed. Her exhaustion had been swapped for vexation and her worry had been replaced by an unforgiving sternness. Even the tears that she shed left no evidence of their existence on her cheeks.

"Finneas Gage Dawson! Where the *hell* have you been?!" Her voice came out as a shrill bark that made Finn immediately recoil into a cower. The single stomp of her tiny foot that accompanied it seemed to make the entirety of the house quake around her.

Monica blinked in surprise, looking her over once again.

Despite being only a few inches taller than Monica's barely five foot height, Finn's mother was a pillar of intimidation. Though she bore the same dark eyes that her son had inherited, hers held no warmth within their brutal stare. Perhaps he'd been right when he claimed her scoldings held a magic of their own. Though Monica wasn't afraid of the tiny blonde woman that now stood before them, fuming, she suspected that that could quickly change if she was to become the focus of her anger instead of Finn. Boy, she did *not* envy him right now.

But, against her instinct of self-preservation, she knew she was obligated to help, out of the promise that she'd made before when encouraging him to come.

Shit, Monica sighed in spite of herself. There wasn't much she could do now, not until his mom calmed down at least enough to listen. Her mission was to give a convincing explanation that his mom would believe, without having to tell her that her son was accidentally whisked away to the magical realm's capital city of Arkynesta and went to work for a djinn who plans to have him aid in the destruction of a corrupt magical dictatorship, because of *Monica's* screw up. She was good at telling believable stories, (even though this one was already going to be a stretch.) She wasn't, however, very talented in the calming-people-down department. She'd usually found it best to let those things run their own course.

Although, from the looks of it, this one was off to a rocky start..

"Well, I—" Finn finally stuttered, wincing as a flush of vivid magenta crept into his cheeks.

She cut him off, shouting, "You had *better* have a good explanation for why you disappeared without so much as a word! For *three whole weeks*, at that! You haven't been answering your phone, you've skipped out on deliveries for your grandad, who's also sick over you vanishing, not to mention that I've got the entirety of Cape Bianca's precinct on watch for you!"

"Mom, I—"

"Your finals are in a few months, but how can you expect to graduate if you're off, who knows where, doing who knows what? And your birthday? You missed your *eighteenth* birthday!"

"Mom, will you please let me explain?"

The fuchsia flush of anger in her skin suddenly blanched, and her voice dropped to a stern monotone as she admitted, "I thought you were dead."

Finn's eyes went wide again when he saw the tears sparkling in hers. He opened his mouth again to speak, only to find that his voice had abandoned him.

"How the *hell* could you let me think you were dead? Do you know what I would've done if I found out that that was true?"

His eyelids fluttered as he gave his head a trembling shake, which was so subtle that it suggested he lacked the strength to give more.

"Mom..." He squeaked softly, punctuating the air with a sharp sniffle as he stumbled into a tearful apology. "I'm so sorry. I never meant to. I never wanted you to worry. It was an accident, but I'm home now. I'm home, and I'm okay."

His mom nodded, burying her face into his chest once more as she ushered him into another hug. He was shaking so hard now, that despite his lanky height, he looked like a child in her arms.

"Mom, I'm so sorry. I'm so sorry." His words muffled into the nape of her neck as she held him. She stretched up onto her tiptoes to stroke his hair with a surprisingly gentle hand.

Finally, after several cycles of his blubbering, she cooed back. "I know, baby, I know."

Chapter 1

Monica's heart ached at witnessing their embrace. Her eyes stung with vicarious tears as she fought against the plaintive memory of her own deceased mother. She had avoided her mom's absence for so long that skirting the accompanying emotions had become easy most days, as long as she didn't think too hard about it. But now, being faced with the reality of someone else's *almost* loss made the rift in her heart sting with a fresh wave of pain.

As she studied Finn's body wrapped in his mother's arms, Monica longed for the long-gone embrace of her own. It had been six years since her mother died. *No*, she corrected herself, it had been six years since The Enclave had murdered her mother in cold blood, which had only been a side effect of the abduction of Monica and her twin brother, Monroe. Their father had been a member of The Enclave, and as a magic wielder, it was forbidden to reproduce with a human. So, because of that, all were punished. At merely thirteen, Monica's family had been ripped apart by forces far greater than her young mind could then comprehend. But things began to make more sense to her when she and her brother were separated after he showed an aptitude for magic, but she did not.

So, instead of being cast back into her own world, Monica had been kept in Vhalta for three years as a slave. Eventually, her brother smuggled her back to their own realm, only for The Enclave to kill him, too, years after their escape.

Monica wondered what it would feel like now, to have any semblance of the family that she had lost. She knew it wasn't something she would likely ever have, but being forced to look on in silence at Finn's emotional reunion with his mom made the thoughts inescapable. The only comfort she found was in the fleeting thought of her growing fondness for both Finn and the siren, Celene, who had also played a part in rescuing Monica from a magical island that manifested her own fears to torture her. Maybe *they* could be like a family to her someday.

Monica's thoughts were suddenly interrupted when Finn's mom cleared her throat and the hug suddenly ended. The intensity of her attention was withering when she finally turned to acknowledge Monica.

Even before his mom spoke, Finn shifted in sympathetic discomfort as he also looked back towards his friend.

Monica, on the other hand, stood as tall as she dared, tall enough to show that she wasn't afraid, but not enough for her stance to be misconstrued as a challenge.

"So, are you gonna introduce me to your friend?" His mom asked, her voice hard and laced with the sting of judgment as she looked Monica over.

Finn stuttered clumsily as the words escaped him. His mother's cadence softened only slightly, but her comment was still pointed. "Don't think I wasn't gonna notice her."

He gave a sudden, eager-to-please shake of his head as if to say, *of course not*.

"Mom," he began tentatively, extending a tremulous hand in Monica's direction, "This is Monica."

His mother studied her with a brazen glare of appraisal, taking in all the small details of her presence, from her muddied and scuffed boots to her faded jeans to her rumpled black t-shirt and drab green cardigan. Then, her gaze rose to linger on the mess of unwashed ebony waves that tumbled about Monica's shoulders. Her expression never changed as her stare locked with Monica's. Even though her face betrayed nothing, her eyes were cold with distrust. It was a look Monica immediately recognized. After all, she had perfected it as a means of surviving on her own, never knowing who to trust.

Even so, Finn's mother gave her polite nod to accompany her curt self-introduction.

"Courtney." She said with a shrug. But her eyes did not let up as she now studied Monica's face, her scrutiny conjuring self-conscious thoughts in Monica's mind about what she would find. "Mind telling me what you're doing with my son?"

Every inch of Finn's skin immediately turned crimson with embarrassment. Flailing his arms, he darted between them, desperate to create some distance.

"She's not *with* me, Mom. Not like *that!*" He squealed.

Courtney stilled Finn's flailing with a firm hand against his chest, but her stare never left Monica; glimmering now, as if she was impressed.

"Even so, Finn's clearly quite fond of you." Her chin inclined in praise, but her words stung more like a threat than a compliment. "And you've brought him back in one piece, but that still doesn't excuse his absence. I hope you have a suitable explanation."

Courtney crossed her arms and her lips thinned expectantly. Monica gave a deferential nod, refusing to look away in an attempt to earn some amount of respect by appearing unwavering. And it must have worked, because Monica thought she saw the faintest shadow of a smile cross Courtney's lips.

Monica didn't mind the silence, even though Courtney's impatience was growing obvious as she hesitated to gather her thoughts. Finn, however, was another matter. After only a handful of seconds, he burst in.

"It's not her fault, Mom. Why don't we—" He wilted as soon as he caught the coldness of her glare, but borrowing Monica's strength with a tentative glance in her direction, he continued, "—go sit down in the living room or something? There's a lot to tell."

She raised a skeptical eyebrow but let the cross of her arms fall when she met her son's gaze. Wordlessly, she motioned him through the archway from which she'd come, only turning to follow after Monica had fallen into step behind him.

The living room was large and breezy, with pale wood floors covered by a baby blue rug with a swooping Victorian design that nearly matched the curtains. The space was decorated with deliberately vintage looking furniture: couches with wooden legs and high-backed chairs upholstered in velvet that sang of a fanciful, if not somewhat suffocating, grandeur. The back wall featured a tall hearth made of pale brick, and of course, all of the throw pillows had tassels on them.

Monica hoped the rest of the house didn't look like this. It couldn't possibly be livable, especially not with a teenage boy in the house. The fact that everything was so pristine suggested that his mother had Finn painfully well-trained. No wonder she was so upset at his disappearance. *Okay, so maybe that last thought wasn't exactly fair,* Monica thought. Anyone could get that worked up over the unexplained vanishing of a family member with whom they were close.

Finn sat in one of the high-backed chairs, and Monica perched daintily in the one beside him. She half-imagined that Courtney might try to serve them tea before she let herself sink into the middle of the couch opposing them.

Even as she sat, Courtney's posture remained rigid. Refusing to let her gaze fall, she acted oblivious to the out-of-place scatter of wadded tissues that littered the coffee table between them. She didn't, however, seem to mind reaching for the half empty glass of red wine that sat at one end.

She regarded them patiently as she took a sip, and then cleared her throat as her attention oscillated between them, as if to say, *okay, which one of you wants to start?*

Finn cast an uneasy glance in Monica's direction, and his nerves seemed to settle as they exchanged a look. He swallowed, shifting the angle of his seat before he finally spoke.

"I was gone because—"

"I think it's best if you start at the beginning." Courtney interjected, gauging what little information she could from the near indiscernible change to Monica's facade. "I want to know *everything*."

Finn watched Monica as she drew in a deep, audible breath. Without looking at him, she nodded for him to begin. Her composure never faltered as he started, his voice but a whisper beneath the uncertainty. But his courage soon returned to him as he unveiled the truth of their meeting, sans a few *tiny* details, all the while keeping a close eye on Monica for any unspoken warnings.

He told his mother of their innocent first encounter, that Monica was a client of his grandad's grocery delivery service while she was in town on business. He described her as a freelance contractor, who was working to procure various artifacts and oddities for a wealthy collector. He didn't, of course, mention the fact that he'd picked the lock when he thought no one was home, so that the groceries wouldn't spoil outside, or that Monica was actually just squatting while the condo's *actual* owner was away, but the details would only get them both into more trouble. Besides, she didn't stop him to elaborate, which he took as encouragement of her tentative belief.

He then recounted their chance second meeting, in which Monica saved Finn from being mugged, and helped him deliver the last package of his shift, to make sure it got to its destination safely. He didn't mention that the muggers were actually goblins that Monica scared off by shouting threats at them in another world's magical language, but it seemed to satisfy her so far.

His mom almost seemed to smile a little at the description of their fun afternoon, eating lunch and walking along the beach, connecting over the loss of someone close to them, and then an unexpected extension at the carnival down the pier. Monica found herself reveling in the childlike wonder of Finn's retelling of the bumper cars and their half-dozen rides on the merry-go-round.

But then, when he got to the part about the party, Finn's discomfort returned in full force, making his voice strain as he eked out the offending word.

"A party?" The displeasure was apparent in Courtney's voice as the word dripped distastefully from her mouth. There was something sharp within it, something forbidding and even a little angry. The tension in her manner had shifted, spiking Finn's own panic in a way that made Monica suspect that Courtney's reaction was something more than the standard strict parent not wanting their teenager going to a party. "You went to a *party*?"

"It wasn't a *party* party," Finn stammered, his eyes going wide as he floundered, "it was— just a casual get-together, nothing major, and definitely *not* a *party*. It was just a few people and some music and some games. Nothing dangerous or—" His stammering fell off into a squeak when Finn met the fire in his mom's eyes, which Monica saw as her cue to jump in. "—illegal."

"And it's a good thing he came after I invited him, too," Monica twisted, sparking a fleeting flinch of surprise in his eyes that revealed that he knew differently. *He* was the one that had invited her to the party. Begged her, in fact. And she wasn't even going to go, if it wasn't for the help of some accidental magic that occurred when she tried to escape the pursuit of three vicious fade hounds after the negotiation for a magical artifact went wrong. With a slight but genuine-seeming widening of her eyes, Monica leaned forwards ever so slightly and added, "In fact, I'm pretty sure I would've been attacked if Finn hadn't come. He helped me escape."

Courtney's eyes narrowed in disbelief as she took a long swig of her wine. She scanned both of their faces in turn, but there were no cracks in Monica's practiced facade, and the tell had already vanished from Finn's face. She inclined her chin as if to say, *go on.*

Monica fought back a smile against the victorious twinge she felt rising in her chest. She wasn't out of the woods by any means, but it was a good start. And if she played her cards right, she could embellish this just enough to make Finn look like a believable hero, without mentioning any of the discrediting instances of magic or other worlds. Actually, it wasn't *too* far off how their journey had actually gone. Finn *was* a hero. He *had* saved her. Maybe his courage would be worth something to his mother. It seemed like a worthy angle to attempt.

"You see, the job that I was in town for went wrong. The seller tried to cheat me, but my boss was set on getting his hands on that artifact. Things get messy sometimes when two sides can't come to an agreement, and I, unfortunately, just happened to get caught in the middle of it. I knew the seller wasn't happy with the way things ended, but I didn't anticipate that he was gonna send guys after me when I went to the *get-together* afterwards." Monica's eyes slid meaningfully to Finn at the use of his word before turning doe-like and innocent when she transitioned to retellings of his heroism. "But Finn was so determined not to see me get hurt, that he helped me sneak away before they spotted me, took me all the way to the bus station, and stayed to make sure I could get out of town safely. It was pretty awesome of him."

Monica smiled and Finn went a little red as she laid it on thick.

"So, that's when I offered him a job. He seemed the type for it, because not everyone thinks as quickly on their feet, but I saw a unique potential in him."

A shift in Courtney's posture alerted Monica to the potential dangers of the story's turn. She wasn't buying that Finn would've gone with her willingly.

Well, Monica decided rashly, *I guess I have no choice but to risk coming off as the bad guy here.*

"I basically didn't take no for an answer. He was insistent though, trying to make me understand just how upset you'd be if he left. I told him that, even if he didn't want to take the position, he should at least come with me to meet my boss, because I was sure there was a reward in it for him, for helping me out on such an important job. And, knowing my boss, his rewards aren't the kind of thing you want to turn down. I promised that it would only take a few hours to go, and he'd be back before you woke up in the morning.

Although, you can see that that obviously didn't go as planned."

Monica paused briefly to give the guise of honesty in the form of stopping for questions. Courtney, fortunately, did not take the bluff and instead seemed intent to listen through to the end before poking holes in the story. Noticing this made Monica all the more cautious, because with Courtney's lack of questions or responses, Monica had much less to go on if she made an obvious mistake, and that would be a lot harder to back track on once she got to the end, and everything was all spun together.

Well, there was no stopping now.

"I found out halfway there that my boss had made an unexpected trip to one of his other headquarters in a much farther city, and, since we were already on the way, I didn't tell Finn that until it was too late."

Finn shot her a nervous glance, clearly not fond of the fact that she was selling herself as an underhanded liar. Not that it wasn't at least *sometimes* true, even if she hadn't lied to him about ending up in the capital city of a magical other realm once they'd already gotten there. Not like the few seconds it takes to go through a rift really gives much time for explaining beforehand, though.

Catching the wordless discourse that was passing frantically between them, Courtney leaned back and pointedly prompted, "Surely that's not all."

Finn gulped audibly as both of their gazes snapped back to her. No, that *definitely* wasn't all. It wasn't even half of it yet.

Chapter 2

Now Monica was starting to get nervous. Even though she was good at keeping her visible cool, she had to hide her hands under the bottom of her cardigan to keep from fidgeting with her fingers as her mind worked overtime on the story.

"When we stopped to transfer to another bus, Finn realized how much longer the trip was going to take than I had originally promised, so I had to tell him the truth.

"His first instinct was to call you, but it was only after the first bus was already gone that he realized that he'd lost his phone. And I don't carry one. We didn't have time to wait around to get it back without missing the second bus. He wanted to try to go back home, but there weren't any more routes headed that way until much later. I convinced him that waiting around the bus terminal alone was dangerous, so on we went.

"The second bus arrived in the city and we went to see my boss. That was when I realized the artifact I was originally sent to get was also missing. I've been in this line of work long enough to know the importance of being careful, which immediately made me suspicious. On top of that, the item was *very* expensive, a one-of-a-kind, and my boss knew that there were other people who wanted it. We determined that it was most likely stolen.

"Needless to say, he was displeased that the job had gone awry, so getting the item back was my first priority. But my boss was grateful for Finn's help and supported the idea of hiring him. Finn was very hesitant at first, but I knew he must've been curious, so I convinced him that since we had already come all that way, it couldn't hurt to hear the offer. It was an incredibly generous offer, by the way."

A partnership between Monica's pause and the subtle glance she now flashed him encouraged Finn to jump in to weigh in, which he did with his usual genuine enthusiasm, despite the apprehension that still lingered in his voice.

"It was." He nodded eagerly, his eyes tracking around the room as he arranged his thoughts. "In fact, I couldn't understand why someone who seemed that powerful would want to offer *me* everything that he did. I don't have any experience doing… the kind of stuff that Monica does. But the offer was promising, Mom. It pays well, it's an opportunity to see the world, and it comes with on-the-job training, so it doesn't matter that I didn't have any experience."

A silent rage boiled beneath Courtney's brow, which had since flattened in anger. Her lips pressed together in a tight line as she set the empty wine glass on the table before reclining all the way into the couch. She inhaled slowly and fully, exhaling with an abrupt volume that commanded the attention of the room.

And then, very calmly she said, "You took the job."

It wasn't a question.

Finn's eyes flitted to her hands, which were now tense claws, digging into the arm of the couch and the cushion beside her. He immediately shrunk into his shoulders, looking like his only desire was to shrivel into the chair and disappear completely.

After a tense minute of silence, Finn surrendered to the admission with a small nod.

Courtney rose to her feet, and her meager height was somehow terrifying once again.

"Finneas, how could you?" She growled, her voice remaining low as she quietly seethed.

Finn's eyes watered and he began to redden as he avoided her penetrating glare. He wasn't sure which part of that story she was most upset about, but he didn't dare answer until he let her elaborate.

"How *dare* you let me think for three weeks that you were dead because you couldn't get up the nerve to call me and confess what you did? You had better just pray that your little stunt doesn't affect your finals or graduating on time. Because that could cost you your scholarships."

Scholarships? Monica looked at him quizzically, realizing the weight of his previous reality and how much she still had yet to learn about him.

He didn't acknowledge the look, instead, springing up out of his own chair with fists clenched as he finally raised his gaze to his mother for probably the first time since the story started.

"No, Mom, you don't understand. I came back because I wanted you to know that I was okay.

"I don't want to go to college. I don't think I ever did, I just didn't have anything better to tell you that would make you change your mind about forcing me to go. But just because I didn't know what I wanted to do with my life, doesn't mean that you get to decide for me."

She rolled her eyes, her tone becoming sharply sardonic as she argued, "Well forgive me for not wanting to see my son end up like his deadbeat dad. You are never going to succeed if you don't know what you want to do with yourself. You're going to waste your time trying to decide and then it'll be too late to do anything of value. I'm trying to do you a favor, one that you will thank me for later in life."

As Monica watched the emotions boiling between them, she suddenly realized that she had stumbled into a long-standing, unresolved conflict.

"No, Mom, I won't. Because I am not going to be happy doing something I don't want to do. I don't want to go to college and I don't want to be an engineer."

"Finn, stop this silliness, now."

"I'm not a kid anymore. Don't talk to me like one. You have never considered what I want. Just because I didn't know what I wanted before was not an excuse for you to take over my life. And now that I figured that out, I'm not going to let you take it away from me. You're already trying to, and you haven't even heard what the job is."

He was right. And that had struck a nerve.

Courtney's mouth puckered as if being tightened by a drawstring. As she regarded him in silence, the air suddenly felt as thick as fog.

For the first time in a long time, Monica didn't know what to say. She knew she needed to intervene, but she didn't know how, not without making the situation even more volatile. But watching Finn stand up for himself now made Monica understand, in retrospect, why he had been so determined to hear out Maal's offer.

Choosing instead to avoid the one question Finn was desperate for her to ask, Courtney turned to Monica with the bitter bite of an accusation on her lips.

"What you're doing is illegal, isn't it?"

"Leave her out of it, Mom." Finn hissed, his lower lip quivering as he peeled it back to reveal a snarl. "Do you really care so little about me that you can't even ask what the job is about, from me?"

His words stung his mother, making the anger on her face numb in favor of a mixture of shock and guilt. She let herself fall heavily to the couch. Anchoring her elbows against her knees, she peered up at her son, who still towered over her. She swallowed hard, her stillness giving way to a reluctant nod that permitted Finn to sit.

"Finneas..." she began haltingly, becoming suddenly more aware and cautious of her manner. "You know I care about you. And I admit, it's probably too much sometimes. But that's the only reason I push you so hard. I want to see you succeed."

"But don't you also want to see me happy?"

"Of course I do! I want you to have both. I'm just scared that you might miss out on one if you only try to chase the other. And it's a lot easier to find happiness after success."

He softened as well.

"I know you care, but it is still ultimately my choice to make. You can't be responsible for my mistakes, nor can you prevent them. And I need you to respect that. Just hear me out. Please?"

She nodded, giving an apologetic flutter of her eyelids as she fell silent again to listen.

"I really like the job so far. I think it's better than anything I'd be able to get here. I've met some great people because of it, including Monica. She always looks out for me. I like all of the things I'm learning and all of the places I'm getting to see. And most of all, I like that I have a chance to make a difference. I have a chance to help people."

Despite the growing softness in her expression, Courtney still looked reservedly unconvinced.

"But what actually *is* the job?" She briefly glanced in Monica's direction, as if doing so would quell her confusion. "Buying artifacts?"

Monica shook her head. "It's more complicated than that, but unfortunately, the nature of the work requires a significant amount of discretion."

"But you don't *steal* stuff, right?"

"No." *Not usually,* Monica thought as she gave a nervous chuckle. "We just facilitate negotiations and deliveries for things that the boss takes an interest in."

And then came the questions, more desperate than demanding. As each one was dismissed unanswered, the frustration began to rise again in Courtney's voice, but Monica's remained cool with understanding.

"How does the job help people?"

"It's complicated." Monica repeated.

"Who is your boss? What company do you work for?"

"We can't tell you that."

"Where did you go?"

"We can't tell you that, either."

Crossing her arms in a huff, Courtney spat, "What *can* you tell me?"

Monica's eyes fixed on hers, leaning forwards as she gave the most truthful evasion she could think of, hoping that her gentle cadence and pleading eyes could convince Finn's mom to understand.

"I can tell you that your son missed you very much. And he's very sorry for hurting you. And while it's not my place to judge, it sounds like you've hurt him, too. But at some point, you're going to have to trust him to know what's best for himself. Especially, since he's an adult now. He's in charge of his own decisions. And he decided to come home and apologize for hurting you by doing what he did. That's an awfully mature and courageous thing for him to do, don't you think?"

Monica leaned back in her seat as Courtney's eyes fell to process the admission. Her face drooped with sorrow, and it seemed like Monica's words *had* made an impact. After a pensive silence, her attention finally returned to Finn. Her facade was only slightly less unreadable now, still clinging to a guardedness that hid all but the emerging forgiveness that tempted in her eyes. But she did look like she was trying.

"And what finally made you decide to come home?" The question came out as a mere whisper, something about it hinting at a fear she hadn't let show before.

Finn's shoulders rounded as the tension within them melted.

His answer came with ease, making a small smile of apology dimple his cheeks as he said, "I didn't want to hurt you anymore. Even if you didn't agree with or approve of my choice, I still respect you enough to give you a proper apology. Even if we don't agree, Mom, it doesn't mean that I don't still love you."

She sniffled, her eyes becoming misty again as she nodded.

"I love you, too, Finn. You know, I only want what's best for you."

The conversation lulled to indulge a tender hug, that ended with both of them crying again.

As she pulled away, Courtney wiped her face with the back of her hand in a gesture that was a near echo of the way her son did it. Her composure flooded back with little hesitation, making her face unreadable again behind a lingering softness that hadn't been present before.

"Well," she said, rising to her feet, "I have to make some calls. Your grandad is going to want to know you're okay, and I should probably call off the bolo so that you're not tackled by any of my officers the second you're spotted outside the house. And then we can revisit this over dinner."

Finn nodded, hovering awkwardly in the space beside the archway as his mom excused herself from the room.

After a long silence, Monica spoke, conjuring a startled expression on Finn's face, as if he'd almost forgotten for a moment that she was still there.

"Well, that ended better than you thought it would, didn't it?" When he didn't immediately answer, she coaxed, "You okay?"

"I- I guess so." Finn stuttered, his eyes wide as he fidgeted uneasily. "Even though I expected her to be upset, I guess I didn't realize how much I hurt her. I- I've literally never seen my mom cry before. Ever."

Monica gave a slight shrug as she rose from her seat, floating across the room to where Finn lingered. She laid an open palm gently on his shoulder, which was bound tightly with stress.

Her voice was gentle with encouragement as she said, "I don't think that's an unreasonable reaction for someone who thought their son was dead."

Finn sniffed, agreeing with a slow, guilty nod.

"Would you have done anything differently?"

After a quiet moment of consideration, Finn lifted his red-rimmed eyes to gaze into Monica's as he admitted, "No. I mean, I would've liked to have maybe called her and told her sooner that I was okay, if it were actually possible to make phone calls from another realm, but otherwise, I don't think so. I stand by the decision I made to start working for Maal, and the choice I made to resist you sending me home without a guaranteed way to come back. And I'm proud that I stood up for myself, even though I was afraid."

"Good. Then that means you did it right. And I'm proud of you, too."

"Really?" The sparkle returned to illuminate his dark eyes as he smiled at her.

"Yeah." She smiled too.

Delight and relief transformed into realization on his face. The tension in his posture morphed into urgency, and he seized Monica's hand without warning, pulling her behind him as he took off towards the staircase.

“What are you doing?”
“I have something to show you! C’mon!”

Chapter 3

At the top of the staircase, Finn led Monica through a hallway and past a door that opened into his bedroom. Once inside, he dropped Monica's hand, leaving her to take in the details of his safe space as he immediately dug for something under the bed.

She wasn't sure how she would've pictured Finn's room, but something about the space that now encompassed them felt somewhat lacking for what she knew of his personality. She thought it would've been brighter and more whimsical, but this was rather isolating for a growing teenage boy who was still trying to figure out his place in the world. But, based on what she now extrapolated had been a rather suffocating existence under his mom's influence, perhaps that accounted for it.

The alternating pale gray and blue-green stripes of the wallpaper was mostly uninterrupted, except for a clock that hung over the head of his twin bed, a wall-mounted shelf of trinkets, and a poster-sized framed print of a mostly scenic picture. Upon closer inspection of the picture, she saw the child version of Finn, no more than eight or nine years old, standing atop a large rock astride a waterfall. He had his fists raised to the sky in a triumphant pose. He was clad in a khaki scout uniform, and the bottom few inches of foreground was cut off by the edge of what looked to be a tent.

Her surveying continued in a broad clockwise sweep.

Atop the dresser, that opposed the foot of the bed, were several model airplanes in various stages of completion. At one end sat a metal tray with raised edges that contained a small assortment of tools and random mechanical bits, and at the other was a stack of engineering books which had begun to collect dust.

The small desk that was sidled up next to the dresser held a pair of computer monitors and a large, rather impressive looking keyboard. Tucked behind one of the screens, Monica noticed a picture frame that held a photograph of Finn with his arm looped around the shoulders of another boy who was similar in age. Monica stole a glance over her shoulder at Finn to compare the photo against, estimating that the picture had been taken no more than three years ago.

Finn's features had thinned and narrowed slightly since then, but he still had the same boyish grin and gleeful sparkle in his eyes when he was happy.

The other boy had bronze skin and eyes so dark they made Finn's look hazel in comparison. The boy's face was wider than Finn's, with rounded features that gave him a softness about his demeanor. Something about the way he held his bushy brow gave him an air of cleverness. A swoop of wild black curls spilled across his forehead and tucked back around ears that were too large for his face, but Monica imagined he would grow into them in adulthood.

Something about the boy's smile made Monica immediately understand that there was something special about their bond. Not to mention how exuberant Finn's was beside him. Though he had a naturally happy nature, Monica wasn't sure she'd ever seen Finn *this* happy. Whoever the boy was, he was clearly important to Finn. But before she could fully consider the thought, Finn roused her from her musings with an announcement.

"Here it is!" He proclaimed, letting a black and red shoebox fall onto his bed with a heavy, jingling plop.

Her focus shifted to the box, watching curiously as he tossed the lid aside and began to paw through its contents.

"What is it?"

The box rattled slightly as his impatient fingers shuffled its contents around, rather than removing anything to unencumber his search.

"Do you remember the weird necklace I mentioned to you the day we met?"

Monica's brow furrowed in thought.

"No."

"I asked you, since you worked with rare artifacts, if you could tell me whether it was worth anything. But I never got around to showing it to you."

"But you know I only know things about *magical* artifacts, right?"

He grinned, his hand stopping mid-air after he lifted his fist out of the box.

"I know."

This piqued her interest, and she came to kneel beside him. Finn's fingers unfurled to reveal a circular ivory coin slightly larger than an inch in diameter. It was strung onto a long cord of wheat-colored twine that had a few simple gold beads braided into it.

He turned the pendant over in his hand, picking at the inlay of dirt that gave its intricate carvings an antiqued look.

The unmistakable design on its face made Monica's blood run cold. The amulet was carved with the outline of a six pointed star atop an askew, elongated shadow of itself, offset so that the star's points alternated with each of the shadow points in a design that was identical to the Riftrider's.

Encouraged by her interest, Finn placed the amulet in the palm of her hand and let Monica inspect it. It thrummed with a subtle magic both familiar yet foreign, an innocuous flow that could've easily gone unnoticed by anyone less experienced with magical artifacts. Whatever it was, it *definitely* wasn't a fake. But it couldn't be what she thought it was… could it?

She knew better than to be so eager to believe, but no matter how much her logic wanted to deny it, the truth was right there in her hand.

"Do you know what it is?" Finn finally asked.

"It's a realm key." Monica said breathlessly. "Do you remember how I said that there are six other realms that are connected to this one?"

He nodded, eyes wide in anticipation.

Monica continued, "Each one requires its own magical key in order to be able to travel back and forth between another realm and Vhenra, which acts as the center point to connect them all."

"I thought so!" Finn exclaimed triumphantly. "It's a Riftrider for another realm, isn't it?!"

"Yes, it's a *key* to another realm," Monica corrected with a pointed tone, "but we can't call it a *Riftrider*."

"Why not?"

"It'd get confusing. Riftriders are the keys that are used specifically for Vhalta, the magic realm. If this is for somewhere else, we have to call it something else."

"Wouldn't the keys to other realms already have names?"

"I'm sure they do," she agreed with a shrug, "but I've never known them. Keys to the other realms are extremely, *extremely* rare, so their names are not widely known. The reason Riftriders are more prominent is because they were made by The Enclave, one for each wielder, so they're not as rare as other keys.

"Also, with the efforts The Enclave have made to restrict access to other realms, I'm sure that if keys to other realms were more plentiful at any point, The Enclave probably tried to collect them all so nobody else could use them."

"Why would they do that?"

"The Enclave wants to keep all the realms as separate as possible. I don't know why, but they always have. So it's honestly kind of a miracle that you have a key to another realm, and even more so as a person who didn't know what it was when you got it."

Finn seemed unconcerned by her shock, as if he'd already connected the dots and accepted what the necklace was a while ago.

"Well, what are we going to call it?"

She flashed him an incredulous glare.

"I mean, you stressed the importance of names giving things power. We should name it, so that we can use it."

Seeing the logic in his fixation, Monica allowed a small nod of tentative agreement. "The name has to be something that makes sense for its powers. So in order to decide what to name it, we first have to determine *where* it goes."

Finn's expression shifted from brief confusion to baffled excitement when he realized, "But I know where it goes."

"How do you know that? Before you met me, you didn't even know that magic existed."

"In retrospect, I thought my dad was joking." Finn shrugged meekly as a shameful knowing invaded his expression. "He said the guy he got it from used it to see ghosts. Dad couldn't figure out how to use it himself, but he gave it to me on the anniversary of my best friend's passing, which was actually only about a week before I met you. I know he meant well. Dad said, if nothing else, it might be worth something."

"A week?" Monica repeated to herself as a brief twinge of concern tugged at her about the coincidental timing. But her subconscious pushed the suspicion away before it could fully manifest, sure that it was nothing, and her thoughts skipped to the next question. "I thought your dad wasn't around."

"He's not, or he hasn't been for a while. But sometimes he'll just show up out of the blue and then disappear just as suddenly, before my mom can catch him."

Monica's brow furrowed as she lifted the coin to inspect it again. In her silence, Finn's eyes watched her expectantly, finally piping up again when she made no effort to break the silence.

"So, what do you think? If that guy was right about using it to see *ghosts...*"

The enthusiasm in Finn's emphasis of the word made something in Monica's mind click.

"No way. There's no way. I wanna believe it, but—" She gasped, her fingers fumbling urgently with the amulet as she turned it over and over again in her hands to study it.

"But what?"

She looked back up at Finn with tears in her eyes. "If you're right, then it's a key to Enderfel, the spirit realm."

"The spirit realm?" Finn echoed inquisitively.

"The place where the souls of the dead go."

Without missing a beat, and as if he hadn't registered the full weight of the existence of a spirit realm, Finn suggested, "We could call it a Soulseeker?"

"I don't *believe* you." Monica rolled her eyes as she pinched the amulet tightly between the knuckles of her index and middle fingers, gesturing with it for emphasis as she continued. “Naming it is the least of our priorities right now. Do you have any idea what this will let me do?”

It only took a moment for Finn to consider it before a smile of childish glee lit his eyes like Christmas lights.

“It’ll let you see your brother?”

“Better.” Monica answered with a new determination invading her voice. “It’ll let me go to him in Enderfel, without losing the physical ability to come back to this realm. If I can figure out how to get it to him safely without having to stay there myself, I can use it to bring him back! This is the thing I’ve been looking for since he died! And all this time… you had one.”

Finn gave a sweet smile, but it was tinged with something that was too quick for Monica to immediately understand. His eyes grew misty and his attention flitted momentarily towards the picture on his desk, which was obscured from view by the computer monitor. The sadness that now seeped into his demeanor made a pang of guilt twist into her gut.

Her jaw clenched and her fingers tightened around the amulet. Even though she sensed that Finn was willing to let the longing pass unspoken, she knew she wouldn’t be able to move past it without addressing the emotion in his eyes.

She turned to peer over her left shoulder, now looking in the direction that Finn had, a moment before. She suspected she knew the answer before the question ever passed her lips.

“The picture… on your desk. Who is it?"

“Akash." Finn said sadly, getting caught up in some distant thought that kept his answer vague.

“He was your best friend, wasn’t he?"

"He was more than just my best friend. He was the brother I never had. He was the one who took away my shyness and replaced it with courage. He was the one that gave me a place to belong when I didn't fit in anywhere else. He always believed in me, even when I didn't.

"Akash was the one that always made me feel like everything was going to be alright, no matter what mess I had gotten myself into. Sorry." Finn sniffled, turning away to hide it as he wiped his cheeks with the backs of his hands.

“Don’t be.” Monica encouraged gently, offering him a bittersweet smile. She put her hand on Finn's knee in a gesture of comfort. "I understand what it's like to have someone who means that much to you taken away. Even though it gets easier to be strong against the pain, it never truly goes away."

Finn's glassy eyes went to a spot on the far wall across the room from them, but as Monica studied his gaze he almost looked to be seeing past it, and into something in the far distance.

"Do you think it's possible that Akash is with Monroe?"

"I mean, I don't know much about how the spirit realm works, but I think anything is possible."

Finn smiled ruefully. "Then I hope they're keeping each other company, like we are."

Turning the amulet over in her fingers, Monica felt the weight of the unavoidable question on her mind. The ivory of the Soulseeker made her fingers itch with the desperate urge to wrap its cord tight around her fingers and never let go. But she knew that it wasn't hers to keep. Gathering her courage with a tremulous inhale, she pushed her fist back towards Finn, opening her fingers in offering.

But he merely looked at it, his face twisting with confusion before his eyes lifted again to meet hers.

"Here." She insisted, pushing it towards him again. "It's yours."

"No." He wrapped his fingers around hers, gently closing her hand back into a fist around the pendant. "I don't think it was ever meant to be. Even if it was, it's yours now."

Her lips parted around a shallow sigh of disbelief as she pulled her hand back in towards her chest. Her heart buzzed with emotion, vibrating like the agile wings of a hummingbird. Even though she knew how sweet and selfless he was, she still couldn't believe that he would give her such an incredible gift.

"You don't want to bring him back?"

After considering this, Finn finally gave a small shrug of his shoulders followed by a conflicted shake of his head.

"I don't.... I don't *think* so. As much as I would like to see him again, I never hoped I might be able to bring him back, like you have. I've accepted that he's gone."

"Even though you might now have the power to change that?" Monica asked fearfully.

"No. I don't want to take that away from you."

"But it's your amulet. As much as I want it, you don't *have* to give it to me just because of that."

"I'm not. I'm not giving it to you because I feel like I have to or because I'm supposed to. I'm giving it to you because I *want* to."

"Oh, Finn." The heat of fresh tears stung her eyes as she breathed his name on a sigh. "I don't think I'm going to ever be able to repay you."

"You already have. Even though you never meant to involve me in all of this, I wouldn't trade this life for anything, and I have it because of you. So we're even."

Monica gave a sniffling chuckle as the dimples emerging on Finn's cheeks made her heart warm with a new bloom of appreciation. As her eyes lingered on his smile, she found herself wondering what she had ever done to deserve him.

Chapter 4

The sweet sentimentality of the moment shattered when Courtney's voice called up to them from downstairs.

"Dinner!"

Finn wiped his red-dappled cheeks, stood from the bed, and then offered Monica his hands to help her up. Once standing, she twisted the Soulseeker's length of flaxen cord around her fingers in a loose coil around the amulet and then stuffed it into the right pocket of her jeans, just above the dagger strapped to her thigh. She readjusted her cardigan, its oversized length easily covering both the slight lump in her pocket, as well as her insurance for the situations that turned combative. Not that she wasn't always careful, but seeing it reminded her that she needed to be doubly so in order to avoid scaring Courtney, or more likely, prompting another interrogation.

Finn led the way down the stairs and into the kitchen, where they were greeted by a spread of sushi in plastic containers and cartons of rice stacked neatly in the middle of the dining table.

The kitchen was a lot homier than the living room. The floor was covered in vinyl, patterned with subtle marble swirls and flecks reminiscent of the texture of stone. The cabinets were painted in keeping with the pale blue motif that

Monica had noticed throughout the rest of the house. The matching print of the wispy curtains and tie-on chair cushions supplied an air of datedness that was not without its own charming nostalgia.

The spotless state of the kitchen made Monica suspect that either Courtney didn't cook much, (or at least she hadn't in Finn's absence), or that she was a neat freak on top of her imperious nature.

Courtney apologized for the lack of a cooked meal as they each took a seat, but her demeanor didn't change to allow even the slightest glimpse of embarrassment, feigned or otherwise.

Monica offered an apology of her own in the form of, "I'm sorry that we dropped in unannounced. I'm sure that you hadn't been expecting company."

Courtney shook her head, offering little in the way of warmth as she wordlessly passed a clean plate and pair of metal chopsticks to each of them. A fleeting observation passed through Monica's mind that Courtney must be quite fond of Asian food to own a set of reusable chopsticks. She had hardly realized that she had gone into information gathering mode, as if preparing for a business negotiation. But then again, until she knew where she stood with Finn's mom, it wasn't a bad idea to be prepared. After all, since Finn had already gotten the brunt of Courtney's scolding, Monica imagined that she was likely next. Needless to say, she was caught off guard when Courtney struck up a conversation with an unexpectedly amiable tone.

"So, Monica, tell me about yourself."

The broadness of the question immediately felt like a trap, but it also gave her an opportunity to be equally vague in response.

"There's… not much to tell." Monica mumbled evasively as she scooped a pile of rice out of one of the nearby cartons and onto her plate.

She handed the carton to Finn, eyeing the half tray of various maki rolls that he pushed in her direction with a reluctant narrowing of her eyes. Not wanting to offend her host, Monica helped herself to two of the less intimidating looking pieces before she began picking at her rice. She had to remind herself that she had eaten far worse than this; between living off whatever leftovers she found in the condos that she squatted in, to the absolute slop she had been fed as a slave. But, even so, she had never been fond of the idea of raw fish. Perhaps she had just gotten spoiled with the options that had been afforded to her in the last several weeks in Arkynesta.

Deciding not to comment on Monica's hesitant manner, if she even noticed, Courtney began with her first question.

"Where are you from, originally?"

Though she knew the question was likely well meaning, Monica felt her chest tighten and her mind become guarded at the feeling of an emerging interrogation. She reminded herself that it was normal for any parent to want to know who their child was associating with. But she also knew that there were enough obscurities about her past that needed to remain that way, that she feared the likelihood of coming off as a liar. Not that she wasn't, merely for the sake of safety, sanity, and privacy, but there was a difference between being reticent and being a liar out of malicious intent. And she wasn't sure that it was a difference Courtney would understand without the unavailable context.

"Uhh… I was born in Crestingate, but I've moved around a lot."

The sudden arch of Courtney's eyebrows betrayed a moment of surprise. Monica assumed that she was likely reacting to the city's implication of affluence in contrast to her worn and slightly grungy appearance.

"Crestingate?" Courtney echoed as she gave Monica a thoughtfully appraising glance.

"Just one of the suburbs."

“How long did you live there?”

“Only until I was thirteen.”

“And after?”

“Like I said,” Monica bit back, trying her best to keep the brevity in her voice from sounding too much like aggression, “I moved around a lot after that. Nothing ever felt much like home.”

Courtney withdrew with a sudden spark of pitying understanding blooming within the confines of her still guarded expression.

“Where do your parents live?”

“Mom—” Finn gave a low growl of warning, but the question was already out.

Monica’s sharp inhale sliced through the air and she set her chopsticks onto her plate with a clink. Keeping her eyes low and her voice flat, she admitted, “Nowhere. They’re both dead.”

“Oh... that’s unfortunate.”

“You didn’t know.” Monica dismissed with a shake of her head, interrupting before Courtney’s apology-adjacent comment could flow into another question.

“But I know what it’s like.” Courtney murmured with an unexpected softness.

The vulnerability in her tone had taken Monica by surprise. Surrendering to her curiosity, she lifted her attention to Courtney’s distant, misty eyes.

“My mother died when I was young. We were close, so it was hard for me. I never knew my father, but my stepdad did his best to raise me on his own. Even though he wasn’t my blood, he would've given me the world, if it were in his power." She broke, turning to Finn with a genuinely warm smile that shaped not only her face, but lit her eyes with that too familiar sparkle of sad appreciation. He returned his mom's smile when she added, "Just like he'd do for Finn now."

A lump rose in Monica's throat. Her guard was slipping, and the feeling of cold, cautious distrust was slowly melting with the warmth of empathy. Even with their differences and disagreements, Finn's mom seemed to be making a conscious effort to relate to her. After she got over the initial shock of it, Monica found that the gesture had sparked within her a new ember of respect for Courtney.

Unsure of how much she was allowed to ask, Monica remained silent beneath a solemn nod. But Courtney's smile, however bittersweet, remained when their eyes locked. Monica wasn't sure if she had merely read the curiosity on her face or was doing it out of a continued effort to make her feel comfortable, but she continued.

"She died of pneumonia. The worst part was how sudden it was. It's never easy to prepare to lose someone you love, but at seven years old, it was almost unfathomable to be playing at the park with her one day and wake up to find her so sick that she's dying the next."

Monica swallowed, her breathing arrested by a sudden twinge of pain radiating through her chest. She was right; the suddenness was excruciating. The Enclave had murdered Monica's mother when she and her twin brother were only thirteen years old, and it was like night and day the way her world had changed. One moment, she was running in the field near their house with no cares in the world, and the next, she was being ripped away from everything she knew and enslaved by a terrifying world of cruel, magical impossibilities. The worst part about the suddenness was how helpless it had made her feel. Now that she was grown, Monica had honed her skills to be able to support herself in any unexpected circumstance, but only because the pain of being blindsided was something she never, ever wanted to experience again.

And knowing that Finn's mom had been made a victim by that same cruelty of fickle fate gave her an understanding far more valuable than she could've hoped for.

"I'm sorry."

Courtney sniffed, but it was drier than it had been for Finn, the sign of a scar rather than a fresh wound.

"Don't be. Even though I wouldn't wish it on anyone, losing her made me strong; stronger than I would've been otherwise, and earlier in life, too. That strength helped me be strong for Finn's grandad on the days he struggled more than others. Just like I'm sure your losses made you strong. You would never apologize for your strength, would you?"

Monica shook her head.

"Good. Don't. Not ever."

Monica gave an obedient nod, and as their eyes met again, she felt the spark of kinship between them. Courtney acknowledged a similar feeling with a briefly widening smile before she turned to Finn with an announcement in her voice.

"Speaking of which, your grandad wants to see you." Her words were sharp with a scolding edge that caught Finn off guard.

"Now?" Finn mumbled through a mouthful of rice.

"No, but first thing in the morning. If he wanted to see you now, I would've been driving your butt over there the moment we got off the phone." Though her inflection was firm, there was an unexpected thread of humor running through her words.

Finn's cheeks reddened and he struggled to swallow the lump of food so that he could respond properly.

"Was he… *too* mad?"

"Well, he didn't say much, but I suspect that he'll be saving his words for you."

Finn nodded nervously. "I'll go first thing in the morning."

Courtney gave a small *tut* that seemed the verbal equivalent of giving Finn a pat on his head. Some of the tension uncoiled from his spine as he relaxed in his chair, but stress still held his shoulders stiff. It likely would for a while.

Giving a half-glance towards Monica, Finn asked, "Do you want to go with me?"

Not even a split second later, he whirled back around to face his mom, as if remembering himself.

"Can she go with me?"

To which, his mom gave a tilt of her head and a partial shrug that seemed to say, *why not*?

His eyes shifted expectantly back to Monica, the anticipation in his smile dimming as he waited for a response. There wasn't fear in his eyes at the threat of what was to come, not like there had been at the prospect of facing his mother. Even though his mom's words had implied another confrontation, Finn's expression promised a gleeful reunion.

Monica deliberated over a slow mouthful of food. She hadn't had this much emotion to contend with all at once in a long time, and frankly, the thought of more was exhausting. But, it's not like she really had anywhere else to be. And it seemed important to Finn, which, she decided, meant that it was important to her.

The "sure" that came after she swallowed made him practically start dancing with excitement. But the controlled apprehension resurfaced to quell his joy when his mother spoke again.

"And Finn? There's one other important thing that we need to discuss."

"Oh?"

"Your party." She remarked blankly, taking another bite of food between phrases to make Finn stew in the silence. "You don't think that just because you were gone when it happened, I was going to forget about your birthday, did you?"

Monica looked up, startled to hear Courtney talking about a party, after how adverse her reaction to the mention of one had been before. And when she looked towards Finn, Monica saw none of the fear that he'd worn before when the subject had come up, only mild exasperation. Clearly they were now talking in different terms that Monica had yet to define.

"Oh, Mom." Finn groaned miserably. "You know I didn't want a party, especially now that I'll have to explain why I was gone for so long. Besides, it's not like I have that many close friends to invite."

Courtney crinkled her nose critically at his objection, allowing Monica to understand that Courtney and Finn did not have the same definition of the word *party.*

"But becoming an adult is a milestone to be celebrated."

Finn shrugged, clearly not seeing the appeal. "It's not really like anything's going to change any more than it already has. Besides, I don't even know if we will have time for a party before we have to go back to work."

Courtney's expression flickered sad before transitioning back to stony. Her movements became immediately restricted, guarded even, as she slowly lifted her eyes to meet Finn's. For a long moment she stared, not saying anything. He gave a nervous gulp, his breath trembling loudly in contrast to the icy silence.

Her words were level when they came, and even though her cadence was nearly devoid of any emotion, her displeasure was sharply apparent beneath it.

"You mean to tell me that you only returned to leave me again?"

Finn's chin dipped in a submissive apology, but he held the courage in his gaze as he dared to maintain eye contact with his mom.

"I told you I took the job, and that I wasn't going to give it up. You can't possibly expect me to stay."

"You can't work from Cape Bianca?" She bargained with surfacing desperation, "After all, you said you met Monica when she came to work here. Ask them to let you stay."

"I can't do that, Mom. I have to go where they need me. And even if I could, I don't want to miss out on seeing all of the places I'll get to see. I'll come back when I can."

"How can I trust that? You were gone for three weeks without so much as a single phone call. I don't like the idea of not knowing if you're okay, not knowing where you are, and not knowing if or when you'll ever come home."

Finn drew in a defeated sigh, but despite the growing weakness he felt against her trembling plea, he did his best to remain both strong and gentle as he reasoned with her.

In fact, his level of composure and maturity startled Monica. Seeing this side of him warmed her with pride to see how much he'd grown in the short time that she'd known him.

"Mom, you know I would never do anything to hurt you intentionally. But I'm an adult now. And at some point you're just going to have to trust me. Can you do that?"

After a long, pensive silence spent in hesitation, Monica chimed in with her own encouragement.

"I know you just want what's best for Finn. We both do. And I wish you could see how happy he is doing this new job. I know it's scary, but I promise to keep him safe while he's away. And I promise to make him check in as often as he can."

Courtney gave a strained nod. Red patches had begun to rise in her cheeks as she held back tears. But instead of saying anything, she reached her hand across the table and wrapped her fingers around Finn's.

Even though it seemed to take every fiber of strength within her being to conjure the words, she at last said, "I *do* trust you, Finn. So if you think that this is what's best for you, I'll let you go." The melancholy in her tone hardened once again to a warning when she added, "But don't think for *one moment* that I won't worry about you the whole time you're gone."

A small smile flitted across Finn's lips as he chuckled in response.

"I know, Mom."

Chapter 5

After dinner, Courtney showed Monica to a guest room located downstairs, beside her own room, which were both at the complete opposite end of the house from Finn's. Though Monica felt that they were off to a better start at getting to know each other then she had originally hoped for, she still experienced a subdued suspicion that she was being supervised.

That didn't bother her like it probably should've. Between Maal's men and The Enclave, Monica was used to being watched. And, trying to see things from Courtney's perspective, it didn't feel undeserved since she was a total stranger who had basically just kidnapped Courtney's son for three weeks.

If anything, Monica was grateful. Being watched by someone that knew she was here was a lot better than potentially being discovered when she was staying in a house that she hadn't been invited into.

The guest room wasn't much to look at; muted colors and sparse patterns, decorated in a lukewarm manner that could have very well been pulled directly from a budget home magazine. But the bed; the bed was a dream. It seemed large for a queen bed, but maybe that was because it had been so long since she'd had one that big all to herself. The spongy mattress gave beneath her weight, reforming to fill every crevice of her body in the most exquisitely comfortable way, like she was laying weightless on a cloud. The sheets were silky and cool when she slipped between them, tickling her nostrils with the refreshing fragrance of a recent laundering.

In the absence of an accessible change of clothes, Courtney had even offered her an oversized t-shirt to sleep in, after having been quite insistent that Monica not wear her street clothes into the bed, which was fair enough. Admittedly, Monica was coming to find Courtney quite hospitable, despite her initially stern manner. After all, it seemed to her that they weren't too different. They both knew what they wanted and weren't afraid to oppose people to stand up for that, or to protect what was important to them.

But despite the luxurious comfort of the bed and the welcoming safety of the house, Monica struggled when she tried to drift off. She wasn't sure what was keeping her from sleep, exactly. After all, she no longer had the fear of being tormented by her previous recurring nightmare that had come nightly for months since her brother's death. That nightmare had gone away for good weeks ago, after she had been saved from the magical island that had forced her to confront her fears.

Perhaps it was just the excitement of the day that was keeping her awake. After all, witnessing Finn's emotional reunion with his mother had stirred feelings of her own that she had gone years successfully avoiding. Not to mention the slight guilt that shadowed the back of her mind at the knowing that she had been the one to originally take him away. But, she also knew that Finn's return to Arkynesta was her choice no longer, so she didn't need to feel guilty over it now.

Her eyes flitted through the darkness, landing on the pile of clothes in the corner, where the Soulseeker slept. Maybe that's why she couldn't sleep. Her mind was too alert, having already begun to churn with possibilities and solutions for the conundrum of bringing her brother back, without sacrificing herself in the process. She knew that she would have plenty of time to work on that problem tomorrow. But even as she tried to quiet her mind, sleep evaded her.

But she wasn't the only one. After over an hour spent tossing and turning in the darkness, she was greeted by a familiar silhouette in the doorway.

"Hey."

"Finn?" She sat up, propping her weight against her elbows. "Why are you still awake?"

The outline of his dark figure shrugged.

"I was just worried that you might be lonely down here, all by yourself."

She choked back a chuckle at his silly but caring offer, sensing that there was something more serious behind the playfulness of his words.

"Nah, I'm fine. Why? Are *you* lonely?"

"A little." He admitted in a near-whisper. "I haven't slept in an empty room by myself for weeks. It feels too weird to start again now."

"Well, I'd invite you to stay down here," she murmured, patting the empty bed beside her. "After all, there's certainly enough room, but do you want to risk your Mom finding us? Because I know she's watching me, and I figure that I could guess how she might react to discovering her son in bed with a girl, even if we're asleep and fully clothed."

"Yeah…" He exhaled a nervous chuckle. From the familiar way his hand had gone to the back of his neck, Monica suspected that a vibrant flush of color was creeping onto his cheeks, hidden by the screen of darkness between them. After an uncomfortable silence, he finally invited, "We could go to my room?"

Though his voice was hopeful, the way it wavered made it seem that he had regretted even asking before he fully got the words out.

"Don't you have a twin bed? That'd be awfully cozy." Monica teased in a husky whisper.

"I'd sleep on the floor." Finn immediately whined, less sheepish in his suggestion after the introduction of humor.

"I'm not sure we'd be any safer up there," She reasoned, but feeling the weight of his anticipation in the air throughout her hesitation, she decided to indulge him. "But I'm willing to risk it if you are."

The warmth of a smile spread across Monica's face in the darkness. She slipped her legs out from between the covers and stood, turning back around to shove a couple of the superfluous pillows into a long lump to hold her place beneath the blankets. Then, with a careful stealth, she crept across the room on her tiptoes, towards where Finn waited in the doorway.

"Well, lead the way." She breathed in a shallow whisper.

To which, he immediately turned around and ambled quietly up the hallway, taking extra care to climb the staircase without making a sound.

The darkness parted as soon as they entered Finn's room, which was lit overhead by the wan glow of a string of white Christmas lights that had escaped Monica's notice before. Additionally, the ceiling was speckled with plastic stars that glowed in a variety of luminescent green hues as they borrowed light from the string of white bulbs that created a perimeter around them, his own patch of makeshift sky. The murky light cast a veil over the rest of Finn's room in a way that seemed cozier and more inviting than before. The vibe of the room was totally different now. It felt more like him.

Finn entered the room behind Monica, watching as she gently lowered her weight onto his neatly made bed. She kicked her feet up, crossing her arms behind her head as she reclined. He made no verbal acknowledgment when she shimmied her body towards the wall to make room for him to join her.

As her gaze lifted again to the stars, her lips pulled back into a contagious smile. Finn lingered in the doorway, unaware that he'd been staring at her until her attention returned to him.

"Well, c'mon. You're not afraid of me *now*, are you?" She patted the bed as she teased him, much like she had that first night they'd spent together in Arkynesta.

His shoulders shook when a small chuckle bubbled up from his chest. Slowly, he approached. He turned his back to her and sat on the bed, glimpsing her over his shoulder as his feet still hung down to the floor. His shoulders shriveled to hide his face after a quick glance had revealed his embarrassment for innocently disregarding the size of the bed.

"You sure you wouldn't be more comfortable if I slept on the floor?"

If it had been anyone else, Monica wouldn't have bought his sheepishness as more than a clumsy cover for lascivious intentions. But she knew that Finn's heart was honest, and he wouldn't have invited her up if he wasn't in need of genuine comfort. Even if some unspoken hope remained within him that she might eventually return his affections despite her previous, misleading admission that she only liked women, Monica knew that he wouldn't cross any boundaries without permission. Her trust in him made her comfortable in what could have otherwise been *too* close for comfort.

"Lay down." She whispered firmly, her tone gently chiding that he was worried about nothing.

He obeyed but still avoided her eyes, laying on his side with his back to her. She wasn't sure if his avoidance was a result of his guilt for any lingering feelings he may have had, or if it was his way of trying to encourage her that he wasn't interested, not that way. She didn't know how he felt anymore; whether he'd moved past the infatuation and just regarded her as a friend, or if he would always have that little crush on her. But she didn't really mind either way.

Finn was a sweet guy. It actually made her feel a little guilty for lying to him before. She hadn't done it to be malicious. And even though it wasn't untrue that she was attracted to women, she was starting to regret telling him that she was *only* attracted to women. But she didn't understand why. It wasn't like she owed anyone an explanation of her sexuality. But lying to him had just felt… mean. Meaner than she had meant it.

Monica tried to make herself feel better by remembering her justification for doing it. She had wanted to let him down easy. She didn't want to hurt his feelings, but she didn't think he would understand why she was pushing him away. The truth had been too heavy then to share with a near stranger, but she had wanted to keep him that way; a stranger, because it would hurt less to lose somebody who wasn't yet her friend. She had been so afraid of losing anyone after her brother that it had been hard for her to get close to anyone, in any capacity. But maybe she *could* let herself get close to him. In that moment at least, she found herself wanting to.

The revelation, when it finally came, sent a shiver through her body. Was she starting to like Finn? Or was she just so desperate not to be alone again that she had forgotten what genuine friendship felt like? Not being able to tell the difference terrified her.

When Finn noticed her shivering, he shifted from his side to his back to fill more of the space beside her.

"Are you okay?"

She gave a reluctant nod, pulling her arms down from behind her head to cross them over her chest.

"Just cold."

"Do you want to lay under the covers? I can get up, so you can."

"It'll pass." He fell quiet again, and after a heartbeat, Monica asked, "Are *you* okay? After everything that happened today?"

"I am." Finn admitted with a sigh. "Even though I know my mom's not happy knowing that I'm going to leave again, I feel good about addressing things with her. It feels strange to be home, though."

"Why?" Monica tucked one arm under her head and rolled onto her side, studying his changing expression as he spoke.

His features grew wistful in the murky glow of the dim, scattered lights. The effect made his skin almost look misty against the dark.

"It's going to sound kind of silly, but after I finally convinced myself that Arkynesta wasn't a dream, I started to wonder if my home was. Is it normal for other worlds to start feeling less real and more like a dream the longer you're away from them?"

Monica thought about it for a while, understanding what he meant but deciding that she had always overlooked that feeling. Part of the reason that she had avoided Arkynesta so fervently after she and Monroe had escaped, was because it had started to feel like nothing more than a nightmare the longer they had been gone, and going back made those things real again.

"Yeah…" She finally answered. "I think it's normal."

"I'll have to work hard to keep my promise to her then."

"What do you mean?"

"The longer I stay away, the easier it will be to get caught up in whatever I'm doing in the other realm. I don't want to leave my mom behind in the haze."

Monica gave an empathetic nod of understanding.

"You won't. I can see how important she is to you. I know how loyal you are to the people who are important to you. And I promised her I'd make you check in, so you'll have help. Even though cell phones don't work across realms, there are other ways. We'll make *sure* it happens."

His cheeks rounded with a smile and his dark eyes fell from the stars overhead to Monica's face.

"Thank you… for your help today."

"Not that I really did much."

"Are you kidding?" The excitement that fueled his words became suddenly apparent as his whisper lifted to an enthusiastic, conversational volume. "I definitely couldn't have done all that by myself! Your story was incredible."

"I don't know that your mom believed all of it, but..." Monica gave a little shrug.

"Even if she didn't, it was enough. It was a lot better than I could have done by myself. Not only that, but you gave me the courage to stand up to her. I've never been able to do that before, alone."

"Yeah, well, you're not the same person that you were before all of this started. You've grown since then."

"I have, haven't I?" His cheek dimpled with a half-smile as he peered towards Monica again. "Thank you."

In the glow of his gentle appreciation, she felt a flutter of warmth rising in her chest. That same flutter made her lungs clench and her stomach twist with a sudden wave of nausea. The longer she looked at him, the harder it was to breathe. A few seconds suddenly felt like an hour, and she had to look away before she was suffocated by the joy on his face.

She didn't like the helplessness that came with not understanding the sudden sensations that were now making her body revolt against her. She had never felt like this before.

Her eyes shifted back to the stars that speckled the ceiling, and she cleared her throat in a desperate attempt to break the moment.

"Are you feeling less lonely now?"

"Yeah." He paused, letting almost a minute go by as he matched her focus. "But I don't think you should go anywhere, you know, just in case."

She succumbed to a nervous smile, feeling a warmth rising in her cheeks with the realization that she hadn't intended to leave. She wanted to stay here with him, beside him, all night.

The flutter in her abdomen intensified. She'd never swallowed a butterfly before, but the irrational part of her mind suddenly feared that she had somehow unknowingly swallowed a thousand. Her shallow, shaky breaths did little to quell the hurricane of wings swirling in her belly as she laid beside him. She genuinely thought she might be sick, but when she turned and saw that his eyes had fallen closed, she stilled to stare.

He looked so peaceful. His chest rose and fell with long breaths that flowed in waves like the ocean. His lips parted around each one, and she watched for so long that she noticed when his eyelids began to flutter. As she studied his face, she forgot her physical disquiet and let herself relax beside him.

Before she knew it, sleep had her in its clutches, and she was finally drifting into the darkness.

Chapter 6

Meanwhile, back in Maal's Tower in the magical city of Arkynesta, their employer was being summoned to an unexpected meeting. The summoning wasn't one of the magical types, which was the most common method that outsiders with no preexisting ties to his organization used to solicit a contract.

To even be permitted access to his tower required an invitation, and those within the tower kept a meticulous count of all who entered. So the opportunity for an unexpected meeting within his tower, with a guest whom he did not already have one scheduled, should not have been possible. Maal was not the kind of man who missed *anything*. The small details were what allowed him to be one step, if not several, ahead of his adversaries. There was little he valued over the upper hand of being perpetually prepared for anything, so the spontaneity of this unplanned meeting was cause for great indignation and disquiet for Maal.

One of his many identical secretaries accompanied him to the meeting room in which the interloper awaited, floundering through an explanation of the situation, as if the oversight had been specifically her fault.

Her voice was flustered and breathless as she tried to maintain the haste of her gait to keep up with his hulking strides.

"We don't understand how he even got in, Master M. He marched into the lobby without an invitation, which shouldn't even be possible since the magic that cloaks your tower only parts to allow visibility to those you have explicitly invited or have other agreements with. Not only that, but he was also able to pass through the lobby's low-level wards without breaking them, and order an elevator *on his own*, after being denied for refusing to describe his business here."

"Who is he?" Maal growled darkly, the length of hallway trembling around him as he stormed onwards.

"The best we can tell is that he's a member of The Enclave. He was wearing an incredibly potent concealment spell over his visible identity when he entered; an enchantment that the wards should've immediately neutralized, but the fact that it didn't means that his level of wielding ability is nothing to be scoffed at. But he made no efforts to hide his telltale veridian mantle, so he either knew that his magic wouldn't be strong enough to even try against the tower's upper wards or—"

"He wants us to know that he's Enclave." Maal snarled through his teeth in disgust.

Yes, that was like them. The Enclave had never been as good at subterfuge as Maal was, nor did they care to be. Whereas Maal was like a viper in the grass whose victim would never see it coming until after the bite, The Enclave was like a lion, making a conceited show of its might with puffed up roars of intimidation and picking impulsive fights with perceived threats. That's all this was. Someone must've caught wind of something that increased Maal's position as a threat, and this wildly ill-advised invasion was merely an attempt to remind Maal of the amount of power The Enclave had amassed as of late.

"What should we do, Master M?"

"Double the wards, and then double them again. He may think he's powerful enough to be able to march in here and flash his fangs, but he's *not* leaving."

The secretary gave an obedient nod and curtsied away mere seconds before Maal slammed through the massive doors of the meeting room that his *guest* had chosen to invade with his presence.

The air in the massive room was dimmed, the sconces mounted on the walls turned down to emit only a mere breath of light. The interloper sat at the near end of the long wooden table with his back to the doors in a display of astonishing arrogance that seemed to boast that he wasn't afraid of anything that could come up behind him. He didn't even flinch when the doors slammed closed behind Maal, followed by the echo of a metal click that locked them both in.

"And what, exactly, is a member of The Enclave doing in my domain?" Maal boomed, both his presence and his voice imposing as he rolled into the room on a carpet of thickly woven tendrils of smoke.

The curly haired wielder picked at his fingernails as Maal approached, fearlessly maintaining that he was neither impressed nor intimidated by the djinn's commanding entrance. When he turned in his seat, the movement was slow and deliberate. His stormy, blue-gray eyes lifted, but he did not stand to bow. In fact, he leaned back even further in his chair, his spine going slack as his body slumped casually to the side to rest an elbow against the table. Any trace of the concealment that he had cast over his facade before was gone, revealing a face that was unknown to Maal, which he took as an indicator of this man's lack of meaningful notoriety.

Maal's eyes flickered from cool luminous blue, to burning amber, vexed by this man's irreverent disregard for any of the usual formalities and appeasements.

"I have a proposition for you, djinn." The wielder crooned in a silken growl.

Maal's entire demeanor radiated a menacing displeasure at the mere presence of this man. After all, he harbored just as much abhorrence for The Enclave as Monica did, if for slightly different reasons. Additionally, the fact that this man could be so nonchalant about the dangers of being within a space under Maal's total and supreme control was an utterly flippant, not to mention arrogant, display. It could've been a bluff, but offended or not, Maal wasn't about to lose his sense of caution in the face of an encroaching nemesis. But the fact that this man was not only here, but so flagrant in his lack of effort to at least put on a superficial mask of diplomacy said that he was either a confident liar, or he had an advantage up his sleeve that suggested he was not to be trifled with.

Maal did allow a moment of recognition for the claims surrounding the wielder's entrance to the tower. Though it wasn't meant to be an easy feat, it still did not conjure the smallest speck of apprehension nor reverence for the act. This wielder may possess real power, but he had more stupidity than magic. And, if he continued on a trajectory as rash as his entrance, it would only be a matter of time until he slipped up, which Maal would ensure would become his demise.

"Oh?" Maal growled, anger swelling in his stare as he searched to meet the impudent wielder's evasive gaze. "How daring of an unknown sorcerer to march into *my* tower and demand an audience with me. The Enclave knows how we *creatures* feel about your mere existence—"

"Yes, yes, and you're all too aware that the disdain is mutual."

Maal cleared his throat forcibly, taking umbrage with the fact that this man would even dare to interrupt him.

"What makes you even think I would entertain such an idea?"

The wielder's lip curled into a slow grin as he regarded the djinn with a cool, contemptuous stare.

"Because, it'll be easier if you're willing."

Maal gave a derisive snort that sent twin streams of smoke spewing forth from his nostrils. "You must be under a curse of impossible grandeur if you think I'd ever even consider consenting to working with The Enclave, for any reason."

The wielder barely flinched at this remark, tilting his head coyly to one side as he continued to stare.

"You wouldn't be working *with* us, but *for* us. Or rather, *me*. And I don't require your consent. I merely said it'd be easier…for *you.*"

Maal's timbre darkened as his eyes flashed to deepening hues of lingering scarlet orange. "I don't have time for this. We're done here."

The man finally stood as if to leave, but he waited for Maal to turn around before he threatened, "We're not done until I say we are, *Maal*."

A faint tickle of magic rose in Maal's chest, making him almost laugh at the wielder's pitiful attempt to control him with the innate magic within names. He had come to use that first syllable of his so freely amongst his contract holders that he had grown nearly invulnerable to its pull.

With the magic's ineffectual sway, Maal felt an unbidden wave of relief settling in his gut. This wielder had far overestimated the value of the treasure he thought he had discovered. Maal suppressed a furtive grin, deciding that the wielder would pay for his foolish mistake with a terror that would ripple back throughout The Enclave.

The djinn's massive shoulders stiffened as he pivoted back to face the green-clad wielder, who, even at his full height looked puny next to Maal. But his expression was definitely not that of a man who felt his vertical disadvantage, or a disadvantage of any kind.

Maal let slip a partial roll of his eyes as he scoffed, “Is that why you’re prancing around like a poodle who thinks it’s a Doberman? Because you’ve learned the first syllable of only *one* of my names? That’ll hardly grant you much control over the most powerful djinn in Vhalta. Get out of my sight, while I'm still feeling charitable.”

“Don’t you even want to know who I am? I would think you would be more interested in learning the identity of the man who is to become either your partner or your master, depending on your choices.”

“You talk a big talk for a tiny, unknown wielder. I knew The Enclave didn’t have a very good sense of humor, but I’m beginning to think that they sent you here as a joke. Is this a test of your initiation or something?”

A twitch of contempt made the man’s upper lip ripple as he paused to compose himself before speaking again.

“I am unknown by face by design. But even so, I am most certain you know of both my history as well as my name. After all, none forget the name of Rowan Drake.” The wielder gave a frivolous bow that was more to feed his own ego than as an act of respect.

Maal clenched his jaw as he fought to keep the momentary spark of recognition from splintering his inscrutable mask. Another thick billow of smoke spilled out of his nostrils with a hiss. But then, he smiled.

“You’ve forgotten that names work both ways, Drake. And by giving me yours, you may as well have handed me the crossbars to your marionette strings.”

Maal's smile immediately soured when Drake retorted, "And you must've forgotten that wielders shed their *real* names when they're sworn into The Enclave. While my reputation is real, that name is not, so it will give you infinitesimal power over me. But do feel free to try if you're so inclined. I'm sure using it won't do me any damage."

Maal's hands balled at his sides, creating fists the size of bowling balls. Not often did he feel like the one at a disadvantage. There was nothing he liked less. Damn this Rowan Drake and his aggrandized self-assurance. There were few things that he could imagine in that moment that would make him happier than to see this pompous, vindictive wielder burn.

Perhaps having sensed this, Rowan decided to indulge the opportunity to rub in his upper hand even more.

"I know you think me stupid for coming here, but I would not have done so without taking *all* of the proper precautions first."

"You're lucky I don't smite you where you stand, Drake. I'm giving you one final chance. Get out of my tower and never return."

"You wouldn't give me that chance if you weren't afraid of me. And rightfully so, *Maalavario."*

Maal blanched. With the utterance of his first name, a flare of magical compulsion ignited within his chest, making his lungs tighten with an immensely uncomfortable amount of force. That same force spread in a band around each of Maal's wrists, squeezing like invisible shackles. The heat of it writhed through him, licking at the essence of his being like a flame licking at a new log being thrown into a fire. Drake's grin widened.

The pressure and discomfort quickly lessened, but didn't completely dissolve, lingering as a reminder of Drake's power over him. The spell was waiting to act on the will of its master. One does not typically cast a spell of compulsion without using it. It would remain, intertwining itself with Maal's essence, hungrily awaiting that command before it would dissipate.

"That's right. I know a full one of your three names, which means, I have more control over your will than you likely ever thought possible. And that's why I came here. I *had* hoped to use your name as an incentive to enlist your services in a way that might benefit us both, but since you have no interest in working with me willingly, my proposition has now changed to a warning. Know that your time is now finite, for soon I will obtain all three of your names, and then you will have no choice but to obey my every command, down to the last modicum of your vast power."

Before Maal could utter any sound in response, the vainglorious wielder gave a snap of his fingers and vanished.

Chapter 7

If Courtney had checked on them in the middle of the night and discovered Monica sharing Finn's bed, she hadn't said anything. Nor did she say anything when both of them finally turned up in the kitchen after having dressed. Monica was grateful that she had not gotten caught returning to the guest room to retrieve her clothes but found it unsettling the way Courtney did not move to acknowledge her when she entered the kitchen mere moments after Finn.

Courtney was already at the dining table, fully dressed and ready for the day. Her eyes still appeared bleary with sleep despite the assumption that she had been up for a while, based on her full face of conservative makeup and the immaculate bun that her mousy blonde hair was pulled up into. Her tiny figure was clad in a distinct navy-colored uniform that made her presence even more commanding than before, even as she reclined in her seat.

"Good morning, Mom." Finn greeted, giving her a peck on the cheek before turning to pour himself a bowl of cereal.

She offered him a wordless hum of acknowledgement, never taking her eyes from the newspaper that held her attention. Finn seemed entirely unfazed by her uniform, which Monica understood, even if she couldn't help herself from staring with a slowly growing unease. Although Courtney herself presented an intimidating demeanor, the sudden spike in Monica's guardedness was more the fault of the uniform than anything. But such was a side effect of living a life in which illicit acts were often a requirement of her survival.

After overcoming her hesitation, Monica echoed an uncertain, "good morning," which was answered with a curt nod as Courtney's eyes continued to move fluidly across the page. The cup of coffee in her hand caught Monica's eye as she moved to take a sip. Just as Monica was about to turn back towards Finn to ask for a cup of her own, her eyes stopped on an unusual space on the back of the newspaper, which bore merely a single line in the center of an otherwise vacant square, clumsily hidden amongst the ad space. But it wasn't *meant* to be hidden, not from Monica, anyway.

"We need to talk. Summon me immediately. -M"

Monica's heart leapt into her throat, rendering her voiceless as she turned to face Finn.

His expression stiffened when he read the urgent disquiet that was sprawled across her face. Leaning towards her, he asked in a hushed whisper, "What's wrong?"

"We have to go." Monica answered, pointing in his mother's direction from behind the cover of her other hand. "Now."

His eyes barely left Monica to search for the cause of her alarm before asking, "Why?"

"You're not going to have breakfast before you go?" Courtney chided calmly, turning the page and reshaping the structure of the newspaper with a controlled flick of her wrists.

Monica bristled at her response. She should have known better than to trust Courtney's sleepy and otherwise occupied facade, but she hadn't expected her to be alert or aware enough to catch her comment, let alone make one of her own. She needed to be careful. And she needed to get Maal's note away from her before she risked having even more to explain.

Clearing her throat, Monica whirled back to face Courtney with a posture that mimicked being at military attention as she addressed her.

"I mean, I certainly don't want to keep Finn's grandad waiting more than we already have."

"Uh-huh." She hummed unamused, keeping her eyes low as one of her eyebrows lifted in judgment. "Monica, he's waited for three weeks. Don't think another twenty minutes is going to change much."

A twinge of conflict rose within her at the sound of her own name. Something about its use was both friendly and warm, but also stirred an anxious feeling that Courtney was winding up to give her another scolding. Monica was starting to grow frustrated by how unreadable she was beyond the austerity of her own guarded mask. Finn's mom wasn't like most people, and that made it difficult for Monica to be prepared.

Monica's pale eyes jumped to Finn as he passed, carrying two precariously full bowls of cereal in each of his hands. He tried to encourage her with a small smile, but it only showed how blissfully unaware he was at the tense urgency that currently threatened her. She knew that that would change as soon as he sat down at the table across from his mother.

"But you said *first* thing this morning." Monica recited dutifully, her tone emollient, so as not to come off as argumentative. "I just thought—"

Courtney gave a dry scoff as one corner of her mouth twisted with a fleeting glimmer of mirth. If she didn't know any better, Monica would've thought that her discomfort was humorous to her. Perhaps it was. Or perhaps it was merely a territorial instinct that had emerged when faced with the realization that there was another female in her son's life now. Even though it wasn't a romantic attachment, it wasn't unreasonable to imagine how Courtney could see Monica as a threat, especially after she had managed to completely separate him from his mother for weeks.

The curl faded from her mouth as Courtney made a gesture for Monica to sit.

"We don't leave this house without having breakfast first." She remarked matter-of-factly. "It *is* the most important meal of the day, after all."

As Monica cautiously approached the table and delicately perched herself on the chair that Finn had pushed out for her with his foot, Courtney's eyes lifted slowly to meet hers. Monica's gaze ducked in past the newspaper but spied no plate or bowl of food sitting before her, only coffee.

"Is coffee breakfast?" Monica inquired innocently, her cheeks flushing with a mild heat when Courtney's gaze finally met hers.

She hadn't meant for the question to sound like the sarcastic challenge she now sensed that it had. But as much as it now made her uncomfortable to persist, she didn't allow herself to wither under the weight of Courtney's focus. After a silent second that felt like an eternity, Monica was stunned to notice the shadow of a smile cross her lips.

"It is for me." She finally said, tipping her cup in Monica's direction in a gesture of respect. "But I also don't have the metabolism of a teenager anymore. So my example doesn't apply to you."

Finn gave an impish smile as he leaned towards Monica and mumbled, "They'll have donuts at the office. It *is* a police precinct, after all."

Monica smiled and her tension eased with Finn's joke. She obediently went to mirroring Finn's eager consumption of the sugar-coated wheat puffs, but the urgency of her previously uncommunicated message still gnawed at the back of her mind. Her gaze rose to the newspaper once more, wondering why Finn hadn't noticed the note yet. Her heart sank with a mix of annoyance and frustration to see that Maal's magical note had shifted back to an advertisement for an injury law firm, leaving no trace that anything had ever been out of place. But every passing second made its words even sharper in her mind.

Immediately, he had said. Summon him immediately. Something was wrong. Something he couldn't say in a written message.

When Courtney turned another page and straightened the paper again with a shake, Monica gave a furtive but clearly intentional nudge to Finn's arm with her elbow. Their gazes locked. Monica, deciding not to risk even the barest of whispers merely mouthed, "We have work."

A flash of panicked understanding lit Finn's eyes before he mouthed back, "Now?"

She nodded, which prompted him to continue with, "What about—"

She gave her head a tight, warning shake, her eyes flitting to the presence curtained behind the lifted newspaper.

"Now."

Drawing in a tense breath, Finn promptly inhaled what remained of his cereal, encouraging Monica to do the same with a movement of his eyes. As soon as she had finished, Finn scooped both of their bowls into the sink and began to usher Monica out of the kitchen.

"Well, have a good day at work, Mom. We're off to Grandad's."

Courtney looked up from the paper with narrowed eyes.

"You know it's Saturday, right? I'm not going to work."

Finn blanched, his nose crinkling in confusion as he peered down at her uniform. "Then why are you—?"

She grinned at him, the glee only serving to widen her lips, but didn't make it to her eyes with the usual light of humor that a smile like that usually carried.

"Just keeping you on your toes. It's Thursday. Do they not have calendars where you went?"

She brushed off the joke before he could answer, draping the newspaper across the table as she stood from her chair. As she crossed the kitchen to refill her now-empty cup, Courtney shook her head and sighed, "My boy, as gullible as ever. You make it too easy to rattle you."

Finn forced an uneasy laugh, accepting a one-armed hug as she leaned in towards him.

"Maybe you could learn something from Monica. She doesn't seem like the type that lets *anything* shake her." Courtney praised, catching Monica's guarded gaze as she pulled back from her son's embrace.

Monica couldn't help but smile in spite of herself at the realization that she'd been triumphant in hiding her unease throughout this interaction. Not to mention the warmth that had come with Courtney's praise. Despite keeping her on her toes, Monica begrudgingly acknowledged the fleeting thought that she was actually beginning to like Courtney. Even though she seemed prickly at first, Monica also sensed that she was the kind of person who would unquestioningly stand up for those who had earned her loyalty and protection. Not only could she always use more people like that in her life, but it was also an attribute that she respected, especially since loyalty was something that was too often bought and sold in Arkynesta.

Smoothing a fallen lock of hair from Finn's face, Courtney continued, "Be good to your grandad, okay? He's had a hard time since you disappeared."

Finn gave an ardent nod and rushed Monica out towards the front door the second his mom's instructions seemed to draw to a close.

As soon as they were out of earshot, Monica remarked, "Boy, your mom does have a weird sense of humor, doesn't she? It's like she likes making people feel uncomfortable."

"She does," he admitted frankly. "It's one of the things that makes her such a good Chief of Police, I think. And it's one of the reasons I was so scared to cross her growing up."

"Fair." Monica shrugged, her tone and her demeanor turning immediately serious as she urged him out the front door. "Now c'mon. We gotta go."

His playfulness shifted also, to panic in response. "What's going on?"

"Maal wants to see us. Now."

"Now? But we're supposed to be going to see my grandad."

"I know." Monica sighed, her haste never slowing as she conquered the length of the sidewalk in a few, determined strides. "But he wouldn't have called if it wasn't important."

"What does he want?"

"I don't know."

"I don't want to get into worse trouble with Mom. We're already lucky she bought yesterday's story. She might just be letting some of it go." He whined.

Monica stopped to whirl on him, her brow pinched in clear distress.

"Look, what do you want from me? This is what you signed up for when you pushed so hard to work for Maal. When he says jump, we jump. Anything he says comes first. And then, we can go see your grandad right afterwards."

When Finn opened his mouth to ask another question, she silenced him with a raised finger and a firm shake of her head. “No, I don’t know how long it’s going to take, but the longer you resist, the more time we’re wasting. Come on.”

Chapter 8

Within minutes, the ocean came into view, curling around the far edge of Cape Bianca in a sickle of iridescent blue.

Even though her lungs burned from the determination that fueled their punishing pace, Monica didn't slow until they had reached the shore. Such discomfort was nothing compared to the increasing apprehension that stabbed needles into the back of her brain as it raced through the variety of misfortunes that Maal's call could come to represent.

She couldn't tell whether Finn was finally starting to understand the foreboding of the situation, or if he was merely being compliant, but he kept up the pace without complaint. He only stopped to question her after they had reached the cave, which was tucked into the craggles of the uninhabited portion of shoreline several miles past the last pier. He hesitated as he hung back to watch her duck in through the squat opening, meeting her gaze with an expression that was twisted with uncertainty.

"Where are you going?"

"This is the cave I keep my summoning materials in."

"Is it safe?"

"It's secluded and well hidden, so the chances of anyone coming around here and asking questions is extremely low."

Finn's chest collapsed as he gave a nervous scoff. "That's not what I asked. Is it safe?"

Monica's brow softened into an arch of encouragement as she offered him her hand.

"Yes." She nodded. "It's safe. Just dark. The worst thing you might find in here would be a colony of crabs, which I'm certain you could defend yourself against."

A glimmer in his eyes acknowledged the humor in her feeble joke, but it died before it could spread to the rest of his face. Even though he took her hand and allowed Monica to lead him deeper into the cave, the fear only disappeared from his face because of the curtain of shadows that had fallen to obscure his features.

Remembering the string of lights and glowing stars that had lit the ceiling of his bedroom, Monica realized the root of his trepidation.

"Are you afraid of the dark?"

Her voice echoed in the small chamber, sounding much louder than it had in the open. It was answered by a single hum of ashamed confirmation.

Monica gave Finn's hand a comforting squeeze before fishing the lighter out of her pocket. It lit the darkness with a click that manifested a small amber flame. The glow warmed her cheeks with a smile that spread to Finn as she wrapped his fingers around the lighter.

"You're in charge of the light."

She turned her back to him momentarily, pivoting back to present a small blue satchel that she had recovered from one of the recesses sunken into the wall near the mouth of the cave.

His concern eased into curiosity as he watched her loosen the braided silver drawstring of the bag and dump its contents onto the floor of the cave with a muted clatter. That same curiosity sparked into a flame of awe as he took in the impossible multitude of items that had come from within the tiny bag. He knew it shouldn't have been possible, but his disbelief didn't alter the reality he saw scattered across the cave floor before him. Monica stooped to gather the several large red pillar candles, which she arranged into a neat row behind a small metal incense bowl, a rectangular metal tin, a glass bottle of oil, and a folded swath of fabric that appeared to be quite large, based on the thickness of its creases. And all of it had come from within a bag that had previously been merely the same size as her tiny fist.

"Bag of holding." She boasted with a smile. "Like the one from the market, remember? Only this one looks different."

A sudden look of understanding flooded across his face, mingling with the wonder that still remained in his eyes. It made Monica's smile widen, enjoying the persistence of his youthful wonder that somehow hadn't faded, even after several weeks of exposure to magic.

The urgency of Maal's command had since begun to dull in her mind, but returned with a sudden strength as she was overcome with the familiar, pensive feeling that accompanied summonings in the past. She took up the large, folded square of dusty, off-white textile and flicked it open with a forceful shake. The banner billowed slowly to the ground, landing to reveal a large circular sigil that measured a grand nine feet in diameter. Finn studied the design in the gently flickering light as Monica walked the perimeter, stooping several times to smooth out any wrinkles.

The circular sigil resembled an all too familiar six pointed star with rounded tips, comprised of six interlocking ovals. Finn quickly recognized it as Maal's star, realizing its vague likeness to the other six pointed stars on both the Riftrider and the Soulseeker amulets. He'd never thought to ask about it before but saw no reason to delay it now.

"Monica?" He inquired gently, garnering a glimpse of her pale eyes before she turned her attention downwards and began stacking the red pillar candles in her arms. "Why does everything have this star on it? I mean, I can see that it's not the same star on the Riftriders and the Soulseeker, but they're similar enough. And I've seen it everywhere. What's the significance?"

"It represents our universe of realms and how they're connected. Even though Maal's star doesn't have them, on both the Riftrider and the Soulseeker, there are seven circles, six at each of the star's points, and one in the middle. That's for each of the seven realms. Vhenra, the mortal realm, is in the middle, because it connects them all and has the strongest bond with each of the other realms than they do with one another. The star symbolizes that connection that allows travel between them."

"What are the other realms? I don't think you've ever told me before."

Monica gave him a wary look as she placed the last of the six candles on each of the points around the star and reached for the small metal tin near his feet.

"We don't have time for too many questions, and that is an awfully big question. I want to answer it well, but I'll have to be brief, okay?"

Finn nodded penitently, falling silent as he watched Monica flip open the lid of the metal tin and remove a small bundle of braided herbs. The herbs were laid in a shallow, palm-sized brass bowl and then placed in the center of the star. Trading the tin for the small glass bottle, she began to speak again as she decanted the oil and generously anointed the herbs.

"You already know of Vhenra, the mortal realm. It's the center point and connecting hub of the network of realms." Her tone grew increasingly somber with focus, as if digging deep into her memory for the words she now spoke. “And of Vhalta, the magic realm, where mythical creatures can exist without restriction. It’s where magic flows freely in the air, and in a far higher concentration than any of the other realms. Enderfel came up when we talked about my brother, because that’s the realm of spirits, the place where the dead go when their souls leave their bodies.”

Monica paused to draw a deep breath as she replaced the cork in the bottle of oil and set it aside. She wiped her oil-slicked palm against her jeans and then she paused. Her brow furrowed in thought, weighing her response.

“I don’t really know about the rest, beyond what I’ve heard, because I’ve never been to the other realms. I don’t even think I’ve met anyone who has, so I’m not sure how much of this is true, but this is the best answer I have.

"There is a realm called The Netherhaven, and that’s where the angels live. It’s said that angels help facilitate the flow of life, by keeping balance between the living and the dead. Then, there’s a realm called Scondera. Some don’t think that it exists at all because no one’s ever seen it. The ones who do think it’s real can’t seem to agree what’s in that realm; whether it’s where the angels go when they die, or maybe it’s even the realm of the immortal gods. No one can really say. Then, there’s The Abyss of Souls, which is more of a black hole than a true realm. It’s a place that takes things and beings out of existence completely and makes them disappear into oblivion. People don’t go there because no one ever comes back. Last, there’s the realm of Haedahl, which is the world where demons live. The demons couldn’t live with the rest of the magical creatures in Vhalta without causing great turmoil and suffering because of their evil nature, so Haedahl is almost entirely closed off. Actually, travel to all of those four realms is quite restricted, more so than even Vhalta and Enderfel.”

"Is that why The Enclave has restricted portals and travel magic? Because of how dangerous the other realms are?"

Monica gave a dry, mocking laugh.

"Doubt it. They're certainly not worried about the danger from anything more than a selfish perspective. I think it's more of a power thing. Besides, The Enclave doesn't usually want much to do with *any* of the realms outside of Vhalta. I honestly think they're happier and more powerful, for that matter, by keeping Vhalta separate."

"Oh."

As Finn quietly contemplated her words, Monica made any final adjustments to the setup of the summoning circle before retrieving the single white taper candle and offered it to him. His nose crinkled in confusion, squeezing the lighter tighter in his fist before realizing that she was likely asking for a light. He lifted the lighter, letting the flame leap to the wick of her candle.

"Put the lighter out." She instructed, and he obeyed.

Then, as his own flame went out, Monica offered him the candle and then motioned for him to approach the circle.

"Wh-what do you want me to do?" He asked nervously, taking the taper from her with careful fingers.

"Perform the summoning."

She nodded towards the circle, and his eyes went as wide as dinner plates.

"What? I can't do—"

"You can. I've taught you how, since you're required to be able to summon Maal at any point during your employment, if the need arises. The spell has already been charged by Monroe when he built it for me, so you don't need to have magic to be able to do it."

"Does the spell last that long?"

“As long as the banner does. It’s the artifact charged with magic. Magic never runs out as long as it has a strong enough conduit, being the artifact that it’s charged to or the wielder channeling it.”

“What if I mess it up?”

Monica gave an unconcerned shrug.

“Then I’ll do it. But I want you to at least get a real opportunity to try, okay?”

“Okay.”

“Oh, and here.” Monica twisted the tiger's eye ring off of her left thumb and shoved it towards him. “You can use this as the offering at the end.”

He opened his left palm towards her and accepted the ring, gripping it tight in his fist as he let his eyes fall to the bowl in which he would place it, after the words had all been spoken.

Finn steadied himself with a long, slow breath before sinking to his knees in front of the bowl of herbs. As he lowered the candle to light the bundle, Monica observed the first tendrils of smoke drifting up from the catching flame. She was silent for a moment as ribbons of fragrant smoke drifted into the air, making the light of the single flame murky as the air thickened.

“Do you remember the incantation?"

Finn swallowed but gave a hopeful nod as his mind turned inwards to recount the words. Though the candle was trembling slightly in his hand, he felt himself steady with a pensive reassurance as the first phrase came easily to his lips.

Just as he opened his mouth to speak, Monica gently reminded, “face north,” making his body snap into alignment. His eyes fell and his body followed, lowering to brace himself on one knee to light the first red candle before rising back to his feet.

"Maal, I call thee. Hear me."

Monica’s chin dipped in approval and Finn pivoted to the next point on the star in a clockwise rotation to light the second candle.

"Maal, I invite thee. Hear me."

Another pivot, another chant. The confidence in his voice became slowly more apparent as he continued after lighting the third.

"Maal, I implore thee. Hear me."

By the fourth candle, the air glowed with a murky orange warmth that made the air opaque as ribbons of smoke rose into the higher spaces of the cave.

"Maal, I compel thee. Hear me."

Upon the fifth, Finn felt himself stifling a cough as his lungs filled with the smoky sweet scent of the incense, which stirred the fleeting image of Monica’s first meeting with Maal, during which he had smelled this same scent pouring out of the canopied alcove that had concealed him.

"Maal, I summon thee. Hear me."

After he had lit the sixth and final candle, Finn had noticed the tension of anticipation returning to tighten his chest.

"Maal, I obey thee. Hear me."

After the final phrase was uttered, his eyes flitted to Monica for a nervous moment in search of a reminder of his next instructions. Mimicking her mimed movement, he snuffed the taper with a quick pinch of her fingers and let it fall to the ground.

His fist unfurled to reveal the ring in his hand, which now emitted a yellow glow from within its circular stone. Stooping forwards, he placed it gently atop the smoldering bundle of herbs, so that the circular tiger's eye it bore now glowed directly upwards, casting an eerie yellow shimmer across the ceiling in a dappled pattern that was very similar to sunlight filtering downwards through treetops.

Monica motioned him out of the trance that had taken him to marvel at the glow pattern, gesturing for him to step out of the circle. He did so, and they both turned to face the southernmost point before they knelt on the bare cave floor. He studied her posture before shifting to match it, bowing low so that his forehead came to rest on his knees.

They waited, eyes averted as the ribbons of perfumed smoke that festooned the air knitted into an opaque veil, lit from below by the glow of the tiger's eye. A breeze crept into the cave, making the tendrils dance briefly before they tangled into scattered clots of smoke that moved with a mind of their own. The smoke then coalesced to create a single form in the center of the circle, so dense it began to appear tangible.

Chapter 9

Just as the smoke had begun to thicken enough to start to look like it might bear a physical presence, a sudden breath of wind dissolved its opacity and made all six of the red pillar candles gutter and die in prompt succession.

Monica and Finn both remained silent in the darkness for several, long seconds before either of them dared to speak. Finn exhaled a shaky sigh.

"It didn't work, did it?"

Without a word, Monica lit her lighter again, letting Finn glimpse an expression of reserved assurance that gave him a sliver of comfort as she stood. Her eyes immediately scanned the darkened scene, motioning towards the center of the circle.

"Help me gather it up."

"W-why?"

One corner of Monica's mouth pulled up into a sly, congratulatory smile. "We don't want a mess when Maal arrives. It should only take him a few minutes."

Finn stifled a gasp and bowed his head in acquiescence and then he clambered to start gathering up the spell remnants. Monica balanced her still-lit lighter within a narrow recess in the wall before she snatched up the meager bag of holding and opened it towards Finn. He stuffed each of the red pillar candles back through the narrow opening, followed by the white taper and the bottle of oil.

"My ring, please."

Finn obliged, turning to retrieve the piece of jewelry from atop the still-smoldering bundle of herbs. He pinched its silver band delicately between his thumb and index finger, studying its dying glow before finally handing it back to Monica.

Her lips molded into a curve of comfort as she slipped the ring back into its familiar place around her left thumb.

Of all the magical artifacts she had ever had the honor of using, this ring, as arguably simple as its powers were, was by far one of her favorites. It wasn't often that Maal let her keep an artifact for her own use, but this one had proven to be of greater aid to her work in service to him, rather than remaining locked away in his personal collection. This ring had the power for removing barriers and making connections between things. Primarily, she used it for stealth; minor lock picking and such, as it was safer and faster than mortal means. But it was also incredibly useful in removing barriers between people, so it was an ideal offering and catalyst for summonings.

Its faint glow hummed briefly brighter, a sign that Maal was near, as Finn gathered up the last few items and dumped them into the bag. Now that only the banner remained, Monica set the bag aside to help Finn fold it back into a neat square. She shoved it into the tiny blue bag with impossible ease and haste. No sooner had she tied the drawstring, and their attention was called upwards by a voice in the darkness towards the back of the tiny cave.

Even though it was the same voice that Finn had heard back in Arkynesta, there was something more powerful about it now. It seemed both frightening and enthralling despite the misleading calm that smoothed its tone, expanding to fill the tiny space with an acoustic embrace.

"Good. You're here. We must talk." Maal's voice thrummed ominously as the remaining smoke eddied around it, rippling with each word.

Maal's emerging presence was marked by a faint, pale orange light at the back of the cave. At first, it was so dim that Monica and Finn's eyes had to strain to discern it, but the light soon swelled to reveal the expanse of his chest, neck, and chin, the only parts of him that were visible from within a tall column of black both above and below, as if he was garbed in a hooded robe made of solid darkness.

Something about the way Maal appeared before them now seemed inhuman to Finn, like he was now merely a partial entity, like a ghost, rather than the more tangible, undeniable man that he had been when he'd stood before them in his tower.

Though the glow of his incorporeal presence was undoubtedly to blame, perhaps more so, that inhumanity came from his eyes. After all, who could look *less* threatening with eyes made of liquid fire? The eerie propane-blue shimmer of his irises ripped through the darkness as he regarded them, their color interrupted by momentary blips of yellow and orange, ever shifting and changing in a kaleidoscope of flamelike iridescence.

Beyond the magical air of their shifting color, his eyes also held a magic of their own, a spell of suggestion that even the strongest willed were helpless but to befall. As before, he wore a cunning concealment spell that would make both Finn and Monica forget the features of Maal's face in favor of being engulfed by his eyes.

Though Finn had been trained for this, finding himself face-to-face with Maal's ghostly projection unsettled him in ways he could not explain. He was more than happy to remain quiet to collect himself while Monica headed up discussion of why they'd been called to summon him.

"What happened?" She asked gravely, her voice so practiced and steady that Finn wouldn't have known her unease had she not expressed it before that moment.

A low growl came from within Maal's throat, a sound of clear displeasure that made Finn shiver unconsciously. Though he couldn't see Maal's face, Finn became even more aware of the djinn's dark mood from the way the smoke that lingered around his feet had thickened and darkened.

"There was an intruder in the tower."

"An intruder?" Monica's voice sharpened. "That's not possible."

"It shouldn't be, no." Maal hissed bitterly, a line of shadow suddenly crossing the glow of his broad chest when he crossed his thickly muscled arms.

"Who was it?"

"Have you ever heard of Rowan Drake?"

Monica's eyes widened and her heart dropped into her stomach. The sting of tears surprised her as fury bubbled up into the back of her throat, making her eyes glow behind a sudden sheen of hatred. She barely noticed that her hands had balled into fists at her sides until the dull stab of her fingernails digging into her palms made her wince.

Divining her answer from the silence, Maal's voice echoed darkly with revulsion mixed with indignation as it filled the cave once more.

"I feared as much." Maal's voice was hypnotizingly smooth, his words controlled and deliberate with the slightest edge of pensive disappointment.

It tickled Monica's consciousness with that familiar compulsion to please him, which quickly sparked guilt at the reminder that she had hidden this information from him.

Though Finn was spared the caress of magic, he too felt the audible pull that made Maal's tone enticing despite his veiled anger.

"Did he really try to go through you to get to me?"

"Dear Monica," Maal snarled as his upper lip curled back to mimic the hatred that burned clear in her eyes. "Don't flatter yourself. He came to bargain with me, but it turned into a threat when I denied him. Why do you believe he has an interest in you?"

"Wait—" Finn chimed in, his cadence lifting with a dreadful and growing realization as he turned to Monica. "Rowan… Isn't he the man from your nightmare on the island? The one who tried to kill you?"

Monica's stomach twisted instinctually as a fragmented image scattered itself through her mind at the mention of the event. Finn was right; Rowan *had* tried to kill her, after boasting his opportunity to take advantage of a lapse in Maal's protection due to being under the control of that dangerously spell-bound island. Even though she had filled Finn, and Celene, in on the happenings of the vision long after they were free, they only knew as much as she had cared to tell. She was thankful Finn hadn't had to actually see it happen. She hadn't even hesitated to kill Rowan when she'd had the chance. Regardless of the circumstances, she didn't want Finn to have to see her as a murderer.

Even though it was a triumph and a liberation for her to have killed the wielder threat at the time, Monica winced at the knowledge that he wasn't actually dead. On the island, Rowan had only appeared to her in a nightmare, which she had since reasoned to mean that he had used magic to appear to her, rather than physically risking getting trapped on that nearly inescapable island. So, even though Rowan's threats had seemed rash and intimidating at the time, they had been more calculated than was originally visible. If Rowan *was* involved, her nightmare had been real, and so had his promise. They would meet again. They had to be careful.

"Monica?" Finn asked gently, shaking her from the haze of her distant thoughts. "He is, isn't he? The man who tried to kill you?"

Sniffing, Monica gave a tight nod.

"Why did I not hear of this?" Maal growled.

Even though his rigid tone betrayed little, the supernatural blue of his eyes flickered with a threatening charge of amber that said more than his voice ever could. His expression was like that of a predator cornered; intimidating and enraged, but also equally and guardedly fearful.

What was she supposed to say? That she had hoped Rowan had been nothing more than a hallucination that would cease to be real when she left the island? She knew how stupid such a hope sounded, even though it had been the truth. But she couldn't help but cling to it after Rowan's threat that he had been the one who had killed Monroe, because she had not so much as remembered his face. And if his claim *was* true, it would not only force her to admit how powerful Rowan was to be able to completely escape her memory, but it would also cast doubt over the sharpness of her own prized awareness.

Not only that, but she also certainly didn't want to admit how scared the prospect of him being real made her feel. The last thing she wanted was for Maal to have to hold her hand if he decided that Rowan was too big of a danger for her to be able to take care of by herself.

If Rowan was real, that was not a vengeance she wanted to give away so easily to someone else.

"It must've slipped my mind." Monica evaded with a tremble in her voice. "Besides, you have bigger things to worry about than my nightmares."

"He's hardly *just a nightmare* now." Maal hissed, his shadowy claws flickering against his arm as his fingers moved in a repeated wave of impatience. "You should have told me when you returned. I respected your wishes to be vague about the traumas that tormented you on that island, but I could not know the dangers of the things you kept from me."

"I didn't know he'd be a problem. He isn't one anymore though, is he?" Monica huffed, the fear in her voice leveling only momentarily as she clung to the fading reassurance of Maal's sense of vengeance. "After all, it was awfully stupid of him to infiltrate *your* tower, knowing full well that he wouldn't leave alive."

Maal went quiet. Monica's desperation sharpened as she searched his inscrutable facade for answers. His eyes went distant, their amber glow fading back to a blue so cold it could've frozen her on a whim.

"He's dead, right? You killed him?" She pleaded, her voice a mixture of hope and dread.

"He knows my name." Maal breathed in a monotone, his cold eyes still distant, as if finally being forced to face the harsh truth of his words for the first time.

"No." Monica whimpered, mouth agape as she tried in vain to draw breath.

Without warning, her knees buckled beneath her, sending her heavily to the floor. Finn crouched beside her, his panicked eyes searching her face for answers.

"Monica?" Finn murmured gently, but even when he lowered himself to block her gaze, her distant eyes looked through him with a desolation that made his heart ache with a desperate need to console her. "Monica, what does that mean?"

Monica's lower lip trembled as she tried to speak, but her voice had deserted her. Her eyelids squeezed closed, wetting her dark lashes as a couple of unruly tears rolled down her cheeks.

When she finally opened her eyes again, she was still and strong, even against the lingering fear that made her voice tremble around the question. Her eyes rolled towards Finn, her words deliberate as she spoke.

"Names have power in Vhalta, and they can be used to control people. If Rowan knows his name, It means that he can control Maal's powers —all of them— for his own agenda, *without* a contract."

"What?" Finn gasped in confusion. "But I thought names had to be given willingly before someone could use their power?"

"Not those belonging to a djinn. A lot of rules are different for djinns."

"Then… what does that mean for us?" Finn groaned as the full weight of the situation finally struck him.

"It means," Maal interjected darkly, "That your number one priority is now to find Rowan Drake. Thankfully, he only knows one of my three names, so he will not have total, unbreakable control over me until he obtains the other two. But that also means that we must hurry, because if he obtains the other two, he will be able to rule Elandis without meaningful opposition. And if he and The Enclave gain inexorable control over the greatest of the nine domains, he will set his sights on conquering the entire realm."

Finn considered this for a moment, his expression now one more of perplexity rather than dread. His head gave a tiny sideways tilt when he asked, "If you're that powerful, why don't *you* rule Elandis?"

"Because," Maal said frankly and without contempt at his innocent but easily twisted question. "I'm a djinn. And as Monica said, a lot of the rules of this universe are different for djinns than for the rest of its inhabitants, be it humans, creatures, wielders, or mythical beings. Even our magic is bound by different rules than the magic that flows freely throughout Vhalta. I cannot use my magic for my own purposes, but I can use it to support the will of another, which is why I make contracts. I can use my powers to support any contracts I hold, so long as it can be justified that the spell somehow ultimately benefited one or more of my contract holders. And at the end of those contracts, I can grant wishes that would otherwise take unimaginable power, but I cannot grant wishes of my own. That being said, in theory, it *could* be done. I *could* rule Elandis, but it would take far more effort and planning than the reign of a non-djinn ruler. Nevertheless, that's not my primary concern right now."

With a soft sigh of mournful realization, Finn remarked, "That's why you need us to take down The Enclave? Because you can't do it yourself, even though you have the power to, and even though they're hurting so many people."

"That's right." Maal purred solemnly.

Their gazes locked, and a moment of reverent silence passed between them as Finn finally understood.

"How did he get your name?" Finn asked meekly, but Maal answered him with only a grim shake of his huge head.

The alarm in Monica's eyes widened in revelation as she processed Finn's question.

"No," She insisted, "That's a *really* important question. Because even if we stop Rowan, wherever that information exists creates a ticking time bomb. Who's to stop someone else from getting it?"

"Not that I don't agree with you, Monica, but *priorities*." Maal growled, the darkness of anger returning to his tone. "Knowing where and how he obtained my name will be of no use if he gains total control over it, and of me."

Her eyes narrowed, studying what little she could of his inscrutable features as they wavered beneath the cover of his concealment spell. Not that he didn't always keep his cards close to his chest, but Monica suddenly couldn't ignore the growing suspicion that he knew more than he was saying. But, didn't he always?

When Monica remained silent, Maal commanded again, "Find Rowan Drake."

"You want me to find him?" She scoffed. "My skills aren't exactly in finding *people*, just items."

"Why do you even need *Monica* to find him?" Finn interjected, the naivety of his tone catching both Monica and Maal off guard. "I mean, Monica said you had eyes everywhere!"

"Not *quite* everywhere." Maal responded, and one corner of his mouth lifted into an impressed smirk. "But even so, The Enclave is often an exception, because, like me, if they don't want to be found, they *won't* be. Unless they're careless or we're clever."

"But what about magic?" Finn insisted, pausing to draw in a nervous breath upon realizing the renewed weight of scrutiny upon him. "Now that Rowan's got one of your names, doesn't that mean you're —I dunno— linked or something?"

Maal cocked his head to one side, studying Finn for a long moment before he gave a pitying shake of his head.

"If only it were that easy." The djinn agreed, with something akin to melancholy in his tone. "Control is different from a connection. It is one sided, only to be felt when it is called upon. Have you felt any extra awareness of me since *our* bond was formed?"

Finn's eyes fluttered as if clearing away tears of embarrassment before he surrendered with a small shake of his head. "No."

"As it should be." Maal acknowledged, allowing a brief additional explanation before turning his focus back to the task at hand. "Magic that links two entities in awareness or communication is extremely rare and exhausting to maintain, so would likely only be feasible with something physical to cement the link, like an artifact. Alas, even if Rowan were to gain *total* control over me —immortals forbid— I would not be able to sense him unless he was actively commanding my powers. Which is why I need Monica to find him."

"So how do you expect me to find him anyway?" Monica asked morosely. "Just ask around and pray I know someone who knows someone?"

"No," Maal chuckled dryly, the faintest curve of a sneer tempting to curl the nearest corner of his mouth. "I have a better idea. One of *my* contacts has alerted me to an artifact in the area that has the potential to be able to trace him."

Her lips had already twisted in contemptuous suspicion that she *wouldn't* like where his idea would take her. But, trying to reserve judgment, she decided to indulge the question.

"Where?"

"Who do you know that carries a sundry of unique artifacts in the area?"

"No, no, no. Absolutely not." Monica spat, vehemently waving her arms as if trying to swat his words away. "After what happened last time, he'd probably sick his fade hounds on me again, on sight!"

"No," Maal crooned, the smile now finally manifesting to show a glimmer of his iridescent shark teeth, which were blindingly white against the darkness. "He'd respect you for having the courage to return. And, after what happened last time, I'd say you proved yourself an adversary not to be tested. I wouldn't discount a grudge, but now that he's down a few body parts, as well as his precious fade hounds since the last time he saw you, I'd just about bet he'll be more cautious before trying to cheat you again."

"Wait… the hounds are gone?"

"Don't you remember? Celene made sure of that."

Though Monica still didn't like the idea of tempting misfortune by meeting with Grunnar again, having direction *did* give her a mild sense of relief.

"Assuming that all works, what in the seven realms am I supposed to do once I get the artifact and use it to find Rowan? Kill him?"

Maal silenced her with a dismissive wave of his long, black-taloned hand.

"Leave that part to me. All I need from you is to do what you do best; obtain the artifact and use it." Sensing the wariness growing beneath her reluctant silence, Maal added, "And Monica, we all know how this has gone in the past, so do us all a favor and wait to use it until you're back within the protection of my tower, hmm?"

Monica shot him a glare of scathing indignance but said nothing.

Then, without warning, Maal's presence winked out in the same way the summoning candles had after they'd been interrupted by the breath of wind from before.

Without so much as a pause, Monica returned the velvet satchel to its hiding place and left the cave and headed back into the city with Finn in tow.

Chapter 10

Once they returned to where the docks began and the streets of Cape Bianca unfurled to meet them, Monica bade Finn to lead the way to his grandad's. He led the way, but the hesitation that had overcome his stride made it obvious that he was suddenly far less concerned about seeing his grandad, and perhaps more eager to get on with Maal's task. After all, despite the gravity of the circumstances, this would still be Finn's first *real* job working for a djinn, not counting Monica's rescue, of course. And, if the enthusiasm that he had channeled into the last few weeks of training had been any indication, he was impatient to put those lessons to use.

"But we can't go to Grandad's just yet!" He argued over his shoulder. "What about the artifact?"

"I thought you didn't want to get into more trouble with your mom? We were delayed enough as it is. Besides, Grunnar only does business after dark. So we'll have to wait until then."

Sensing the tension in her clipped tone, Finn allowed his pace to quicken, but their new haste hadn't distracted his mind from the looming questions as he had hoped.

"Monica?" He began cautiously. "What is this artifact, anyway?"

Monica gave a single-shoulder shrug, seeming unperturbed by the lack of information that they had been given.

"As always, I'm sure *I'll know it when I see it.*" Monica remarked wryly, parroting the phrase that Maal had repeated to her all too often whenever she asked such questions.

As infuriating as that phrase had become, Maal was right. She *had* always known what she was meant to obtain when she saw it. And though she never fully understood the root of that instinct, she had never doubted it, and it had never failed her. Her skills in negotiation and reading people had been learned and carefully honed, but her instinct about artifacts —which ones were valuable, discerning the relics from the replicas, and even *how* to use them— was all innate.

"But wouldn't it help to have more information?"

"Of course it would," she huffed, the irritation apparent in her voice. "Unfortunately, that's just how Maal operates. The less we know now, the less we have to accidentally give away if something goes wrong later. But I'm not concerned. He has never set me up for failure by hiding anything important enough that it would've changed the outcome of any of my tasks so… I trust his judgment."

Finn weighed this for a few moments, his curiosity itching even more with her talk of deception, trust, and failure. It made Maal's words ripple back into his mind from the summoning, specifically about how her last job *had* gone wrong. With the things that he had learned about Monica, it struck him as odd that she wouldn't have a grudge over that incident, unless what had caused it to go wrong was her fault instead of his.

Either way, even though she likely wouldn't want to indulge the question, he decided that if they were going to be returning to the scene of that mishap, it would be wise to ask about what they were getting into.

“What… happened *last* time?”

Even through his partial sideways glances back at her as they walked, Finn caught the tension returning to her shoulders. Her posture squared and her gait became rigid as her steps quickened, prompting him to match the pace in order to avoid hindering the direction of their course.

"Last time," Monica admitted haltingly, her voice sharp behind a new edge, "we ended up in Arkynesta after being chased by Grunnar's fade hounds."

"I meant… before that. Leading up to it."

She let out a heavy sigh. She wanted nothing more than to remain reticent and evasive, but something about Finn's genuine and well-meaning curiosity made it impossible for her to stay angry with him.

Sensing his eyes upon her, Monica gave a permissive nod as she summoned her courage to admit the gritty details of the failed job.

"Grunnar is one of the few artifact dealers in the area who consistently has at least one unique or rare item every time I've had to work with him. He has a crew that pillages what's left of the ancient magical ruins of this realm and then they bring the bounty back to him to sell here. I've had several previous dealings with him, during all of which he has tried to swindle me. He has never succeeded. But, he *thought* that last time was going to be different."

"Why?"

"Last time, he got a glimpse of my Riftrider and then got cocky. He thought he was going to get rich by extorting a member of *The Enclave*." Monica made mocking quotation marks in the air with her fingers to highlight the bitter sarcasm of the concluding phrase.

"He thought you were a wielder?" Finn echoed with a humorous chuckle at the absurdity of such a notion.

Monica indulged in a brief chuckle of her own.

"Ridiculous, right? And I told him as much! But *no*, he wouldn't let it go. So by virtue of The Enclave's reputation, he decided that doing business with me was suddenly so dangerous that I should be charged ten times the original rate we had agreed upon, you know, for *insurance*." Monica rolled her eyes. "Well, when Maal wants to buy an artifact, he usually already knows what it is and has a rate set. I'm just there to enforce the deal and to ensure the item's safe delivery. He gives me the amount up front, so I didn't exactly *have* ten times the asking price. Nor was Maal willing to pay that when I alerted him of the issue. So instead, Maal concocted a little punishment for Grunnar, under the guise that we were *actually* going to pay him. Careful planning let me get away with the artifact. But as you can imagine, Grunnar was less than happy that the tables had turned on him. He tried to have me mauled in order to get the dagger back."

"And what was his punishment?" Finn asked with eyes wide in wonder as he hung off her every word. "Maal said he *lost some body parts*?"

Monica shrugged like it wasn't a big deal, but then she flashed him an impish grin and said, "An eyeball, at least."

"An eyeball?" He gasped, both enthralled and disgusted. "How?!"

As Monica considered the wording of her response, she realized that his gleeful enthusiasm had suddenly made her feel like her story was more intriguing than she'd originally thought. And what's more, she was actually enjoying telling it. She knew she shouldn't let herself get carried away, but it had been months since her last opportunity to tell the tales of her escapades. But, even so, Monroe had never been *this* excited to hear them.

"Have you ever heard of a Medusa Viper?"

He shook his head.

As Monica indulged him with the rest of the story's thrilling details of revenge, danger, and the magic that led to him being involved in her escape, the distance that remained to their destination elapsed in the blink of an eye. Monica had barely gotten to the part about accidentally arriving at the party when the storefront of *Dawson Deliveries* sprang up before them.

Finn slowed to a halt, his expression overcome by a new austerity as he peered up at the logo sprawled across the overhead sign. Monica was only absently aware of his sudden stop until she was in the middle of her next statement.

"I asked for a drink. And that's when you said, *I'm not exactly old enough.* And then—"

"We're here."

Monica's story and stride both halted at Finn's announcement. A prickle of nervous anticipation raised the hairs on the back of her neck and she pivoted to take in the sight.

The storefront was an add-on to a much larger warehouse building. It was not unlike several of the other warehouses that existed along this portion of town, which separated the piers and loading docks from the rest of the city, other than the fact that its metal siding was painted a bright robin's-egg blue. The broad side of the warehouse was lightly speckled with salt residue from exposure to the sea air but was otherwise crisp enough to make the color look like a recent improvement. The roof was edged in navy, a shade that matched the add-on's tall plate windows and the lettering on the large overhead sign.

As Finn still stood frozen in reverence, Monica took the opportunity to survey the scene. She couldn't see anyone through the tall windows, only glimpsing towers of boxes and shelves and a vacant counter, where she suspected a cashier should've been. She tilted to the side, just in case said cashier was merely hidden by the edge of the wall, but still saw no one.

Finally, she turned to Finn and asked, "Are you sure he's here?"

Finn's brow furrowed and he gave a nod of quiet assurance.

"Of course he is. He's the first one here every day, even before the sun is." Finn's seriousness eased with a small smile and he made a gesture towards the building. "Well, let's go."

Monica nodded in agreement, falling into quiet step behind him. A cluster of tiny bells clattered against the top of the frosted glass door as Finn barged inside, his head spinning to and fro in search. Instantly, a man's voice with a vaguely southern accent called out through an archway that was behind the empty counter.

"Be with ya in a minute."

"Grandad? It's me."

The door jangled closed behind Monica. She only had time enough for a single glance towards Finn before he was swept away into a strong hug. Monica tensed, alarmed that she had barely even registered the man's swift and noiseless assault. But her muscles slackened as she observed the details of the man now hugging Finn.

Despite not being genetically related, the man that now stood before her held a remarkable physical resemblance to Finn. He had the same lean musculature and slightly gangly build, despite the slump of age that had begun to hunch his shoulders. His white hair was trimmed short in a cleaner version of Finn's ruffled, touchably spiky style, and when he pulled back from the hug, she was met by a hazel version of similarly warm, sparkling eyes.

The man's expression was already alight in joy, but his exuberance brightened even more when he saw Monica. His eyes narrowed dramatically behind the rise of his rosy apple cheeks and his head gave a little sideways tilt as he studied her face, as if trying to figure out where he knew her from.

Though the attention initially gave her a twinge of discomfort, it quickly abated in the shadow of his overwhelmingly friendly demeanor. His eyes were so honest and safe and inviting that— after noticing the needling urge to tell him everything about her life in a single breath— she wondered if this man had some kind of magic of his own.

Then, with none of the assumptions that had been present in Courtney's version of the phrase, he said, "You brought a friend with you."

The lilt of his voice was graceful and melodic despite the slight droop of his drawl, but the accompanying openness of his expression accommodated for the meaning of any deformed syllables.

Finn's toothy grin reflected his grandad's delight when he turned to present her.

"Grandad, this is Monica."

"Pleased to meet you, sir."

Monica stuck out her hand, only to be swept into a bear hug that trapped her arms awkwardly at her sides as he squeezed her. When he finally released her, he said, "None of that *sir* business here. You can call me Scott, or hell; you can even call me Grandad, too!"

An involuntary rush of color surprised Monica as it flooded into her cheeks, making her shrink into her shoulders as Finn interjected.

"Grandad," He laughed, but not with the same discomfort he'd had when correcting his mom. "Monica's just a friend."

Scott's face stretched with immediate horror, making Monica realize who Finn had learned his *embarrassed* face from. Had he learned to blush from his grandad too? Because based on the color now leaching into his age-dappled cheeks and forehead, she deduced that Scott may have been a red head before age had whitened his hair.

"Nah, I didn't mean it like that," He chortled back. Something was now more restrained about his voice beneath the addition of self-consciousness. "I was just bein' friendly."

His watery hazel eyes rolled back towards Monica, his animated face now melting into a mask of penitence.

"I hope I didn't offend you, miss." He said honestly. "I didn't mean it to sound like I was assumin' anything."

The color quickly fell from her cheeks as she excused his misstep with an easy shake of her head.

"You can call me Monica… Scott."

He beamed at this, confirming her words with an ardent bob of his chin.

"Nice to meetcha, Monica."

Then, with barely a moment's pause, his attention snapped back to Finn. His smile melted into a firm line, conjuring scowl lines at the corners of his mouth, even though he wasn't actually scowling. His bushy brow plunged forwards with a new sternness and his expression sobered like a switch had been flipped.

At least ***he*** *wasn't hard to read,* Monica thought. The opposite, in fact. While she certainly didn't have the energy to keep up with the committed level of emotions he had already exhibited, she appreciated seeing someone who was unafraid of displaying the nuances of every genuine emotion that crossed their mind. Kind of like Finn…

Anchoring a fist against one hip, Scott scolded, "Boy, you just 'bout gave your mom a heart attack, going missin' like that."

"I know, and I'm really sorry. I never meant to hurt her."

"D'you tell her that?"

Finn gave a solemn nod, and the furrows in Scott's brow smoothed into clemency. "What happened?"

A spark of hope returned to Finn's eyes and his mouth pursed with a daring, pleading smile as he announced, "I got a job."

"Really?" Rather than looking slighted or put out, Scott looked genuinely taken aback before his demeanor evolved into vicarious pride. "Well, let's sit down. You can tell me all about it."

Chapter 11

The fact that Finn's grandad didn't seem the slightest bit upset after that brief moment deeply baffled Monica. But then again, even though his expressions of emotion were overt and unrestrained, she imagined that he wasn't the kind of man to hang on to any of them for too long, especially his anger. Not to mention that, knowing his daughter, Scott probably figured that Courtney had been furious enough for the both of them. In fact, he fleetingly said as much at one point, along with his opinion that Finn's mom was inclined to dramatic overreactions borne from her overprotective nature, or something like that.

But as Finn bravely told his story, a reiteration of Monica's fabricated cover, moments of concern *had* resurfaced across his grandad's face. He cared, deeply and genuinely, only it seemed that he preferred to care in the moment rather than to cling to the emotions of even the recent past. Which is why he wasn't angry, not anymore. He was relieved and happy for Finn.

Monica decided that she not only admired that but envied it. How freeing it must've been not to have to hide one's true thoughts and emotions from the world, and to be able to live without the constant sorrow of a tormenting past.

She remained relatively quiet throughout the story, sensing that Finn wasn't concerned about handling this one on his own.

When Finn had finished, Scott inclined his chin in consideration. He was silent for a moment before he asked, "And how'd your mom take it when you told 'er you'd be leavin' again?"

Finn drew a sharp inhale, but his smile didn't waver when he admitted, "Hard. She wasn't happy about it. But I told her that I'm an adult now, and I asked her to respect my decisions."

At this, Scott looked both surprised and impressed.

"*You* stood up to your mama? And she listened?"

"I mean, she didn't like it," Finn said with a shrug, "but yeah, she listened."

Scott's lips parted to allow a forceful exhale of surprise, accompanied by an incredulous shake of his head. He leaned back in his chair and his eyes shifted to Monica. A flicker of realization made one of his eyebrows arch like a fuzzy caterpillar climbing up to a higher branch.

His watery gaze fixed on hers, and though he said nothing, a quiet understanding passed between them. *She* had been the variable, the change that had facilitated both Finn's courage to stand up for himself, as well as Courtney's reluctant willingness to listen. A glimmer of appreciation warmed his eyes, filling Monica's chest with a faint echo of the sensation of nervous butterflies she had previously experienced. But this time, the sensation was pleasant to her, and even joyful.

Then, Scott turned back to Finn, his mouth creased in a reluctant half-smile of disappointment.

"Ya know son, even though I'm proud of you for going after the opportunity that you wanted, I'm gonna miss ya."

"I'll be back to visit," Finn whined before adding sheepishly, "ya know, periodically."

A small chuckle stuck in his grandad's throat, but as he shook his head, the mournful gleam in his eye briefly suggested that he knew differently. And though Monica was determined to try her best to help keep Finn's promise, she anticipated that Scott was more right than she wanted to admit. After all, seeing Finn's explosion of enthusiasm when he talked about the job and the new places, and all of the new experiences that his new life was offering him, she knew it would only get harder and harder over time for him to come back. It would be too easy for him to get wrapped up in those experiences and lose track of what he had left behind in this world.

Scott gave a thoughtful hum, as if reading the thought from Monica's face with no more difficulty than she had reading his. But, instead of acknowledging it, his gaze went distant and his facade drooped with a changed melancholy.

"I'm not worried about you, Finn. I can see your determination, and I know you'll do great things." He gave a sigh and his dark eyes lifted to flit past the towers of boxes that now sprawled out around them from where they had gathered at the edge of the warehouse's opening. "But I am worried about who I'll get to replace you."

Concern creased Finn's brow and his chin dipped in shame.

"But I've been gone for three weeks. In that time, you kept my job open for me?"

Scott shrugged, but his smile was one of reassurance. "I mean, I had to have someone cover your route in the meantime, but yeah. I knew you'd come back, eventually. I just didn't think it would be to say goodbye."

"It isn't goodbye, Grandad."

Scott gave a wave of his wrinkled hand, in a gesture that seemed to say, *I know, I know.*

"Even so, it is to this job. I mean, I knew it was on the horizon. You'd be leaving for college soon anyway, even if you came back to work. But it's gonna be different without you around. It's not often that I find employees who work as hard or care as much or as honestly as you do. You're a big part of why I have so many loyal customers." To this, Finn blushed a little, but it faded as soon as a change of tone made his grandad's words turn ominous. "But to be frank, that's not all I'm worried about. Crime in this town has doubled since you left, and it's affecting the deliveries. There have been five routes robbed since you took off, and two of those occurrences happened on yours."

A muscle in Finn's jaw feathered as he grit his teeth. His face flushed red with intense indignation and his eyes burned with angry tears. Tension bound his broad shoulders as he shot his eyes sideways towards Monica. The look was a question. Had this rise in crime been caused by the same hoodlums that she had scared away when she saved Finn from a similar fate?

Her own jaw tightened and she folded her arms over her chest. It wouldn't have surprised her, honestly. If word got back to Grunnar from the goblins that she chased off, it would've been a prime opportunity for them to continue after she disappeared. And it wasn't unlike ogres to hold a grudge. Even though the first robbery could have been a random occurrence, her rescue of Finn and then subsequent slight against Grunnar could have put a target on Dawson Deliveries. It wouldn't have mattered to them that she wasn't involved with the delivery company before saving Finn. Goblins and ogres don't exactly have a reputation for being the most logical of creatures. All that would have mattered to them is that at one point, she seemed to care enough to stop them, and now she had wronged them.

Her eyes narrowed with the spark of a plan she turned away from Finn.

She leaned forward in her chair and addressed Scott with a cautious and conspiratorial tone.

"What if I told you I had an idea of who was doing that? And even how to stop them?"

Scott's eyebrows lifted to reveal a moment of interest before he reassessed this and gave a more measured response. His eyes jumped briefly to Finn and then back to Monica, his face growing skeptical.

"Now, I appreciate you kids wantin' to help, but I do *not* want you putting yourselves in a dangerous situation on my account. If you tell me who you think it is, we can just get the police involved instead."

"No!" Finn shouted, immediately shrinking back from his vehemence as the attention turned to him.

But Monica was smooth to recover the conversation with, "Finn's right. Police wouldn't do much in this situation."

"Then what makes you think that *you* can?"

Her gaze shifted back to Finn's, translating the pleading expression that was now forming on his face to match the forbidden thought that had briefly crossed her own mind.

When she remained silent, Finn leaned towards her and whispered urgently, "We have to tell him."

"We can't. You know that."

"He's different. He'll believe us. And he won't tell anyone else."

Scott cleared his throat, and when the two looked up, they were met by his expectant eyes.

"Tell me what?" He asked hoarsely, as if failing to mimic their whisper.

Finn's eyes bore back into Monica with an even more intense expectancy than his grandad's. His brow was slowly knitting together, his lips pursing to plead with her once more.

Monica took a long moment of silence to deliberate, giving his grandad a long, appraising look as she decided whether trusting him was worth the trouble it could likely cause her. His eyes were honest, but the ache of reluctance in her chest was too great. It was a knowledge that could put him at even more risk. He seemed like a nice guy, and she didn't want that for him, or for Finn to have to worry about him. Besides, she saw no edge that telling him the truth would give them towards improving their chances of success in stopping the goblins.

Her breath caught when her lips parted to allow a shallow exhale. Avoiding both of their eyes, Monica shook her head and whispered back to Finn, "We can't. It'd be too dangerous."

"We'll be fine." He tried to reason, earning the returning wrath of her glare.

"It's not us I'm worried about." Monica bit back, her tone immediately making Finn draw back with mortified understanding.

"Oh."

"Will one of you *please* tell me what's going on?"

Monica shook her head apologetically as she addressed him with a casual tone.

"I'm sorry, Scott. I don't want to make any promises, and I certainly didn't mean to make you worry. We'll help if we can, but we can't tell you what we're going to do. It's better if you didn't know, just in case the perpetrators decide to retaliate."

A great, sorrowful concern swept across his face.

"But you kids aren't going to do anything *too* dangerous, are you?"

“It’s nothing more than what we were already going to do.” Monica admitted honestly.

“It’s not anything illegal, is it… what you two are involved in?”

“Of course not!” Finn joined in, missing the furtive sideways glance from Monica that warily suggested otherwise.

But seeing how his grandad’s expression and posture both wholly relaxed with the reassurance, she didn’t dare try to amend the statement. Her mind returned to the inkling of a plan that had emerged before.

Tentatively, she said, “There *is* something that you could do for us that might help, though.”

“Anything.” Scott nodded vehemently.

“Do you have a spare uniform that would fit Finn?”

“Sure.” He motioned towards a short line of metal lockers stacked against the wall on the opposite side of the open archway. “There should be a couple of spares from past employees in one of them unassigned lockers. I do wish you kids would tell me what you’re plannin’ though.”

Monica dipped her chin in appreciation and immediately stood and strode over to the lockers.

"So how long are you planning on staying in town?" Scott asked.

Monica heard Finn give a nervous chuckle from behind her, but her focus remained on the lockers. Her mind filtered out the clanging of the metal doors opening and closing as she looked through them, keeping her auditory attention split from her vision to continue monitoring the conversation that unfolded behind her.

After a hesitation, Finn said, "I'm not sure."

"Probably not long." Monica interjected between locker slams. "If things go according to plan anyway, we'll need to deliver that *thing* right away."

Scott cleared his throat, but merely gave a wordless hum instead of the question Monica suspected that had crossed his mind. She gave him points for suppressing his curiosity to maintain their privacy. Few people had that much control, not to mention, respect. Questions came as an impulse to most people, and nosiness caused an itch that was often hard to ignore.

"Well, d'you think you can come for dinner tonight?"

Monica didn't even need to turn to register Finn's hesitation. Even with her back turned, she felt his eyes upon her, waiting for permission. But, just as she was about to dismiss the question entirely, she succumbed to an unexpected tug of emotion. Without even looking at him, she could *feel* how important this opportunity to spend more time with his grandad was to Finn.

After a pause, she asked absently, "What time?"

"Uhh, about eight?" Scott offered.

"Well, we do have work tonight." She answered, her focus resolving into the fleeting flicker of a smile when she finally found an appropriately sized uniform. She folded it across her arm, latching the locker door behind her before turning to rejoin the group.

"What?" Finn whined. "That early? I thought we didn't need to be there until later."

"We have some preparations that will need to be completed first if we want things to go well. But," She hesitated, catching a glimpse of the melting sadness in his pleading eyes as she placed the uniform in Finn's lap, before turning her attention back to Scott. "Maybe we could swing by earlier, if we're not too long."

A smile overtook Scott's face and he exclaimed, "Hell, it's not like I've got anywhere to be. Does six work better?"

Monica's eyes lingered on Finn's still hopeful face, only pausing for a moment before she gave a small nod.

“Great! What are y'all in the mood for?"

Monica shrugged. "As long as it doesn't involve raw fish, I'm easy."

He answered with a hearty laugh. "I take it that means Courtney ordered sushi. I'm not surprised. Why my girl likes that stuff, I will *never* understand. But don't worry. Even though I'm not a great cook, I have a couple of family favorites memorized." His index finger tapped twice against his temple. “You are good with *cooked* fish, though, right?”

“Sure.” Monica chuckled.

“Great!” Scott beamed. “Then we’ve got a plan.”

“Great.” Monica echoed as a reserved smile danced across her lips. “We’ll be looking forward to it. But we should head out for now and let you get back to your work.”

With a polite nod, Scott stood and walked them back to the front of the shop, waving at them through the window as the door swung closed behind them.

Chapter 12

Finn's eagerness barely waited long enough for them to get out the door before he started prodding Monica for details about her plan.

"So you really think we can help my Grandad by stopping those robbers?" His voice was bright with hopeful anticipation.

"If they're Grunnar's men, like I suspect, it's definitely a possibility. But we'll have to be careful."

"What did you have in mind?"

"Well," Monica glanced at her watch, squinting before her other hand could rise fast enough to block the penetrating rays of the noonday sun. "We've got several hours to kill before Grunnar will be open for business. But I don't think it's a good idea to go after the goblins before our job, just in case it goes wrong and somehow messes up our chances with Grunnar even more. But it *does* give us an opportunity to hammer out a plan, so that we can go tomorrow."

"But what if the job goes *so* well that we get the artifact and have to go away tonight?" Finn asked with a clear nervousness in his tone.

"Even though the possibility of that exists, however small, I don't think it's *at all* likely. If Grunnar is as pissed as I suspect he'll be, it'll be a miracle if he's willing to say *anything* useful to me. But if we can get enough of a confirmation that he even *has* such an item, we can go about it another way."

Finn's eyes narrowed and his lips nearly disappeared as they rolled together in a thin, contemplative line. He clearly didn't like what Monica was implying. But, before he could argue, she gave him a pat on the arm and continued walking away from his grandad's shop.

"C'mon." She called out over her shoulder, prompting the eager patter of his stride to resume behind her as he skipped to catch up.

"So what do we do in the meantime?"

"We work on the plan." She said with a shrug.

"Which plan?"

"What can you tell me about your old route?"

"It varies based on the day of the week, but if we go tomorrow, that would be the same route that they tried to rob me on before."

So, the two spent the afternoon canvasing the loop that constituted Finn's old Friday delivery route, which started along the pier and covered several blocks of shoreside condos, like the one she'd been squatting in when they'd met. Then, the route went up into the city, catering to a couple of the smaller mom-and-pop shops before looping around a quiet park and hooking back to a block of apartment buildings that had a cluster of several stops that marked the end.

Finn thrilled at the sensation that came from their furtive research and made careful note of all of the places Monica pointed out as potential ambush spots where the muggers might hide. This was the first time he'd really gotten to see her working up close. He was enthralled at the glimpses of the inner workings of her mind that this allowed him, stunned by how cleverly she read into small details that he'd never noticed lurked just below the surface of the daily life he'd known for so long. Though her explanations were laconic, they were also efficient and educational.

After their excursion, Finn retrospectively understood why she had wanted to wait to confront the goblins. The information that they had gathered today would dramatically increase their chances of success in finding and confronting them in a way that would give them the upper hand in negotiations, something they wouldn't have by charging in blindly.

Monica and Finn returned home shortly before his mom got home from work. Monica decided to use some of that time to clean herself up for their dinner, not realizing until after her shower that she actually felt the need to impress Finn's grandad. But she decided not to let herself think too much into it, as she'd already had to deal with more vulnerable and frankly, exhausting, emotions over the last few days than usual.

Finn invited his mom to tag along to dinner, but Monica found herself secretly thankful when Courtney declined. Monica thought she'd noticed a flicker of longing in Courtney's eyes after the refusal, but respected her restraint when she explained that she didn't want to cut into Finn's time with his grandad. That didn't save them from the somewhat uncomfortable car ride with her when she insisted on driving them to Scott's house, but at least it was over quickly, and didn't contain too many new questions that needed answering.

Monica noticed their destination from blocks away. Though the little house didn't stand out amongst the quaint, residential neighborhood in an obvious way, something about it seemed to sparkle with an inviting warmth, even at a distance. Courtney's suburban slowed as they rolled up to one of the corners towards the East end, at which stood a white brick farmhouse with dark shutters and matching trim. A warm glow shone from all of the large windows that ran along its face, as if Scott had turned on every light in the house to welcome them.

The house was set back from the street to make room for a large wrap-around porch lined with white railings that stretched up to connect to the overhang that covered it. The yard was lush and green, but without much decoration beyond the grass and a pair of young aspen trees that framed the cobblestone walkway.

"You two have fun, okay?" Courtney said as they began to climb out of the back seat. "What time do you want me to pick you up?"

"Oh, don't worry about it." Monica dismissed with a shy gesture, trying to make the response sound casual and innocuous despite the suspicious narrowing of Courtney's eyes suggesting that it was already too late for that.

Finn was quick to rescue her with, "Monica's right. You know how Grandad and I get when we're together. There's no sense in you waiting up that late. I'm sure he won't mind bringing us home after."

After a long moment of uncomfortably reluctant silence, she groaned, "Oh, alright. But call if you're going to be much later than ten?"

Finn smiled and nodded, waiting to turn up towards the house until after his mom started to drive away. Monica tried her best not to look nervous when his eyes went to her, choosing instead to mirror the infectious smile that was slowly spreading across his face.

Why am I nervous? She thought, realizing the strangeness of the reaction as she followed Finn up to the front door. Well, perhaps it wasn't all *that* strange. After all, she wasn't used to meeting this many new people so quickly, especially people she didn't inherently need to be distrustful of. These weren't people who wanted something from her or wanted to hurt her; a concept that was admittedly rather foreign to her. People weren't this friendly in Vhalta, especially not to strangers.

But the way Finn paused to smile at her before he lifted his fist to knock made her anxiety ease. Her heart warmed for just a moment before it began fluttering again with a different kind of nervousness.

The front door of the house swung open under the motion of Finn's knock, and the pair were greeted by the smell of savory fried food and the far-off sound of Scott singing show tunes from the back of the house.

"Grandad?" Finn shouted, cupping one hand at the side of his mouth. "We're here!"

The singing stopped momentarily, only to continue with his own improvised lyrics of, "Come in, come in, the food is almost done," to a somber tune that Monica *almost* thought she recognized. Then, just as they started up the hallway, Scott's face popped out through an archway towards the back, plastered with an exaggeratedly creepy, but clearly joking grin. He gestured them nearer with his farm-animal patterned oven mitts as he sang another refrain of, "come in, come in, let's eat and have some fun."

This earned immediate laughter from Finn before he retorted, "Only if *I* get to be Jean Valjean this time."

Deciding not to comment on the joke she was clearly missing, Monica asked, "What are we having? Smells good."

Grandad grinned proudly, stepping aside to let them into the kitchen.

"Cornbread, collard greens and—"

Finn's eyes lit up with delight as both the and Scott said, "Fried catfish!"

"Oh, Monica, if you liked the fish and chips from Jojo's, you're in for a *real* treat now."

"You didn't have to go to the trouble." Monica began, but Scott shushed her with a shake of his head before handing them each an empty plate.

"No trouble, really. Besides, I knew how excited Finn would be."

Monica surrendered to a small smile that only widened as she hung back to observe Finn's expression as his grandad helped him dish up a heaping helping of each. Watching them together filled her with an uncomfortable mix of wistfulness, longing, and perhaps even a touch of envy. It was no wonder he wanted to come tonight. They both looked so at home in each other's presence, as though all they needed to be happy was each other.

And, seeing the way his smile grew when he turned his attention to her, Monica was stunned and a little frightened when she saw the way that Finn wanted to share that with her. She should've been happy, grateful even, but in that moment, a sudden twinge of guilt overshadowed those things in knowing that this wouldn't last. In seeing his childlike joy, all of a sudden, all she could think about was how they'd both be leaving soon, and how that was ultimately her fault.

Sure, Finn had fought hard to stay, and even though it was his choice to return, those options would've never existed for him if she hadn't accidentally brought him to Vhalta in the first place. Was it really fair of her to let him choose to put himself in danger and risk losing his family because of her mistake? But was it also fair of her to make that decision for him, especially after fighting so hard to prevent his mom from doing the exact same thing?

She swallowed hard, desperate to push the thought from her mind as she traded places with Finn to fill her own plate with food. She thanked Scott with an atypical shyness before she turned to follow Finn to the dining room. The realization that her normal, practiced austerity and cold guardedness wouldn't work here left her feeling vulnerable. She'd faced far harder challenges than this. In fact, playing nice at a dinner with a friend should've been a cake walk for her. But as the three of them sat down to eat, she found herself wishing instead for her admittedly warped sense of normal. Bargaining with an artifact swindler, pickpocketing a creature three times her size, or even hunting a member of The Enclave all instantly seemed like things she was far more prepared for than this.

As the boys began to sing and eat, she decided that the best thing to do would be just to keep her head down and act as quietly agreeable as she could manage until it was all over.

Of course, nothing was *ever* that easy.

Chapter 13

As dinner drew to a close, Scott excused himself to get dessert from the kitchen.

Monica took the moment to draw a concealed breath of relief, but soon discovered that she was clearly not doing as good of a job acting as she usually did. In her defense, she was only used to maintaining her more convincing masks for ten or twenty minutes at most, and this encounter was already approaching an hour. Not to mention that it was a lot easier to fool a crook than it was a sweet old man that had welcomed her into his home. But, maybe that was just her conscience talking.

The smile on Finn's face dimmed with concern the moment his grandad was out of sight.

"Monica?" he whispered. "Are you okay?"

Though his question was innocent and well meaning, her pre-decided guilt made it feel like an accusation. She kept her gaze low to avoid him and focused on the remaining bites of food on her plate.

"Mmm-hmm."

"You don't like the food?"

"It's delicious."

"Then what is it? Are you feeling left out that you don't know any of the songs, or our jokes? We can stop if you want."

The mere offer that Finn would sacrifice his grand time for her comfort made her heart ache.

"No, Finn," she mumbled, focusing hard to keep her voice steady as she felt the sting of unbidden tears pricking her eyes. Thankfully, a sharp intake of breath before she spoke again numbed them, at least momentarily. "I love that you're enjoying yourself."

"Then what?"

"I just… feel a little out of place, that's all." She instinctively lifted her head at the sound of footsteps approaching from the hallway, pressing the corners of her mouth back in a forced smile. "But I'll be fine, really. Thanks for including me."

"I've got peach pie!" Scott sang, placing the pan in the center of the table. "Who wants some?"

"Me!" Finn squealed.

"Yes, please." Monica agreed politely, not wanting to offend, despite not having much of a sweet tooth.

"Oh, before that," Scott caught himself, turning to Finn with an impish gleam in his eye as he produced a small, flat package wrapped in shiny green paper from behind his back. "I know it's a little late, but you can't fault me for that. Happy birthday, my boy."

He placed the package on the table in front of Finn before he sank back into his seat. Finn looked up at him with wonder in his eyes, a look of genuine surprise that quickly morphed into gratitude.

"Oh, Grandad, you didn't have to get me anything!"

"Well, honestly I didn't; not when you were still missing. You know how I always tend to be late with gifts and such anyway. I went out and got this after you two came and saw me this morning. I wanted to make sure you were really back, with my own two eyes, before I got too carried away." He laughed. "It's not much, but I think you'll like it. Well, go on, open it."

Monica eyed the package, cringing a little as Finn haphazardly tore into the paper with no regard to how neatly it was folded and taped. His fingers peeled away the shell of shiny green to reveal a notebook bound in supple black leather, barely larger than his phone. Its pages were rimmed in gold and its spine crackled as he thumbed through it.

"There's more."

Scott waved a hand towards the discarded wrapping, which Finn promptly upended until a long, thin box thudded to the table out of one of the halves. Brushing the paper aside with his arm, he lifted the box in his fingertips to inspect it before removing the lid to reveal a metallic dark blue pen with silver accents.

As he inspected the pen, Scott explained, "It's a tactical pen. It can do all sorts of neat stuff— open bottles, break glass— it also has a screwdriver, a flashlight, and a little knife inside it. Plus, it's supposed to write *real* nice. I figured you could use 'em to chronicle the adventures you have at your new job."

"Really?" Intrigue lit his face as Finn took a moment to fiddle with the pen. "Oh my gosh, that's so neat. Thank you!"

"I also figured, since you'd probably be too busy to call me and your mama all the time while you're working, you could maybe write us letters instead."

Scott's smile had shifted to bittersweet, his honest expression doing nothing to hide the gleam of tears in his eyes. His lower lip plunged forwards into a pout that Monica fleetingly acknowledged made him look like a hound dog, before the wave of contagious emotion forced her to turn away.

"Oh, Grandad, thank you so much."

Finn sprang to hug him, and a crushing fist of guilt wrenched Monica's heart in her chest. The sharpness of the sudden pain startled her as she bit back a cry and sprang from her own chair, causing the attention to immediately shift to her before she could choke down the sting of tears.

"Monica? Are you okay?"

She couldn't look Finn in the eyes as she answered, clutching her fists at her sides as she unsuccessfully tried to force the words out of her mouth. The sudden lump in her throat choked her, making it hard to swallow. Realizing that no words were going to come, no matter how hard she tried, she reluctantly lifted her eyes, letting him glimpse their glassy surface for only a second as she gave a stiff nod.

Finn's expression didn't ease, the concern sapping the joy from his face more with each passing second. His eyes were now studying her so intently that the scrutiny made her skin itch. The absence of her normal mask made her feel naked.

"Are you sure?" A bubble of panic rose in her chest at the sound of his unconvinced question.

She gulped against the lump in her throat, earning only a shallow breath that felt stale in her lungs. But it was finally enough for her to choke out the words, "I just need some fresh air."

Finn began to ask if she wanted him to go with her, but barely got the first word out before she had darted out of the room and up the hallway. She was out the front door before her next breath.

A whirlwind of chilly night air swirled around her as soon as she crossed the threshold. The front door slammed behind her and she threw herself down on the top step of the small staircase leading down from the porch. Even though she could breathe, she was still shaking so badly she had to anchor her elbows on her knees and rest her head in her hands to keep it from spinning.

The first thought that she became fully aware of as the mists of panic cleared from her murky mind was how trapped she felt, just then. And then, confusion. Why should the kindness of a stranger make her feel trapped? Sad, sure. Lonely, she could understand. The envy made sense, but the guilt; the guilt was the one thing she was unable to reason with. Guilt was one thing she had long since been without. After all, part of the grief and pain that had come with losing her brother was because of the crippling realization that his death had been at least partially her fault. But maybe it had been easier to cope with since she hadn't had to face that guilt until after the choice had already been made; until *after* it was too late.

But now; now, she could see the choice so clearly that it hurt. Two paths had unfolded before her, neither of which she liked. But this wasn't about her now. It wasn't about what she wanted, and she knew that. Even if what she wanted *was* what Finn wanted. She never thought she'd be able to admit that to herself, that she *wanted* Finn to stay in her life, that she actually valued and treasured his company, but maybe it was selfish to keep him in it.

Her mind flashed with images of Scott and Courtney, their faces, their fear and relief, and she knew she couldn't face the thought of knowing what those faces would look like if she allowed Finn to come back to Vhalta with her and somehow lost him in the process.

That won't happen, a small voice in the back of her head tried to convince her, but it struggled to be heard over the voices of her own fear, guilt, and perceived morality. *Finn's stronger than I initially gave him credit for. He surprised me once. He can do it again and come out alive against the odds.*

Then, a second, stronger voice spoke over it, saying, *but that's not my choice to make. I don't get to choose to let him endanger himself. What if it were me? What if someone was trying to take me away from my family? Would I want them to?*

Monica knew the answer, and that hurt her, almost more than the weight of her denial. She knew what she had to do, and she hated it.

Her gaze lifted to the sky, dark and speckled with stars. The misty glow of a waning moon filtered out from behind a smudge of stormy clouds, and a breeze caught the ends of her hair, making them tickle at the nape of her neck. Before now, she'd only been dimly aware that it was dark. But now looking up at it, she was consumed by the call to action, knowing that the dark was all that she had been waiting for.

She stood, finding her limbs no longer trembling with weakness.

Her focus panned towards the distant coast, which was obscured behind blocks of houses and a dark line of jagged buildings beyond it. Her thoughts shifted to Finn. Her stomach knotted with regret as her muscles tensed.

He'd forgive her if she left, wouldn't he?

Twisted up in her own thoughts, she barely felt the warmth of his hand on her shoulder until the force of it pulled her back from taking the first step down the stairs.

"Monica, what's going on?"

"Finn." Her eyelids fluttered as her gaze lifted to find the curve of his face, glowing warmly in the scatter of ambient light that flooded out from inside the house. Her heart leapt with a momentary and involuntary hope, but immediately sank into the pit of her stomach like a brick as she tasted the confrontation brewing on the tip of her tongue. So much for slipping away unnoticed.

"You've been out here for fifteen minutes. I was getting worried. What's wrong?"

Breathless, Monica shook her head as the lump returned to her throat. Frustrated, she fought it back, determined not to sound as weak as she felt despite the tremble in her words.

"I can't do this anymore."

"Do what? The dinner? I'm sorry, I should've asked—" He stammered, his thoughts becoming fragments as he scrambled for an apology. "I just thought you'd—"

"No," she whispered, lifting her hand to cup his upper arm as she fixed her stare on his. "Thank you for including me. I like your family, and I like getting to see that you have what I so dearly miss. But that's exactly why I can't do this with you anymore. I thought I could, but I can't. I can't take you away from them again. It isn't right."

"Monica?" Finn whimpered, his voice small and frightened. His wide eyes searched hers, frantic to understand. "What are you talking about?"

"I think you should stay."

"What?"

"Permanently. I don't think you should come back to Vhalta."

"What? No!" He pulled away, his expression twisting with the horror of betrayal in his confusion. "You said you wouldn't force me to stay."

"And I'm not. I'm not *forcing* you. I'm asking you. I know it's your choice, but I think that coming back with me is the wrong one."

Coming to grips with the initial shock, Finn slowly sank, letting himself rest on the stair that she had before pulling Monica down to join him. With a voice much calmer now, but no less frightened, he pleaded simply, "Why? After everything we've done, why now?"

"I just… keep seeing you with the people who love you so much and I can't help but think of everything I would do to keep that if I still had it. And it would be wrong for me to take you from it and put you in danger. I can't let you risk losing everything you have here."

"But what about you? I don't wanna lose you, either."

"You never *had* me, Finn."

Tearfully, his eyes fell. He shook his head, only looking away for a second before his eyes snapped back to her. His voice trembled with hurt, causing the ache in Monica's chest to reawaken.

"I don't understand."

"I don't know what you think this is, but I never wanted to hurt—"

"I thought you were my friend."

Monica paused, and a shallow breath escaped her lips as the meaning of his plea struck her. Even though, before now, she had suspected his feelings had changed, or even dissipated, the sudden lack of more intimate affections stung her with a sharpness that her blunt, heavy grief did not have. She didn't have the time or the focus to rationalize it now, but there was almost a fleeting twinge of resentment that passed through her before she spoke again.

"Oh, Finn… I am. And that's why I can't let you do this. If I go after the Enclave, even if we bring them down, it'll likely be at the cost of my own life by the end of it. I wasn't exaggerating when I said how dangerous working for Maal is. And just because you don't have a contract doesn't mean you're any less likely to die. I can't let you throw your life away because you're beguiled by the magic of the other world."

"I'm not throwing my life away," he pressed, his voice suddenly becoming stoic as he straightened beside her. The warmth of his hand encircled hers, and before she could process his touch enough to react, he continued. "I want this. I want to help. I want to be there for you."

"Why?"

"Because I'm also *your* friend. Isn't that what friends do? They help each other?"

Monica froze, her mind stalling as whatever words she wanted to say fluttered out of her grasp like startled butterflies. But, instead of fighting for her deserter voice, her mind was overcome with the throbbing sensation of the way her pounding heart now filled every inch of her. Her veins thrummed hot in a way that made her shiver against the cool night air. Her skin prickled with goosebumps as she stared into Finn's sweet, gentle eyes, like a deer transfixed in headlights.

In a rush, she became uncomfortably aware of the sensation of each exhale as it slipped out of her mouth, mingling with his as he leaned towards her. She hadn't realized how close they were before now.

Her eyes dropped to her hands, now both of which were encased in his. He was so warm. Her attention returned to his face, and, seeing that he hadn't moved, considered with brief alarm how the moment suddenly seemed to stop.

They were frozen in that moment, frozen in her grief, fear, and desperation.

Her eyes fell to his lips, watching them slowly form around each whispered word as he said, "I wanna help you."

With a hot swell of tears, her vision blurred. In that moment, she suddenly didn't care about any of the unpleasant feelings that had plagued her before. All she wanted was not to lose him, ever.

"And I want you to live." Her voice cracked under the weight of the words, and she was suddenly nauseated by the intensity of how genuine and vulnerable they felt as they flew from her lips; a single butterfly escaping her.

"Nothing says I won't." Finn whispered sweetly, his voice like a song as it thrummed low in his throat.

His eyes were pleading and soft, sparkling with wistful promise. She didn't want to see the horrors of her reality steal that sparkle.

The look in his eyes scared her. She wanted to read it as comfort, but her own emotions were growing quickly undeniable to the point that she worried she couldn't trust herself to read only the truth. She pulled her hands out of his, standing in a desperate attempt to get some distance between them. But it only served to pull him closer. He stood immediately as she did, looming so close that they were practically chest to chest on the step.

She felt herself trembling as he looked down at her, his dark eyes full of a gentle determination as he said, "I know you're scared. I am, too, but I know that I don't have to be as long as you're there. I want you to know that everything you're doing to take care of me and keep me safe, I would do the same for you. That's part of the reason I wanted to stay. I wanted to be able to help you. And I still do. Please don't take that away from me."

A shallow exhale of disbelief fluttered from her lips as her knees went weak. She squeaked in surprise when Finn caught her, frightened by how safe she felt with the warmth of his arms around her.

"Monica?" His tone was instantly sharper with alarm as he held her upright. "Are you okay?"

Silently, she sought his eyes, feeling so small in his embrace. Before, when she looked at him, she'd only seen a lost boy who needed protecting. She had forgotten how strong he was, before now. He wasn't just a boy. And she didn't know why, but that realization, that shift of perspective scared her so much she thought she might be sick.

She nodded weakly, her voice failing her as she felt herself being drawn into the soft care in his eyes.

“What’s wrong?”

“I feel… strange. Like my stomach wants to jump out of my mouth.”

"Are you sick?"

Monica steadied herself with a ragged inhale, forcing the weakness to leave her knees with a sheer mental determination she probably shouldn't have been capable of in such an otherwise weak moment. Her stomach also settled, though not completely, as she pushed herself away from Finn with a hand planted firmly on his chest.

Finally, as she stood independently on wobbly legs, she gave a decisive shake of her head. The austerity returned to her face as she endeavored to return to her usual state of guarded strength.

"I'm fine," she announced. Though to her it sounded more like she was trying to convince herself instead of just him. "Whatever it was passed. We should go back in now. I don't want to keep your grandad waiting."

As Monica turned to approach the door, Finn reached for her, hooking his fingers in the crook of her elbow to stop her from leaving.

"We don't have to go back in if you don't want to."

"No, I want to. Besides, I want you to have that time with him, too, since you don't know when you might get to see him again after we return to Vhalta."

Finn smiled a little, and though it was an uncertain smile, his eyes sparkled with gratitude.

“You’re letting me?”

“It was never my choice to make.”

Chapter 14

After dessert, they thanked Scott for dinner and shared several hugs before saying their goodbyes. Finn claimed that they were going to walk home, since the weather was so nice. Scott seemed quietly skeptical at first but dismissed it with little question and a clever glint in his eye that seemed to suggest an assumption of the pair wanting some time alone. He even agreed to play into their cover by calling Courtney to let her know they would be staying longer, so she *hopefully* wouldn't stay up worrying.

The mood shifted instantly as they crossed the front edge of the lawn. Monica's mind blanked with the instinctual transition to work mode. Finn skipped at her heels to keep up, nervously looking back over his shoulder towards his grandad's house, for fear that it would look too much like they were running. As soon as they were sure they were out of sight, their pace quickened as Finn's stride also shifted to one of haste.

Though the coast was at least a few miles away, their journey to the pier blurred behind a screen of apprehension and laser-like determination. The minutes blurred into seconds, and the shoreline was in view after only a few blinks.

The air became increasingly acrid with a brine-and-fish stink that grew as they trotted down the shoreline towards the pier from which Grunnar did business. Reaching the end of the sandy bank, Monica whirled around, halting Finn in his tracks before the sound of their footsteps against the wooden pier could give them away.

"I want you to wait here," she instructed in a gruff whisper, motioning him towards the overhang of the back of an opposing warehouse.

"What? No! I wanna go with you."

She gave a grave shake of her head, keeping her focus locked on Finn in the hopes that her austere demeanor would assuage his eagerness.

"Tell me we haven't come all this way, just for you to tell me it's too dangerous." He pleaded desperately, the whites of his eyes reflecting a growing sheen of silver in the partial moonlight that filtered down from above.

Monica let her mask soften as she said, "No. It *is* dangerous, but that's not why I want you to stay behind. Here." She produced an item from beneath the length of her cardigan and offered it to Finn. He hesitated for a moment as his mind processed the presence of a familiar wooden rod, which was retracted, making it only about six inches in length in its current form.

"My staff!" He gasped, surprise igniting in his eyes before quickly becoming muddied beneath his growing nerves. "Where—"

"You forgot you brought it through the rift with you, didn't you?" She scolded softly as he cradled it to his chest. "You left it at your mom's house. You can't do that. Even if you think you're going somewhere safe, as long as you work for Maal, nowhere is truly safe. You have to be prepared for anything, anywhere, at any moment, okay?"

Finn swallowed hard and gave a solemn nod. The tension in his shoulders eased slightly as he clutched the condensed staff tightly in his hands. His veins thrummed with the rush of familiar adrenaline that came from its presence, his training, and the welcome yet terrifying reminder that he was no longer helpless.

"Do you really think I'll need to use it tonight?"

"I don't know. I hope not, but this could go *really* wrong, so I need to know that you can help if it does. I've always worked alone as far as Grunnar is concerned, so he won't be expecting me to have brought backup. But we'll lose the advantage of surprise if they see you, okay?"

Too nervous to speak, Finn gave an eager nod and pulled the staff closer to his chest. His mind tingled with the instinct of how to unfurl it from within the spell that binds it to a more convenient size for travel. He always struggled with that, and while he hoped he would not have to use it, the fear still loomed over him that if he did, his nerves would make his memory falter.

Finn's heart fluttered erratically and his lungs grew tighter around each breath that passed as he watched Monica turn to walk away. His eyes lifted to the spot on the pier beyond her, where he could just glimpse the edge of an ear and the outer curve of a face poking out from behind a tower of crates. Beyond the figure, several goblins clambered back and forth to unload a bevy of crates.

Monica braced herself against her own rising tide of anxiety that nearly succeeded in pulling her under when the heel of her boot thudded with her first step onto the pier. Though his eyes hadn't yet caught her, she was painfully aware of Grunnar's sudden attention to her presence as his head pivoted to acknowledge the sound.

She reached into the depths of her mind as she strode up the pier, desperate to summon the confidence that usually came so easily to her before situations like these. She found her gait faltering when that usual, cool self-assurance evaded her. Her gaze flitted, unbidden, to Finn for a mere moment before she forced her stride to resume.

A sudden wave of stench rolled over her, twisting that familiar knot of revulsion into her stomach that miraculously made her relax as it transported her mind back to the all too vivid memory of her last encounter here. The air no longer smelled of only salt and sea life, but was ripe with stale booze and body odor, which marked that only seconds remained before she would be face to face with—

"Grunnar!" Monica greeted, praying that her apprehension wasn't apparent from beneath her forcedly amiable tone.

His head spun to meet her as she rounded the corner and came to stand before him where he reclined into his makeshift throne of crates. The intensity of his scathing scowl made her blood turn to ice as she surrendered to his attention. His appraising glare lacked the lecherous hesitation that it normally contained, only regarding her with unadulterated animosity.

Monica tried not to stare back as he looked her over, but it was hard not to admire the handiwork that Maal's vengeance had exacted upon his face. Admittedly, Grunnar had been a disgusting beast of a man before; sporting a gnarled, scarred mug with bulbous, ogrish features and avaricious eyes that could make most people's skin crawl with merely a look. Not to mention his dramatic, jutting underbite that parted his gray-green lips with a pair of grimy, yellow tusks. But now, the spiderweb of black veins that spilled out from beneath the eyepatch resting across where his right eye used to be made him look downright villainous. The skin of his cheekbone was swollen with bulbous, festering pockets that made the web of veins ripple around the disfigurement.

The injury extended up into his wide forehead, fading just as it reached the crest of his dappled scalp that was visible through a thinning halo of graying charcoal hair. It too was raised, though not as dramatically as his cheekbone, giving the illusion of such depth beneath the eyepatch that it looked to Monica as if the Medusa Viper had torn a hole clean through his face. A morbid flicker of curiosity made her cringe at the idea that it might be possible to see all the way to his brain through the hole, *if* he had much of a brain to begin with.

"Half-blood." He growled darkly, his upper lip curling back into a shiver-inducing snarl as he met her presence with such quiet animosity that Monica fleetingly imagined steam lifting from his forehead. "You've got a lotta nerve coming back here after what you did."

He didn't bother to greet her like he usually did upon their dealings; rising from his seat and descending to the pier to meet her. Instead, he remained seated and slouched on his throne, glowering down at her from the top of the dais of boxes. And for this, she was thankful. Not only did it give her a more comfortable buffer between her personal space and the stench of Grunnar's repulsive rotting meat breath, but it also gave her ego enough room to swell back into the nonchalant and perhaps somewhat imperious air that gave her the comfort to be audaciously direct in her dealings. And, most importantly, it also meant that he didn't yet have plans to assault her; at least not himself. That was enough for now.

Suddenly and without thinking, her instincts came flooding back to her, replacing her anxiety with indignation as she anchored a fist on her hip.

"Me?" She scoffed derisively. "You should be thankful. You got off easy after I warned you that I wasn't with The Enclave, and not to cheat my boss. Not to mention that we had a deal, one that *you* chose to ignore. You brought it on yourself."

Grunnar's shoulders swelled and his face became flushed with offense. Noticing his distress, a couple of goblins who had returned with empty arms stopped by to watch instead of continuing back to the ship to get another load.

"Easy?" He hissed through his bared, splintery teeth, before making an angry gesture at the eyepatch. "Easy? Does *this* look like I got off easy to you?"

Her lips pressed forward into a mocking pout as she feigned to consider this.

"Oh, be honest. You like how intimidating it makes you look, don't you? Don't try to tell me your new look hasn't been useful in negotiations. I'd say, all things considered, we did you a favor. But that's beside the point. I've come looking for an artifact."

Grunnar snorted as he reclined on his throne, bearing his tusks in a sneer that was more irritated incredulity than animosity.

"You must be much dumber than I thought if you truly think I'm going to even entertain the idea of ever doing business with you again."

"C'mon, Grunnar." Monica enticed in her best sultry sing-song tone, pairing each over-accentuated syllable with a flutter of her thick black lashes. "I know you're not one to turn away the chance of becoming a *very* rich man."

Unfortunately, despite his typical lustful proclivity, he wasn't falling for her coquettish provocation. Not this time.

"But I *am* one to turn away a lying anomaly. And that's not all I'd like to do, but I'm hardly in the market to lose my other eye in the event that it would anger your boss to find you dead."

She was impressed to hear him talk such a big talk despite the fear she knew accompanied his anger. But, irate as he may be, she knew that his threat was nothing more than bluster. After all, Maal had been right about the severity of the impression that his vengeance had left in its wake. Despite any desire that Grunnar harbored for his own revenge, he also knew that he did not want to risk the price that had been declared if he crossed them again.

"You're not even going to hear my offer?" She tempted again, in vain.

"I'm not interested in wasting my time when you've already proven you can't even keep your word."

"*I* wasn't the one who went back on a deal that was already set. We have no deal as of yet. Once we do, you have my word that I will hold to it. Now, are you really going to turn away the opportunity to *name your price*?"

Grunnar's eye narrowed and his mouth flattened into a line that was still soured by his anger as he considered it. Though she knew her chances were slim, Monica found the pause in his manner promising. He was tempted. But of course he was. Scum like him only cared about one thing: money. No matter how severe the misdeed, you can make them forget with enough of it.

"And what, exactly, is it that you're looking for?"

Monica suppressed the small twinge of victory that frolicked through the back of her mind, desperate to keep her cool as she strung together the words of her response. She had to be precise. She knew that, already being on thin ice, Grunnar would likely be unwilling to show her a spread of items if she told him she'd *know it when she saw it.* That would also risk her coming off clueless, like she was merely fishing for information. Not that it was untrue, but he certainly didn't need to know that. If she was going to get anywhere, she had to pick her words very, *very* carefully.

"What do you know about an artifact that would let me trace another person? A magic wielder."

His face remained blank for only a split second before a subtle spark of recognition flared in his remaining eye. The tell that cracked his guarded facade was indisputable despite its brevity. He knew *exactly* what she was talking about.

"Well, I guess that depends on just how badly you wanted to find this person."

Here we go. She thought, sensing that this question was his wind-up before naming a truly outrageous price. So it surprised her when Grunnar delayed, only to seek sensitive information of his own.

“And just who is it that you're trying to find? I have contacts everywhere, you know, so you may not even need an artifact for that.”

Monica's stomach clenched into an immediate knot of distrust. Barely a minute ago, he didn't so much as want to even speak to her, so the fact that he was now offering not only his assistance, but perhaps an easier alternative, seemed like a trap.

Deciding on the cautious approach, Monica lowered her head, looking warily towards the group of goblins that had now collected to observe them.

Making her loose obsidian waves sway around her head with a shake that looked more like a flinch, she finally said, “The boss said that wasn't for *me* to know.”

“He must not trust you much, anomaly.”

Though Grunnar’s insult made her skin itch with indignation, as she was sure he had intended, she noticed something else beneath his words. Something more cunning, more calculated than his usual strategy. Not to mention, the way he had started calling her *anomaly.*

The first time, she barely noticed it, having attributed it to his state of vexation, since *anomaly* is typically a derogatory term. With his knowledge of her illegal lineage, coming from one human parent and one wielder parent, he’d taken to calling her half-blood in all of their prior interactions, since she’d been unwilling to give up her actual name.

There was only one other person in recent memory who had called her *anomaly* so insistently. She froze as a flash of his villainous face passed through her memory, the image taken from their encounter on the island, during which he'd tried to kill her. Rowan.

The fear that rose within her burned with the white-hot heat of lightning. But she pushed it down, smothering her sudden panic beneath a blanket of denial that she was just overthinking an impossible coincidence. Rowan had so much power that it was nonsensical for him to stoop to using an ogre in the mortal realm to trap her. Not to mention, he was likely now in a race to obtain the rest of Maal's name, so that he could become too powerful to be stopped before he trifled himself with such small concerns as her. And she took comfort in realizing that she was likely no longer his priority, for now, at least.

Snapping out of her haze of alarm, Monica demanded, "My only task was to obtain such an artifact. So, do you know of it or not?"

"Not." He finally sneered, looking pleased that he could tell he'd rattled her. "I don't know anything about an artifact that's specially meant to track somebody down."

Then what was his reaction from before? She was so sure it had been recognition. Either he was lying, or she simply wasn't asking the right questions. But would he even tell her if she was?

She considered what he'd said about the situation depending on how badly she wanted to find this person… What if that *hadn't* been his wind up to ask for money? What if he had been hinting at the artifact's powers?

Not often were such things so simple as to have a single, straightforward intent. Her gaze absently fell to glimpse the tiger's eye ring encircling her left thumb, subconsciously using it as an example. It removed barriers, but that could be extended to physical ones, allowing her to use it to pick locks, or abstract ones, such as distance. That's how it helped her bridge the gap between realms in order to be able to communicate with Maal through a summoning.

As she considered this, her confidence returned that Grunnar *did* have an artifact that would help. She just had no idea what its caveat was.

Trying not to sound too desperate, Monica turned to another question.

"What about something that—"

"Look," Grunnar interrupted in a huff, "You clearly don't know what you're looking for, so get outta here. Quit wasting my time."

Now *this* is more what she'd expected from him. But the shift back to prickly was so abrupt that it only fed her feeling of suspicious unease. Something was going on here, and Grunnar didn't like that she was asking questions.

"I know you have it. My boss wouldn't have sent me if he wasn't sure."

"Look," He repeated, the annoyance mounting in his tone as he rose from his seat, "Everyone makes mistakes. Your boss doesn't know what he's looking for either."

She was losing him. Her heart thumped erratically as she watched the window of opportunity closing right in front of her eyes.

"But if you could just help us find it, something that would help, you would be ineffably rich!"

He didn't even register the content of her desperate promise, continuing down the make-shift crate stairs as he waved the gathering of goblins away.

"Piss off. This has gone on long enough. Besides," He hissed, turning his single, beady eye towards the cluster of goblins that had now accumulated nearly his entire crew. He threw up his hands in anger and they reluctantly dispersed when he said, “You’re distracting my crew. Get back to work.”

“But I need—”

“No.” Grunnar spat, crossing his girthy arms over his chest to obscure the sweat-soaked semi-circles underneath them. “You should’a thought of that before you ripped me off. Now, you ain’t gettin’ *anything* from me. Not artifacts, not information, nothing. Now get outta here. If I see you again, it’ll be very bad news for you.”

The venom in his words made the blood in her veins swell until she felt like her whole body might explode. She hated that there was no winning this, not this way, at least.

Monica’s jaw clenched as she stormed away. Her feet clomped violently against the pier and her mind clouded with a clamber of anxious, desperate thoughts. *What am I going to do?* She wasn’t sure who she was madder at; Grunnar for being such an *ogre*, or Maal, for not seeing it coming and not believing her about it. She understood him wanting to exhaust all of his possible options, but she didn’t need his enigmatic strategies to see that something like this was practically inevitable after how things were left earlier.

It wasn’t like Maal to waste her time, or be so willingly stupid, especially with time as a limited commodity. She fleetingly considered that this was perhaps a punishment, a guaranteed failure meant only to make her look stupid, but such punishments were rare, since they held no ultimate gain for Maal. There was something she was missing, a reason she was made to do this, but she was too angry now to see it rationally.

A haze of furious heat settled across her brow, dissipating only slightly in the cool night air as she made her way back towards Finn.

He greeted her with concerned eyes, his knuckles blanched from how tightly he was still gripping his staff.

She didn’t stop, merely making a tight gesture for him to follow as she stormed by.

"What happened?"

"Says he doesn't have it." Monica growled through gritted teeth. "But I'm pretty sure he's lying."

"What are we going to do?"

"The only thing we *can* do. We’ll have to get more information about this artifact and where he might be hiding it, and then find a way to sneak in and take it."

"Oh?” Finn questioned uneasily, clearly not fond of the suggestion. "How are we going to do that? Please tell me you already have an idea."

"Of course I have an idea," she scoffed. "I *always* have an idea. But we're going to have to pray that those goblins robbing your grandad's company actually *do* work for Grunnar."

"And if they don't?"

"We'll have to cross that bridge when we get there. But I think the chances of that are unlikely, as magical creatures tend to run in packs in Vhenra. It wouldn’t make sense for there to be two random goblins off on their own.”

“But if they are?”

“Then at least Cape Bianca will be down two muggers, even if we're wrong."

Chapter 15

The pair returned to Finn's house in the wee hours of the morning with no incident. Fortunately, whatever Scott had told Courtney had worked, and for this, Monica was indescribably thankful. She was *so* sure that, with her personality and her penchant for finding amusement in making others uncomfortable, that finding Courtney waiting up to lecture them would be an inevitability. So being able to slip off to sleep without confrontation was a sigh of relief, for both of them. After all, there'd certainly be more than enough confrontation to make up for it when they hunted down the goblin muggers after they awoke.

After Finn's mom left for work that morning, Finn donned the delivery uniform his grandad had loaned him, and the pair set off to apprehend some goblin thugs.

Goblins weren't known for being the brightest creatures by a long stretch, not to mention that they were painfully predictable. Monica had decided that, since it had almost worked for them before, it wouldn't be unreasonable to expect them to be planning to ambush the replacement driver from the same place they had used to sneak up on Finn. After all, it wasn't a bad spot, hidden by some buildings near a quiet park that didn't see much traffic mid-day.

They waited around until the delivery truck came into view at the far end of the street, and then split up to set the plan in motion.

The goblins crouched in the shadows at the mouth of a narrow alley, unaware as Monica snuck up from behind. They practically started dancing in anticipation when they saw the delivery truck pull up and park down the block.

Knowing that this route had several stops along this street, Finn expected his replacement to do as he did; park and walk the block before leaving, rather than moving the truck only a few feet between each one. He was right, because when the driver went inside the first building at the far end of the road, Finn had a prime opportunity to sneak into the truck with his knowledge of the old combination lock and make off with the delivery for old Mrs. Mallory at the opposite end.

He tried to subdue the triumph in his smile, painfully aware of the unbidden jaunt in his stride as he headed towards the alley. Too focused on Finn's approach, the pair of masked goblins never so much as noticed when Monica lifted their dagger from their possession.

In surveying them carefully, she was able to determine that they had come with no other obvious weapons.

Typical, she thought, *just like goblins to come without a back-up plan.*

She grinned at the realization that this was going to be an easy fix, and suspected that the only reason they had even resumed after her first scare *was* the fact that she was gone.

As Finn neared, the goblins' bodies lowered into a squat as they prepared to pounce. But before they could take even their first step out of the shadows, Monica had unsheathed her own dagger and held them back with the flat of each blade resting along each of their throats.

While Monica had a special talent for moving with a swift, soundless efficiency, the fact that they hadn't noticed her reaching around their necks until the cold metal of the blades chilled their throats was a testament to just how little they had been paying attention.

Monica felt the entirety of their wide, stocky bodies tense as she brought her chest to rest just above their backs, in the small space between them. A slow smile unfurled across her lips as she brought her mouth to hover between the gray-green tips of their ears. One of them suppressed a snort of alarm, while the other failed to conceal the beginnings to a frightened squeal.

Hearing the noise from the street, Finn sprinted into the alley to join Monica.

"Etus, vinardus." Monica purred in Elandian, her voice so smooth that it sent shivers through their bodies. "Remember me? You tried to rob my friend. And you didn't listen to what I warned you would happen if you didn't stop."

Finn set the box aside and strode over to where she had the goblins pinned, dwarfing all three of them with his slightly taller than average frame. His smile evaporated instantly from his face as he took in the scene, and the innocence that usually shone within his eyes had hardened into a mature determination, tempered by his anger.

The squealing goblin began to whimper, much to the chagrin of his friend, who had decided to talk tough despite their clear disadvantage.

"You're *not* Enclave." The first goblin grunted, his voice muffled by the thick knit of the balaclava obscuring his features. "You tricked the boss to try and get a better deal, and when it didn't work, you ran away."

"So you *do* work for Grunnar. I'll have you know that I never told him any such thing. In fact, it was one of *you* who assumed I was with The Enclave, and it caused him to try to con me. I'm not happy about it."

“It wasn’t us, it was Robert.” The goblin groaned, sounding suddenly less confident than before.

Unconcerned by the accusation, Monica changed the subject.

“So why does he have you doing robberies now? Is extortion for artifacts not paying as well anymore?”

“He’s not!” The whiny goblin croaked, “It’s just us.”

“Grunnar keeps the biggest cut for himself.” The gruffer of the two elaborated, his voice an impressively low hum for the diminutive size of his body.

The other goblin’s voice was less impressive, drilling out into the air in a nasally whimper as he chimed in, “A cut that keeps getting bigger."

“We’re just doing what we gotta do to get by.”

Grunnar was cheating his own workers! Monica rolled her eyes. She was disgusted, but not surprised. Of course an ogre would do whatever he could to get ahead, even if it meant costing him the loyalty of his team.

Monica saw an opportunity in their response, beyond just merely getting information from them. If their loyalties to Grunnar were as weak as they sounded, it wouldn't be hard to turn these two into allies. And, given the desperation of what the situation was likely going to make her do, now that Grunnar clearly had no interest in giving anything up during standard negotiations, she could use all the backup she could muster.

"I'm going to offer you a deal." She began cautiously, her eyes lifting momentarily to catch the sparkle of surprise that now lit Finn's eyes. "I'm going to put the daggers away, and you're going to listen to what I have to say. And if you decide not to take me up on my offer, I will let you leave under the conditions that none of this gets back to Grunnar, and you swear not to rob any of these innocent people again."

"Or what?" The first snarled, his vehemence immediately dying as Monica reminded him of the blade against his throat.

"Or I'll make good on my first promise to get The Enclave involved. And you *won't* like it."

"But you're not *of* The Enclave." The second goblin squeaked.

"I'm not." She cooed assuredly, "But I don't have to be. They don't like me very much, and if they knew where I was, they would cause an awful lot of pain to try to get to me. All it would take is me making them think that I'm with you. Hmm?"

"Fine!" The second goblin cried out, waving his hands in a gesture of desperate surrender. "We'll listen to your deal. Tell her, Crognak."

"We'll listen." The gruffer goblin, apparently called Crognak, agreed, straining to pull back from the blade digging into his neck.

"And I have your word that you won't try anything?"

"Yes." They squawked in unison.

With cautious movements, Monica withdrew her arms and stepped backwards a few paces to create enough space between her and the goblins that would give her an edge if they tried anything, but not so much that they would be able to outrun her if they decided to make a break for it. She sheathed her own dagger before handing her stolen spare to Finn.

A nervous gleam shone in his eyes as he wrapped his long fingers around its hilt. His stance straightened, as if to make up for it, and the shadows that now streamed across his face made him look almost menacing. Monica smiled in spite of herself, impressed at his composure.

The goblins turned to face her and their beady eyes lifted expectantly. They studied her through brief, mistrustful squints, grumbling to themselves with displeasure as they waited for her to speak.

"What would you say to a job that pays a hell of a lot more than this one, working for a boss who'd actually treat you fairly?"

"I'd say, where do we sign?" The second goblin asked, earning an immediate glare of admonishment from his cohort, Crognak.

"Not so fast, Wurick." Crognak warned before glaring back at Monica to ask, "What's the catch?"

"The catch is, you have to betray Grunnar and work with me in order to prove yourselves worthy before my boss will offer you a job. A contract, actually."

Both of the goblins' faces lit up at the phrase, clearly unaware of the more sinister magical agreements that went by the same name, to which she referred.

"A contract?" Crognak whistled. "So it's a long-term thing?"

"You bet it is." Monica promised slyly. "If you do well enough for my boss to offer you a job, you'll be set for a good long while. You won't have to worry about the scarceness of work that causes you to resort to petty thievery like this. Not to mention, you certainly won't have to worry about running low on funds if you succeed."

They both looked at each other with expressions of amazement and interest.

“What do you want us to do?” Wurick brayed.

“First, I want you to take your masks off, so I can see who I’m working with.”

Crognak’s beady black eyes narrowed in distrust, but his hesitation ended as an eager Wurick put an elbow of encouragement into his ribs.

“Alright, alright.”

Though the absence of their masks revealed truly unappealing faces, they were still nowhere near as grotesque as Grunnar. Both of the goblins that stood before her looked on from behind bulbous, exaggerated noses and squat heads that resembled footballs, if those footballs had skin the color of bog water. Their ears were long and crooked, extending further up and back than the elegant tips of elven ears. Crognak's bare head glinted with a sickly sheen in what little of the watery sunlight that filtered into the alley, while Wurick wore a full mop of dark, wiry kinks that frizzed out from his head in disorderly clumps.

She smirked, pleased at how easy their obedience had been to tame.

"You just gonna stand there and stare, or are you gonna tell us what's next?"

"To start, I want some information from you. What do you know of an artifact that would let its user track the location of someone else? Say, a magic user, if that makes any difference."

They both looked at each other and shrugged.

"Grunnar keeps the contents of his stock pretty close to his chest, but even so, we don't know anything about anything like that."

Wurick agreed with a nod before adding thoughtfully, "But if it's something that he has currently, the only other workers that would know anything about something like that would be the plunderers."

"Plunderers?" Finn asked, stiffening again as their attention turned briefly to him.

"The crew that goes out on the ship and actually brings the stuff back. And we're no plunderers. Our job is to schlep boxes and unpack or repack the ship between voyages."

"Do you know of any plunderers who might want in on this action?"

Wurick’s beady eyes shifted towards Crognak in a suspicious way, but the other goblin only shrugged in response.

“Even if we did, there’s no guarantee they’d even know much, either. The boss doesn’t say much to no one about nothin’ except the people with money.”

And she already proved *that* was no longer a viable option for her. Monica crossed her arms and sighed.

“I offered him money, loads of it. He didn't bite. I knew he was going to be pretty pissed at me, but I kinda hoped enough money would pay off his grudge."

“Good luck with *that*.” Crognak cackled sarcastically. “It'd be different if you hadn't also hurt his vanity, taking his eye and all, but you disfigured his whole damn face! That kind of hate doesn't just go away. I mean, he’s a little happier now that he has that shiny new eye that the plunderers brought back a week ago, but there ain’t no way he’d tell *you* anything, no matter how happy he gets.”

“Not even if— Wait.” Monica stopped, struck by the curious thought that if the plunders brought him a new eye, and their job was to bring back magical artifacts, then what were the chances that said eye was an artifact itself? And if so, that would also explain his unwillingness to continue the conversation when she started probing about artifacts, if he had decided that whatever it does is worth more to keep for himself than whatever she could pay him. “What does it do? The eye?”

The goblins seemed unperturbed by the question, but still seemed to offer it proper thought before they both dismissed it with a shrug.

“Don’t know.” Crognak admitted. “I *did* overhear him talkin’ about it a few days after he got it, though. He said that it helped let him see how to get what he wanted. Called it the Eye of Desire, or some shit like that.”

"It lets him *see* how to get what he wants? How?"

Crognak thumbed at the tip of his nose before shaking his head defensively. "I don't know much about artifacts, nor do I care to. I'm just repeating what I heard."

Monica's heart warmed with a sudden surety that returned to her after the goblin's confession and things started to make a lot more sense. However, the glow of triumph was fleeting and soon succumbed to a sense of dread that swelled in the pit of her stomach. Not only was she going to have to steal the eye, sneaking in and leaving unnoticed was no longer an option if she had to take it out of his head, as she feared.

When she glanced at Finn, for some reason, the concern on his face assuaged her own panic. He didn't look afraid in the same way that she felt. It looked more like empathy, perhaps a wish to free her from hers. She had to be strong.

There was no promise that this would go well, but at least now, there was hope.

She turned back to the goblins.

"What does Grunnar do when he's not open for business?"

"He's *always* open for business." Wurick sputtered, as if he didn't understand the question.

Monica's brows knitted in frustration.

"No, he's not. I have to wait until after dark to deal with him."

"You're not one of his VIPs." Crognak sniffed. "They come and go whenever they please, so he doesn't leave the warehouse cabin, like, ever."

"Ever?"

They both nodded, and it was all Monica could do to resist the grin that fought to spread across her lips. If Grunnar never left, the chances of apprehending him would be much higher if she didn't have to guess where he'd be. If she played her cards right, this could be like shooting fish in a barrel. All she had to do was determine the perfect moment to strike.

"Okay." Monica sighed, trying not to let her relief be as apparent as it felt. "What can you tell me about his daytime schedule?"

"Schedule?" Crognak erupted into a sputtering laugh. "Grunnar has no schedule. He eats when he feels like it, deals with the VIPs whenever *they* feel like it, and gets his sleep whenever he can between the two. Not much else worth mentioning."

"Oh, he *does* run gambling games with the crew in his cabin sometimes during the day." Wurick interjected thoughtfully.

"When?"

"Whenever he feels like it." He echoed Crognak's sputtering laugh in mutedly nasally tones. "But more likely on days after his sales don't go so good. Those days, the crew doesn't leave when the work's done, and instead, they drink and gamble all morning until everybody's either broke or passed out."

Knowing what she did of last night's interaction with Grunnar, she prodded, "So today, probably?"

The goblins looked at each other and shrugged. "Probably."

Monica didn't know if they were just agreeing to agree, or if they'd been among the audience that her clumsy attempt last night had garnered, but she didn't care enough to mention it.

"When he's *not* running these gambling games, how often is he alone?"

"Rarely."

"More like *never*!" Wurick corrected. "Whether it's a VIP, a handful of crewmates, or, ya know… one of his *pretty* girls, there's usually always somebody with him."

Monica bit her lip in a moment of contemplative frustration. While it'd definitely be safer to try to get him alone, time was of the essence. And if such a thing was a relatively rare occurrence, she reasoned that it probably wouldn't be worth it to wait around for the right time. At least, if his crew was gathered for a game, their locations within his cabin were likely to be more static and predictable. That could actually *be* the better option, with appropriate planning.

"This game, will either of you be there?"

"As if." Wurick gave a snort of derision. "You think that somebody desperate enough to rob grocery men to even be able to eat, would have enough money to be squandering it gambling? Especially with a crook like him? Naw."

Monica lifted an eyebrow, flicking Finn a thoughtful glance that suggested an idea forming.

"What if I wanted you to be there?"

"Well, uh," Crognak began, pausing to glance up at the sky, "If you wanted to pay the buy-in, I suppose we could try to make an appearance, assuming it hasn't ended yet."

"How much is the buy-in?" Monica asked flatly, lowering her gaze in a stare that said she meant business.

Crognak stared back, scratching one of his dry palms with the crusty, yellow fingernails of his other hand as he narrowed his eyes in deliberation. Wurick squinted at his partner from the side, as if trying to communicate something non-verbally, but Crognak knew better than to break that stare. And, by the way that the tension suddenly left his shoulders, she noticed when he'd decided better than to try to squeeze her for more than necessary, too.

"Fifty bucks oughta do it." He finally sighed. "For each of us."

Without breaking the stare, Monica apathetically fished a couple of crumpled bills from one of her pockets, only giving it a split second of unconcerned attention as she flipped through them and then handed the money to Crognak. He snatched it from her with an ill-concealed grin that only faded after he pocketed the cash. Then, his expression turned serious again.

"And, uh, what is it that we're meant to do while we're there?"

"Win, if you can." Monica sneered, and both of the goblins cocked a quizzical eyebrow at her.

"Seriously?"

"Yeah. You think it'd be enough to get Grunnar to storm out angry if he loses?"

"I mean, sure," Wurick squawked, "He's got a short temper, but we already said he cheats. It ain't likely he's gonna lose."

Monica looked unconcerned by this fact.

"That's fine." She dismissed cooly. "While I'd love to see that scumbag be the one coughing up money for once, it's not gonna hurt anything if not. Just be at the game. When you see our distraction, try to keep the group focused on it for as long as you can. Grunnar's probably not gonna be at the table when it happens, so just try to keep the rest of the players from noticing and asking questions about how long he's been gone."

Crognak narrowed his eyes at her distrustfully, while Wurick was distracted with a dreamy grin that broadcasted his likely fantasy of Grunnar's fit if they won.

"And what's *the distraction*?" Crognak growled, making his last few words warble with exaggerated flair.

"You'll know it when you see it." Her scheming grin widened as she thumbed over her shoulder towards Finn. "Okay, you're free to go."

But as Finn collected the box and the pair turned to leave, Crognak called out with an emerging anger in his voice.

"Wait! That's it?"

“Pretty much.” Monica answered with a shrug, twisting to offer a passing glance over her shoulder. “Hurry and get down there as fast as you can. Join the game and try to make everything seem like business as normal. And no more robbing. Can you do that?”

A hesitant glance passed between them before Crognak decided aloud, “We can do that.”

As she spun away on her heel, Crognak called after her.

"Hey! What about our dagger?"

Monica gave a brief pause of deliberation.

"Well," She considered, "It's hardly valuable enough to be considered recompense towards your crimes, but it's a start."

"You're not going to give it back?"

"Not even as a token of good faith?" Wurick chimed in.

Her eyes flitted towards Finn, who gave an empathetic nod. The wordless look lingered between them before a dip of Monica’s chin permitted Finn to return the dagger, which he did with guarded care. Then, the pairs parted and went their separate ways without another word.

Chapter 16

Finn dropped off the box he'd swiped at Mrs. Mallory's before they left the neighborhood. She was overjoyed to see him, exploding into a fit of tearful delight when she peeled back the door. Monica itched with second-hand discomfort as she watched him break the difficult news to her that, even though he was okay, he was only back temporarily, and would be leaving the job permanently to move on to other things. He assured that his replacement would take care of her, and even though she was adamant that it wouldn't be the same without "Finny as the bright spot in her week," the conversation ended with closure, as well as a double tip, despite Finn's polite but firm refusal.

As the two clambered back up the street in the direction of the pier, tension crept into Finn's shoulders, until the fabric of the blue delivery uniform was stretched visibly tight over his shoulder blades.

Catching Monica's sideways glance of inquiry, he nervously sputtered, "So, uh, what's the plan?"

"You're the distraction." She huffed humorously. Though he was relieved to see Monica looking more like herself after her breakdown last night, the coolness of her clever expression did little to quell his nerves.

"Why do I feel like I'm bait?"

"C'mon, you wanted to help. And you know I wouldn't set you up for anything *too* dangerous."

"Then why aren't you telling me anything?" Her apathy broke into a grin that made Finn realize, "You're having fun?"

"Yeah," she admitted, blinking as she seemed to be realizing it for herself, as well. "I am. And why shouldn't I be? Getting to give a smug crook their payback *is* fun."

Finn indulged a reserved, if not bemused smile, eyeing her in a way that suggested that he was suddenly struggling to figure her out as they walked.

"Fair enough. I just thought that after last night, you'd be more anxious."

Her grin faded and the playful glimmer in her eyes melted into sadness as her tone went serious.

"I *am* anxious. All I've been since we've returned to this world is *anxious*. And I'm sick of it. It's exhausting. This is the one part of my job that I really enjoy; getting to stick it to the bad guys."

He paused, his head giving a sideways tilt as he considered this. Even though he looked open to the concept, it clearly still confused him. "Why?"

"Because, I guess it makes *me* feel like less of a bad guy."

Finn's forehead rumpled in confusion, and the corners of his mouth sagged under the weight of a sad frown.

"You're not a bad guy."

"You don't know that. You've only known me for a few weeks. You don't know all of the things I've had to do to survive in this way of life."

"Oh." Finn realized sadly. "That's what this is about? You're still trying to convince me to get out while I can?"

"No," Monica retorted passionately. "I just want you to know what you're getting into. I mean, what you're *really* getting into. These last few weeks have gone easy on you, and I don't want you to think that's all there is. You're right that it's your choice to make, I just... I don't want you to regret whatever that ends up being. All I feel somedays is regret, that is when the guilt isn't too overwhelming to feel much else."

"You *regret* living like this?" he asked haltingly, earning a contemplative but honest nod from her. "Would you have done anything differently?"

Her eyes turned skywards, her pace slowing as they walked.

"Of course I would've. But I don't know if any of it would have made a difference. I was too selfish and oblivious back then to realize what I was doing. And while I know that you'll make better choices than me, I don't want you to do anything that you'll regret."

After a moment, Finn nodded, a smile of reverent gratitude creeping slowly back onto his face.

"For what it's worth, I don't. I don't regret anything so far."

Monica's gaze locked with his before she gave a small nod.

"Good. Then keep it that way. Now, about this plan..."

The pier was vastly different in broad daylight. Monica had never been here during the day. It was so quiet... too quiet, almost. Except for a few shrieking gulls that circled lazily overhead, the docks were deserted. There were no boats in the harbor, no workers in any of the bays, and all of the warehouses were locked and shuttered.

This part of the shore wasn't like the friendlier end, which buzzed with food vendors, attractions, and people with nowhere to be who were just soaking up the sun. The business end was the total opposite, only coming alive after dark, and only catering to the shadiest and most unsavory of the town's lurkers. Monica decided that, purely by virtue of the nature of her business, she was always meant to be a lurker herself. After all, she felt more comfortable amongst them than she ever had while trying to blend into a crowd of "normal" daytime people.

And, it was that instinct that urged her to skulk around the area and take in the scene before settling in to wait for the perfect moment to ambush Grunnar.

As they tiptoed down the pier towards Grunnar's warehouse and attached cabin, (a setup which was not unlike Dawson Deliveries, save for the fact that the attachment housed living quarters instead of a storefront), Monica began briefing Finn on his role in the plan.

The cabin's windows were crusted with a thick layer of crystalized sea spray that made it hard to see much more than the movement of indistinct shapes through them. They stopped only briefly, just long enough for Monica to confirm her intel before moving on in search of a better vantage point.

Through the first window, Monica was able to spy the woozy outlines of several squat men, milling around a circular table in a room that was crowded with stacks of crates. Good. That meant two things; one, that Crognak and Wurick were not only right, but truthful about the gambling games, and that those crates likely held items that Grunnar deemed more valuable than whatever was in his warehouse. Even though the item she sought was not likely to be in one of those crates, it meant he kept the things he valued close. So if she could distract him long enough to lure him out and get him alone, he'd likely be keeping the eye on him at all times, even when he wasn't using it.

"How many of them do you see in there?" Monica tested, squatting below the bottom of the window frame as she waited for Finn to survey the blur.

"Three... no, four small ones and a big one."

"Are any of the small ones either of the two we just saw?"

Finn took an extra moment to squint at them, but ultimately only came away with a frustrated shake of his head.

"It's too blurry to see their faces, but I don't think so."

"That's okay." Monica cooed. "Even though we intentionally didn't rush to get here, I still figured it might be too early for them to be here yet. Besides, I wanna get a better look before we do anything."

"What do you want me to do?"

"Find somewhere comfortable that you can be patient and inconspicuous." She waved her arm towards a haphazard cluster of stacked crates that formed a small alcove, the inside of which was shielded from the door and windows. "I just want to take a look around to see what we're dealing with."

They exchanged a silent look before Monica slunk away around the far corner of the addition that constituted Grunnar's cabin.

She held her breath as she shimmied along the narrow edge of the pier that wrapped around behind the building, which dropped off completely several yards before where it joined to the warehouse, the length of which jutted off in a parallel direction. It didn't give her much room to work with, but thankfully, it also meant that there wasn't nearly as much opportunity for someone to sneak up on her.

There weren't any windows on the back of the cabin, but there was a small, enclosed balcony across the gap after the pier ended. It was barely big enough to turn around on, and only appeared accessible through a single door. Monica wondered if it led into a private back room or private sleeping quarters, which could be an option, but it wasn't a risk she was eager to take without first exploring safer alternatives.

She inched towards the pier drop-off, focusing to get a better sense of the distance. The balcony wasn't *too* far—enough to make her nervous, but not enough that she entirely doubted her ability to make such a leap. It'd be a challenge, especially with the noise the landing would make, but it wasn't impossible. If she missed, the worst case scenario would be landing in the water below, which would be unpleasant, but definitely wasn't a deal breaker.

Her focus returned to the pitted metal siding, which was rusty and crusted with as much salt as the windows. She studied the obvious imperfections in the building's facade; specifically a spot of wear where a particularly deep groove held the promise of a small hole. Large enough to look through perhaps? If she could even reach it, since it was a good two feet beyond the end of the pier.

She sighed to herself, frustrated that she saw no better options, but quickly decided to make use of what she could.

Monica balanced on the lip of the pier's edge and dug her claws into the grooves of the siding before slowly leaning over the water towards the hole. A flutter of excitement sparked within her chest as she pulled her face to the gap, gratified when she found it large enough to look through with one eye.

Her vision panned around a room that was relatively unfurnished, and except for a bed, used wooden crates in lieu of real furniture. She had to give it to Grunnar. Why spend money on tables, chairs, or even shelves when boxes worked just as well?

The wall to her far left was lined with them; a staircase of boxes that were littered with partial bottles of booze, sheets of rumpled paper strewn about with no discernable logic, and a couple of pieces of leather armor that looked large and worn enough to belong to the ogre himself. Based on her perception of the space's depth, the door to the balcony matched up with the wall that ended just before the crates. The room looked innocuous enough. If she could lure Grunnar into it alone and manage to somehow make it in quiet enough to allow her the element of surprise, it was looking like a decent option.

Unfortunately, it still left the challenge of getting in, *and* being quiet, not to mention that it put Finn on the complete opposite side of the building, making it impossible to communicate inconspicuously once things started to go down. But, it did lend itself to a quick escape as long as she didn't mind getting wet, especially since goblins did. They're infamously averse to even approach ankle-high water, due to the fact that they sink like stones. Which made it all the more baffling that Grunnar's crew stuck around, especially with the increased risk that working on a pier posed to their kind, and without better compensation. Perhaps tricking them into staying was a testament to his cunning. But, then again, goblins weren't bright or difficult to trick to begin with. And Monica certainly didn't want to credit Grunnar for being clever. Manipulative, sure; but the bar to appear smart wasn't high amongst a crew like his.

Monica's vision slid to the other side of the room, noting little of interest. Three crates were arranged in the middle of the space, one of which was cluttered with chicken bones, scraps of bread, and two large jugs of mead. A colony of flies danced over the bones, and her nose crinkled at the passing dread of the likely stench that awaited her inside the cabin. Grunnar's malodorous presence was already bad enough in the open air, so the thought of having to bear it in concentrated stagnancy made her gag in anticipation.

Along the right wall were a pair of mealy twin mattresses on sagging metal frames, their bars lashed together with a length of rope at both ends. Only one bed meant only one man, indicating that the crew bunked elsewhere. Seeing as he was the man in charge, Monica grew confident that this was Grunnar's room.

Her knuckles groaned for her to release her hold, but just as she began to pull away, the crate beside the head of the bed caught her eye. More specifically, the bulging leather satchel that had tipped over, spilling out coins. Amongst the scatter, gold coins outnumbered bronze and pewter ones by three to one. That was a *ton* of money for a man in his line of work. Even if he *was* extorting his clients and cheating his workers, the amount seemed unreasonable, even for that.

Not to mention, they were *coins*, not bills. Stennas; money from Vhalta. He was doing business with someone from the magic realm. Why were they coming here, though? There were plenty of artifact dealers in Vhalta, which meant that he had something specific that someone wanted.

Not that that was what Monica was here for, but it was useful to know things, even things that didn't *seem* useful at first. Secrets made for good leverage. And secrets involving *that* much money could be very motivating to somebody like Grunnar.

Monica's grip threatened to quit, but that didn't stop her from lingering for a final look for more clues. A letter was buried beneath the coins, which only revealed a scattering of words. The script was narrow and swooping, a style that suggested affluence, if the money laying atop it did not already do so. It was hard to make out the content of the letter, but a few familiar phrases *did* catch her eye: *Artifact, projection, cloaking ward, bypass without disruption.*

Cloaking ward? That was suspicious. From what Monica knew of wards, they were usually meant to act as a barrier to keep something out, so making it *cloaking* as well— to make it unseeable from the outside— seemed like overkill. Although, it occurred to her that *that* was exactly what Maal did to his tower. And there wasn't any way to get past a ward without convincing the person who cast it to modify it to allow access, short of totally breaking the ward. So the phrase, *bypass without disruption,* seemed equally suspicious to her.

It was worth investigating if she could manage it.

That's when Monica made a decision. With one deft motion, she pushed back from the wall and flung her weight back onto her feet. She swayed just a little with the landing, quickly leaning back to press her weight into the side of the building again as she caught a glance over the sheer drop to the water below.

Her chest heaved with a breath and she let her muscles relax for a moment. The satisfaction of her realization upturned the corners of her mouth as she overturned the details of the opportunity in her mind.

She'd been going about this all wrong. She didn't need to lure Grunnar into the back room and *then* sneak in. She needed to get in first and wait, and maybe even satisfy her curiosity while she was at it.

Chapter 17

Monica's sudden reemergence startled Finn when she burst from around the wall of boxes that hid him.

"Finn!" She panted in a hushed, but still clearly excited whisper as she threw herself into the alcove beside him.

His expression did acrobatics between horror, surprise, concern, and relief, only to settle on confusion as he studied her wild facade. The sound of her panting filled the small space with an added sense of panic before he registered it as excitement instead of alarm.

"What's wrong?"

She shook her head, gulping in a huge breath before she exhaled her hushed confession. "Nothing. In fact, I think we just got *really* lucky."

"What did you find?"

"A way in." She said with a mischievous grin. "But it's not a graceful one, so I'll need your help."

"What are you planning?"

"There's a balcony on the back with a door that leads into Grunnar's cabin. I'll have to jump to it, which I can do, but the landing will be loud. I figure if you're able to distract the group when I jump, then not all of them will come looking for the source of the noise. And since it's Grunnar's cabin, he'll be the one that comes looking for me. All I need is to be able to get him alone."

"How are you sure it'll be him?"

"Are you kidding?" She gave a little chuckle. "That ogre's got more trust issues than anybody I've ever met, and that's saying something, considering how many crooks I've worked with. But rightfully so, with the way it sounds like he's cheating his crewmates. There's no way he's going to want them to be able to have access to any of the money or valuables he's hiding in his own cabin."

"How do you want me to distract them?"

"However you can. If you're able to get them out of the building completely, that would be ideal. But if not, just try and keep them distracted for as long as possible."

“And then?”

“Then, I do what we came here to do.”

Finn swallowed nervously. “I don’t like this. It sounds risky.”

“Yeah, well, welcome to the job. Pretty much everything we do is risky.” She sighed, her tone softening with a mix of apology and reassurance. “Look, I’m sorry, but this is just how these things are. I know what I’m doing, and honestly, it could be a *lot* worse.”

“Well,” Finn started hesitantly. “If you think it’ll work…”

“I do. I’ll *make* it work.”

“Okay. Then I'll do my best, too.”

In seconds, they were both in position. Monica balanced on the edge of the pier’s drop off, crouched to make a leap for the balcony just as Finn lifted his fist to knock on the cabin’s door. It was barely even a door; more just a jagged piece of siding sawed off and reattached with hinges. He could already hear the sounds of chatter and raucous laughter from inside from several feet away as he approached. His apprehension made time lag when he lifted his fist, but he forced himself not to hesitate so he couldn't change his mind.

Finn held his breath as his knuckles rapped against the door, making it clang and rattle louder than he'd anticipated, enough to make him bristle. The voices immediately stopped, but only for a moment before one of them asked, "Boss, you expectin' somebody?"

"No." A deep voice growled, the one he thought he recognized to be Grunnar's, even though he'd only heard it once before. "Not till after the games, at least. Send 'em away."

Then came the sound of wood scraping against wood, followed by the shuffling of movement. And then, another voice chimed in.

"What if they've got something valuable?" He laughed, a small but gruff voice that Finn hoped was Crognak's. "Might be worth it to see if we can help relieve them of it?"

But, as a couple of them exchanged cackling laughs, another voice came that made him realize the last one wasn't Crognak's, because *this* one more certainly was. "Boss, ain't you got somewhere to be?" It wasn't overly apparent, but Finn noticed that he sounded nervous.

"Naw," Grunnar guffawed. "You ain't gettin' rid of me that easily. At least not before I clean out yer pockets first."

Finally, the door peeled back to reveal a pudgy goblin with tribal tattoos along half of his face that swirled down across his neck and both arms. His scalp was pulled tight by a cap of cornrows that twisted into a short, stubby braid dangling an inch past the nape of his neck.

Beyond him, four other goblins and Grunnar sat on crates, huddled around a circular wooden table. The new addition to the group was Crognak. Finn didn't know how he'd gotten in, or if he simply hadn't seen him before, but he was hopeful that their new ally's presence would be helpful as things unfolded. He didn't have time to fully wonder about the whereabouts of Wurick before the goblin at the door snarled, "And who are you?"

Just as Finn opened his mouth to reply, his senses were swarmed by an onslaught of stench— the mingling odors of sour liquor, stale sweat, piss, and probably several kinds of rot. His eyes rolled back in his head as he fought not to inhale the stink, but it was already too late to hold his breath. His lungs burned with the urge to cough and gag all at once, but he feared if he did either, he might also lose the contents of his stomach. Not that the addition of bile would do much to cover the smell.

"Delivery." Finn croaked, struggling to compose himself enough to give a relatively convincing response.

The one unexpected benefit of the rampant stink was that the shock of it had wiped away the nervousness that had plagued him before.

The goblin at the door narrowed his eyes, giving Finn a long, sweeping glare of appraisal.

"Where?" He growled guardedly, peering past Finn for any evidence to support his claim.

"You see," Finn began, clearing his throat to buy time as he fabricated an excuse. "This is just the pre-delivery. I was sent to make sure you'd be here to receive it when it came. Or, maybe not *you* specifically. We just require someone to sign off on it before it can be delivered and unloaded."

"What is it? We ain't expecting no delivery."

Finn's hand went to the back of his neck in a nervous gesture, channeling his unpreparedness into a dopey smile that he hoped would read as innocent cluelessness.

"I dunno, man. Probably groceries? I think that's what this company does. I'm just doing what they tell me to do."

"Groceries?" The goblin shot a skeptical look towards Grunnar, who looked less than pleased by the interruption. "What company are you with?"

Finn's finger flicked towards the logo embroidered across the left breast of the uniform, right above a name tag of a former employee that incorrectly identified him as "Jordan."

"Dawson Deliveries."

"We ain't never got anything from you before. What's the name on the delivery?"

"Don't turn him away." One of the goblins at the table called out. "We're hungry! If he wants to bring us food, let him."

"Yeah," another chimed in, before a low chorus of chants began, "Free food, free food!"

"Shut up." Grunnar snapped, slamming his fist down on the table with enough force to make the bottles and coins atop it rattle, and the goblins all immediately fell silent. "You sound like a bunch of idiots."

The goblin at the door looked to him for direction. Grunnar wore an inscrutable scowl, so both the goblin and Finn responded with surprise when he finally said, "Yeah, let him bring the stuff."

Just then, a muted *thud* came from the back of the cabin with enough force to make the front walls shiver.

"What was that?" A couple of the goblins and Grunnar stood in alarm.

Monica.

Finn tensed, but he did his best to cling to an inscrutable expression.

"So, uh," He resumed, raising his voice in an attempt to reclaim their attention before they decided to go investigate. "What time should I tell them to bring the delivery by?"

Finn watched Grunnar with divided attention as the goblin before him turned back to address him with renewed authority. “Uh, how ‘bout an hour?”

Grunnar grunted and waved to the other two that had stood to sit back down before he turned and began waddling towards a door behind them.

Finn’s mind exploded with the need to communicate his approach to Monica, but how?

Panicking, Finn obeyed the first impulse that entered his mind, and kicked the wall beside the door frame as hard as he could and then stumbled, belatedly trying to sell the action as a clumsy mishap.

The impact rattled back through the thin walls of the cabin, making the air shiver from the sound of the metal.

He choked on a sigh, brief relief at the promising likelihood of the sound traveling back to Monica in time to warn her. Then, overcome by a swell of embarrassment, Finn belatedly reacted to the impact, shaking his foot as he apologized nervously, “Oh, oww, sorry! Clumsy me.”

Grunnar glared at him before disappearing through the back door, which he slammed closed behind him.

The knot of apprehension tightened in Finn's stomach as his thoughts leapt to Monica. All he could do was hope that she was okay.

No. He shook himself, realizing that that's *not* all he could do. He had a job to do. She was depending on him to keep the goblins distracted so that she could handle Grunnar on her own. Even though the thought of that also made him even more nervous as he subconsciously measured the way Grunnar's massive height nearly doubled Monica's in his mind, Finn knew that he had to trust that Monica could take care of herself. After all, she had for so long before him that she knew her own limits better than he could. The best thing he could do to help her was exactly what she told him to do.

Keep the goblins distracted.

Chapter 18

Monica's fingers ached as she clung to the pier, hanging out of sight off the side of the balcony. She held her breath and waited for the inevitable, praying her strength would hold. She'd been fortunate enough to make the leap and stick the landing, but the *thud* that doing so had created had made the whole building rock from the impact.

Thankfully, even with nowhere to hide atop the tiny balcony, her instincts had kicked in. No sooner had she lowered herself over the edge and the back door had swung open. Grunnar peered out, his mug contorted with wary irritation as he scanned the back of the building. He quickly disappeared back inside when he saw no one. Since Monica was hanging from the side of the balcony behind the door, Grunnar hadn't even noticed her.

After he'd gone, she hoisted herself back up onto the balcony, flexing her aching hands. She could still hear him shuffling around inside the cabin, and knew she'd have to be both quick and silent in order to grab him before he decided to abandon the search.

In one swift movement, she burst through the door, ripping her dagger from the holster strapped to her thigh as she lunged at him. His back had been turned to her, but, hearing her enter, he whirled as she charged. One of his thick arms slashed at her, but she easily ducked in order to put herself behind him once more. As he turned, Monica swept his foot with her ankle, using his established momentum to make him stumble backwards into the wall of crates stacked along the left wall.

Even as he caught himself, the impact from his massive weight slamming into the boxes with even partial force sent shock waves rippling through the thin walls of the cabin. Monica grit her teeth, knowing she'd have to pay for her impulsive entrance.

Grunnar delayed pulling himself back up to stand as the tip of Monica's dagger came to point directly at his Adam's apple. Panting, he let his weight rest against the crates, dispersed across his spread arms.

"Anomaly," he snarled through bared teeth. The hot, fetid miasma of his vile breath steamed into the air between them. His single black eye glinted with hate as it studied her. "I warned you that it'd be bad news for you if I saw you again, but you just don't listen, do you?"

"I hate to break it to you Grunnar, but your threats don't exactly sound intimidating while you've got a dagger to your throat."

Just then, a knock came from the door that separated this room from the front cabin, where the quake had surely reached the goblins by now. And Finn. Monica spared him a split second of fleeting hope before her focus returned to listen.

"You okay in there, boss?" A goblin called from the other side.

"Get rid of him." Monica demanded in a harsh whisper, making Grunnar flinch when she nudged the sharp point closer to his throat.

"Fine!" Grunnar called out, feigning a grunt of pain between. "Just dropped a crate on my... toe."

"Oh." After a brief pause, the goblin, who still sounded wary but clearly had other things on his mind, asked, "You comin' back to play soon, or what?"

"Deal a round without me. I had something *come up* that I have to handle right quick, first."

The goblin's voice muffled as he relayed this to the group before being drowned out by a chorus of laughter and snatches of the crude jokes they'd twisted out of Grunnar's words. Monica only offered a fleeting expression of disgust before she returned to the job.

"Where is it?" She growled beneath her breath as she stared him down.

"I don't know what you're talking about."

"Bullshit." She leveled the edge of the blade against his gray-green skin with enough controlled force that the dagger drew the thinnest thread of blood to the surface where it pressed. "Even though you decided to play dumb about it last night, you know exactly what I want."

Grunnar drew in a sharp, wincing breath, but he didn't back down. Even with the knife pressed to his throat, the way he stared down at her, towered over her, made his thoughts too painfully easy to read. He knew that all he needed was the right moment to turn the tables. If she so much as slipped, it'd be over.

"Who are you looking for?" Grunnar asked in an equally menacing whisper.

The unexpectedness of his question shot a bullet of panic into her heart, which exploded upon impact, sending a storm shrapnel careening through her veins. Her muscles tensed as she recovered, but the alarm never made it to her face.

"None of your business. Now where's the eye?"

"That's interesting, because someone has been looking for you, too. I just thought it might be a convenient coincidence for you, and then, you wouldn't need the eye after all."

Rage stung her eyes and she bit back a snarl, trying not to let his words shake her. Negotiators and salesmen were always full of bullshit. That's how they made a living. Hell, that's how they *existed.* There was no reason for her to believe anything other than he was just trying to do what he did best in order to shake her enough to gain an advantage.

She told herself that this was a lie. Everything coming out of his mouth was and always would be lies. After all, he'd do anything to bargain for his own sorry skin. But it only worked if she believed it.

"It must be a *very* powerful artifact if you're doing this much to try to dissuade me from taking it. But it's not gonna work. My boss gets what my boss wants, so if you wanna keep your other eye, your *real* one, I suggest you tell me where this one is before I lose my patience."

The dagger pressed back against his neck with enough force that the thin thread of crimson coating its edge widened, making Grunnar wince.

"All right!" Grunnar finally surrendered, gritting his teeth in a feeble attempt to disguise the pain that threaded through his voice. "I'll show you. But you're gonna feel like a total fool when I do."

One of his hands started to rise, but stopped as soon as Monica spat, "Don't move. Just tell me where it is."

"Where would *you* keep an extra eye if you only had one?"

Monica grimaced in disgust when the dreadful, but admittedly obvious revelation hit her. Seeing this, Grunnar smirked, the stench of his breath once again growing as he huffed, "Not so eager now, are you?"

"Don't stall. Take off the eyepatch, real slow, and give me the eye. Now."

As his hand began to oblige, his smirk smoothed into a mockingly sweet, even placating smile before his fingertips ever reached his face.

"What if I make you a deal instead?"

"I don't want a deal. All I want is the eye, and I'm not leaving without it, even if I have to pry it from your damn filthy head myself."

Grunnar's lips pulled back into a snarl of frustration that Monica only observed for a second before a sudden explosion of muffled noise demanded her attention. Unbidden, her head swiveled in its direction, realizing in horror that the cacophony was coming from the front cabin. Finn.

Before she could snap back to Grunnar, his arm shot out to chop her wrist away, causing the dagger to go flying across the room. It landed with a clatter at the foot of the bed.

Monica let herself fall before Grunnar could grab her and then flung herself across the room. The floor came up so quick to meet her chest that it knocked the breath from her lungs, but she didn't stop. The world trembled around her with each quaking step that the ogre took in her direction. As soon as her fingers closed around the dagger's hilt, one of his massive feet came barreling towards her head. She rolled out of the way just in time for his toes to catch only her hair.

She sprang to her feet and he lunged at her again, his gait clumsy and labored. Dodging him was no strenuous task, merely annoying and draining. She couldn't do it forever, but she also didn't have the brute strength to face him squarely. Her agility was her best advantage. A passing worry reminded her of the fight Finn was facing just on the other side of the wall as the noise continued beyond it. She knew he wouldn't last long either against at least four goblins, but there wasn't much she could do with an ogre in the way.

Not to mention, that she still needed that eye; otherwise, this entire endeavor was pointless. She couldn't help Finn until Grunnar was out of the way. Forcing the thought of her companion from her mind, she dove at Grunnar in a flurry of swipes. A few of them caught him, but the wounds were superficial, doing little more than aggravate him further.

He paused long enough for his hand to go to one of the deeper cuts on his left forearm, pulling away with a renewed rage when he saw blood coating his fingertips.

But before he could charge her again, Monica caught him off guard with a daring demand.

"Tell me how the eye works."

Grunnar only responded with a grunt as he charged her again. His size and clumsiness made him the perfect bull in a china shop. Monica leapt out of the way, sending Grunnar slamming head-first into a tower of crates that went toppling with the impact.

Dazed, he hesitated, which gave her the perfect opportunity to dart behind him. This was her chance.

She flung herself at his back, gripping his waist with her legs as she climbed to take hold of his stocky neck. He grabbed her arms as she tried to bring the dagger to his neck, but this only made her squeeze more to secure purchase. His thick fingers wrapped around her forearms, making Monica even more painfully aware of the contrast in their sizes as he tried to pluck her off.

As he tugged at her, she shifted all of her strength into holding on with her legs, digging her knees into his ribcage as if atop a wild bronco. Her fingers clamped down on the dagger, desperate not to lose it again as her arms fought to get free of him. Her left arm flailed in an attempt to evade his fingers, and in turn, ended up repeatedly swatting his face.

After surviving several seconds of the struggle without being unseated, her confidence returned and she shouted again, "Tell me how the eye works! Now!"

This time, when she spoke, her dagger met his neck, its edge sharp digging into the hollow just above his clavicle. Begrudgingly, realizing that his own strength was waning, Grunnar grunted, "It lets me see how to get whatever I want most."

"How?"

He thrashed, trying to throw her off, but to no avail.

Her left arm closed around his neck in a tight knot. Her muscles trembled as she tried to force more strength than she had left into an attempt to seal his airways.

He stumbled, and in a labored growl, he allowed, "When it's installed, all I have to do is focus."

"On what?"

"On whatever I desire most. There has to be a single, clear point of intention before the eye's magic will illuminate the location of the desire."

"Is that it?" She snarled into his ear, trying hard not to think about the way her limbs were threatening to give out as she squeezed.

"Sometimes." He paused to pant, bracing himself against the wall with his hand. And from the way Monica could feel him swaying and shaking beneath her bolstered her resolve to endure. "After I got real good and used to it, I could make it let me see *how* to get things. In sales, it made me see what things to say and how to say 'em. Made me see when someone was hiding something crucial in getting that thing I desired."

"Give it to me." Monica hissed, slowly pulling the dagger away in the hopes that he wouldn't notice its absence as she moved to remove his eyepatch.

He not only noticed but took the opportunity to send himself staggering backwards into the wall. The weight of his body slammed hard into hers, momentarily crippling her strength and knocking the breath from her lungs so hard it dizzied her.

Panicking, her dagger arm squeezed down around his throat to join the other. Soon, it was all she could even do to hold on. Her options were running out. Time was running out. In the haze of panic and desperation, Monica became dimly aware of the temporary lull in the noise outside the room. Her stomach twisted, fearing the worst, but she dodged the thought before it could be fully realized in her mind enough to shake her focus. Instead, she ripped the dagger back towards herself, gouging hard under Grunnar's chin.

A sticky spray of hot liquid melted down across her hand as Grunnar cried out, a noise cobbled together from jagged fragments of pain, fear, and frustration.

The ogre's knees buckled, sending him stumbling as he fell. One hand went to his neck on instinct, trying to cup the wound above where Monica's arm still squeezed. His other hand caught the lip of a crate, on which he stalled to brace himself on the way down. Somehow, he managed to remain up on his knees, even as the blood continued to seep from him.

"Last chance," Monica trembled, though her voice sounded more exhausted than anything else through her gritted teeth. "Give me the eye now and spare yourself any more damage. If you cooperate, you just might live."

"Ha." Grunnar snarled breathily, trying hard to still sound tough despite the clear wooziness in his voice. "Like you think I'll let you leave in one piece after all this."

"You're in no state to fight me. Give it up. It can't be worth more to you than your life."

"You're right. It's not." He snapped, nudging off the eyepatch with his forearm, which revealed the festering hole in his face, now inches from Monica's. "Take it."

His words were a dare, knowing that the mere sight of the pulsating pustules and snaking black veins that swirled around the ghastly hole would sicken her on sight. The muscles in Monica's throat clamped down in a desperate attempt to deny her stomach from emptying its contents right then and there. But then, the smell hit her.

Salty and sour, like a bouquet of rotting meat and feet and bile, the stench that wafted up from the depths of his face was enough to make her retch. Though Monica was unwilling to relinquish her hold on Grunnar, she couldn't deny the impulse to turn away when her stomach purged itself. It did little to help because the smell hit her again the moment she turned back.

The queasy realization of how close her face was to his sent ripples of nausea through her. Monica fought to detach her mind from the repulsive reality of what she was about to do.

She transferred her dagger to her left hand, mentally steeling herself before she reached in with the fingertips of her right. She fought the gasp that clawed up her throat when she failed to avoid contact with the squishy, sticky inside of the hole. Finding nothing but flesh, her hand was forced deeper, sinking past the knuckles before she touched something solid. The eye.

Why in the seven realms was it so deep? She wondered, mortified. Of course, the size of his head meant it occupied more space than hers, but she suddenly gauged the fact that her previous thought that the hole could have been torn all the way back into the cavity that held his brain, didn't feel too far off.

Not unlike the contents of her stomach, she forcefully ejected the thought from her mind as her fingers tried to twist around the hard surface of a circular object inside.

Grunnar groaned uncomfortably, and the vibrations of his voice tickled up her arm like spider legs.

She didn't stop, twisting her hand in an attempt to wrench the item free. *Why is there so much resistance? It shouldn't be connected to anything.*

She didn't try to reason through it too much, only for the sake of her sanity. Instead, she doubled down her efforts to pull.

Another angry groan boomed forth from Grunnar's throat. She felt the eye finally sliding forward, coming loose.

With renewed effort, her hand emerged with a pop, but before she could register the triumph, her body was thrown across the room.

As she flew, her limbs curled into themselves, desperate not to lose the things in her hands.

She landed with a brain-rattling *thud.* The room spun around her, and for a moment, her mind stalled. Her awareness returned just in time for her to find Grunnar towering over her, blood streaming from his throat. His dark eye rolled backwards in his head and his mouth gaped, tinting his hesitation with a zombie-like mindlessness.

Terror bubbled up in Monica's throat as she clutched her gooey hand to her chest. Barely able to move as the weight of her previous exertion hit her, she turned the dagger in her left hand towards him. The silver length of its stiletto blade sparkled in the dim half-light of the cabin as her hand quaked.

"Don't come any closer!" Monica squealed, her voice suddenly devoid of the authority of her previous demands.

In the moment that Grunnar remained frozen, there was only silence. Even the sounds from the front room had stopped, a realization that made tears sting her eyes. *Finn.*

"I warned you..." Grunnar growled, his voice barely audible.

But he didn't move. And the silence until his voice came again was deafening. Monica's mind searched for the sound of his breaths, suddenly but couldn't even find that.

"I warned you." The words trailed like a hollow echo as his body finally began to tip backwards. He fell in slow motion, as if trying to prevent it despite lacking the strength.

Grunnar's body collapsed to the floor with a monstrous *thud* that reverberated with such force that the walls rattled around her. No, they *hummed.* The hum continued long beyond when the force of the impact faded. It hung in the air, transforming into an uncomfortable droning that quickly increased to a maddening volume.

Something was wrong, Monica realized. *What was happening? What did Grunnar do?*

Chapter 19

The door that led to the front of the cabin swung open.

"Finn!"

Monica scrambled to her feet.

A quick glance permitted Monica's lungs to fill with a breath of relief. He appeared unharmed, despite the spray of blood that stained his uniform. His stance was still charged with combative energy in spite of the clear exhaustion that made his shoulders sag, clutching his extended staff— the ends of which were scuffed with evidence of use— so tightly that his knuckles were white.

Monica only noticed the two goblins standing behind him once she approached. The sight of them sent a jolt of defensive impulse through her limbs, but the way Finn's presence separated them forced a pause long enough to register their faces before she could strike.

Crognak sported a black eye and busted nose, and Wurick's lower lip swelled around a gash that still seeped fresh blood. Their faces both glistened with a sheen of sweat and they were panting heavily.

"I hope this'll be worth it." Crognak huffed in greeting when he saw Monica.

"What happened?"

Monica’s eyes skirted the ground, where the bodies of four unnamed goblins were strewn about behind them. A moment of observation revealed that they were still breathing, despite the otherwise total lack of movement.

“The kid had it under control until he tried to convince them to leave the building. When they couldn’t make sense of his reasoning, things got violent.”

The droning in the air had risen to a level at which Crognak almost had to shout in order to be heard over the din.

“Typical.”

“We have to get out of here.” Finn interrupted, fear apparent beneath his gasping. "Did you get the eye?"

Monica nodded, squeezing her hand even more tightly around it. It was warm and hard, as firm as a marble despite being the size of a small plum. Though curiosity prickled the back of her mind, with her stomach still threatening to revolt, she didn't dare look at it now.

"Good." Finn huffed, giving a hurried motion for her to follow him. "We have to go."

"What's happening?"

"That'd be the boss' backup." Wurick announced, his voice flat with annoyed resignation, rather than the fear his next phrase should have conjured. "Piranha bats."

"What?!" Monica squawked, instinctually crouching forward and lifting her dagger arm to guard her head, despite the fact that the ceiling still shielded them. But not for long. “Why didn’t you mention that before?!”

"Yeah, we kinda forgot about those."

"Forgot?! How the hell do you forget about something like that?"

"There wasn't no risk of being on the other side of them before today. Besides, he hasn’t had ‘em for long; just since the hounds—"

The hum broke as a storm of sudden pings rained down from above. The explosion of noise was like a torrent of steel golf balls had been poured out onto the metal roof. A series of several punctures began to open in a scattered pattern across the ceiling, offering threatening glimpses of tiny, black-taloned feet and gnashing white fangs through the holes.

A sharp chorus of squalling shrieks stabbed into the air as soon as the bats began to catch glimpses of their prey through the litany of growing punctures.

Shit, shit, shit! Monica cursed silently in her mind. *That's what I get for taking the stupidity of goblins for granted.*

"We have to run!" Finn said.

"We can't." Monica argued, her voice on the edge of breaking. "They'll pick our flesh clean from our bones in minutes. And we don't have long till they'll break through the ceiling."

"Then what are we going to do?"

Monica's face sobered with determination. Her spine straightened and she holstered her dagger.

"The only thing we can do."

She palmed The Eye of Desire to her left hand before her right lifted the amulet that hung around her neck by its cord. Finn's hand flew to her wrist, grabbing her before she could activate the Riftrider.

"Wait! What about them? Each Riftrider only has enough power for one person. And I'd be dead without their help."

"Yeah, well *all* four of us will be dead if we don't. And then this whole thing will have been pointless." Monica tore her arm from his grasp, looking apologetically to the goblins. "I'm sorry. You must understand that sacrifices must be made in order to destroy The Enclave."

The goblins' eyes widened with incredulity.

"*You're* going to try to destroy The Enclave?" Crognak asked, dumbfounded.

"We're not going to *try*. We're going to succeed. And it wouldn't have been possible without you."

Wurick grimaced, his split lip trembled as it continued to ooze. His eyes glazed as if preparing to cry. But then, despite what Monica would have expected otherwise, Crognak was the one to break.

"But I don't wanna die!" He wailed, dropping to his knees in a display of despair that was equal parts pathetic and guilt-inducing.

"I'm sorry. I really am. I wish we could have repaid your service. But perhaps you will find peace in Enderfel, knowing that you both made a difference."

Wurick sniffled and gave a stoic nod, laying both of his hands on Crognak's shoulders as the kneeling goblin exploded into a convulsive fit of sobs.

"Do what you gotta do." Wurick said.

Fighting the unexpected lump in her throat, Monica mirrored the nod. Her attention shifted to Finn, whose face was dappled red with the threat of tears. Even so, he said nothing, lifting his own Riftrider in solidarity.

Monica linked her arm through Finn's, pressing her knuckles into the surface of her amulet, centering her focus. She nodded to the goblins once more, her face surprisingly soft with genuine gratitude. And then, she and Finn both closed their eyes and vanished.

The metal of the roof roared as it gave way to a cloud of winged bodies that spilled into the building like liquid. Their wings roiled like a massive black wave as the swarm collapsed inwards to occupy the once-empty air.

In Monica and Finn's minds, they still heard the echoes of ravenous shrieking and agonized cries as the swarm devoured any organic material within the building.

But thankfully, the magic of the Riftriders spared them the sight of the gruesome scene, instead, making the world open up around them. Any lingering images of their previous location peeled back, and in the blink of an eye, they were transported into a space that was only occupied by an inky, hollow blackness.

Then, the blackness ripped open, spilling forth streams of blue and purple light that rippled through the air like colored ink through water. The light sparkled with flecks of shimmering silver and opalescent white, dancing like stars in the space around them. It reached forward, welcoming them, enveloping them as it pulled them through the space.

When it spilled over them, the rift's energy made everything else melt away. The distant cacophony of screeching metal and crying goblins wilted into the background as the rift melted closed behind them.

Monica and Finn were only dimly aware as it happened, but all of the unpleasant sensations and emotions that they had endured in the recent past dissolved and drifted away, no longer anchored to them from within the weightlessness in the rift. Their hearts and breathing slowed, temporarily free from the influence of any passing dreads or doubts. As they floated, their bodies were absolved of the pain and exhaustion of battle.

Soon, they were no longer floating, but falling, tumbling forwards through the rift. It seemed like hours until they finally hit the ground, but the instant the wind was knocked from their lungs, their minds realized that their journey had happened in only a flash of seconds instead. The tunnel of swirling space was sucked away, lifting to reveal the glistening city of Arkynesta before them.

It was no less jarring for Finn than the first time he had ended up here. He lifted his head slowly, still dizzy from the fall, and was greeted by the enormous, breathtaking city.

Seeing it made his eyes prickle with unexpected tears that absolved the subconscious fear that he might never return. It was even more beautiful now than the first time he had seen it.

Monica took no time to recover, as if she had traveled through rifts hundreds of times instead of less than a dozen. She towered over Finn as he sat and gawked, her hand extended in an offer to help him to his feet. He took it, suddenly aware of the mystified bewilderment that had twisted onto his face.

Monica's mask had never faltered, though something about her cool indifference seemed more hollow now. Perhaps it was because he had come to see so many of the things that she used that mask to hide. Though her eyes were empty as she looked him over, Finn almost thought that he could observe fragments of thought crossing her face beyond them.

When Finn got to his feet, they immediately began walking in the direction of Maal's distant tower without a word passing between them. After all, what does one even say after the willful sacrifice of unlucky pawns turned unexpected allies, without whom they would not have succeeded?

Before Finn, Monica wouldn't have so much as batted an eye at the loss. Crognak and Wurick hadn't been her friends. In fact, they had started as her enemies. And even though she had partially tricked the goblins into working with them, she wouldn't have felt guilty for the fates of those originally wicked creatures. But even without words passing between them, Monica could feel Finn's reverence in the silence.

She wondered if he felt guilty, which ignited an empathetic flame of disquiet within her own heart. Yet another burden he would not have had to bear without her accidental interference in his life.

Why did he make her feel this way? The question resurfaced again, but she pushed it back without a second thought, only increasing her pace as she used the tension of her stewing emotions to fuel the haste of her stride.

Monica's left hand remained a tight fist around The Eye of Desire as they walked. At first, she ignored the subtle sensations that crawled through her, the first of which was a soft, throbbing warmth inside her fist, but her mind wrote it off as a combination of the tightness of her prolonged grip and the beat of her own heart. But then, a gentle force began to tug at the base of her skull, like a rope was attached to her, pulling tighter with each passing second. It wasn't until she noticed the faint glow of a fuzzy crimson light out of the lower left reaches of her vision that she realized something was off.

Her pace slowed and she lifted her eyes to the cool blue sky overhead. The sun hung high above them, casting a warm, golden hue over the city. Surveying the light glinting off of the windows of nearby buildings, Monica only saw the pale, silvery white of the reflected sunlight, but no justification for a light as vibrantly red as the one that still lingered in her periphery. Even as her attention turned more fully to the red glow's edge, it showed no sign of fading.

Reluctantly, Monica finally glanced over her left shoulder in search of the light, sure that she was imagining things. It was probably just a side effect of how taxing the day had been. But when she glimpsed Finn out of the corner of her eye, her heart leapt into her throat. His entire silhouette was hemmed with a gentle crimson glow, unobtrusive but undeniable, all the same.

"Finn?" Monica questioned cautiously, making him stop in his tracks when she turned to inspect him. "Do you see that?"

"See what?" His expression was one of startled obliviousness. "Why are you looking at me like that?"

"You're... *glowing*."

Finn's brows knitted and his eyes darted to his arms, which he raised between them for inspection. He turned them back and forth several times before letting them fall before giving a confused shake of his head.

"I don't see anything. What does it look like?"

"Like—" Before she could answer, her notice caught the movement of a couple of passersby cautioning her to think better of it.

What if the crimson light was the side effect of someone trying to cast a spell on them? Monica turned to scan the faces of the passersby, but they seemed unfazed by her sudden attention. She whirled around to survey the scene for the possibility of anyone watching them but saw nothing worthy of note. Nevertheless, she decided that now was not the time or place to start announcing the notice of anything potentially dangerous in the midst of someone wishing to harm them, lest they retaliate.

After the people passed, Monica glimpsed a momentary blip of a second red silhouette, standing just behind Finn. The outline clearly belonged to a man, but the form was empty inside, obscuring who the second person was meant to be.

Noticing her shift in focus, Finn turned to look over his shoulder towards the silhouette, but his reaction revealed that he still didn't see what Monica had. Even if he could have, the outline had vanished before he turned, winking out just as fast as it had come.

In the far reaches of her mind, Monica felt an itch of Deja vu as the echoes of a fragmented voice called to her.

Brother... brother...

She barely recognized the sensation as a clear word, but rather, the memory of the feeling of when it had been spoken before. It was that pull of strange obedience, that feeling that she was meant to be somewhere else, that had accompanied the call of the dripsies when her brother had summoned her.

But, just as quickly, even that was gone.

After the second silhouette had vanished, Monica became suddenly aware of another point or origin for the red light; the right pocket of her own jeans. The light didn't envelop her like it did with Finn. Instead, it outlined the definite shape of the amulet that was tucked away in her pocket. Her right hand flattened against it with the panicked instinct to try to obscure the light. She certainly didn't want anyone else to be aware of the Soulseeker. And it worked, because the light immediately faded beneath her hand, as if her touch had somehow dismissed it.

She was relieved to find that the light did not return when she lifted her hand away. But Finn was still glowing. Not only that, but his confusion had sharpened into genuine concern.

"Monica?" He asked haltingly. "*What* are you seeing?"

Instead of answering him, she reached her right hand towards him. Flattening it, so that her palm was parallel to the ground, she jabbed his arm cautiously with all of her fingertips, sucking in a small gasp of surprise when her touch also dismissed the glow from around him. She peered down at her hand, eyes wide in wonder before they lifted again to Finn. Her wonder narrowed into wary skepticism that lasted only a moment before she shook her head and reclaimed her mask of indifference.

She turned away, resuming her stride towards Maal's tower as if nothing had happened.

But even though Finn's feet pattered on the pavement behind her as he skipped to keep up, he wasn't about to act like nothing had happened.

"Monica, what did you see?"

"I don't know." She answered in a small voice.

"Is it dangerous?"

"I don't know." She said again, her voice sharpening defensively. "But it's gone now, so we won't know unless it returns."

"That's super weird, right?"

"Yes," She growled under her breath, stopping to shoot Finn a glare of warning. "But this is *not* the place to discuss it. Hurry up, okay? We can't keep Maal waiting."

Chapter 20

"It's about time you showed up," Celene huffed as Monica burst through the doors and into the tower's lobby with Finn at her heels. "We've been waiting *forever*. I almost thought I was gonna have to come save you *again*, damsel."

Despite the edge of irritation in her tone, Celene's honey-hazel eyes gleamed with humor as her attention followed Monica. A curtain of long red curls bobbed loose past her shoulders as she turned to accompany them. Her long-legged strides made her graceful pace seem a far more casual saunter than Monica's determined haste.

"Glad to hear you missed me." Monica sneered, her stride never slowing as she crossed the empty expanse of the lobby and approached the reception desk towards the back. "But I told you not to call me that."

"Well, the shoe fits," Celene retorted with a playful pout of her full lips.

Realms, she was irritating, Monica thought with a roll of her eyes, though she was hardly aware of the unbidden smile that now tugged at the corners of her mouth. Irritating or not, Monica would be lying not to admit that it *was* nice to be missed. Especially by someone who was as attractive as they were annoying.

Noticing the shift in Monica's demeanor, Celene seized the opportunity to lay it on even thicker by adding a sultry drama to her voice. "Shame on you for making me wait. Do you have any idea how *lonely* I was getting?"

"I'm sure you found *some way* to entertain yourself." Monica sighed, shooting a teasing glance back in Celene's direction. "I know how good you are at that."

"True." The siren chuckled softly, and even *that* sounded like music.

The simplistic seating of the lobby passed in a blur as Monica led the charge to the reception desk, where Maal's six identical secretaries, or rather, a splitter and her five copies, sat working in robotic synchronicity. They were unchanged from the last time she had seen them, outfitted in their uniform pastel-blue dress suits, and each with their long, blonde locks pulled up into an impossibly smooth high ponytail that was held by a gold cuff. Their dark eyes were rimmed with crisp cat-eyed wings and their heart-shaped lips were painted with the same pale pink that emphasized the startling uniformity of their faces.

Unsettling as always, Monica thought. As useful as it would be to be able to make identical copies of herself, Monica had always found such a power disconcerting. At least it was rare, so she didn't have to think about it often.

The clicking of the nearest secretary's rhythmic typing ceased and she lifted her head with a friendly smile, signifying her as the original splitter, since the copies, fragments of her consciousness, were really only suited to menial, muscle memory tasks that didn't occupy too much conscious effort.

“Greetings, Lady Elliott.”

“Inform Master M that we've arrived,” Monica instructed before the secretary had even fully risen from her chair.

She forced a breathy chuckle through her enduring smile before bowing her head in acknowledgement.

"He is already aware. I will summon an elevator for your party." She extended her palm towards the few pairs of gold metal slats that were inlaid in an alcove of wall beyond where the desk ended, before sinking back into her chair and fell back into the continuing chorus of rhythmic typing that the others had maintained during her intermission.

As the three turned to approach the elevators, they were greeted by another friendly face.

Even though his pale jade eyes scanned all three of their faces, only one name crossed his lips.

"Finn." The curve of his mouth deepened and his lips parted to reveal a white flicker of teeth. "You're back. Or should I say," he paused, eyes falling briefly to the nametag on Finn's soiled uniform, before correcting himself with a playful note of amusement in his voice, "Jordan?"

"Davhi!" Finn's voice was breathless with joyful surprise. It took Finn a moment to register the second half of the centaur's comment, but when he did, his own gaze fell to the patch embroidered over the breast pocket of the borrowed uniform. Finn shook his head, chuckling to cover his embarrassment as he unbuttoned Jordan's shirt and shrugged out of it to reveal his own t-shirt beneath.

When Finn wadded up the uniform but awkwardly continued to hold it, eyes glancing to and fro in search of somewhere to stash it, Dahvi joked, "So you're not Jordan after all?"

"Not anymore," Finn gave a breathy laugh.

"*Anymore*? I'm intrigued."

Without interjecting, Monica snagged the shirt from Finn's hand and deposited it into a tall gold cylinder that, upon first glance, had looked far too fancy to be a trash can. Regardless, Finn was glad to be rid of it. He thanked her with a shy nod before turning back to Dahvi, saying, “It’s a long story.”

“I’d like to hear it when I’m not so busy.”

“Busy?” Realizing Dahvi’s choice of words, Finn asked, "Why are you here?"

The centaur gave a cool shrug that betrayed nothing, but it didn't hide the clear nervousness in the shifting of his stance, particularly the soft clacking that his hooves made against the marble floor. The tapered edge of his silky white hair danced down along the length of his neck with the movement.

"I received a letter, a summons. When it mentioned that you were involved, I knew I had to come."

A soft smile carved dimples into Finn's cheeks as he inclined his head to look at Dahvi, suddenly reminded of how strikingly tall the centaur was in comparison. Sneaking a furtive glance back at Monica, he wondered if that's how she felt when she looked up at him.

"This is where we work." Finn explained, hoping that the details might bring Dahvi some comfort in the face of the unknown. "Well, not directly; this is where our boss works. Maybe he wants to hire you? That'd be cool. Then we could all work together!"

Monica cleared her throat, giving Finn a glare of warning that immediately dampened his enthusiasm and forced him to remember the risks that came from working for Maal. As he considered this, he was struck by a pang of shame in realizing that she was right. He shouldn't want someone he considered to be a friend to willingly be put in an unnecessary, dangerous situation. Feeling that shame manifesting as a sudden wave of heat rose in his cheeks, Finn gave a nervous chuckle and said, “Never mind. That might not be a good idea, actually."

"Why not? After all, if you're using my weapons training for whatever it is that you do, I might actually be well suited to help, especially with the depth of my varied combat knowledge."

Finn swallowed nervously, and, seeing that he clearly was at a loss as to how to respond, Monica interrupted.

"Let's just not get too ahead of ourselves, okay? We don't know why you were summoned yet, but there is no sense in making assumptions when I'm sure we'll be finding out very soon."

On cue, the elevator arrived and the nearest set of gold panels slid open for them to enter.

Dahvi nodded in agreement before trotting onto the elevator at her gesture. Finn followed him, trailed by Celene, and then finally, Monica.

Once they had piled into the elevator, everyone did their best not to move, in what was perhaps a futile attempt to respect the little buffer of space that remained between them now that they were so tightly nestled together. Even despite Dahvi being relatively small for a centaur, it was honestly an impressive feat that all four of them had managed to squeeze into the tiny elevator without touching one another. The quiet remained for only a moment until the doors closed and the upwards momentum of the elevator jostled them, shattering their careful separation.

Finn's heart raced. He wasn't sure if it was from the nerve-wracking closeness of Dahvi's body behind him, Monica's beside him, or if it was merely from the nerves building at the knowledge of seeing Maal soon. After all, even now that Finn was working for him, Maal was an intimidating being, especially more so in person.

Then, remembering Monica's warning from his first time here, Finn turned to Dahvi and murmured in a low voice,

"You know, you probably shouldn't tell our boss your name if he asks."

"Oh?" Dahvi inquired coolly, his expression lifting slightly with the question, but it never hinted at even the barest amount of concern. "But he already has my name. It was on the summons."

Finn stiffened at this, immediately turning away in the hopes of concealing the alarm that had overcome his face. A warm hand unfurled atop his shoulder, which was likely meant to be a comfort to him, but the unexpected touch only made his muscles clench even tighter.

"You know," Dahvi answered in a low, comforting purr that was barely loud enough for Finn to hear, "I appreciate your concern, but I've worked with Maal before. Not in the way that you do, but at least enough to know what to expect."

“What?” The single word was all Finn could manage in his startled state.

His head spun with questions, but he didn’t have the opportunity to process any of them before the elevator stopped and the doors peeled back to reveal a new space. Monica and Celene took no time to disembark, standing off to the side as they waited for the boys to join them.

The room was an odd amalgamation of Maal’s first suite with its high walls, inlaid with carved arches, domed ceiling, and open air, and Maal’s basement lair, with its walls made of large bricks and its dimmed, ominous lighting.

The air was warmed with an orange glow that, as their eyes adjusted, the group realized was attributed to the army of candles that speckled the area. The taller ones that sat in groupings along the marble floor came as high as their knees, while many of the smaller ones were cluttered atop shelves and in little alcoves that set back into the walls between hangings of wispy gossamer silks that dripped from the perimeter of the vaulted ceiling.

Despite the lack of natural light, the air was filled with gentle currents of movement that made the flames flicker as if caught in a breeze.

The room was spacious with sleek, yet simple furniture scattered in sparse groupings across the expanse. Their unsystematic groupings amongst an otherwise open space suggested that this room was meant for parties, where smaller groups of guests could break off from the crowd to find some privacy amongst a throng. It seemed like an odd choice to meet with only four of them here, given that the room was currently empty.

Monica's eyes scanned the room before she took the first cautious step forwards, clearing the way for the other three. She thought it odd that Amadarus was not present to greet them and took the absence of Maal's androgynous assistant as an indication of the gravity of the situation. Maal had cultivated many binding loyalties with his immense power, and Amadarus was among those he'd trust with almost anything. So, either Amadarus had been called to assist with other duties, or, as Monica dreaded, whatever Maal was planning for them was meant for them alone.

"Maal?" she finally called, her voice rippling throughout the vast emptiness of the room, which amplified even what she had measured to be barely a whisper.

No sooner had she spoken his name and her nostrils swirled with the familiar, musky, sweet aroma of smoke perfumed with vetiver, iris, and neroli. The flames of all of the low, distant candles began to flicker with suddenly more movement before several tendrils of opaque white smoke began to spread low across the floor, creeping forwards like spider legs.

Monica’s eyes lifted to follow the ribbons of smoke, up to where they eddied around the legs of a massive figure striding towards her. Even from across the room, his height was nauseatingly imposing. Her eyes had been on him for barely even a second before she noticed his magic take hold. She could feel it, writhing inside her brain as she tried to recall the last time she had seen him standing. She knew she had, but as she stared at him now, she found it difficult to believe that she could have ever let her awareness of his impossible height slip from her mind. As if realizing it for the first time, her gaze instinctually flitted upwards to allow a moment of brief recognition for the necessity of such high ceilings.

Monica was only dimly aware of the sounds of her party's footsteps behind her, her attention instead consumed by the effort that it took to process the details of Maal’s appearance against the compulsion of his cloaking magic. His outfit displayed the suggestion of affluence. Ivory silk harem pants concealed the girth of his massive tree-like legs amongst its airy folds, and its high waist was embellished with ornate designs embroidered with a gold thread that matched the metallic sheen of the many rings that glinted along his long, claw-tipped fingers. His broad, muscular chest was bare, and his sculpted shoulders swirled with a dark pattern of ink that almost seemed to move on its own across his gray-blue skin.

Twisting deeper into her mind as she looked at him, Maal's magic soothed Monica’s guardedness, which soon ebbed away in favor of the spell of the familiar reverent obedience that his presence always cast over her.

When she stared directly into his face, her mind was arrested behind an almost tangible wall of suggestion that denied her true recognition of his magically obscured features. She fought the inclination to squint and focus on his face, knowing that such an impulse would be pointless to pursue. In all the times she’d ever seen him, she’d never won against his impressively unobtrusive concealment spell, even when she was allowed a much closer proximity to him. The hazy consideration of whether her friends were also as aware of the concealment crossed her mind but disappeared the moment her eyes locked with his.

His eyes, which flickered electric blue with pops of amber and orange, seemed to blur the air as their glow caught the wisps of smoke that drifted across his features like blue headlights glaring out from behind a screen of fog.

Maal lowered his chin to look down at Monica as she approached. His mouth was framed by a dark, well-groomed mustache that transitioned into a small triangular beard of wiry black. The tip of the beard was pulled into a small gold cuff and ended only an inch below his chin. Even though his features were impermanent in her mind, she still read the expression that curled his lips as he studied her.

“You have it?” He asked, though his intonation seemed more congratulatory than inquisitive.

“Yes.”

She raised her arm, overturning her left fist in offering. But before her fingers could unfurl to present the eye, Maal turned and gestured towards a nearby alcove, made of a sofa, a long chaise, and three small ottomans.

“Come, then. Let us discuss.”

Chapter 21

As soon as they were seated, Maal turned to Dahvi. His stern expression and calculating eyes did little to dislodge the centaur's charming yet relaxed smile. In fact, other than the awkwardness of the way his horse half was leaned crookedly against one of the ottomans, Dahvi looked impossibly nonchalant. It was as if he'd been completely unaffected by Maal's intimidating demeanor, reputation, or the unwelcome prickle of magical suggestion that Maal emanated.

Only Monica seemed to notice this; thinking it odd, but then reluctantly deciding that it could merely be Dahvi's way of being guarded, especially since this wasn't exactly the time or audience in which to question it.

It *did* seem unusual that he was here, though. While it wasn't unlike Maal to try to obtain new contract holders wherever and whenever he could, bringing somebody new into a group of existing agents, especially with the severity of the current circumstances, seemed like an unusual risk.

Maal must be getting desperate, she thought, dreading whatever was to come if that *was* the case. While she was in no place to question Maal's judgment, a wary concern made her aware of the passing thought that she hoped Dahvi was trustworthy enough to merit his presence.

"You'll have to forgive my brevity," Maal began, "but unfortunately, we have little time for the usual pleasantries that would normally precede a business arrangement."

Dahvi gave a gracious nod, encouraging Maal to continue.

"Those within this room are the only individuals who know of my true intentions. I have invited you here because I think you would be a valuable asset towards achieving our success. Especially since I became aware of a particularly unique and valuable ability that you possess. I have been looking for someone like you for ages, but to no avail.

"I must commend you for keeping yourself so well hidden for so long, especially in a city under so many watchful eyes. But I must also concede that such a feat is not unexpected for one with abilities such as yours."

Dahvi gave a grin that made his teeth sparkle when he chuckled at the flattery. Maal's eyes seemed to sharpen at Dahvi's unspoken confirmation of whatever Maal had been insinuating. Looks passed between Celene and Monica, then between Monica and Finn as the three tried to wordlessly discern the clearly sensitive information that they had not yet been made privy to.

Ignoring their curiosity, Maal continued, "I am prepared to offer you great compensation for your services and the use of your abilities towards our objective."

"Such as?" Dahvi inquired cooly.

"Why, it could be nearly anything. So tell me," Maal grinned, letting his own gleaming teeth become visible from within the telltale smile that, despite whatever pageantry he'd intended to forgo, he simply couldn't resist the particular question, "What is it that you desire, *centaur*?"

The glint in Dahvi's eye turned knowing. He shifted to adjust the splay of his legs, molding his posture to look even more relaxed as he retorted, "I simply wish to know how your objective would involve my skills. You can't expect me to just go on agreeing to things without knowing what I'm getting myself into, hmm?"

Maal's smile tightened in annoyance, his eyes growing dark with a wary deliberation. He remained silent for a long moment, as if trying to judge just how much information he would need to give in order to convince Dahvi, while still holding his cards close to his chest. Finally, Maal answered. "Fine. Since you seem a clever being, I see no sense in sugar-coating this for you. My objective is treacherous and its cost will be high to achieve; likely resulting in the loss of one or more lives of the people in this room. That being said, its success will result in a far superior existence and quality of life for nearly everyone residing within this realm."

"You say it as if you expect to persuade me to do it simply for the *good of the people.*"

One of Maal's eyebrows rose in judgment at the challenge.

"You would not? Even if it benefitted an entire world?"

"I'm not convinced that it will. Such a promise sounds grand, believe me; but why should I trust such an outcome when I'm still blind to the means intended to achieve it? And why should I trust you to have a similar motive, doing this for the good of the people? The powerful people of this world do not do something so risky if there's not something bigger in it for their own personal benefit."

A muscle in Maal's jaw feathered as his teeth clenched. His head turned to the side momentarily, as if deciding whether or not to remain offended by Dahvi's concerns.

Monica's breath caught in her chest as she watched the negotiations unfold, stunned to see someone who could challenge Maal so easily and still seem so graceful and unconcerned while doing it. He was asking the right questions; questions that she herself had wanted to ask but had made no progress against Maal's vehement persuasions that he had earned enough of her trust that she needn't question his motives. But she did. She questioned everyone, *doubted* everyone, and to see someone taking the time to do the same impressed her. Not to mention, she was enjoying being a spectator at the bargaining table, for once. It was like watching a good game of chess but not having to worry about anticipating all of the hard moves herself.

Maal's jaw finally unclenched as he turned back with a smile of renewed determination that barely curled the corners of his thin-pressed lips. He seemed pleased at the thought of whatever it was he was about to say.

Therefore, everyone was surprised when he admitted, "That's perceptive. And you're right. There *is* a matter of personal retribution at stake. And though it is not my primary motivation, it would be deceitful to deny the fact that *that* is what inspired this."

Monica couldn't believe what she was hearing. Shock shivered through her and she surrendered to her objections without thought.

"What?" Monica gasped, struggling to keep her voice below a shout when she demanded, "Why have you waited so long to say this? All this time I've tried to get answers from you, and you only ask me to trust you. But now, this near *stranger* comes along, and you sound about ready to spill your guts to *him*!" She paused, gesturing towards Dahvi with emphatic indignance. "And we don't even know why. Why *him*?"

When Maal's eyes rolled towards her, their usual cocktail of intimidation and coercion intensified. Despite the resulting prickle of magical inclination that now clawed at the base of Monica's skull, the edge of Maal's voice had dulled with understanding, and perhaps even desperation.

"Monica, I have always appreciated your obedience, even when your curiosity has made it a challenge, but you know that I have never kept anything from you that would cause you direct, substantial harm in doing so. But I, as well as anyone, am entitled to my secrets, regardless of the reason. Even though I am powerful, I am not infallible. And I am running out of time, as well as options."

"So you've chosen to trust this newcomer over me? I've given you years of loyal service. I know I've failed you a lot lately, but it hurts that you would ask so vehemently for my trust and not return it. We don't even know what abilities he has that you're referring to. Why all the secrecy?"

"That is *because* of what they are. Dahvi's abilities are rare and coveted but are not ones that help prevent him from being taken advantage of, like Celene's. So, while I know enough to judge their usefulness for myself, it is not my secret to tell, especially before he has committed to any kind of agreement to work with us. You speak of trust, and my respect for his privacy is a token towards proving that he and I can foster that same trust. Additionally," Maal purred, something almost startlingly sentimental, and even paternal, within the gentling of his following response. "I have never withheld my trust from you, Monica. In fact, the reason that all of this was finally set in motion, was *you*. In knowing that I could trust you to pursue my objective with unquestioning and unrelenting tenacity, despite any possible obstacles, is what decided that this team was ready to be assembled. Because a team cannot be expected to succeed without a trustworthy leader."

"L-leader?" Monica squeaked hesitantly, tears of surprise pricking her eyes. Her heart fluttered, shocked to find just how much she had craved such validation from the man she'd only ever thought would see her as a tool to be used. But, as much as finally hearing it satisfied her, it also equally set her on edge. Why should she have to beg to hear him say he trusted her? Sure, Maal was a guarded man in almost every respect, but that made it hard to know where she stood with him, regardless of how long or successfully they had worked together.

"Yes." He said, a low shell of his voice sending fragmented reverberations throughout the room. "I've been waiting for you since everything began. And…"

Maal paused, closing his eyes as he pulled in a breath so deep that it made his chest balloon outwards. He shuddered as he released it, suddenly looking far more human than he ever had, despite the unchanged impossibility of his features.

"...in order for all of you to *truly* understand, I have to tell you how it began." Turning briefly to Dahvi, Maal explained, "We are going to bring about the fall of The Enclave. Their cruel, unjust reign here in Elandis has gone on for too long. Not to mention that there's talk that The Enclave has plans to conquer even more of Vhalta. Once they do, there will be no stopping them, so we must act now.

"You asked for details, so listen well and decide. I merely require that if you decline, you consent to having this knowledge stripped from your mind before you leave here."

Dahvi hesitated, a moment of apprehensive consideration flickering across his face. Maal's requirement clearly unnerved him, but what other choice did he have? He seemed to realize this, and gave a wordless hum of agreement, so Maal continued.

"Most people forget that the near immortality of djinns leads to a lot of grudges, but then again, so does the length of such a reign as that of The Enclave. Some grudges are justified. Some are not. While that would not usually be up to anyone outside it to determine, this grudge happens to be on the behalf of nearly an entire realm's worth of people, both existing and past.

"If we succeed in this plan, we bring down the tyrants who overtook this domain over three hundred years ago— having stolen it from a docile people who had initially welcomed them despite being interlopers— and seek to expand their regime to the whole of this realm, so that no peace is left to be had.

"You see, magic wielders are not actually native to this realm. They originated in Vhenra, as humans with unusual, selective gifts. But unfortunately, many humans have a tendency to destroy what they fear and do not understand, so rather than attempt to educate non-gifted humans and to strive towards a state of tolerance, wielders formed a group, pooled their magic, and sought a cowardly escape. That escape brought them to Vhalta, which at the time belonged only to creature races, including sirens and centaurs, such as yourselves.

"But the wielders quickly proved to be no better than the humans, killing and enslaving the natives of this land and instilling a hierarchy of power for those that held any sort of magical aptitude. Creatures who could do magic were able to maintain a small amount of comfort in their new world, but only if they submitted to the wielders' new way.

"And since creatures were not generally as magically gifted nor as practiced as the wielder invaders, they were unable to fight back to expel them. None of the neighboring domains have seen fit to intervene in Elandis' plight, fearing their own enslavement or destruction as a consequence. So, the wielders stayed. They stayed, they took over this domain, and became what we know today as The Enclave, reigning over all, to preserve their cowardice and destruction by simply displacing their own suffering to the people of another world.

"And I had to watch it all happen. It was before any of my contracts, which feed my ability to utilize my powers on behalf of another's will, so I was also powerless to do anything to stop them. I'll never forget all of the cruel things they did and continue to do for as long as their reign exists. They don't belong here. They never did. So now, with your help, we will bring down The Enclave, prevent their influence from spreading, and take back Elandis for all who originally lived here."

"I'm sorry you had to live through all of that," Dahvi reverently acknowledged. "I cannot imagine what it must've been like. I understand and admire your desire to set things right. But I'm still not clear on *how* we will do this."

"We?" Finn piped up, a clear brightness to his hopeful voice that seemed to cut through the existence of any of his former trepidation. "Then you'll help us?"

Dahvi paused a moment before giving a thoughtful nod.

"Despite how dangerous it sounds, it seems like the right thing to do."

"Just like that?" Celene asked, with a curiously dubious edge to her question. "You haven't even heard details of the plan, or anything that Maal may offer as compensation in return, and you're so willing to dive head-long into a situation that could end in your potential death? C'mon, nobody's *that* good of a guy."

"Hey!" Finn barked, offended. "It's not like *I'm* in it for the money, either. I wanna help people. Dahvi's a good guy, too."

Dahvi smiled at Finn's defense, though there was a sparkle of something in his eyes that had shaken his previous ease.

"My family," he said somberly. "If I have the opportunity to make this world safer for them, I will. I would do anything for them. And The Enclave is a ticking time bomb. Just because they haven't hurt my family yet, doesn't mean they won't. So it's far better for them, and for me, if The Enclave were brought to an end, and quickly."

"You would risk your life for them?" Celene asked.

"Wouldn't you do the same for yours?"

Celene fell silent, her urge to argue or question his motives vanishing in the face of the emergent soberness that overshadowed his answer. She *was* doing the same for hers. Celene's mother was also a siren. Living in the mortal realm made her vulnerable to some severely disagreeable side effects. Namely, sirens were cursed with a bloodlust that periodically caused them to lose control. It was specifically triggered by prolonged existence spent in close proximity with males of any human-like species.

So, even though Celene's parents still loved each other very much, they couldn't be together without the risk of her mother accidentally killing her father. But that wouldn't be a problem if they could move to Vhalta. In this realm, no creatures suffered the side effects of their magical existence the way they do in Vhenra. But, with her father being human, that posed a whole new set of challenges. In order for her parents to live a comfortable and safe life here, she knew that The Enclave must first be removed from the equation. Despite her shallow knowledge of Dahvi's familial circumstances, his motives seemed no different than her own.

Monica quietly assessed their reactions after the conversation closed. Still more interested in, and wary of Dahvi, Monica now noticed the faintest hint of apprehension surfacing in his manner that hadn't shown through before. There was now a nervous twitch to his tail, which shifted with a sudden, fidgety frequency. Additionally, the cool charm had left his smile, and his lips were now pressed into a narrowed line. Despite the lack of emotional sharpness in his words, his admission *did* seem genuine, perhaps even edged with a sense of desire that she didn't understand. There was a perceived lack of urgency in Dahvi's determination compared to hers, Finn's, and Celene's.

Still, any allies.could be useful against such stacked odds. *After all,* she reminded herself, *look at how beneficial it had been to partner with Crognak and Wurick to pull off the artifact heist at Grunnar's.* That wouldn't have been possible without them. Perhaps the same would soon be said of Dahvi.

"Then we have an accord?" Maal asked, and Dahvi's chin dipped in staid acceptance.

"If I can be of service, it sounds like a worthy cause. What will you need me to do?"

"Wc will all rcconvene to discuss the logistics of a plan shortly, as well as the specific expectations of your employment, including compensation, as Celene mentioned. But first," He paused, turning to Monica with a large hand outstretched in her direction, "The eye?"

Monica felt the eye pulse once in her still-clenched fist as she looked down at it. She'd nearly forgotten that she was still holding it. Her fist had long since dried from the gag-inducing goo that had sheathed it upon emergence from Grunnar's putrid wound. Her knuckles groaned with an ache as she unfurled her fingers, scales of the dried ichor flaking off with the movement.

Even as the group barely moved, Monica became claustrophobically aware as heads turned and bodies shifted around her to get a better look at the orb in her hand.

She didn't register that she hadn't even gotten a decent look at the eye herself until the shock of its unusual appearance struck her. When she observed the sphere in her palm to be nothing even resembling an eye other than its shape, her intrigue grew. The ball's surface swirled a creepy, slow-moving mix of galaxy black, flecked with coils of gunmetal-colored micro-shimmer that mingled with veins of crimson and burgundy. The pattern churned and pulsated with energy that felt *alive*. It had no iris or pupil to show, uniform across its surface with the gradual but ever-changing movements.

It wasn't difficult to become so mesmerized by the eye that she could've lost hours looking into it if she hadn't been interrupted by the sudden pull of Maal's voice.

"Very good." But when Monica's hand rose to offer it to Maal, he shook his head and motioned it away with a forward-facing palm. "You will be the one to use it. Do you know how?"

"Me? Why must it always be me?" Monica asked wryly, but only as a disguise for the newfound uncertainty churning in her throat.

"You *are* my artifact expert. And, admittedly, based on what little prior knowledge I was able to obtain of that artifact, the one thing I was certain of was that, of everyone here, you had the best chance of being able to use it successfully. What did you learn about wielding it?"

Monica stared down at the orb as she drew it back into her chest, now cupping it with both hands, as if it were an egg. After a heartbeat's hesitation, she gave a regretful shake of her head.

"Not much. But to be fair, it's awfully hard to get a detailed explanation from an obstinate ogre who was only made compliant in the first place by my blade in his neck."

Giving an understanding yet unconcerned nod, Maal encouraged, "What did he say?"

Monica's eyes narrowed in thought.

"He said... it let him see how to get whatever he wanted most; that when it's installed, all he had to do was focus." Monica swallowed disdainfully. "You don't mean I'll have to—?"

She winced, squeezing one eye closed to demonstrate her question.

"No, no, my dear." Maal answered, the humor returning to his voice. "If it's attuned to focus, it only needs direct skin contact. I'm interested in the aspect of its functionality as it relates to the user's desire. Since it shows you how to get the thing you want most, I knew you would be key, since your desire for vengeance against The Enclave rivals my own.

"And, since Rowan seems to be targeting you *specifically*, I believe that your growing desire to enact his demise will be enough to locate him, if channeled successfully."

"I- I understand all that, but focus artifacts take time to master. We don't exactly have much of that to spare right now." Monica worried aloud.

"You're right. Which is why my contacts will still continue to search for him, but I'm confident that if your desire is truly as potent as I estimate, we shouldn't need much time for mastery. Desire magic tends to be a hungry one and is substantially more powerful with abundant fuel. It feeds like fire, so you needn't do much to light it, only to stoke and guide it."

Monica gave an obedient nod of understanding, lifting her head slowly as the tentative question crossed her lips.

"When?"

"Tomorrow. You have undoubtedly had an exhausting day. It is wise to wait until you are rested and your emotions have the energy to be expressed freely."

Monica's lips pressed together in an expression that held some semblance of appreciation, but the rest of her reaction was distant and hollow. Distraction churned within her and she pondered over the emergence of several stoked emotions. After the initial shock of pride, Monica realized just how unsettled Maal's validation had made her feel. She hated that she had had to push him to say such things, and despite sounding genuine, she suspected that even this was somehow a calculated move. Perhaps her rising mistrust was merely a defense in order to keep herself numb to the uncomfortable, increasing awareness of the weight riding on her shoulders. But she couldn't help but feel that if there was no other motive behind his confession, Maal would've told her those things much sooner.

She returned from her musings as her eyes fell to The Eye of Desire once more. She opened her hand wider and she pushed it towards him, only to be rebuffed with a shake of his head.

"You will keep it on you. Focus artifacts work better when given an adjustment period in close proximity to attune to their user's energy flow."

"What if I lose it?"

Maal's cheeks lifted with a mirthless smile that Monica wasn't sure was meant as reassuring or mocking.

"You ask me to trust you, but you can't even trust yourself?"

Her eyes narrowed with indignance at the comment, but she wordlessly reveled in the way it pulled her out of the stormy mood of uncertainty and back into the clever guardedness and cool, practiced apathy that she usually wore.

Maal's smile endured, brightening with something akin to amusement, which Monica had not expected to see on his face, especially now. With further scrutiny, she was surprised to read what she thought was relief on his face, as if the joy he usually took in being enigmatic was actually a farce. Even though she would have never expected such a reaction from him, she understood it. Secrets were heavy to hold, and even heavier alone. She was sure that after she had time to process it, she would find comfort looking back at this encounter and remembering Maal finally unveiling a modicum of vulnerability.

Maal rose from his seat, again reminding them all of his impossible height.

"You're all free to go, until I summon you again. Dahvi, be prepared to come again tonight to discuss our formal agreement. Then tomorrow we will discuss the detailed plan and put it into motion."

Chapter 22

A gust of crisp, cool air rushed to meet them as the four stepped out of Maal's tower and onto the street. The sky was already growing dark behind a screen of dusky pink and gray, leaving Monica blinking in surprise at how much time had lapsed. This was confirmed by a growl that came from her stomach, audible and unbidden.

"I was just thinking about the same thing." Celene giggled. "Why don't we all grab a bite to eat?"

Before she could answer, Monica was overcome by a sudden visceral tug at the base of her skull, followed by the reemergence of a murky edge of scarlet light in her periphery. She glanced down at herself, seeing the light outlining the Soulseeker in her pocket. *That's weird.* It couldn't be a coincidence. Her gaze turned to The Eye of Desire, still clasped in her left hand, and suddenly realized a pattern.

The weird red light hadn't started until *after* she'd obtained the eye. And it seemed that she was the only one who could see it. Doing a double take of the crimson glow that emanated from her pocket made her recognize its striking similarity to the red parts that ebbed across the artifact's surface. No, it certainly couldn't be a coincidence.

She shoved The Eye of Desire in the other pocket, and the light immediately faded, but her mind was now suddenly and unavoidably overwhelmed with thoughts of her brother. Maal said that the eye's powers would feed off of her greatest desire. And, despite what he'd hoped of her desperation to bring down The Enclave, reuniting with Monroe was actually her *strongest* desire. That was going to be a problem.

"Well?" Celene chirped, nudging Monica with an impatient elbow.

Monica startled and shook her head, turning to the group before she started to back away.

"Actually," She began, trying to hide the tension that was now invading her shoulders. "There's something I have to take care of."

"What? You just got back."

Monica's hands made a dismissive gesture that fluttered like a pair of butterflies, uncertain of where to land. "It's important. Why don't the three of you go? I'll meet up with you later."

Seeing past the distractedness of her changed demeanor, Finn caught threads of concern woven through the muscles of Monica's expression.

"Monica, is everything okay?"

"Yeah..." She bit her lip, keeping her eyes low. "Go have dinner with Dahvi and Celene. I won't be gone long."

"But where are you—"

Before Finn could finish, Monica was already halfway up the block. His voice muffled into the cool air as he called to her, but she kept her head down and pretended not to hear him. As soon as she was out of sight, she broke into a sprint and hooked a sharp turn that let her disappear into a nearby alley.

She ducked into it, pressing her back against the side of a brick building as she stopped to catch her breath. Only a handful of seconds later, fast approaching footsteps broke the quiet, and Celene emerged from around the corner.

"Monica, what the hell?" She panted, folding forwards to brace her hands on her thighs.

"Celene?" Monica's voice steeled with an edge of annoyance that did nothing to mask the apprehension that snagged in the back of her throat. "Why did you follow me? Go away."

"After what happened to you the last time you ran off? As if! This situation calls for some damsel insurance."

Monica's mouth puckered in a scowl, but she decided against wasting her breath to chastise Celene for the continued use of the unwanted nickname. If anything, Monica's irritation would only serve to encourage her more.

"What are you doing, anyway?"

"It's none of your business."

"It *is* my business. We're a team now. We're supposed to help and look out for each other. You don't have to keep secrets from us. It'd be a lot easier to do whatever it is that you're doing with help, wouldn't it?"

Monica hung her head in defeat. A faint sigh escaped her lips and she shook her head.

"You wouldn't understand."

"Wouldn't I?" Celene challenged, straightening now that she had finally caught her breath. "Or do you just not want to give me the chance? Look, I know you don't know me that well yet, but I've given you no reason not to trust me. I helped save your life, for crying out loud."

"Only because your contract—"

"Bullshit. I've been helping you long before my contract. What about how I kept Finn safe after you ran off the first time? Or how I took care of the fade hounds you brought into a venue full of teenagers back in the mortal realm? Or how I collected the magical artifact that you dropped when you ran away and kept it safe from anyone finding it who shouldn't have?"

"You didn't even know me then."

"But I know you now. And I wanna help you."

"Why?" Monica huffed, finally feeling brave enough to lift her eyes to meet Celene's in the brief silence that followed.

As their gazes locked, Monica felt a warmth within the siren's sad eyes that she'd never noticed before. Celene blinked, her thick, dark lashes doing a coquettish dance to clear away welling tears as she studied Monica's expression with a pleading pout.

"Are you really gonna make me spell it out for you, damsel? It's because I like you."

For a second, the whole world froze. The air stilled, and Monica suddenly found that she couldn't breathe. But the warmth rising in her chest made her feel like she didn't need to.

"I like you *a lot*. I've liked you since the moment I first saw you. Why else do you think I tried to get you to come dance with me?"

In a blink, Monica's mind was silent, empty. She was no longer filled with obsessive thoughts of her brother, or the ache of foreboding knowledge of their looming destiny. Her body felt suddenly light, and the warmth in her chest rose into her cheeks, making them tingle with a strange shyness that was unfamiliar to her. But most of all, there was no apprehension to follow Celene's admission; no worry of hurting her because Monica knew that Celene could take care of herself, and no guilt, because even though she *had* had a hand in bringing Celene here, it wasn't the same as it had been with Finn. And, more likely than not, Celene would've ended up here, one way or another, because of Maal's plan.

Monica swallowed, suddenly choked by a lump in her throat that she hadn't noticed forming.

"Aren't you gonna say anything?" Celene asked solemnly, making Monica realize just how much uncertainty her expression had betrayed.

Celene was a siren. She could have anything she wanted at the easiest request because of her magic, so it baffled Monica that she was asking without it. Monica fleetingly recalled asking Celene never to use her powers on her or Finn, but the fact that she was still honoring that was… unusual. But maybe not a *bad* unusual.

"Why didn't you say anything before?" Monica's voice was barely a whisper now. Although she kept her eyes low, her muscles had lifted her body from against the wall, and her feet were now carrying her towards Celene with achingly small steps.

"I don't know…" She began, her voice quivering. "I guess I was scared you wouldn't like me back."

"But you could make me if you wanted to."

"I don't want to. I promised not to use my powers on either you or Finn, and I especially don't want to if it means I'd hurt you. Either of you."

Celene bit her lip and turned her head away, searching for some distance as Monica now loomed within an arm's reach.

Standing so close to the siren in such an intimate moment should've scared Monica. It was the exact kind of moment that usually strengthened her guard, not lowered it, but something within the siren's confession had warmed her, and made her want to believe it.

"You care about him too, don't you?"

"Of course I do. How can I not, with those damn puppy dog eyes of his?" Celene bared her teeth as a laugh bubbled up her throat, a sound that Monica briefly echoed. Then, as the air fell quiet again, Celene admitted, "He's the reason I didn't tell you before. That boy was so in love with you that he could barely see straight. And you never noticed."

"I *did* notice. But I didn't want to hurt him. And I just… didn't like him like that then."

"What about now?"

The question pierced Monica's heart like a dagger, forcing her to draw a sharp intake of breath. The sudden realization exploded in her mind like a firecracker, and all at once, she was forced to confront the reason for the butterflies she still got whenever she thought about him. She hadn't wanted to admit it to herself before, but now, everything seemed so clear that guilt stung her as she pondered the mess that was her heart.

She couldn't do this. Even if it had been his choice to stay, Monica knew she'd never be able to look at him again without the guilty worry that her unspoken affections had somehow swayed him. Even if they hadn't, if she told him, any chance of him changing his mind and going home would vanish. Whether he knew how she felt or not, anything that happened to him in Arkynesta would always be her fault. And she knew, despite her strength, she'd never be strong enough to love him fully because of that guilt, not like he deserves.

"I can't." Monica finally said, turning away on her heel.

Celene grabbed her arms and spun Monica back to face her with such force it made her head whirl.

"You can't, or you won't?"

"I don't even know if he likes me that way anymore."

Celene's stare trembled but remained fixed on hers, an unashamed demand buried within her eyes. Monica knew what Celene wanted, but she also knew that there was no way to make the siren understand. Monica *needed* her to understand.

"Don't do that to me. I've been alone for so long that this is where I'm comfortable. I don't even know if *anyone* can like me like that, because I don't think I'd be able to let them in. I'm afraid I'd hurt anyone who tried. I'm better off alone."

Monica tried to pull away, but Celene only held onto the sleeves of her cardigan even tighter.

"I've been alone. I know what it's like to feel like you'll never have someone who is able to care about you for real, without the influence of magic, or without wanting to use you because of it. I know what it's like to lose the people you love and be too afraid to let yourself love again for fear of losing them, too. No one should ever have to feel like that. Now, if you can't bring yourself to confess to Finn because you don't want to hurt him, or if you genuinely don't feel things for him, I understand. But you can't force yourself to remain alone forever. It hurts too much to be alone. And I don't want that for you."

Monica only fleetingly registered the heat rising within her before an impulse passed through her limbs like lightning. She didn't stop to think, otherwise she'd fight it, and she didn't think Celene would've wanted that. *Seven realms*, Monica didn't think she, herself wanted that. So before she could change her mind, Monica threw her body flush against Celene's, and let their lips crash together as she tasted the forbidden sweetness of physical affection.

Celene's body tensed from shock but was quick to relax when she realized that Monica wasn't letting up. Monica's hands rose to cup the sides of Celene's face, indulging a new urgency in the kiss that sucked the breath from the siren's lungs. Monica's fingers curled through Celene's silken red hair, hardly believing what she was doing.

Monica couldn't remember the last time she'd actually *wanted* to do that. During the darkest days just after losing

Monroe, when she was well and truly alone, Monica *had* allowed herself a few brief, casual flings, but not one of them made her feel like she did at that moment, with Celene. Not even her butterflies for Finn compared to the battery of fireworks that were combusting in her head, her chest, her veins, *everywhere*. Monica's every nerve was so on fire with desire that after their lips parted, she held her breath for the ridiculous fear that she might exhale smoke.

Maybe it was the siren, her magic somehow, but no… Monica knew Celene hadn't coerced her into doing that. Nor had she coerced Monica into wanting to do it again. And she *did*. She kissed Celene with so much fervor that it momentarily let her forget the fear humming through her veins and the way her mind screamed for her to withdraw. Fighting against those impulses made the second kiss even sweeter, but it also depleted Monica's strength so that she soon had to give in, despite the immediate chill of regret that swept over her the moment their lips parted.

When Monica pulled away, her cheeks were wet with tears. Celene's eyes widened fearfully, but before her fingers could rise to smear the droplets from Monica's cheeks, she had already turned away with her face buried in her sleeves. Monica gave a soft sniffle as her head rose again. Her expression was soft and strangely vulnerable in a way that made Celene's heart skip a beat.

"Wait…" The siren began, her voice still containing music at even a whisper. "I'm confused. You *don't* like Finn?"

"They're not mutually exclusive."

Celene hazarded a small smile before she persisted, "That's not what I asked."

"Honestly, I don't know." Monica said with a slow shake of her head. "But I *do* know that you're right. I can't keep doing this. As scary as it is to let someone in, it's exhausting being alone. And…"

"And?" Celene echoed hopefully.

Monica's eyes lifted again, breathtaking as they sparkled a nearly colorless blue. She bit her lip in hesitation as her focus returned momentarily to Celene's lips.

"I like you, too." She admitted with a tentative nod. "When I first saw you dancing, it was mesmerizing. But I wasn't there for you."

"You were there for him," Celene finished with a thoughtful tilt of her head.

"No!" Monica answered, almost too vehemently. "I wasn't supposed to be there at all. It was an accident. If circumstances would've been different…"

"You would've danced with me?" The siren tempted playfully.

"Hell, no." Monica laughed, her demeanor softening as the seriousness left it. "I don't dance. But I could've watched you all night."

Celene gave a timid smile that warmed her eyes with sweetness.

"So where does this leave us?"

"I don't know." Monica admitted again, "But I wouldn't mind finding out if you're okay with letting me take my time."

The way Celene's smile endured was all the answer she needed, but still, Celene whispered, "Of course."

Monica's heart fluttered with the realization that someone liked her, despite her circumstances, and that wasn't something she ever planned on finding. It was nice, having someone to trust and to not be afraid of.

But could she trust *herself* in such a situation? Her tangled uncertainty of emotions made Monica worry that her heart was a ticking time bomb. And while the last thing she wanted to do was hurt another person she was starting to care about, maybe the siren had a chance at diffusing that bomb.

"...and with me being a mess." Monica added sheepishly. "I'll do my best not to hurt you, but you have to know that I can't make any promises."

Celene chuckled cooly. "Then luckily for you, I'm not asking for any… yet. Let's just see what happens."

Monica's expression faltered, only half-registering Celene's joke as she remembered herself and the thought of Monroe came flooding back without warning. Turning away again, she said, "I have to go."

"Wait." Celene called, rooting Monica to the spot, even without the aid of her magic. "At least tell me where you're going. That way we know where you are if something happens and you don't come back."

"I *will* come back."

"But if you don't—" Celene repeated firmly.

After a short hesitation and a long sigh, Monica relented. "Fine. But you can't tell Finn, unless I don't come back tonight, okay?"

Celene's eyes narrowed in judgment, resting a fist on her hip as her weight shifted to emphasize the stance. "Uh-huh?" She asked, less of a confirmation and more a wary accusation that insinuated that she knew she wasn't going to like Monica's answer.

"Look, I just don't want him to worry, okay?"

Celene nodded, as if to say, *go on.*

"I'm going to Enderfel."

"What? Why? How?!"

"With this." Monica pulled the ivory amulet from her pocket, looping the braided twine of its cord around her neck. "It's a key to Enderfel; a Soulseeker. It'll allow me safe passage so that I can come back with a physical presence when I'm done."

"Why?"

"My brother's there. Monroe. You met him on the island. The Eye of Desire keeps reminding me that I want to go, so I don't think it'll work to find Rowan until I do."

"And what in the *seven realms* do you think you're going to accomplish while you're there? It's not like you can bring back the dead."

"I mean, maybe." Monica answered firmly. "I have a way, I just don't know how to make it work yet."

"What do you mean?" Celene trembled, the concern clear on her face. "What are you talking about?"

"Look, I just need to talk with him, okay? I need him to know that I'm working on it, and then maybe it won't feel so urgent, so my desires can be redirected to find Rowan instead."

"You can't." Celene pleaded, her voice now trembling with fear. "No one knows what Enderfel is like. Do you have any idea how dangerous that is; going alone and leaving us with no way to contact you?"

"Since when have you ever known me to take the safe option?" Monica asked wryly. "I have to do this."

"You can't leave Finn. And you have no idea how long you'll be gone. Have you ever even used that thing before?"

"It can't be any different than my Riftrider. I'll be able to come back whenever I want. And I promise, I'll only stay until I find Monroe. Then I'll come right back."

"No." Celene growled with tears welling in her eyes. "You'll come back *tonight.* I don't care how long it takes you to find him. Do what you've gotta do, but don't leave us in the dark, with no way to gauge your safety. That way, if you're gone longer, we know there's a problem, and we can try to help. Besides, Finn's gonna start asking questions that I can't answer. And I can't lie to him with those damn puppy dog eyes of his. Come back tonight."

"Okay." Monica conceded with a nod as she drew back in towards Celene. "I'll come back tonight."

After Monica's promise, Celene rejoined Finn and Dahvi, who both waited on the sidewalk with casual smiles and easy stances. As she approached, the air was filled with gentle bursts of laughter. She caught a glimpse of something in Finn's eyes as he looked at Dahvi, but whatever it was vanished behind a curtain of concern when he saw her running towards them.

"Where's Monica?"

Celene shook her head, doing her best to smile though her breathlessness. At least the effort of running was a good cover for her still-flushed cheeks and racing heart.

"She's fine. She's running an errand, but she'll be back tonight. I made her promise."

"And you believe her?" Finn asked expectantly, his tone edged with nervousness.

"I do." Celene encouraged softly. "Now, how about the three of us go get dinner, like we planned?"

Chapter 23

The rift created by the Soulseeker was far different than that of the Riftrider. Rather than a liquid galaxy lit by the light of a thousand stars, Monica felt as if she was being dragged into a vacuum of darkness, the weight of which pulled at her limbs. The sensation was not at all like floating and then falling, but merely sinking, as she was being dragged under by an undertow made entirely of molasses. The deeper she plunged into the darkness, the colder the air grew, until soon, her body was assaulted by waves of an icy stinging that her mind likened to being poked by thousands of needles of ice. The icy, aching ripples rushed up and down her limbs, until finally, she began to numb to the discomfort.

The rift peeled away and spat her out onto the hard ground of a foreign realm. Monica picked herself up with a groan, and her hands subconsciously went to shield her upper arms from the sharp air that penetrated the knit of her cardigan. Upon standing, she found that the air was no colder than the slight chill of a brisk, spring morning, melting to give way to an ambient temperature barely below a comfortable neutral. It was a shift her mind didn't have time to ponder as her gaze lifted to take in the shock of her changed surroundings.

The sky was an inky, starless black, not too unlike the night that draped over the glistening spires of Arkynesta, apart from the clear lack of a moon. But this sky was far different, filling Monica's stomach with a sinking dread that she couldn't quite put her finger on. Something about this sky seemed inherently wrong; cold and lifeless, crushing down on her with a weight that the normal night sky did not possess. Below the empty void of obsidian sky, the horizon was etched with the thinnest line of dusky, pale amber. Monica squinted at it, half-wondering if the color was merely a trick of the light, but it didn't waver, no matter how long her focus held.

Then, scanning the sky once more, she puzzled at the source of the light, following the band of amber around her in a perfect circle. The ground that met the horizon was a stark contrast against the dark sky. All around her stretched an endless expanse of white, ridged with cool undertones of gray. The ground was soft and featureless, covered in a substance that looked like ash; what little of it she could see, anyway. The flat plains of this new realm was crowded with people, all gathered together in makeshift camps like a settlement of homeless people. Her head swung to and fro, but everywhere she looked, they surrounded her.

There were no buildings to be seen, no trees, mountains, or cities. Just people. Millions of them, fading into the distance beyond where her sight ended.

That's when the sound hit her. A swell of murmurous voices wove into a thick blanket of white noise all around her, so dense that she almost hadn't noticed it until after she saw all the bodies that accompanied the voices.

Why were there so many of them?

The sight was troubling to her. She suddenly couldn't remember if she'd ever spent time deciding what she believed happens to people after they died, but at least, she would've imagined that they had to go somewhere. She didn't picture that somewhere as stagnant or combined, but a place where people could have their own place. But that clearly wasn't the case. Instead, it looked like they all came here, and simply stayed.

That's when the dread hit her. How in the seven realms was she going to find Monroe amongst so many people?

Before she could surrender to the hopelessness of such a thought, she ran to the nearest person and asked, "How do I find somebody here?"

The person, if she could even call them that, stared up at her with hollow, black eyes that sat vacant above two deep crescents of sunken purple exhaustion, which made the rest of the being's face glimmer with a waxy, white pallor. Their wizened face was wreathed in a haphazard halo of dark, unwashed hair that peaked out from beneath the hood of a ratty age-worn coat.

After a lengthy delay that made Monica suspect that the person wasn't going to answer at all, they finally drawled, "Why would you wanna do that?"

"I've lost someone important to me. Please." Monica begged, but the stranger seemed unfazed by the crack in her voice.

Without meeting her eyes, the being gave a heavy shrug.

"Nobody here is important anymore. Once they come to Enderfel, they become shadows of their former selves. Nowhere to go but right here, forever." The stranger made a lazy gesture of outstretched arms, indicating the crowded area around them.

Monica's brow furrowed, repulsed at the thought. It didn't make sense. If all the dead went to Enderfel and nowhere else, what would happen when it got too full to hold any more? It couldn't be this way on purpose, could it?

"Why?" She demanded sharply, barely rousing another response.

"No more Guardians to take us away."

"Guardians?" Monica asked. "What are you talking about?"

The stranger shrugged again, this time, lolling over to the side like a sack of potatoes, as if the mere weight of their spindly body was too much to bear. Their eyelids began to flutter without warning, and their mouth drooped open to expel a tired sigh. And just like that, they were asleep.

Deciding that it wasn't worth trying to wake them to ask for any more information from this stranger, Monica moved on. Her eyes scanned the crowd, zoning in on anyone who seemed to be maintaining more movement and consciousness than her last target. Most of the crowd appeared half dead. Bodies were strewn out across the ground or piled together in mounds, making Monica worry that some of them had actually died again, but that wasn't how Enderfel worked, was it? Spirits shouldn't be able to die. But if they can't die, then they need to be able to go somewhere. Even though she knew next to nothing about this realm, its observable details made no coherent sense, filling her with the suspicion that something was wrong here.

Her focus landed on a plump lady who was hunched forwards as she tended a pot sitting over a fire. Her still-nimble hands tore apart some sickly looking roots, which she tossed into the bubbling pot of gray-brown liquid before her heavy eyes lifted towards Monica.

"Hello, dear." She said in a soft, kindly voice that still lagged with a tired lilt. Her eyes were the same coal-black shade as the previous stranger's, but were creased at the edges, as if she wanted to smile, but lacked the energy to maintain the full expression. Her skin was a soft gray, and the color of the hollows beneath her eyes were far less pronounced. “You must be a new arrival.”

“I’m looking for somebody.”

“Yes, yes, you all are. As soon as you realize you’re dead, your first instinct is to find somebody dear that was lost before you.”

“I’m not— "

Monica stopped herself, glancing warily from side to side before she decided to hide the Soulseeker hanging at her heart. With a slow, contained gesture, she lifted it by its cord and let it duck behind the fabric of her shirt, falling to where it clattered against the warm metal of her Riftrider. The last thing she needed was for someone to get the idea that they could get out of Enderfel if they took the Soulseeker from her.

“And it’s normal to be in denial at first, too. It’s hard to adjust to being dead.”

Monica gave a respectful nod, pausing to pretend that she was letting the woman’s words sink in.

“How long have you been here?”

“It’s hard to know something like that. Time doesn’t move here in the same way that it does elsewhere. Or, perhaps it does, and we just lose track of it after experiencing so much of it.”

“Does everybody here talk in riddles?” Monica huffed, trying to mute the exasperation within her voice.

“You’re an impatient one, huh? Well, don’t worry. It’s not like you have anywhere else to be, or any time to lose. Here, all we have left is time. You can see how long someone’s been here by the state of their face. After all, spending hundreds of years with nothing to do and nowhere to go is mind-numbingly exhausting. It wears on us all after a while.”

“Why is there nowhere to go? Somebody said something about no Guardians to take them away?”

"Yes." The woman cooed gently, her eyes falling as she took up a wooden spoon to stir the contents of the bubbling pot. "Enderfel wasn't always like this. It was never meant to be a final destination, merely an in-between, where souls of the dead went in order to await judgment. Guardians were meant to help souls pass though that judgment before they could move on. But they don't come here anymore. They haven't for a long time. Though, perhaps, not as long as it seems."

"Why not?"

The woman shrugged and shook her head. "Nobody knows. All we can do is hope they'll come back, so we can all move on."

Monica chewed at her lip as she thought about this. Even though she didn't understand, she knew that the woman's words meant that Monroe *had* to be here somewhere, since there was nowhere for souls to go. That was her primary concern over asking more questions about the state of the realm.

"How do I find somebody here?"

"Good luck." The woman crooned kindly despite the bitterness in her tone. "I've been looking for my boys since I arrived. Lost two of 'em in the war, and another as a baby, stolen away by a cruel sickness. As far as I can tell, they're nowhere that I can find."

"So you've just *stopped* looking?"

"No." The woman hissed, as if somewhat offended by this, but too tired to hold onto it. "I decided that if they're looking for me, I'd be better off staying in one place."

"I don't have time for that." Monica spat in frustration.

"Then, like I said, good luck."

Monica whirled around, taking several steps away from the woman as her eyes scanned the crowd in search of where to go next. But they were all the same. Their faces, gaunt with exhaustion; their eyes, hollow with listlessness. Why should she hope that any of these people were going to be any different? Why should she believe that any of them were going to help her?

Her eyes roved over waves upon endless waves of faces. A cold pit of overwhelm opened in her empty stomach, radiating the taste of bitter defeat up her throat.

A tremble of fear hit her, making her knees buckle as she collapsed to the ground.

No, she thought, *I don't have time for this. This can't be happening.*

She threw her head back and let out a scream that sucked every ounce of breath within her.

"MONROE!"

Echoes of his name shook throughout the realm. Monica prayed it'd be enough to reach him.

Chapter 24

After an enjoyable dinner filled with laughter and growing familiarity, Celene reluctantly parted ways with Dahvi and Finn. She offered to accompany them to make sure Finn got home safely out of courtesy to Monica, but Dahvi was quick to point out the lack of sense doing this would make, since Celene's apartment was at the other end of town. Besides, with Dahvi headed for Gulfport, and Finn's apartment not being far from there, it's not like Finn would be alone.

Celene was just about to protest when she noticed a glint of playful suggestion in Dahvi's gray-green eyes that she recognized all too well. Beyond even her own vast backlog of experience, sirens had an especially keen eye for spotting attraction. Not that Dahvi was being particularly subtle about it, by any means. After all of his covertly amorous quips during dinner, Celene knew better than to stand in the way of their privacy.

After one final glimpse at Finn's almost painfully oblivious face, Celene hesitated just long enough to offer a passing wonder at whether Finn knew what likely awaited him after she left. But, then again, it's not like she worried that Dahvi would take advantage without permission. She prided herself at being a good judge of character, and despite not knowing him for too long, she decided that he didn't seem like that kind of person.

So, without much resistance, Celene hailed a taxi and offered a genial goodnight. The taxi darted away down the road, leaving Finn and Dahvi alone in each other's company.

"Do you want a ride?" Dahvi offered with a grin. "It's a long walk from here."

"I don't mind." Finn said with a shake of his head before his eyes lifted to the darkening sky overhead. "It's a nice night for a walk."

"Okay. But let me know if you get tired."

Finn let out a hum of agreement as they set off. The quiet air was punctuated by the rhythmic cycling of six-footstep refrains, made up of four hooves and two feet, clopping along with a steady stride.

"It feels weird being with you without having done training first."

"Weird?" Dahvi asked. "A good weird, I hope?"

Finn gave a nervous laugh. "Yeah. I had fun tonight. And I think it's gonna be fun working with you, too..."

"But?" The centaur interjected curiously, sensing the weight of concern within Finn's pause.

Finn's dark eyes lifted, now heavy with worry beneath the shadow of his furrowed brow. "I don't know if it's a good idea for you to."

"To work with you? Why not?"

"Working with Maal is… dangerous."

"I know." Dahvi answered coolly. "You remember how I said I've worked with him before, right?"

Finn nodded, sticking his hands into the pockets of his jeans as his neck seemed to shrink into his shoulders with a shameful, growing discomfort. "You don't… have a contract or anything, do you?"

"No," Dahvi gave a vehemently reassuring chuckle. "I most certainly do *not* have a contract. Nor do I intend to agree to one. The things Maal has needed me for in the past have been on a very case by case basis, and have usually only been in regards to weapons or classes, rather than my special skills. But, based on the sound of it, he wants me to work for him badly enough that I think he'll just about let me outline my own terms."

"What are your special skills?" Finn asked without thinking, panic immediately making his cheeks flush pink as he backpedaled, "Not that you *have* to tell me. I was just curious."

"It's okay." Dahvi reassured with an easy nod. "I don't mind. But this isn't exactly the place to talk about something like that, only since I have to be so careful with it. Unfortunately, Maal was right in saying that what I can do is rare and coveted, so if I reveal it where someone who wants to take advantage of it could see me, it could be dangerous for me. But you will know soon. Especially since it'll be an important part of working together."

Finn's alarm eased as he peered up into Dahvi's cool expression, admiring the way he could be so cautious and yet so calm at the same time. But even so, he couldn't shake the itch of the encroaching guilt that came with his new friend's involvement in their potentially life-threatening scheme.

"You're really okay with the risk of dying by the end of this?"

"I wouldn't have agreed if I wasn't."

Finn paused, thinking back to the explanation he'd given before.

"Your family really means that much to you?"

Dahvi smiled softly. Something about it was wistful, warm, and still somewhat melancholy, all at once. His eyes were distant, dancing as if he was able to see a picture forming somewhere far off in the sky above them. Letting his gaze return to Finn's face, he murmured, "Yes, they do. Doesn't yours?"

"Of course." Finn's lips pulled back into a wide grin, anchoring itself to his cheeks with a deep dimple at each corner. "I'd do anything for my mom and grandad."

"Anything." Dahvi agreed with a sad sigh.

"Dahvi, tell me about your family. Please?"

He paused, his stride slowing somewhat in thought before he gave a decisive nod. For a moment, his eyes almost seemed to glint with an increasingly glassy sheen, but before Finn could question it, Dahvi cleared his throat.

"My father, Brahn, is probably one of the most intimidating centaurs you'll ever meet, until you get to know him. He's taller than me by a good head and a half, with arms that could pull an entire tree out by the roots. But, once he opens up, he's just a huge teddy bear. He's got an entire arsenal of clever jokes and his belly laugh is infectious. He's also got probably the best beard you'll *ever* see."

"Is that why you didn't seem intimidated by Maal?"

"Oh, I was. I've just gotten good at not projecting it because of my dad. Intimidating people tend to respect you more if you can hold your ground without coming off as conceited or irreverent. What about yours?"

"Oh, I don't get to see my dad much anymore. He's… not a great guy most of the time. I think he means well, but he makes a lot of dumb choices. My mother left him when I was still pretty young."

"Oh." Dahvi paused apologetically. "I'm sorry."

"Don't be." Finn reassured with a shake of his head. "Keep going. I wanna hear more."

"Okay. There's my mother, Leela. She's the sweetest, kindest soul you'll ever meet, and she'll dote over anyone who gives her the chance. She's an amazing cook, too. Her pies would knock your socks off. When I was growing up, she was the first person I'd go to with a problem because she's so good at listening without making you feel judged, or like she knows better than you."

"That's funny. She sounds almost the complete opposite of mine. I know mine cares, but she's so protective and strict that it's easy to forget sometimes."

"Do you have any siblings?" Dahvi asked. When Finn shook his head, the centaur chimed back in with, "Well, that's probably why. You're her only chance to get it right, so of course she's gonna be firmer with you."

"I take it that you do?" Finn asked.

"I do, indeed." Dahvi beamed. "Three siblings: two older brothers and a baby sister.

"Taurok is the oldest; competitive, serious, but always has your back when you need him. The other one is Soren; adventurous and always getting into trouble, so it's no surprise that he's the prankster of the family. And then, there's my sister, Willow. She'll be eight this year, and she's got the wildest imagination of anyone you'll ever meet. If you wanna lose an afternoon like that," Dahvi paused to give a snap of his fingers to emphasize the point, "request a tea party with the queen. She'll bring out her entire kingdom of stuffed animals and make you help her dress them, arrange them, and then she *has* to make you a flower crown before she can finally serve the tea. But you'll be so entertained, you won't even realize you've been there all day."

The sparkle of joy that shone in Dahvi's eyes was infectious, but Finn still couldn't help but fixate on the slight shimmer of sadness he noticed beneath it.

"When was the last time you saw them?"

"It's been about a year. Unfortunately, I don't get out of Arkynesta as much as I should, and it's a long trip back to my village."

"How far is it?"

"My village is in Orsawl, just beyond the Northern border of Elandis. It's about two days on foot for me, if I hustle, but planning for three is a more reasonable pace."

"Wouldn't it be faster if you didn't go on foot?"

"It would…" Dahvi sighed, one corner of his mouth lifting in a wistful grin that seemed to say, *if only it were that simple.* "The people of Orsawl are very protective of their quiet, rural lifestyles. They don't have the infrastructure to support the kind of roads needed for most mainstream methods of mass conveyance; though, even if they did, I don't think anything would change. Uncomfortable and inefficient roads make for significantly fewer casual comings and goings."

"Wouldn't family members want to see each other though? It seems like not having other options for travel would discourage visiting."

"They usually don't have to go very far. Those born in Orsawl rarely ever leave their village, let alone the domain. In fact, before me, there were only ever two people that moved out of my village across its entire history, so…"

Dahvi's voice trailed off in a sigh that made Finn's heart clench with the suspicion of loss. In his hesitation, Finn considered abandoning the question altogether, but something in the curve that lingered absently on Dahvi's lips as the centaur's eyes sought Finn's in his silence not only promised forgiveness, but encouraged his curiosity.

"Did…" Finn began tentatively, clearing his throat. "Did something happen?"

"No!" Dahvi said with an exaggerated brightness that sounded oddly akin to relief. "No. My parents always knew I was drawn to more than what our little village had to offer. Even though it was hard for them to watch me go, I am eternally grateful for how they always encouraged me to honor my heart by doing whatever I thought would bring me happiness, even before I left."

Finn rolled his lips between his teeth, briefly fighting the smile conjured by Dahvi's bittersweet admission before he surrendered with a nod. "I bet they miss you."

Dahvi gave a sad smile. "It's mutual. I wish it were feasible for me to go see them sooner, but as soon as all of this is over, I know I'll see them again."

After a moment of quiet reflection, Finn added, "They sound really wonderful. Do you think I might get to meet them someday, too?"

"Perhaps. And they are truly wonderful. I don't know where I'd be without them." After a sudden and almost painful pause that lasted the rest of the block, Dahvi admitted softly, "I don't know my real parents. They abandoned me when I was a baby. Brahn and Leela took me in without batting an eye. As far as they're concerned, I'm one of them."

Finn sensed the reservations in Dahvi's pause, but a wave of uncertainty crashed against one of curiosity as he internally debated whether it was appropriate to ask about. Noticing Finn's hesitation, Dahvi turned to him with a nervous smile and timidly explained, "I guess, even with as much as I love them, I don't always feel like I fit in. Kinda like I'm… just pretending?"

"I'm sure they don't think that." Finn encouraged.

But before Finn could say much more, Dahvi's clear discomfort took over. His gaze scanned the stretch of sidewalk that still remained in front of them before turning to Finn and, almost pleading, he asked, "You sure you don't want that ride? It's still a long walk."

Sensing that this was perhaps Dahvi's way of asking to move on from the current conversation, Finn agreed.

After several weeks of practice, Finn was no longer embarrassingly clumsy in his climb onto Dahvi's back. In fact, once he settled into place, he was overcome by a wave of comfort that he almost hadn't realized how much he had missed until now. Dahvi's skin was warm against his chest as Finn laced his arms around Dahvi's toned torso.

The storm of disquiet immediately lifted from the centaur's face when he turned to give an impish grin and warned Finn to hang on. Dahvi took off like an arrow, whizzing through the air more like he was flying rather than running.

Within minutes, Finn's apartment building was in view.

Finn had almost forgotten the near impossible exhilaration that came with their rides, relishing in the contrasting mix of both closeness and freedom. The cool night air turned to needles of ice that stung his cheeks and neck and ruffled his hair as they rode. Too quickly, the ride was over, but long after he dismounted, Finn's heart continued to race as he caught his breath.

As he turned to enter the building, Dahvi stopped him with a gentle grip on his upper arm.

"Wait."

"What is it?"

Finn turned, only to be grabbed by the magnetizing quality of Dahvi's soft jade-green eyes. That look rooted Finn in place, and he found himself unable to pull away as he tried to decipher it. It sparkled like gratitude with a hint of lingering wistful sadness, but when Dahvi's lips finally parted again to speak, he understood.

"Thank you, for everything."

It sounded like a goodbye, but when Dahvi's gentle touch continued to rest on Finn's arm, a flutter of confusion raced through his chest.

"For what? I didn't do anything."

"For just being you." Dahvi's head fell slowly to the side, tilting as he stared at Finn's face with an intensified wonder, like he was trying to paint a mental picture to hold onto after the moment faded. "I've always felt like that… like I'm pretending to be something I'm not, no matter who I'm with. But it is so easy to speak with you. And you've never made me feel like that. You make me feel like you don't care what I am."

Finn's brow furrowed in confusion as a feeling of disquiet churned in his stomach.

"I *don't* care." He answered meekly with a shake of his head, still not understanding.

Why should he care what Dahvi was? Sure, it was hard adjusting to it first, to the fact that he was a centaur, but only because Finn had no prior experience with creatures of *any* kind. But since he'd gotten to know him, he'd learned what a kind heart Dahvi had. He was a great teacher, a clever person, and someone Finn had come to trust. Dahvi was his friend.

But before he could give voice to any of the several questions that now spiraled around his head, he found Dahvi fast approaching, pressing Finn's back into the wall beside the door of the apartment building as the centaur towered over him.

"I know." Dahvi murmured sweetly, his breath creating a hiss of steam that billowed warmly against Finn's cheek in sudden contrast to the increasingly chilly night air.

The sudden absence of distance between them wasn't intimidating, like he'd fleetingly feared, but instead, felt strangely intimate. One of Dahvi's arms rose to brace against the wall astride Finn's head, and his other hand moved to Finn's shoulder with a contradicting touch that made him feel both nervous and safe.

Though his eyes had a clear view of every movement and progression of the moment, his mind stalled, wholly oblivious to what was happening until after Dahvi's lips brushed softly against his. Finn's body tensed as electricity jolted through his muscles, filling him with the impossible feeling of floating. Finn's heart took off in a gallop that made his blood pound with the same rhythm as Dahvi's hooves against the pavement during their rides.

Chapter 25

As the reverberations of Monroe's name faded in the air, the memory of faint, crimson light tickled at the lower edges of Monica's vision, reminding her of the solution that she'd overlooked in her desperation. Her frantic fingers scrambled to her pocket, momentarily stunned to find that the eye was still there. She was in no place to question it, but retroactively realized her fears regarding limitations of the Soulseeker's magic regarding any physical objects that remained on her being.

Doing a quick pat-down of her person with her other hand, Monica felt the small bulge of coins that remained in her right pocket, as well as the dagger still strapped to her thigh. Her hand then went to her chest, which expelled a sigh of relief as her fingers found both of the amulets hanging at her heart. Her immediate belongings were all present, a blessing that she only spared a passing second to be grateful for before returning her attention to the eye.

Her mind flailed with the realization that she didn't know how to control The Eye of Desire. Sure, she'd used it before, but until just a little while ago, she hadn't been fully aware of what was happening. How was she supposed to control it when she didn't even know where to start?

Not only that, but Maal had warned her not to use it outside his tower, where she could be supervised in case anything went wrong. And he had a point with that. After all, look what happened with the Portalslicer dagger. Unexpectedly ending up in Arkynesta had been one of the best case scenarios that could have happened, compared to all the places in the universe *that thing* could have taken her. Even though she had enough knowledge to identify and figure out magic artifacts on a basic level, it was, in truth, just enough to get her into trouble.

But it's not like she had much of a choice now. She was already in Enderfel, so there was no sense in wasting the trip. Not to mention, if her suspicions were correct, she wouldn't even be able to use the eye for what Maal wanted until she found Monroe. There was a reason she was here. She had to do this. She *wanted* to do this. And that was enough.

With nothing more than her focus turning inward to study her thoughts, the eye responded to the emergence of her primary desire. It hummed awake in her hand, the entire surface of the orb now alight with a pulsating red illumination.

Her eyes lifted out of cautious instinct, but as she scanned the crowd, she was relieved to find that none of the tired spirits were even phased by the obvious magic she now wielded. Realizing this allowed her an exhale of relief before she channeled her attention inward.

Her mind offered her a glimmer of memories of her summonings. That quiet, meditative focus was exactly what she needed now. A small voice in her head worried that such a thing would be difficult to achieve in a place with so many people, as she was usually only to find such a vulnerable state of surrender when she was alone. But she forced the doubts from her mind, motivated by the thought and if she could achieve it, that focus was exactly what she needed here.

Staring hard into the orb, Monica let all of the images in her periphery muddle together beyond the growing screen of misty red. The shapes crawling across its glassy surface lifted, jumping out of the orb like a hologram as its textures wove into a mirrored image of the face in her mind. Though he was only portrayed in hues of black and red, Monroe looked just like she remembered him.

This sparked a flutter of hope within her heart that translated into immediate motion. Her feet carried her forwards with renewed haste as she darted into the crowd. Without pause, the haze of light around her coalesced back into the eye, only momentarily, before it streamed out in front of her, funneled into a single string that led her onwards. The thread of scarlet light wove through the crowd with seemingly no rhyme or reason, but she didn't hesitate or question it. Under the driving influence of her now uncontainable desire, she didn't care. She didn't care about the people she pushed past, or the mindless circles she turned. She didn't care that everything looked the same, or that she couldn't tell how long she'd been chasing that thread. Her desperation made it feel like only minutes, but her aching legs tempted her to consider the possibility of the chase occupying hours. None of it mattered. The only thought that she allowed to remain within her conscious mind for more than a second was that of finding Monroe, until she was repeating it softly to herself, like a person maddened by obsession.

"I have to find Monroe. I have to find Monroe. I have to find—"

She stumbled when the string unexpectedly ended. She looked up, broken from her trance, only to find herself face to chest with her brother.

"Monroe?" His name came out as a breathless whisper, her voice breaking as tears stung her eyes. It felt weird, addressing him with his proper name instead of the nickname she'd given him when they were little, but it had been an important factor in finding him. She didn't doubt that the power of his name had acted as an anchor to guide the eye.

"Mo?" He murmured, just as breathlessly. He peered down at her with wide unblinking eyes of sparkling, ice-like blue. "Monica? Is it really you? Or am I dreaming again?"

He was just as she remembered him, if not slightly more bedraggled. The shorn sides of his dark top knot had grown out, lessening the contrast of his typically sleek haircut, and his chin was shadowed by a layer of stubble. His outfit was even the same, consisting of black tattered jeans, a white band shirt, his trademark leather jacket of dark navy blue, plus maybe a couple of new scuffs and stains.

A small groan escaped Monroe's chest as Monica slammed into him with a force so unbridled that her embrace nearly tackled him to the ground. He was real. Feeling the warmth of his skin for the first time in almost nine months sent a shiver of relief coursing through her. She was almost too scared to believe it, especially with the worry that he would only be taken away from her again, but she couldn't help it. She'd been scared for so long that she couldn't help but be overwhelmed by the relief, even if she feared it was only temporary.

No. She steeled herself with the resolve that she wasn't going to let that happen. She had worked too hard to get here for this to be temporary, regardless of the reason. She wasn't going to let anyone take him away again, and she wasn't going to fail in bringing him back, for good.

"You're real." Monica sobbed into his chest, melting at the feeling of his warm palm cupping the back of her head.

When she breathed in, her nostrils swirled with the lingering sense of summoning incense that clung to the lining of his leather jacket. Even though it had been months since he'd likely lit any, she couldn't imagine him smelling any other way.

"And you're here." Monroe sighed, his voice trembling with an echo of the relief that overwhelmed Monica's disbelief still apparent in his cadence. He pulled away, his eyes misty as they sought hers. "How?"

Monica's fingers fumbled for the braided twine that hung around her neck, untangling it from the black cord of the Riftrider as she pulled the ivory amulet from beneath her collar.

"This."

"Is that—?"

Before Monroe could finish the question, Monica let the Soulseeker return to its hiding place with a heavy *thud* against her chest.

"Where did you get that?" Monroe demanded in a hoarse, frightened whisper, holding her back at an arm's length as his strong hands now clutched her upper arms.

"Finn."

Monroe's grip eased, his face a sudden wash of too many emotions for Monica to accurately decipher, even with her talent for reading people. That's when she noticed the pale purple crescents resting under his eyes. She noticed them, but she didn't want to see them. She didn't want to believe that her brother could end up like these weary spirits, even though such a fate was inevitable if he stayed for long enough.

"He just *gave* it to you?"

She nodded, her wide eyes glistening like that of a child as she stared up at him.

"Do you know what this means? You can come home."

"If that's what I think it is, then it's not that easy," Monroe growled.

His hands released her, and his shoulders fell with the new weight of something unspoken as he turned away. Her heart ached with the bitter coldness that now snaked through his expression.

“What do you mean?”

"Come here," he motioned, turning to walk towards a small alcove of people. "Let's talk."

Chapter 26

Finn remained frozen and speechless as Dahvi's lips parted from his, his only visible reaction rising with the redness that now burned his cheeks. The centaur's jade green eyes greeted him with a caring, if not slightly alarmed, expression when Finn finally opened his again.

"Was that the first time you've ever kissed a guy before?" Dahvi asked without judgment.

"Uh," Finn stammered nervously, his words taking off in a gallop as his embarrassment took over, "that was the first time I've ever kissed *anybody* before, unless you count running mouth-first into Danielle McKenna during an eighth grade dodgeball tournament, *kissing.* Well, I guess there was that one time during my junior year that I was dared to take a French fry out of Samantha Jordan's mouth with mine, and our lips barely touched for like, a second."

"Finn," Dahvi said gently, calming his nervous rambling with a warm hand returning to cup his shoulder. "It's okay. You don't have to explain yourself to me."

"Really? Because I think I have to explain it to *me.* I don't think I like guys. Not like that."

"Oh," Dahvi answered sadly, taking his hand from Finn's shoulder as he tilted his head gently to the side. He lifted his other arm from the wall beside Finn's head, backing off to allow the space to grow between them. "You didn't like it?"

"I—" Finn exhaled suddenly, his eyelids fluttering and his heart pounding so hard he could barely hear the voice of his conscience inside of his own head. Was this how Monica had felt when letting him down? She'd barely reacted at all. But then again, he hadn't *kissed* Monica. If only he could be as cool as her. He certainly didn't want to hurt Dahvi's feelings. Finally catching his breath, he admitted, "It was nice, but, I— I don't know."

"You know," Dahvi murmured softly, his manner still kind despite Finn's faltering rejection. "I can be a girl, if you'd prefer."

"What?" Finn scoffed, but it turned into a laugh in his chest as his apprehension suddenly cooled in favor of amused disbelief. "Very funny."

"I am funny, thank you very much." The centaur retorted, his humor quickly returning to a weightier seriousness as he preemptively studied Finn's face for a reaction. "But I'm not joking. Not this time. See?"

Gently, so that Finn might not have noticed if he hadn't watched the full shift happen right in front of him, Dahvi's features softened, melting into feminine lines that somehow changed his entire presence, despite not warping his familiarity. His lashes grew thicker and darker, his lips swelling and blushing into a simpering pout. His face rounded, the angles of his jaw and cheekbones fading slightly as he smiled. His silvery-white locks unspooled around his shoulders and melted down his back with striking new length.

Transfixed by the transformation, Finn gawked as everything about Dahvi's presentation shifted to one that was unmistakably feminine. But Dahvi's eyes never changed, still holding the same, knowing flicker of personality as they watched Finn's expression shift through stages of confusion, startled interest, and finally, cautious intrigue.

Finn slowly lifted his fingers to hover just above one of Dahvi's changed cheeks, hesitating as if he worried that the illusion would break the second they touched.

Dahvi gingerly leaned into Finn's hand, so that the warmth of Finn's fingers now rested against skin.

"But you're—"

"I'm a shapeshifter." Dahvi confirmed in the smooth soprano tones of a voice that had also shifted to match his changed appearance.

"I thought you were a centaur."

"That's simply how I choose to present."

"Why?" Finn asked innocently.

"That's how I grew up. It's what I was comfortable with, because of my family." Dahvi explained with an easy shrug, and the cadence of his voice softened with nostalgia. "They're centaurs."

Finn's lips parted to let in a small gasp of understanding as Dahvi's previous comment about feeling like a pretender suddenly made so much more sense.

"Then this is… your power? The thing that Maal wants you to use to help us?"

"Yes."

"How?" Finn asked, intrigued.

"Lots of ways. I can be anything you want me to be." Dahvi offered sweetly. "Watch."

Sweeping into a partial curtsey, Dahvi's horse half suddenly vanished to give way to a pair of seamless human legs beneath a flowing skirt of shimmering white that couldn't have looked any more natural with his new feminized form. Dahvi leaned back towards him, bringing Finn's hand back to nuzzle against the curve of Dahvi's face as their eyes locked.

Do you want to try again? The thought passed wordlessly between them, hanging in the quiet air as Davhi's lips inched painfully towards Finn's, watching his tremulous gaze intently for a response. As Dahvi leaned in, Finn finally consented with a slight nod, succumbing to a kiss that lasted twice as long as the first.

Dahvi's lips were so soft that Finn thought he might melt. His fingers found their way into a silky tangle of hair, falling to Dahvi's cheek once more as they parted.

"What do you think?" Dahvi asked gently, with no weight of expectation or obligation within his searching green eyes.

"I think it's incredible. And I understand now why you needed to be careful."

Dahvi gave a coy chuckle, still clearly more occupied with the emotions of the present moment. "No, I meant, do you prefer me like this?"

Dahvi's gaze fell meaningfully to indicate his current presentation.

Finn's hand lingered a moment more against Dahvi's cheek, studying not only Dahvi's changed features, but searching for something beneath them. Finn's brows creased, briefly perplexed by the question, and when it finally came, his response was so candid and honest that it made Dahvi startle.

"Do *you* prefer being a girl?"

Dahvi was rarely ever at a loss for words, but his reaction made it clear that this was a question he had never been asked before.

Realizing this made Finn's heart sink.

Dahvi's eyes fell away for a long moment, considering. Then, with a sad smile, he softly admitted, "No. But I don't mind if it's for you."

"No." Finn said emphatically with a stiff shake of his head. When he pulled his hand away from Dahvi's face and returned it to his side, the flicker of panic that crossed the shifter's expression sparked a twinge of regret in Finn's chest. The last thing he wanted to do was hurt Dahvi, but based on the shifter's willingness to endure his own discomfort in order to please someone else, it was clear to Finn that someone in the past already had. Which made his next words all the more important. "That's not for me to decide. You should get to be who *you* want to be. You deserve to be with someone you don't have to change for; someone who loves *all* of you, regardless of form."

"Would you not?"

"I—" Finn began breathlessly, startled by the warmth he felt when looking into Dahvi's eyes. "I don't know. This is all so new to me."

"It's okay not to know." Dahvi encouraged graciously with a dip of his head.

Finn's admission had brought a slight smile to Dahvi's lips, which faded back to their normal shape, soon followed by the rest of his face. His hair slithered back up to his shoulders and his height stretched upwards so that he was now towering over Finn like before. In an instant, Dahvi had shifted back to his preferred masculine form, complete with the gray horse half that returned to take the place of his former human legs and skirt.

Dahvi's eyes sparkled with a bittersweet gratitude as he thanked Finn with a nod and backed away.

"It's rare to find someone as honest as you. Don't lose that, okay?"

Dahvi turned, but Finn caught him by his elbow with a new panic rising in his voice.

"Where are you going? I didn't hurt you, did I?"

“No. I just know that Maal will be expecting me to return to hammer out the details of our agreement.”

“Oh, yeah,” Finn acknowledged, looking both a bit embarrassed as well as sad.

“What about you?”

“Me?” Finn gasped, caught more than a little off-guard by the question.

“Is this going to hurt our friendship after today?” Dahvi asked. Finn’s gaze went sad and distant for a moment as he considered this, which Dahvi interrupted with, “Because I can act like none of this ever happened if you’d like. I’m nothing if not a good actor.”

Finn let a small smile lift his still-rosy cheeks as he finally shook his head.

“I think it's fine.”

“Very well,” Dahvi nodded, unable to tear his interested gaze from Finn even as he shrugged out of his grasp. But before the shifter pulled away or turned to leave again, Dahvi murmured, “Even if you can’t see this becoming anything serious, know that my powers are available for your amusement if you ever change your mind; even if you just get curious, or anything.”

Dahvi gave an impish wink, but before Finn could find enough of his voice beyond a renewed bout of flustered embarrassment, Dahvi’s shape had lifted off the ground and shifted into a vaguely hawkish blur that flew away into the night.

Chapter 27

"Talk?" Monica squawked, her voice sharp with distress. "We'll have plenty of time to talk when you come back. This isn't the time or the place for it. I have to get back. *We* have to get back."

But Monroe ignored her, shrugging her off as he continued a slow shuffle weighted with weariness; early stages of the same affliction that troubled the other people around her. This observation made her brow wrinkle in concern. She hadn't noticed the exhaustion in his manner before now, or perhaps she had, but had chosen to ignore it. Either way, it was not a fate she wanted for her brother, and she was determined to get him out of here before it became a problem.

In his silence, an obedience set in that made Monica fall into step behind him.

The alcove that awaited them was a semi-circle made of three bodies, gathered around a dying campfire that sat in the center of the space. Even its flames seemed tired, sputtering as it lapped at the several tiny twigs and handfuls of dry leaves that sat within a ring of smooth stones.

The nearest was a boy of similar age to Monroe, who lay curled on his side with his arm tucked under his head like a pillow. Long strands of greasy brown hair spilled down across his gaunt features, sunken to reveal a more advanced state of exhaustion than Monroe's. His broad jawline was softened by a spray of patchy stubble, and the outer edge of his right eyebrow was slashed with a white line of scarring. Despite his grizzled facade, the boy's inky black eyes were troubled with an air of tragic wisdom that gave his youthful face a contradictory look of age. Monica found his eyes particularly unsettling. She didn't know what color they should have been. But seeing the black so reserved for those who had lost the battle against their hopelessness seemed wrong for someone with such painful knowing in their eyes. Worse still was the intensity of his gaze as he stared at her, unashamed and even tinged with judgment as she entered their space.

The second body belonged to an older man with shorter hair the color of gunmetal. He stretched out on his back opposite the first boy, with his vacant eyes upturned towards the sky. His irises weren't completely black, but a deep charcoal gray, as if still in the midst of a transition. But, unlike the first boy's, they only held a pitiful sparkle of the life this soul used to possess. His paper-thin skin was wrinkled with age, particularly around his eyes, and the bottom half of his face was obscured by an unkempt beard.

The smallest and youngest presence was a boy of no more than sixteen, with warm brown skin and a guarded demeanor. His back was turned to Monica, so she couldn't get a good view of his face as he hunched over the fire, but even so, she couldn't help but sense a certain familiarity about him.

She tried not to make it obvious that she was inspecting him, taking him in with only a furtive glances as she walked. His frizzy raven curls spilled over his forehead, lazily tucked around a pair of ears too large for what she could glimpse of his soft, rounded features. For a moment, she thought she caught him looking at her too.

Monroe sat across from them, folding his legs beneath himself with a grace almost too stealthy for his tall, muscular frame. He patted the ashen ground beside him, and Monica lowered herself to her knees; a position that would allow her to easily spring back to her feet if needed.

Her eyes finally returned to Monroe's face, searching as she whispered, "You wanna talk? *Here*?"

"They're fine." Monroe murmured with a soft shake of his head. "I trust Brady and Akash. And Guy's not really there enough anymore to repeat anything important, even if he wanted to. Besides, it's not like we'll have any more privacy elsewhere."

Akash. She repeated the name silently to herself, stealing another glance towards the boy as she realized why he looked so familiar. *There are too many people in this realm for that to be a coincidence*, she thought, remembering what Finn had hoped about his best friend and Monica's brother keeping each other company. *Well, fate does have an unusual sense of humor.* A moment of guilt squeezed her heart, but she wasn't here for him. Besides, wouldn't it be cruel to mention the best friend he'd never see again, just for the sake of the connection? Akash didn't know her, and he didn't need to.

Shifting back to the priority at hand, Monica demanded in a harsh whisper, "So, tell me why you won't come back with me."

"Mo, don't be rash. You haven't thought this through. I *know* you know how Riftriders work; specifically their limitations and carrying capacity."

"And?"

"You *don't* have two of those." He said bluntly as a brief flicker of his eyes moved to indicate the hidden amulet. "There's no way. And unless you did, I don't see how bringing that here could possibly work."

"What are you saying? You don't want to come home?"

"No. I'm saying that I *can't* come home at the expense of *you.*" Monroe explained with pleading eyes. "C'mon, Mo, I know you lose all sense of rational thought when you're excited or desperate, but I *know* you must've thought this through before now."

Monica's jaw clenched in irritation at the undeniable thought that he was right. She *had* thought about it before now. And, despite her impatience to have her brother back, she knew coming into this that it wouldn't be so easy. She was in denial, so desperate to simply just *see* her brother again, that, in coming here, she'd fallen into the old habit of believing that her brother could fix anything she didn't know how to.

"Can you blame me?" She finally asked, her voice a mix of wryness and melancholy. "I've been looking for a solution for so long that once I got even the barest possibility, I had to jump on it. I've been holding onto it for days, and that's been killing me. The first free second I got, I had to come see you with it, even if I knew, deep down, that it couldn't be permanent yet. But it will. I just needed my brother to help me find a way."

"Monica…" he answered with a sad sigh, but his eyes were bright with tears of gratitude. "I appreciate that you'd do anything for me, but I just don't think that you can expect someone else to, too. In order for this to work, you'd have to find someone who was not only willing to sacrifice their life for mine, but who was actually loyal enough to see through trading places with me, and not taking off as soon as they got the amulet. Not to mention, the hazards of getting that thing to me without getting it stolen along the way."

"Stolen?" Monica asked with a dry chuckle from beneath a raised eyebrow. She gave a glance around the crowded clearing, a sea of apathetic lethargy that posed no obvious threat even comparable to what he was suggesting. "You think anybody here would even notice it?"

"You'd be surprised. But more likely than them, are the magpies."

"Magpies?" She asked with a scoff. "Seriously?"

"Metaphorical magpies. It's what we call the predator spirits here— nasty things like wraiths and wendigos—hungry spirits who would jump at the chance to make a meal out of anything with that kind of power. They see even a sparkle of energy, and they don't hesitate to try and take it."

"Energy?" Monica echoed, glancing around with a new understanding of the throng that surrounded them. "They'd *eat* the amulet?"

"Yeah," Monroe mouthed with a nod, his eyes darting to and fro, as if he feared that even speaking their names might conjure one. "And whoever had it if they got the chance. Everything here feeds on energy, even the realm itself. The longer souls stay, the more it saps them, until they finally fade into nothingness. That takes a really, *really* long time, though. Usually, people get eaten way before they make it to that point. Magpies feed on the freshest ones first; those who hold onto their hope. So it's easier to act broken to hide yourself, but then it gets hard sometimes to forget that it's just an act. It wears on you."

"Is that what happened to—" Monica paused, gesturing vaguely towards the older man with the hauntingly vacant eyes.

Monroe gave a wordless nod of reverence before turning back to Monica with a new urgency in his voice.

"And that's why you have to go." He said, abruptly standing. "You got to me impressively quickly, but even you only have so much time until they sense you."

"Go?" Monica squeaked, springing to her feet beside him. "You can't tell me something like that, and then just expect me to go. I knew you were dead, but I didn't think you'd *still* be in danger here."

"There's a reason I didn't tell you. But there's no point in you staying and only putting yourself in danger, too. Do us both a favor, and don't come back here, ever, if you can help it."

Monica's lower lip trembled as angry tears swelled in her vision.

"I don't understand. Why would you put in all that effort to contact me to tell me you're here? You risked my life by calling me to that dangerous island. And then, you even asked me to come to Enderfel, so we could be together! The brother I used to know wouldn't have asked me to put myself in danger, not once, but twice, in order to be together. Why did you do it?"

"I didn't know everything then that I know now."

"But you've been here for months. And it was only a few weeks ago that I saw you on the island. It doesn't make sense. What aren't you telling me?"

"Time moves differently here. And I—"

Suddenly, a piercing, birdlike screech resonated from somewhere in the distance. The edges of the sound were warped, warbling with a darkness like something possessed. It stirred an immediate wave of reaction from the sounding souls. Bodies snapped upright and light returned to vacant eyes, only to become panic. And then, as one, everyone collapsed around her, falling like dominoes to create a tapestry of feigned sleep.

"What was that?" Monica trembled, her eyes falling to Monroe as he tumbled to the ground out of instinct.

With his body limp and squeezed closed, all he did was utter two syllables, laced with more commanding desperation than she could've ever imagined.

"Go. *Now*."

Chapter 28

Monica landed back in Arkynesta with a *thud* so hard that it rocked the breath from her lungs. Her knees ached as she stood, certain that her shins would be *beyond* bruised in the morning. But, contrary to the expected challenges of returning from Enderfel, at least she still *had* a physical body to bruise.

A chill pricked her skin, making the hairs along her arms and neck rise as a burst of cold night air bit through her. Though the shiver had had a tangible trigger, her mind chose to pivot and focus on the lingering terror that had chased her on her too-close escape instead of the mere cold. She hadn't seen the magpie, or the wraith, or whatever it was, but she had felt it. It had possessed an energy that seared her own with an abstractly painful sizzle, like it had tried to reach inside her and rip her apart with fingers made of electricity. Fortunately, the rift had sucked her away before it could fully seize her, making her grateful for the uncomfortable experience of its frigid transport.

But what about Monroe? He was right beside her when she left. *What if that thing—*

She stopped the thought before guilt could encroach any further, knowing that adding to her already existing mountain of regret would serve no purpose but to slow her down. All she could do was pray he was okay, that he was practiced enough in playing dead like he'd explained and turn her own efforts towards solving the Soulseeker's sacrificial puzzle.

Monica's head whirled around as she reclaimed her bearings, baffled at her good fortune of how close her trip back had brought her to the apartment that she and Finn had begun to call home. Maybe that was a sign that her skills controlling the Riftrider were more transferable than she had originally hoped for.

Or maybe it was the eye. She glanced down at her left hand, a claw of aching fingers that clutched The Eye of Desire with such force that she was immediately thankful it wasn't more fragile.

She shoved the eye back into her pocket, its light already dimming from exhaustion. The only illumination that now filtered into her eyes was from a scattering of streetlights that lined the empty street. Monica had only been dimly aware of how dark the sky was before now. How long had she been gone? She had promised Celene that she would be back the same night. Was it still tonight?

She peered briefly at her watch, whose delicate silver hands indicated a time slightly more than halfway past two a.m. A flash of relief crossed her mind, only to be tackled by a burst of annoyance. Well, it *technically* wasn't tonight anymore, but hopefully it hadn't been enough time to make anyone worry about her too much to lead to questions.

That was unlikely. They would worry about her regardless, and the questions were likely inevitable. Monica took off, deciding not to waste any more time.

The apartment building was only a few blocks away, and her brisk pace had her there in minutes. No sooner had she opened the front door of her own apartment, a sudden wave of physical exhaustion overtook her, pouncing at the heels of the relief that had come. This apartment, though it was still new to her, was somewhere that she was slowly learning to allow herself to feel safe. But that also meant that her guard was down against all the subconscious things she usually forgot she was resisting; like the after-effects of an energy sucking realm as well as the creature that had almost devoured her there.

Monica's lowered guard also allowed her worries about the logistics and likelihood of Monroe's successful rescue to quickly flood back. But before she could give any of them her proper attention, her eyes fell to the peaceful face of a sleeping Finn. He was curled up on the couch with a small blanket wrapped around his head and shoulders, as if to block out the light that was still on in the front room.

He'd been waiting up for her; or trying to, anyway. Monica's chest tightened with mild alarm at noticing the urge of wanting to go to him, to wake him and tell him everything. She wanted someone to empathize with her challenges and comfort her against her fears, and it felt vulnerable to realize that she felt safe enough to want to let that someone be Finn. She knew she couldn't do that, for many reasons, but the tranquility in his expression was disarming enough to stand as an independent excuse.

The tufts of hair that hung over his forehead fluttered gently as his slow breaths seeped from between his lips, at one corner of which rested a faint shadow of a smile. She almost didn't realize that a reflection of his smile had infected her too, as she stood observing him.

Monica closed the door softly behind her, careful not to wake him. But she still wanted to tell *somebody.* Turning back around, her eyes caught the outdated phone mounted to the wall at the mouth of the hallway, and another name crossed her mind. *Celene.* She was probably on the edge of anger and worry, with as late as Monica was in returning. A fragment of lingering disquiet remained at the thought of trusting *anyone* with her problems, but maybe she didn't have to say everything. If she had to call anyway, maybe Celene would be a willing ear to listen. She was so desperate, she'd tell anyone at this point. But with as unusual as it was, she was sure that feeling of vulnerability wouldn't last.

No sooner had Monica lifted the phone to dial, she was startled by a series of noises coming from up the dark hallway. First, a muffled toilet flushing and running water. Then, a light switch clicking off and a door opening. Finally, a pair of graceful, bare feet padding up the hallway. Celene emerged from the darkness, her hazel eyes widening with relief beneath a brow still pinched with worry. But then, in all of half a second, her expression blanched with indignation.

"Monica!" She gasped in a hoarse whisper, a dramatic hand flying to her chest to emphasize her claim. "Finally! You scared me!"

"You?" Monica echoed the siren's sentiment with more authentic surprise. "I scared *you*? You're the one hiding out in someone else's apartment with no warning!"

"No," Celene scoffed, her eyes maintaining a faint glint of amusement as they narrowed to scold Monica, "You scared me because I thought you weren't coming back."

"Oh." Monica's tense muscles eased at the genuine worry in Celene's now soft and disarming eyes. "Then why—"

"And I wasn't hiding. I was waiting for you. When Finn made it home and you still weren't back, he called me. I didn't want him to worry, so I came over to keep him company while we waited."

"So you decided to worry about me *for* him?"

Celene gave a shrug of acknowledgement that wasn't quite an admission, but it wasn't quite a denial either. A pang of guilt hit Monica as her eyes briefly flitted to Finn's undisturbed face before returning to Celene's.

"Is he okay?"

There was a split second pause before the siren's answer, but before Monica could assume the cause, Celene sighed, "Yeah, he'll be fine. What about you?"

"*He will* be?" Monica growled, trying to keep her voice low despite the panic that now emerged. "What happened?"

Celene's full lips curled into a tight line as she shook her head. Her arms crossed, the weight of her stance shifting defensively as the accusing question came out, "I'm more interested about what happened to you. Spill. *Now."*

Monica exhaled a sharp sigh. "Fine, but can we not do it in the middle of the hallway?"

Celene nodded, stepping aside for Monica to enter the dark hallway before she turned to follow.

Monica planted herself at the foot of her bed, not bothering to close the door behind her after Celene had entered. She folded forward and began unlacing her boots in order to avoid the siren's expectant glare.

Displeased by the several seconds of silence that Monica had taken to gather her thoughts, Celene prompted, "So, what took you so long?"

A sigh of annoyance left Monica's lungs, but when it finally came, her voice only resounded with despondency.

"Enderfel is not what I thought it was."

"Oh?" The edge of Celene's accusation dulled beneath renewed concern.

"Even though it's the realm of the dead, I thought Monroe would be safe there, or at least, safer than here. I thought it was a place where souls could rest until— I don't know— they moved on or something. Knowing what I know of these worlds, maybe it was foolishly optimistic to hope for something more and better beyond an eternal existence in the realm of the dead, but I never thought spirits were supposed to just stay there forever. There were so many of them. It was so crowded, stretching on beyond the end of my sight. There were more spirits in Enderfel at once, than as many people as I've seen across my entire life."

Though she spoke with a flat, level voice, by the time she was done, Monica's breath quivered with the threat of tears. She kept her head low as the discomfort of vulnerability squeezed her heart, suddenly making her second-guess her previous desire to confide in someone. This wasn't Celene's problem.

Celene sank to her knees between Monica's feet, forcing her to stop before she could remove her second boot. Monica tried in vain to avoid her eyes. Celene's head tilted to the side as she peered up into Monica's face, her searching expression bearing a mix of determination and concern. Monica nervously shook her head, now hating that she was unable to avoid the siren's penetrating stare.

"I'm sorry." Monica sniffed, leaning back to pull away.

But Celene stopped her, placing a hand on her knee in gentle encouragement for her to stay. *Stay*, the gesture seemed to say, *I'm listening. Stay and be vulnerable.*

"I think you're right." Celene whispered. "Not that I can claim to be even remotely educated on the workings of the realm of the dead, but at the very least, I'm pretty sure that it's not meant to be permanent."

Relaxing a little with the reassurance, Monica's evasive urge eased enough to let her chin rise.

"Someone said something about there not being Guardians anymore to take them away? I don't know what they meant by that, but I'm more worried about the realm itself."

"Why? What did you see?"

"Prey." Monica forced the word out with a tremble in her voice. Before she continued, she slipped off her second boot, setting them both aside before letting her full attention return to Celene. It was a struggle to continue, as if saying it aloud confirmed that it was real. "The spirits there are little more than food for predator spirits that feed on energy. Those who survive them are drained by the realm itself. The longer they exist there, the more their hope and will to exist is sucked away, until they become vacant husks."

Celene's hand rose to rest on Monica's other knee, but the gesture of comfort did little to quell the tension that remained in Monica's body. Worse, she had started shivering, shaken to the very core by the unsettling truth. Monica tried to hide it, turning her head away. Celene's hesitation was respectful, but it didn't last. They both knew that her next question was unavoidable.

"And Monroe?" The siren whispered carefully.

"He's—" Monica's voice abandoned her before she could say *okay*. After all, she didn't know if he was since she'd left. And, even if the magpie *hadn't* gotten him, he most definitely *wasn't* okay.

Something was going on with him. He wasn't acting like himself, and there was clearly something he wasn't telling her.

Swallowing hard, Monica forced a nod. "He's there," she finally said. "He was in better shape than most when I saw him, but I don't know how long that's going to last."

After another respectful silence, Celene asked, "What are you going to do?"

And there it was. It was a question that Monica had known was inevitable, but never wanted to face, nonetheless. What *was* she going to do? For the first time in recent memory, she didn't have a clue. The realization crippled her like a ton of cold stones had just been dropped into her stomach. Her shoulders collapsed and she hung her head, curling into herself.

"I…" Monica began, her chest convulsing as a single sob slipped past her defenses. "I don't know."

Celene stood. Monica's eyes followed her, if only in surprise at her sudden withdrawal. But the siren didn't leave. Instead, she gestured for Monica to stand, which she only did with great reluctance.

Looking Monica square in the face, Celene gave a confident nod as she said, "I know what you're going to do."

The confusion that was plain on Monica's face sharpened when she found herself enveloped in a tight squeeze. Celene's arms were warm around her, cradling her body with a gentle strength that forced the tension to leave her all at once, like an exorcism of doubt. Monica's knees quaked with weakness, forcing her to lean into the hug. She barely noticed the hand cupping the back of her head until it pressed her chin to rest in the crook of Celene's shoulder.

The siren rested her lips against Monica's ear and cooed, "You're going to save him."

And, for a moment, Monica believed it. She wondered if Celene was compelling her with magic, but she didn't feel the grip of a command or the silk of compulsion in her words. But still, the courage was there. Celene spoke those words with such assurance, as if she knew, beyond any shadow of doubt, that she spoke the truth. And whether it was or not; for that, Monica was grateful.

Monica wanted to believe it herself, but the more she tried, the more her doubt returned. Her chest ached as the sobs crept back in, but Celene only held her tighter.

"You will," Celene said, as if feeling the doubt radiating from Monica.

Though every fiber of her body wanted nothing more than to let herself melt into Celene's soothing encouragement,

Monica could only cry. “But I don’t know how. I don’t know if it’s even possible.”

“Then tell me.” Celene said, still holding Monica flush against her. “Tell me everything and we’ll find a way. Together.”

Chapter 29

Monica told Celene what she knew of Enderfel and the details of Monroe's predicament. She confided her fears of the requirement of the Soulseeker's impossible sacrifice, and how she knew she wouldn't be able to find someone trustworthy and willing with enough time to save Monroe before something catastrophic happened. After all, Enderfel was just as much a ticking time bomb as were their current circumstances in facing The Enclave.

Though Celene listened intently and without judgment, it was clear in her troubled silence that she didn't have concrete answers to offer Monica. But that didn't stop her from suggesting, "Have you considered telling Maal all of this?"

"No." Monica answered bluntly, with no indication that she cared to say anything more on the subject.

"Why not?" Celene began, choosing her words carefully as she sensed Monica's guardedness returning. "He could help."

"No." Monica snapped, perhaps a little too loudly before she remembered that Finn was still sleeping in the other room. "Absolutely not."

"Why not? You know he's got the resources. And if anyone has a chance to help you, it's him."

"It's not his problem." Monica spat, her words still sharp with a bite that made Celene's brow pinch in concern.

"That doesn't mean he'll refuse to help. You keep forgetting that you don't have to do everything alone."

"But *this* I do."

"C'mon," Celene tsked, folding her arms. "You don't really believe that. If you did, you wouldn't have told me."

"This…" Monica began, gesturing between the two of them for emphasis, "*This* is different."

"Why?" Celene urged softly, searching Monica's eyes with a forgiving softness that was so disarming that Monica had to turn away.

She swallowed audibly, searching for words that never came. When she finally found enough strength to turn back to face Celene, tears welled in her eyes.

"Don't make me say it," Monica pleaded, searching the siren's features meaningfully. The tiniest shadow of a smile crossed Monica's lips, the expression meant to harken back to when Celene had spoken that same phrase to Monica before.

Celene's lips mirrored the smile, making it clear that she understood the phrase's intent, and though her expression that started off sly and pleased, it quickly changed to something sadder.

"Because you like me? That's not what this is," Celene pressed softly, her eyes sparkling with sage understanding before the suspicion crossed her lips. "You don't trust Maal, do you?"

Monica's jaw clenched, revealing the accuracy of Celene's gentle accusation.

After a long silence, Monica admitted, "Maybe with his own business, but not with mine."

Celene's tone remained placatingly tranquil as she questioned, "Why?"

"Gee, I don't know, Celene, maybe because he's a djinn?"

"You mean like I'm a siren?" She snapped back, matching Monica's newly rising tone. "Just because the stereotypes have *some* truth doesn't mean they're gospel."

"That's not what I meant," Monica bit back.

"Really? Because that's how it sounded."

"Look, I just mean that he's *never* been straight with me. Nine times out of ten, when he tells me to do something, he either won't give me the full details, or he won't tell me *why* he wants it done. And, when I express perfectly sound objections on why something won't work, he doesn't care and orders it anyway."

"I know it's frustrating, but you have to accept that he has his reasons. Despite what it may feel like, he's never intentionally set you up for failure, otherwise, you might not be here. Everyone's entitled to their secrets. And after everything he's done for you, you still don't think Maal is different?"

"Shit, not you, too." Monica rolled her eyes in exasperation. "Look, I have a contract. That means that no matter what he does for me, it's only because he has something to lose if he doesn't. At the end of the day, I'm still an agent; a tool to be used to get what he wants because he can't use his magic to satisfy his own purpose directly."

Celene gave a small sigh, her voice soft with supplication when it returned. "But what about all those things he said about you being the one he was waiting for to put all this in motion, that he trusted you to be our leader? You don't believe him?"

Monica froze, her expression shifting between desperation, disgust, and perhaps even an edge of hope.

"I want to, I *really* do, but I can't. He's too good at pretty words and emollient suggestions for that. I've seen how he works— how he gets what he wants— for too long to think otherwise. And I know you haven't seen what I have, but you can't possibly think that, if given the choice between me and his own motives, he'd seriously pick me. You saw how willing he was to sacrifice you and Finn in order to save me from that island."

"To save *you*," Celene pointed out.

"Because he decided that I was more valuable to his plan than you were at that point."

"No. I can't deny that you're valuable to him, but I honestly think it's more than just strategy."

"Why?"

"I don't know why." Celene sighed. "Call it a feeling. Maybe you should ask him yourself."

"A *feeling*?" Monica sputtered. "You want me to trust him based on a *feeling*?"

"Why not? That's what normal people do. That's why you're even talking with me now. Admit it, Damsel. Even though trusting people is hard for you, it's possible. But you're making this harder than—"

"Do you *actually* trust him?" Monica interjected, her voice sharp with guarded desperation.

"Enough," Celene said with a shrug, followed by a frank nod.

"Then you don't," Monica challenged.

Celene only shook her head, her argument one of pity rather than urgency.

"Trust isn't black and white. I trust him enough to work with him. I wouldn't have agreed to a contract if I didn't believe in his goals."

"You agreed because you were desperate. You'll get things that *you* want out of that contract, too."

But, rather than denying this, Celene simply asked, "Why did you agree to yours? What did you want?"

Monica drew back, trying not to let the shock show on her face. The last thing she had been expecting was for Celene to turn that on her. Monica was too used to being defensive, and having people respond in kind. It was so easy that it usually didn't even register when she was doing it anymore. But Celene. Celene was not only *not* returning her guarded brevity, but she was also opening up even more to it, as if to show she wasn't afraid of letting Monica see her vulnerabilities.

When Monica felt the siren's eyes boring into her as Celene awaited her answer, it was all Monica could do to fight the heat of tears stinging her eyes. Her chest tightened with a pressure that made her anxious. Her skin prickled with the dread of an impending threat. Everything within her fought against that question.

Until finally, forcing her eyes to meet Celene's, she whispered in a near inaudible register, "Something impossible."

Saying nothing, Celene stared into Monica's eyes with so much understanding that Monica feared the siren's empathy might break her. All at once, Monica wanted to collapse into tears, but the realization made her feel effortlessly stronger against the urge.

Despite poking at her defenses and digging around in her fears, Celene made Monica feel safe, rather than weak or ashamed. This was perhaps the first time that Monica didn't entirely feel that her fears were only something to be exploited.

With the same gentle understanding as before, Celene asked, "Is it impossible because it is, or because you want it to be?"

Startled, Monica stammered, "W-what do you mean?"

"You have a knack for making things harder on yourself than they need to be. Like now. Why are you making this situation harder by not asking Maal for help? *Why* won't you trust him?"

Monica paused, realizing that Celene was right, even though she didn't want to admit it. Trusting people was hard for her. After all, it was a defensive mechanism. She likely wouldn't still be alive if she had let her guard down. There had been too many people who had wronged her, and that made her angry. But as the tears burned her eyes, Monica realized that, even though she hated and resented everyone who had ever forsaken or taken advantage of her, it was nothing compared to the degree she harbored the same feelings against herself.

Sniffing, she slowly peered up at Celene with suddenly shy eyes. Did she really want to tell the siren all that? Even though part of her fought against the yearning, Monica realized that it was in vain. After all, she wouldn't be telling Celene *any* of this if there wasn't at least a part of her that wanted to.

Monica didn't ask for this. She never asked to be part of a team, to be forced to learn to look out for them and trust them. But here she was. And maybe it was time. As she had admitted before, carrying all of her burdens alone was exhausting.

"Maybe..." Monica began tentatively, "it's because... how am I supposed to trust anyone when I can't even trust myself?"

"What?" Celene asked, eyes widening as she drew back in bewilderment.

"Ever since I lost Monroe, I've questioned everyone, but especially myself. It was because of my own dumb decision that he's dead. And, for a really long time, he was the only one I *could* trust, because he's the only one who has never betrayed me. With everyone else, it was always just a matter of time before I got hurt again. Even if it was unintentional, and even if the pain was self-inflicted. I decided that I can't go through it anymore, so I don't trust in order to protect myself. And Maal's been around the longest, so he's overdue to betray me before anyone else."

"This isn't about trust," Celene realized aloud. "It's about loss. You're so scared to lose anyone that you'd rather push everyone away than even risk the odds."

The siren's revelation was so disarming that it sent a shiver through Monica's entire body. As the hairs on her arms rose, a wave of fear rolled through her. She felt the urge to clam up again but fought it with every ounce of strength she had.

"What are you doing?" Monica began defensively, trying to keep the accusation out of her voice. "How do you know that?"

Celene's solemn mask cracked with a clever smile that lit her eyes with pride.

"I think you forgot that I was a hypnotherapist in Vhenra."

Monica shook her head. "But there was no compulsion magic in your questions. I would have noticed."

"You're right, there wasn't. I *am* persuasive, but everything you said came out willingly. Therapy isn't always about the hypnosis. Sometimes, it's just about the talking."

Monica swallowed, narrowing her eyes to give a wary sideways glance. "I didn't ask for this."

"Maybe not out loud, but I didn't make you do or say anything you didn't want to. And I think the progress you're making is long overdue. Do you want me to stop?"

Monica's sharp intake of breath cut the silence as she considered this. Sure, the vulnerability was wildly uncomfortable, but strangely, it wasn't as bad as the pain she had held onto for so long. She didn't know how she felt about that. After only knowing pain for so long, there was a part of her that almost wanted to keep holding onto it, only because it was familiar. And even though familiar didn't always mean safe, it wasn't as scary as change.

But the relief was also undeniably liberating. Maybe change didn't have to be scary if she had someone to help her through it.

Lifting her head, Monica cautiously asked, "Do you think it'll help?"

"I think it already *is* helping." Celene encouraged with a gentle smile.

"I meant my other problem— saving Monroe. Do you really think it'll help if I talk to Maal?"

Monica couldn't believe she was even considering it. But Celene was right about that, too. He hadn't done anything to betray her… *yet*. Though her guardedness remained, maybe she could try it. After all, if nothing else, he *had* earned her trust so far.

"I don't think it could hurt. What's the worst that could happen?"

That's what she was afraid of.

Monica bit her lip, drawing in a deep breath before she finally relented, "Okay."

"Okay?" Celene's voice brightened with optimism. "Then you'll talk to him?"

"*Maybe*," she said firmly. "When I'm ready."

Even though they both knew that Monica didn't have much time, Celene didn't press the issue. She gazed at Monica with kindness in her eyes. Her hand rose to smooth a stray strand of ebony hair from Monica's face, studying her with unabashed focus.

The touch made Monica shiver, and even though the intensity of Celene's attention was uncomfortable, Monica didn't pull away. Her heart skipped a little when Celene's thumb trailed down around the curve of Monica's jaw, coaxing her closer with a pressure so slight that it was more like an idea than a suggestion.

As the warmth of their breaths mingled in the closing space between them, a sudden sound from the hallway startled them out of the intimate trance. Monica stood without thinking. Her heart pounded as she stared into the darkness outside of the bedroom door.

After a second, Finn emerged, his hair mussed and the blanket still coiled around his shoulders and chest, like a wildly oversized scarf.

"Monica?" He asked with a sleepy voice that didn't match the clumsily disguised alertness in his dark eyes, which was lost just as quickly beneath the tidal wave of relief that crashed over his expression. "You're back!"

"Finn." The tension fell from Monica's shoulders when his name crossed her lips as a sigh. "Sorry, did we wake you?"

Completely ignoring the question, he demanded, "Where were you?" Despite the insistence in his inquiry, something about his voice almost seemed a little sad. "Why didn't you tell me you were leaving?"

"I'm sorry," Monica sniffled, cradling herself in a half-hug as one of her hands rose to grab her other arm. "I didn't think I was going to be gone long and I didn't want you to worry."

"Then you should have told me."

Fighting her instinct to brush it off as *not his problem*, Monica looked to Celene for reassurance before she submitted to a small nod of admission.

"You're right. I'm sorry."

Finn looked both surprised but somewhat placated by this. His brow eased but concern still twisted one corner of his mouth as he murmured, "Are you okay?"

Monica nodded, but Finn appeared unconvinced by her evasion.

"I'm just tired. Can we talk about it tomorrow?"

Finn remained quiet as he entered the room and sat on his own bed across from them. Keeping his eyes low, he finally said, "We don't have to."

"You're right, though." Monica admitted. "And I want you to know."

After a long, sheepish pause, Finn said, "I *do* know. Because I heard everything from the hallway."

"You were awake? For how long?"

Finn shrugged. "I woke up when you two were still standing in the living room."

Finn's chin dipped with the shameful admission. A heat of indignance rose in Monica's cheeks, but it was brief following the awareness that she probably wouldn't have told him *at all* before Celene's unlikely persuasion. It made sense for him to want to know, especially since he so often wanted to help her. But he couldn't help. Not here. Not with this.

"I'm sorry." Finn finally said, but no sooner had the words crossed his lips and Monica dismissed them.

"I understand why you listened. Oh…" she paused, a new worry creasing her brow as her eyes darted to Celene, remembering what the siren had insinuated about Finn earlier. "Are you okay? Celene made it sound like something happened?"

Finn's cheeks flushed a soft shade of pink that he hid by sinking his further into the coil of blankets around him, like a turtle retracting into its shell.

He mumbled something that Monica couldn't discern before forcing a rushed nod. Then, clearing his throat, he parroted, "I'm okay, I think. But I'm tired, too. Can we talk about it tomorrow?"

After a pause, Monica finally agreed with a wordless hum. Celene rose from the bed beside Monica. The siren glanced at Finn briefly before pivoting back to plant a fond kiss on Monica's forehead. Monica's eyes shot to Finn as soon as Celene withdrew, baffled by the apparent lack of emotion on his face. He wasn't good at hiding his feelings, which, to her, meant that he didn't mind Celene's affection towards her. Which she also interpreted to mean that he didn't like her anymore, at least, not *like that.* She had no idea that his side was just as complicated as her own.

Monica's chest tightened with a transient twinge of sadness.

"I'll just let myself out." Celene said, flicking the lights off before she vanished through the door. "Good night, both of you."

Chapter 30

For the first time in weeks, Monica's sleep was tormented by nightmares. They weren't the full, vivid images as she had been accustomed to before meeting Finn, just fragments—faces, voices, feelings. But the theme was painfully unavoidable: Monroe.

She tossed and turned, fighting the invasion as her mind made a desperate attempt to work through the barrage of recent fears. It only came to an end when Monica was finally jerked out of her fitful sleep by the aggressive knock that came from the apartment's front door in the early hours of the morning.

She stumbled to the door in a haze, barely conscious as she accepted the summons letter from one of Maal's messengers. Finn greeted her from the hallway with sleepy eyes and sleep-mussed hair.

"Is that from Maal?" He asked with a yawn.

Monica wordlessly shoved the envelope at him, which clearly displayed a telltale six-pointed star in the gold wax of its seal. Not awaiting his response, Monica lumbered past Finn and back up the hallway to get ready.

Suddenly uninterested in the letter, Finn began in a small voice, "Monica? Can we talk about last night before we go?"

Deaf to the concern in his words, Monica only grunted, “No. Maal doesn’t like to wait. We’ll have time later.”

Finn didn’t argue, though it was clear that he wanted to. The sharpness of Monica’s tone was enough to dissuade any of his normal perky persistence.

Despite her cranky tone, Monica hid her exhaustion well, as she did with most afflictions. But even though nobody else seemed to notice, or at least chose not to acknowledge it, Monica was painfully and constantly aware as the symptoms of her unrest manifested as a splitting headache that was exacerbated by the blinding rays of the early morning sun. Why Maal had insisted on meeting on the roof of his tower, she didn't yet understand, but loathed it all the same.

“Couldn’t we have gotten coffee, and maybe some sunglasses first?” Monica let slip as a groan moments before Maal arrived to join the group.

“Good morning to you too, sunshine.” Celene goaded.

Monica shot her a short-lived snarl that quickly melted when Celene answered the look with a charming curve of her lips and flutter of her long, dark lashes. Behind the siren, Finn flushed a bright shade of magenta when his eyes met Dahvi’s before pulling away. The look lasted only long enough for Monica to get suspicious, but not long enough for her to pursue the question before Maal emerged from the elevator behind the group.

His hulking frame was dressed head to toe in black; an outfit consisting of a sharp, simplistic suit, leather gloves, a fedora, and even a pair of dark shades that made him look like either a giant bodybuilder vampire, or a secret service agent at a funeral. His normal miasma of fragranced smoke lingered at the edge of his presence but dissipated in the open air barely an inch from his body. Despite the opacity of his black glasses, a glimmer of blue still pierced out from behind them, casting a wavering, dulled version of his typical compulsion spell to persuade any who viewed him to immediately and completely forget his features.

Beside him, Amadarus stood on tiptoes, stretching their already impressive height to accommodate the large, black umbrella held over Maal's head.

Monica's immediate instinct was to suppress a snicker, a welcome lightening to her otherwise bitter mood. She never thought she'd see Maal in a hat of any kind, other than the hood of a cloak. Nevertheless, he still somehow managed to look menacing in a fedora, once his attention was upon her.

That's when his spell took hold. Though it was milder than normal, Maal's magic still robbed Monica of the opportunity to strain to discern his forbidden countenance.

"Your haste is appreciated, all of you," he acknowledged, never taking his eyes from Monica even as he addressed the group. Though the booming resonance of his voice still tickled the air, it didn't carry with quite the same commanding power that it usually held. "Monica, the artifact?"

Without a word, she freed the orb from where it strained the fabric of her pocket, lifting it and twisting it between her fingertips for his inspection.

Maal's lips peeled back in a grin that made his sharklike teeth glint threateningly in the sunlight.

"Very good. Let us begin."

He strode past her with hulking yet graceful steps, shadowed by his seer assistant as he made his way towards the roof's edge.

"Wait," Monica said, her loose grasp on the eye turning into a tight fist as disobedience bubbled up her throat. "Not before you tell us the plan."

Maal stopped, gravel crunching loudly beneath the sole of his shoe as he pivoted to face her. His grin was tight, his chin lowered in a dare for her to continue, waiting as if he wasn't sure he'd heard her right.

The familiar itch of compulsion made Monica's heart race as she stumbled into an apologetic justification.

"Look, I just mean, we can't go looking for Rowan if we don't even know what we're going to do with him after."

"After..." Maal purred in feigned consideration, "Let me worry about after. Just do what you've been asked, before I decide to *command* it."

There was already magic in his words, but it remained surprisingly gentle despite its sharpening persistence. An intake of breath cut the quiet as Monica was compelled to march through the gravel to come up to Maal's side, opposite Amadarus. Maal's back turned to Finn, Dahvi, and Celene, who were still gathered behind them. Leaning towards Monica with the slightest movement, Maal hummed, "Patience, Monica. You know I will tell you everything soon enough."

The stress in her shoulders was unbearable as she fought the spell enough to ask in a pitiful squeak of a voice, "Why not now?"

Maal made a sound somewhere between a hum and a chuckle. Monica wasn't sure if it was humor or praise, but it didn't sound like the admonishment she expected after her brazen defiance.

"I know you endeavor to be as prepared to complete your duties as possible, which is laudable, but your mind must remain clear for the eye to have the best chance of success. You don't need to stress yourself with details of a plan dependent on this initial task. Locate Rowan, and as soon as you do, I will tell you *everything*."

A shiver wracked Monica's body, making her achingly aware of just how tiny she was beside Maal. She wasn't aware that his hand had come to rest on her shoulder until after it had pulled away, but something about his touch shifted her focus back to determination and obedience. She knew she shouldn't believe him. After all, he's never told her *everything*. But now, she found herself wanting to believe. Maybe opening up to Celene last night *had* made a difference. It scared her, but this desperation didn't feel like magic. She *wanted* to trust him, without fear. Was that even possible? Maybe it was time to try. And how better could she demonstrate her trust for him than by doing her job?

Her fist tightened around the eye, making her whole arm throb, which she wasn't sure was from the pressure or the magic. *Yes*. She would find Rowan. She wanted that, too. She wanted him to be brought to justice.

"I will. I'll find him."

"Good." Maal purred before gesturing towards Amadarus with a gloved hand. "Entertain the other three. This may take some time."

Amadarus nodded in obedient acknowledgement, handed the open umbrella to Maal, and strode away to collect Celene, Finn, and Dahvi, despite their grumbles and protests. The silence was stark after Monica's associates disappeared into the elevator with Maal's assistant.

It felt oddly comforting to be alone with Maal again, after so long of being accompanied by at least one other presence. Admittedly, a few weeks *wasn't* all that long, but it had come to feel that way lately. Everything was so different now.

Monica drew in a deep breath, inhaling the tranquil expectation that hung over her in the silence. She felt Maal's eyes upon her, and that should've made her anxious, but in that moment, it didn't. It only lasted until her thoughts shifted to the eye. Her fist unfurled and her gaze fell to look upon the orb, which glistened with the movement of liquid rubies and black diamonds writhing in billows below its glassy surface, but as she studied it, she became quickly dismayed to find the artifact unresponsive to her intent or attention.

She swallowed hard, hearing the lie in her head before she tossed a nervous glance back over her shoulder at Maal, who had made himself comfortable in a newly conjured chair that was large, straight-backed, and upholstered in black velvet.

"I don't know… how to use it?"

Maal's face was impassive in the several seconds of uncomfortable silence that followed before his large head tipped thoughtfully to one side.

"Monica," he chuckled, "you know better than to lie to me."

She grit her teeth, clenching her hand around the eye in annoyance. Not his old games again. Was he really going to be cryptic and fish for information in order to get her to spill her unintentional disregard of his instructions *not* to use the eye outside of his tower?

"I—"

"I know you have enough knowledge about focus artifacts to understand and apply the basic principles, even if you've never used this one before."

The praising edge of his comment twisted her stomach with instinctual apprehension, and her first thought was that this, too, was somehow a trick.

Am I that cynical? Monica realized, making a conscious effort to release the growing tension from her muscles that accompanied the suspicion that she'd been barely aware of as it was forming. After she relaxed, she tried again, frustrated again to find that eye would not respond.

After several, long minutes spent straining, Maal inquired darkly, "Monica?"

To which she sputtered breathlessly, "I'm trying, I really am."

"You're thinking too hard. Desire should be easy, instinctual. You shouldn't have to think. Just want, *crave*, and let yourself go."

Expelling her breath in a huff, Monica nodded and did her best to empty her mind. She closed her eyes, cupping the orb between both hands, which gradually rose to hover just in front of her chest.

Maal was right. This was easy before. So easy, in fact, that she hadn't even realized she had been using The Eye of Desire, until well into the second activation. It *wanted* her to use it. She just had to open herself to it.

A fleeting fear flitted through the back of her mind, but she quashed it, like an ant beneath her mind's boot. Then, she merely stood, feeling the breeze in her hair and the warmth of the sunlight on her face as she let herself be vacant for the awakening of her desires. Her head pounded, but it was quiet. She remained until the pain of her headache dulled into a mere pressure, which slowly began to trickle down her scalp and accumulate at the base of it. When the pressure finally became a gentle but familiar tug, the thinnest smile crossed her mouth.

Her eyelids slowly lifted, confident that she would open her eyes to the red glow of magic. Which she did; only, it still indicated the dominant desire that she had hoped to dissuade with yesterday's trip to Enderfel. Her smile immediately soured, but she let her eyes silently follow the edges of the scarlet illumination to its source before she spoke, just to be sure. Her neck craned until it was obvious that she was looking down at where the Soulseeker hung over her heart. Though it remained obscured by her shirt alongside her Riftrider, it was unquestionable what the glow indicated.

She was thankful for the reassurance of her previous use of the eye, which demonstrated that she was the only one who seemed to be able to see its magic. That meant that to Maal, it likely only looked like she was staring down at the eye in her hands. But even if he couldn't see *what* her desire was indicating, she knew better than to try to lie her way out of the fact that it wasn't working the way he wanted it to.

"Damn it." She snarled under her breath.

"Monica?" Maal asked, but before he could continue his line of questioning, Monica snapped back, the frustration apparent in her voice.

"What?"

"What is it that you desire?" The smoothness of his question disarmed her, making her frustration sharpen to panic before it fluttered away with the coercion of his voice. The question was no different than when he asked it of a soon-to-be contract holder in the midst of being charmed into servitude.

"Why would you ask me that?" She quipped, though far less defensively than it had sounded in her head. This version of her response sounded honest, vulnerable, and perhaps even a little scared.

"Answer the question," Maal pushed, calmly but firmly.

Monica's eyes fell to the orb as she held it low in front of her chest, genuinely unsure of what to say.

Well, if there was *ever* a time to trust him…

"You don't know?" She finally asked, her face timid as her gaze rose to meet his.

His smile was softly paternal, and she almost managed to convince herself that whatever warmth she saw within Maal's expression *must* be a product of her pathetic desperation. But no matter how long she looked, it didn't fade or waver.

"Of course I do. But I wouldn't waste time asking questions that I already know the answer to if they weren't important. I want to hear you say it."

"I desire Rowan's de—"

"The truth," he corrected firmly, but without judgment. "You will not be punished. You cannot control what your heart desires. But this will not work without your honesty and cooperation."

Monica surrendered with a solemn nod before she began again, with great hesitation, "I desire… that my brother be returned to me. To Vhalta."

Maal's head bobbed with a slow, sagely nod. And then, after what felt like a full minute of silence, he said, "I desire that, too."

"You do?" Monica's eyes narrowed. Her initial thought was, *why would he be trying to make me feel better?* But as she analyzed his enduring and unnervingly human expression, she couldn't help but believe his candor. "Why?"

"When The Enclave murdered Monroe, I lost the single most powerful wielder I have ever had the fortune not to be on the wrong side of. Your brother was a great ally. Additionally, my best non-wielder agent lost a lot of her focus when that happened." Monica hung her head in shame, but before she could fully realize it, Maal continued unexpectedly, "But worst of all, I lost part of my pride in knowing that I failed him. I wanted redemption for you and your brother. I wanted for us to be able to bring about the fall of The Enclave *together*, given as a gift to those who needed it most. I wanted to drink in the sweet satisfaction of being able to offer revenge to those whom they had most wronged. I wanted to protect you both until that happened, after which you might both finally be able to protect yourselves."

Monica couldn't believe what she was hearing. Sure, there were parts of his admission that were selfish, but still more that were unexpectedly not. And it scared her, just how much she believed *all* of it. Her whole body was shaking so hard that she had to sit down, for fear that she might otherwise topple off the edge of the roof. She wrapped her arms around her thighs and let her forehead rest gently against her knees.

Celene was right. What if she'd had this conversation before? What could she have accomplished with the help of Vhalta's most powerful known djinn if she only would've trusted him sooner?

Sniffling and almost too afraid to ask, for fear that she was dreaming, Monica finally questioned, "Can you help me bring him back?"

"And how are you hoping to accomplish that?"

Monica let her knees fall away from her chest as the fingers of her empty hand fought to separate the Soulseeker's braided twine from the black cord of her Riftrider. Every impulse within her suddenly screamed and burned for her *not* to show him, but she forced it down. She wanted to trust him. She was desperate to. And now, despite all rational instinct and drive for self-preservation, she believed she could. "With this."

He didn't even pretend to be surprised when he laid eyes on the ivory coin that sparkled as it hung from her fingertips. Instead, he just smiled that unsettling, shark-like grin again, and congratulated, "My, my, it seems you're definitely off on the right start. How in the seven realms did you manage to obtain a realm key to Enderfel?" Maal asked approvingly.

Monica shook her head, not knowing why, but deciding to obey the strong protective instinct to obscure the amulet's true origin. "Just got lucky, I guess."

"That's an understatement. But it *does* pose some additional challenges, you realize?"

"I know." Monica sighed. "That's...actually what I was hoping you could help me with. I don't know how to get this to Monroe in a way that would let him come back without trading places with him myself. Anyone I hire would likely run off with it, sell it, or change their mind about sacrificing themself for a stranger, and that's before they even made it to Enderfel."

"So what are you asking of me?" Maal began, his voice laced with the barest trace of ridicule. "Surely, you don't think *I'll* trade places with him."

"No!" Monica scoffed, shaking her head at the ludicrousness of the assumption. "No, I'm hoping you might help me find someone trustworthy enough to hire to do it."

"You can't *buy* trust, Monica." Maal reminded morosely, making Monica nauseous at the irony of the thought that he was now the one giving her advice about trust. "It's only ever earned, honestly or… otherwise."

"What about someone with a contract? They have to obey *anything* you command, right?"

"That's assuming that I'd even be willing to sacrifice another contract holder at your behest, which is awfully presumptuous of you. But, even if I *was* willing, no. Contracts aren't enforceable for agents who do not exist in one of the living realms. Even if they haven't actually died, my control does not extend to Enderfel, so there's no guarantee they still wouldn't back out once they got there. Your best— perhaps only— option is to ask someone you trust; someone close to you, someone who would do anything you asked."

Monica's brow furrowed. "I don't have anyone like that." She said with a quick shake of her head.

To this, Maal gave a shrug. "Well, until you do, you're at an unfortunate impasse. But, since it's no longer an urgent issue, shall we try again to—"

"Not an urgent issue?" Monica spat, frustrated but not surprised that he'd be so anxious to pivot back to his own motives. "Do you know *anything* about the way Enderfel works? For every second Monroe's there, he's in danger of being eaten."

"Oh," Maal groaned, though Monica could no longer tell how much of his tone was genuine and how much of it had returned to his standard, superior affect. "That *is* unfortunate. But there's no sense in wasting any more time—"

Monica threw up her arms in exasperation. "I should've known you wouldn't help me. You're only interested in getting me to let this go enough so I can do what *you* want me to do."

"Look," he hissed, a sudden bite of offense entering his tone. "I would help you if it were within my power to do so, which you would know if you had been *listening*. But since you are not, let me put this another way. Monroe isn't the only one who's running out of time. What happens when that wielder bastard gets ahold of even my second name, hmm? Do you really want to wait long enough to find out whether he'll be too powerful to stop by that point?"

Monica's jaw clenched in aggravation, knowing that Maal was right.

"Fine." She relented. "I'm here, and I can't do anything for Monroe at this moment. So command me to use the artifact to find Rowan, so I can go."

"While I appreciate even your begrudging permittance, I can't do that. I can only compel you under the terms of your contract so far as the abilities of your own body and mind. I cannot command your heart, nor can I will you to use any magic as a non-wielder. So, to be successful with the artifact, you must focus your own desire to use it as intended."

"Seriously?" Monica scoffed. She crossed her arms in annoyance, turning away for a moment before she forced herself back to her feet. "Then what was all that about, *just do what you've been asked, before I decide to command it*?"

"Ahh, yes," Maal chuckled, looking more pleased that Monica had caught him rather than being embarrassed in such a clumsy bluff. "Motivation doesn't have to be honest to be effective. And, sometimes you just need a little push."

Finally, she gave a heavy sigh of defeat, peering down at the artifact nestled in her hand as it rested in the crook of her elbow. Her shoulders ached as she turned and lifted her head to look back at Maal.

Her voice had lost nearly all of its former strength and agitation as she asked, "So what am I supposed to do now? How do I make this work if it's clear that saving Monroe is my strongest desire?"

Maal inclined his head, wearing an expression that was no longer readable to her. His stiff shoulders hinted at pride, but the tenseness of the way his claws dug into the arms of his chair read as apprehension. But neither detracted from the surprising assurance in his voice.

"You will do as you have always done—overcome."

He sounded so certain as he said this that it only made Monica more sick to her stomach. She wasn't sure if he really believed it, or if he was just trying to make her feel better. But nothing about his manner suggested any uncertainty.

"Overcome? How?"

"It will take a lot of mental strength, but the benefit of focus artifacts is just that; they are controlled through the focus of their user. Frankly, this is the part that you expressed concern for since we don't have the time for you to be able to properly master the *focus* part of this endeavor. I had rashly hoped that your desire to end Rowan would be potent enough to overcome the artifact's querulous nature, but it appears that this will come down to *your* self-discipline."

Great, she thought, her internal sarcasm suddenly fading as her mind caught something unexpected in his tone. *Wait, was he actually admitting that he'd been wrong?*

"But, no matter," Maal continued, "because, though it is not your greatest desire, there is still powerful emotion behind your adversarial connections to Rowan. So, if you focus enough on that, you should be able to cultivate it, bring it to the surface, and find him."

The finality of his words made her veins pound with a boiling rush of anxiety. Her mind raced with fear and self-doubt, finally settling on a mild, but still wary resignation. Whether it was genuine, or just a tactic to make her will more malleable, Maal *really* did seem determined that she could do it.

Could she?

"Do I even have a choice?"

"My dear," Maal growled with a returning ominousness to his voice, "neither of us do."

Chapter 31

Monica spent several, grueling hours on countless attempts that all invariably ended in failure. It was only after the sun had begun its descent that Maal finally called for an intermission.

"That's enough for now."

By this point, Monica's pale skin was radiating the heat that had gathered from her prolonged exposure in the sun. Her scalp was uncomfortably steamy with sweat, and she did not look forward to the likely sunburn that awaited her. She glared at Maal as he stood from his seat, suddenly envious of his large, black umbrella. The massive velvet lounge vanished into a wispy puff of blue-gray smoke the second his weight had left it, dissipating quickly in the stagnant afternoon air.

Though part of her was undeniably eager for a break, the other part; the one more inclined to listen to fear over reason, had her calling out, "But I haven't found him yet. I haven't made any progress."

"And continuing will accomplish nothing that you have not already attempted. There's no sense in depleting yourself further. Come," he gestured with his large, gloved hand, making Monica fall into step behind him as he floated towards the elevator. "Besides, I believe I'm due to make good on your request."

At the very least, Monica knew better than to question him on that. Maybe now she was finally about to get some answers.

Monica's feet stumbled a little as she walked, finding her legs heavy and weak with exhaustion. She chided herself for this, knowing that she had endured far more strenuous and uncomfortable things than standing in the sun for a few hours, even if it had not been for a while.

Upon entering the elevator, her stomach gave an audible groan, making her suddenly aware of the undeniable lack of nutrients her body had been given today. Maal made no obvious recognition of the sound but displayed his awareness just the same in the form of a rather lavish lunch laid out for them in the dining hall of his lair.

Maal indulged no conversation until after he motioned for Monica to take the empty seat alongside her comrades before he did the same on the opposite side of the table.

Maal and Monica were greeted with three pairs of eager eyes in the tense silence, staring mostly at Monica with an unabashedness that made their anticipation clear. She lifted her gaze only briefly enough to meet Celene's, who's full lips were curled in question. Instead, Monica only gave a blank-faced shake of her head before turning her attention to the cloche laid before her by one of the several serving girls that had shuffled in.

A wide, shallow bowl of chicken alfredo was unveiled before her. Glancing around the table, there was no clear pattern to the meals that were being served, other than perhaps, personal taste. Celene was offered a banquet of seafood and steamed vegetables. Finn lit up at a carefully constructed artwork of pancakes, chocolate chips, whipped cream, and cherries that resembled some kind of creature with a grinning face. Dahvi was served eggplant parmesan and a cup of fruit salad, alongside a beverage that looked suspiciously like beer with chunks of fruit in it, but that smelled far more pungent and acidic, even from across the table. For Maal, only a glass carafe of red wine and a single silver goblet were supplied.

After everyone had been served and the servants had retreated, Maal finally broke the hungry silence with a chill-inducing growl that made the air shiver from the strength in his voice.

"Thank you all for indulging your patience today. I wish I could announce that things are progressing as planned, but given that you are all still here, that's obviously not the case."

Despite the lack of accusation in his words, Monica couldn't help but feel her shoulders sag under the weight of self-blame.

"So…" Celene began, casting cautious eyes around the group before voicing the question that was on everyone's tongue. "What's the plan?"

"The same as before. Our first priority is to find Rowan."

"And then?"

"And then," Maal answered coolly, eyes downturned to inspect the swirl of burgundy liquid within the goblet in his hand before taking a small sip. "We use his absence from The Enclave to our advantage."

"Absence?" Monica slowly lifted her head, narrowing her eyes as she gingerly tugged on the thread dangling from her question. She felt a prickle of humorous incredulity invading her voice, but the sheer ice in Maal's enduring austerity squashed any dare she had of entertaining it. "You say that like you're planning to abduct him."

"More or less," Maal shrugged.

Monica bristled. "You're not serious."

"Why not? After all, what better way to keep him from obtaining any more of my names, as well as limiting his threat to us, than taking him as our prisoner?"

"Why not just kill him?" Monica sputtered, both confused and a little frightened by Maal's idea. "Why go to the effort of capturing and then keeping him contained?"

"You really think a wielder with that big of an ego wouldn't have put countermeasures into effect if he dies?" Maal scoffed. "If we're to be successful in facilitating The Enclave's undoing, we mustn't tip them off. Besides, keeping him alive and in our control could greatly improve our understanding of The Enclave's motives, inner workings and, most of all, their weaknesses. And, don't tell me you wouldn't love the opportunity to interrogate that smug weasel yourself?"

"I *would...*" Monica sighed hesitantly, pausing to consider more thoroughly what it would take to make such a thing possible, and feeling suddenly guilty for her admission.

"How would you do it?" Celene interjected in Monica's pause, seeming genuinely curious at Maal's proposition. "Not that I doubt your power, but can you be certain that you can harness it with enough success to rival his, and actually hold him, after he's already proved strong enough to successfully threaten you in your own tower, without recourse?"

"Well, for one, he got lucky. Which *won't* happen again." Maal answered Celene's question with a tight sneer that soon turned into a clever and somewhat pompous grin. "As for our retort, the trick is in the capture. If we can take him by surprise, holding him will not be as difficult in its sustained nature, as long as we are careful."

"How do we capture h—?"

"And that's where the other part of our plan is set into motion," Maal continued, entirely ignoring Celene's interrupted question. "As long as he's our prisoner, there will be an obvious absence within The Enclave. If we leave that gap open, the other wielders will get suspicious fast. But, if we insert one of our own to take his place, not only will it buy us time to keep him within our control, but it'll potentially give us access to more information about The Enclave that we would not otherwise know. Which is also a valuable fallback to have established in the event that interrogating him proves less fruitful."

A tense silence fell over the group as the promise of more information suddenly became an unspoken threat. A look passed between Celene and Monica, confirming a shared fear that neither of them wanted to voice. Dahvi's quiet presence and low eyes excluded him from the silent discussion. When the leftovers of the girls' apprehension flitted to Finn, it only seemed to make him more curious than afraid.

"And who—" Finn began, nervously looking around at the others when no one else dared to ask the question. "Who'd take his place?"

His eyes saddened slightly as he realized the answer to his own question the second it had left his mouth.

"Me," Dahvi announced firmly, taking the opportunity to show off his powers when all eyes turned to him.

He pressed the shadow of a sly grin into the corners of his mouth as he seamlessly shifted from his familiar facade to the sinister mask of Rowan Drake, only wearing the illusion from the waist up.

Monica nearly sprang out of her chair in response, looking ready to tackle him until her eyes fell to study the gray horse half of his centaur body that still remained. Even Celene looked visibly shaken, though not enough to remove her from her delicate, cross-legged perch on the edge of her seat. Finn, on the other hand, had to remind himself to look surprised, which was delayed and clumsy at best, but was just enough to fly beneath Monica's watchful eye in the face of her own extreme alarm.

"So you're a—" Celene began with her head cocked to the side as she studied his mask for any cracks.

"A shapeshifter," Dahvi answered in Rowan's smooth voice. "*Not* a centaur."

"Well, that makes a lot more sense." The siren sighed, relaxing her guard as she continued to slide her gaze up and down appraisingly over his features. "Not bad, either."

Monica leveled a suspicious glare at him, her posture still visibly on edge despite the shifting of her shoulders in an attempt to force herself to relax.

"Wait..." Monica began tentatively. "How is this supposed to work if you're not also a wielder? You're not, are you?"

Dahvi shook his head. "I'm not. But it's my understanding that Maal has *alternatives* for me that'll circumvent that issue, at least at an observational level."

"There's... no way that'll work." Monica looked to Celene and Finn for any hint that she'd missed something. "Artifacts can only do so much, and there's *no* way that a trained wielder wouldn't immediately be able to tell the difference."

"I didn't say it would be an artifact," Dahvi said matter-of-factly, from behind a stare that made Monica shiver in disgust.

Her lip curled in a snarl of controlled contempt as she leaned back in her chair, desperate to create some space between her and the shapeshifter's illusion. Logically, she knew it was merely that; an illusion, but the conjured likeness was so sickeningly accurate that she had to continually remind herself that she *wasn't* face to face with the man who had claimed to have killed her brother. After all, that's all he had been the first time, on the island: an illusion.

"Can you stop doing that?" Monica glowered, crossing her arms tightly over her chest. "It's unnerving."

"Sorry," he sighed, the menacing chill wilting from his smile as Rowan's features morphed back into Dahvi's familiar face. "Sometimes I just can't help myself. Better?"

Monica sniffed, her arms immediately uncrossing as the tightness in her posture eased. She offered a small nod before reminding with a still-steely tone, "You haven't answered my question."

"I don't recall there being a question, merely a discussion."

Though Monica was well acquainted with Dahvi's playful predisposition, she had also gauged his ability to be serious when the matter called for it from his inclusion in their last group meeting with Maal. So was he being pedantic for a reason she had missed, or merely for the sake of it? Either way, she was finding it exceedingly irritating. But, perhaps that was a lingering side effect of how perturbing his unexpected demonstration had been. Restraining the temptation to release a more forceful retort, Monica held her breath for a handful of seconds before she finally spoke again.

"Regardless, I don't understand how you're going to be able to trick The Enclave into believing that you're *actually* Rowan, without any powers."

Dahvi glanced towards Maal before giving a small shrug. "It's my understanding that I won't have to try very hard."

Monica glared at Dahvi. "And what does that mean?"

Maal interjected, allowing only a split second's glimpse of an odd expression that passed between him and the shapeshifter before he took over. "Dahvi won't need magic of his own, because I'm sending someone else with him who does."

Monica was not expecting that. After a moment of stunned silence, she finally managed to mutter, "Who?"

Maal cleared his throat, indicating Celene.

"Her?" Monica gasped, echoed by the siren's own cry of alarm.

"Me?"

"Yes," Maal answered with a nod to each of them, before turning to face Celene. "You. Even though you're not a wielder in the traditional sense, as a siren, you still have access to an amount of flow magic. And, you've been making great strides in your training, making you this team's best candidate. Not to mention that you may not even need to use any flow magic, considering your *very* persuasive ability to bend men to your will."

"No." Monica shot back, struggling to remain in her seat as her legs tensed with the urge to stand in dissent. "Absolutely not. You have plenty of other wielders on staff. Why not send one of them? And how would that even work?"

"I would not trust any of them to be up to this task the way I trust *this* team. And I have a handful of viable options to make this possible." Maal said with a shrug, beginning to count off on his fingertips as he recited, "Invisibility elixirs—"

"Temporary," Monica challenged, and all eyes turned to her.

"—shrinking tinctures—" Maal continued as the focus bounced back to him, unfazed.

"Also temporary; and *dangerous.*"

"—cloaking artifacts—"

"Which they'll catch with search beacons."

"Or an imperceptibility talisman," Maal concluded with a grin, as if this had been the *real* option that he'd merely been building towards for effect.

“That they— wait…” Monica paused, a thin line sinking between her brows as she pondered his final suggestion. Finally, the group’s focus settled, no longer bouncing between the two like spectators at a tennis match. “You actually *have* one of those?”

“Why, of course.” Maal smirked like it was no big deal.

And maybe it wasn’t to him, but talismans *were* a pretty big deal in general. Talismans were like artifacts in that they were supercharged with a magical ability, but unlike artifacts, which had to be actively and consciously used in order to work, talismans were basically always “on” as long as they were being worn. Not only that, but talismans didn’t require the recharge period that most artifacts did after strenuous use. Instead of having a single set capacity of expendable charge, talismans were still set to only perform one magical task, but they were instead tuned to the ambient flow magic, letting them run tirelessly and indefinitely within their measured limitations. This included the standard, "one user per item" constraint.

Because of their nature, talismans were generally used more for defensive effects or subterfuge, rather than some of the more interesting or dangerous purposes of artifacts. But even so, talismans remained one of the more valuable and coveted items in any magical arsenal.

Forced to admit defeat, Monica sighed, “That might *actually* work.”

“It *will* work,” Maal comforted, letting his eyes roll towards Celene. “Otherwise, I wouldn’t have suggested it. Besides, Celene’s a big girl. She can decide for herself. Celene?”

The siren’s eyes went wide with sheepish pause, and for once, she seemed a little hesitant at the proposition.

“*Decide*? You’re *asking* me?” Celene pondered aloud when her voice finally returned to her. When Maal nodded, she clarified, “If I think it’ll work, or if I want to do it?"

“You seem surprised,” Maal replied, evading her question.

“Well, yeah,” Celene paused, though her wits quickly returned to her in the form of a rising guard, tinged with indignation. “In fact, it’s awfully rude of you to pretend like my opinion matters at all."

Maal’s grin wilted and his head tipped slightly to the side as he regarded her with a new seriousness. Something akin to hurt sharpened his tone, but it was still more chiding than reassuring. “Celene, my dear. I would not ask your opinions if I did not value them.”

“When did I become *your dear*?” She scoffed, and the seriousness of the situation seemed to dissolve a little with the introduction of humor.

“When you became my agent."

"Oh, right. The same time you began to *own* me. You never offered me such a courtesy before you commanded me to join Finn in rescuing Monica from the Isle of Reflection," Celene retorted, her voice touched with a bitterness that revealed that Maal's conciliatory gesture was backfiring on him. "That makes me nervous, djinn, because you're either asking merely for flattery’s sake, which means that this won’t end well for me, or you're really concerned it won't work *at all* and you’re looking for reassurance.”

That seemed to touch a nerve. Even though Maal’s expression barely changed on the surface, his mouth seemed to tighten and the glint in his eyes became cold. After a long, pensive silence, austerity flooded back over Maal’s impassive expression.

"I would not instruct you to even attempt it if I did not foresee this plan's probability of having a favorable outcome that would ultimately further our cause."

Though the coy, calculating flicker in Celene's eyes never dimmed, a fleeting twinge of contempt flickered at one of her nostrils. She had her answer.

"So…" she began haltingly, keeping the tone of her voice level as if trying not to tip her cards. "I'm to be sacrificed, then?"

"There's no certainty of that," Maal stated with a fabricated softness, meant to reassure her, even though the content of his words did not. "There's no certainty of *anything* yet. But there is always that chance. I'm sure that one as clever as you understands that no endeavor is ever immune to the element of chance. Sometimes, the unexpected can serve just as dutifully if one is able to adapt. And that is why I'm sending *you*. Between your powers and Dahvi's, the two of you have the strongest chance to gain an upper hand if something goes wrong."

"You mean *when*." Dahvi groaned morosely, something in his tone hinting that his retort held more knowledge than blind suspicion.

Maal brushed this off with a shrug of his shoulders as his smile dared to return.

"Have more faith in yourself, shifter." Maal's eyes narrowed and his voice was laced with the sharpness of a threat, rather than the soft tones of reassurance. "And your team. After all, it's impossible to know how things will turn out with unshakable certainty. That is why all of you must be prepared to adapt at a moment's notice."

Chapter 32

And without warning, Maal stood, turning to leave.

"Where are you going?" Monica growled, her voice still tense with too many unasked questions.

"What kind of leader would I be if I didn't follow my own example?" Maal asked, followed by a wave of his hands. "You're dismissed."

"But what about finding Rowan?"

"We will. But since you have thus far been unsuccessful with the eye, my resources will begin exploring alternative options."

"That's it?" Monica scoffed in disdain. "We went through *all* that trouble to get the eye, only for you to give up on it so quickly?"

Maal gave a growling chuckle. "Monica, when have you *ever* known me to give up? The clearest path is not always the one most easily traveled. Therefore, I'm merely scouting as many paths as possible. You will return to use the eye again after you have practiced. But you'll make no progress in your current state."

"Practice? But there's no way of knowing how long that'll take."

"Hence, seeking alternatives," Maal reminded with a sharp gesture, flicking his finger as if to make a mark in the air. "Really, Monica, it's like you haven't even been listening."

Monica withdrew, crossing her arms over her chest to make her pose match the sullen expression that had crept onto her face. "Well, what do we do in the meantime?"

He smiled at Monica, though something about it almost seemed like a pitying smile.

"I'm sure you'll find something to keep yourselves occupied." Giving the group a broad sweep of his eyes before his focus returned to Monica, he concluded, "Rest. And just try not to get yourself into any *more* trouble. Not like last time."

Monica's expression tightened with the indignance of a child scolded. Their stares remained locked for a long moment, but Monica struggled to find the strength to question him until after the compulsion of his eyes had left her and his back had turned.

"If the eye doesn't work… What other options are there?"

He paused for only a moment to peer back over his shoulder at her.

"Monica, will you never learn not to concern yourself with such things? They're not yours to worry about. Let me do what I do best, and I will let you know when you can do yours."

Before she could say anything more, Maal vanished, fading beneath a combination of the weight of darkness and a new bloom of smoky tendrils that muddied the air.

An aura of stunned confusion descended on the group as they departed, finding themselves listless without an immediate objective. Everyone, except for Monica, that is.

Monica, exhausted as she was, should have found herself grateful for another opportunity to rest, something that was often rare and limited. But her mind would not give up the churning desperation to reach for a solution that dangled just out of her grasp. Sure, she had a million other things to worry about: the conversation she had promised to Finn and the subtle implication that something concerning had happened to him, Dahvi's and Celene's possible demise, and planning for everything else that awaited their team, but they all paled in comparison to the worry of how she'd left things with Monroe. So much so, in fact, that she barely allowed a fleeting semi-conscious thought for any of those other things before she took off again, the moment she was free from other duties.

The group called after her, but to no avail. This time, she didn't so much as offer an explanation or a rushed promise of return. She just ran. And pursuing her made no difference, because the second she was out of sight, the magic of the Soulseeker had already whisked her away.

The silence that immediately followed Monica's disappearance was fraught with tension. Even with no view of Finn's face as she stood behind him, Celene read the tightness in his shoulders as worry, and the slow way his head fell when Monica ignored his calls as defeat, or perhaps even guilt.

Wanting to comfort him, Celene laid her hands on his shoulders as she came up behind him. Despite his stoic stance, he was trembling. His head tempted a turn of acknowledgement towards Celene, but he didn't take his eyes from their distant point of focus, as if staring would somehow bring her back.

After a long moment, Finn audibly swallowed before exhaling a gravelly, fearful whisper.

"She went to Enderfel again, didn't she?"

"I don't know." Celene cooed, wishing she had anything more to tell him that might ease his mind. But she knew better, and she wasn't going to lie to him. "Probably."

He dropped his head, and when it finally lifted again, he offered a shy glimpse of dark eyes sparkling from behind fearful tears.

"Is she avoiding me?"

"What would make you think that?" Celene's voice came out genuinely baffled.

"She didn't want to talk this morning, about last night… I didn't get to tell her what happened."

Finn's eyes lingered on Celene for only a moment before his gaze turned to Dahvi, the two exchanging a look that ended with Finn lowering his eyes in a way that communicated a shadow of his sadness onto Dahvi's features.

"You're worried you're going to hurt her feelings?"

Finn gave a guilty shrug. "Maybe."

"She's got a lot going on right now that doesn't involve you."

"I still wish we could've talked about it —about everything— before she ran off."

"I know," Celene offered. "But with everything she said last night, are you really that surprised?"

"Surprised…? No. Scared…" Finn's head dropped as he nodded pensively.

"I know. I'm scared, too. But so's she. That's why she's acting like this."

Finn gave a heavy sigh. "I know. And I think part of that's my fault."

"What? Finn, that's ridiculous. You had nothing to do with her losing her brother. You didn't even know her then."

"But I *am* contributing to her fears. I heard everything last night about what scares her, about how she doesn't want to lose…" He stopped, jaw tightening as he pulled in a haggard breath. Lifting his eyes again to Celene, he admitted, "Before, she begged me not to come back to Vhalta. She didn't want to lose me, and she didn't want my family to lose me. And I came back anyway."

"Finn, she's not going to lose you."

"We don't know that. I didn't want to see it before, but as Maal said, there is no certainty of anything. And, despite wanting to help her more than anything else, I don't want to end up hurting her more."

With eyes wide in genuine apprehension, Celene haltingly asked, "Where is all this coming from?"

Finn was quiet for a long moment. His eyes were distant, as if searching for something. His brow furrowed before his attention transferred to Dahvi, who remained sagely silent, his own expression sparkling with sympathy at Finn's clear distress. After the boys shared a lingering look, Finn shook his head.

"Never mind," Finn finally sighed. "I guess I'm just frustrated. I wish she could see that she doesn't have to do this alone. I want to help her. I wish she would let me."

"Let you?" Celene's eyes narrowed slightly as she studied his face, her hazel irises glinting in the light of new suspicion. "Finn, do you know how to help her?"

The question made him immediately shrink and brace himself before he could fully turn away.

"Sorry," he sniffled and shook his head. "It's probably just desperation and wishful thinking. I didn't mean to get your hopes up."

Celene tried to hide the unconvinced look that had surfaced behind a mask of practiced reassurance. Finn was scared. He was talking out of hopeful desperation, so of course he wasn't making sense. He needed someone right now. Celene took his hand in hers, hoping that her forced smile looked as comforting as she meant it to be.

"It's okay. I wanna help her, too. And I know it sucks feeling helpless, but right now, she's too determined that she has to do this alone. We can't do anything except wait and be there for her when she's ready to let us, okay?"

A sharp sniffle came from Finn as he nodded.

"Do you want me to walk you home?"

The nod turned into a quick shake of his head that ended when he turned to glance at Dahvi.

"No, I'll... be okay."

At this, Dahvi smiled, but the light of the expression never fully rose to erase the sympathy glimmering in his eyes. Celene's gaze broke to study the shifter's expression with a reserved wariness that reluctantly gave way to permittance. There was nothing she understood better than seeking comfort in physical affection. After all, doing so made up a lot of the dumb choices she'd made growing up. But, in evaluating the softness in Dahvi's eyes, she didn't see any signs that made her worry for Finn's innocent heart.

"Okay..." She finally sighed, letting her grasp dissolve through Finn's fingers like sand as she pulled away. "But call me if you need *anything*, all right?"

Finn nodded, turning towards Dahvi, who was quick to offer an arm outstretched in comfort. Finn didn't hesitate, tucking himself under Dahvi's arm to accommodate an awkward stride that made him look like a child next to the towering centaur.

Celene wished she could do more for him, but now, seeing as he was in good hands, there wasn't much left that she *could* do, except silently curse Monica's dangerous impulsivity and wait for her to return in one piece.

Chapter 33

"Damn it, Monica! I told you not to come back here." Monroe met her with a scowl as he rose, slowly and deliberately.

Monica's expression softened to show only a flicker of relief before squaring off with a glare of her own. She was unfazed by his towering height, despite the foot of vertical advantage it gave him over her diminutive stature.

"And since when have I *ever* listened to you?" She shot back, fists balled at her sides as she challenged him. "I'm not leaving until you tell me what in the *seven realms* is going on, Monroe."

"Mo," he pleaded, hushing her with a harsh whisper and a small, placating gesture. His head lifted to take a brief, apprehensive sweep of their surroundings before his focus returned. "Keep your voice down!"

"Fine."

"Sit." Monroe nodded towards the ground beside him as he sank and crossed his legs.

Monica obeyed, but the bite in her tone when she spoke again threatened that she was far from surrendering.

"What happened before the island? Why did you call me to such a dangerous place when the you I knew before would *never* have done that?"

Monroe's broad chest rose and fell with a frustrated breath. He chewed his lower lip as he thought, uncertainty filling his pale eyes as he mulled over his response. Turning slowly back to face Monica, his shoulders sagged with shame. "Because… I got scared, okay?"

"You?" Monica's nose wrinkled in disbelief as she repeated the unsettling word, "Scared? Since when?"

Monroe's lips parted around a forceful scoff.

"I know. I've never let you see me scared, but this…" He growled, pausing to gesture at the world around them with a shrug. "This has all been too much."

The weight of his final phrase made her guard immediately fall. Monica tilted her head away, not wanting to let her brother see the doubt creeping across her features. Monroe had never been good at talking about his problems. If he had one, he dealt with it alone. Or, more often still, he ignored it, as if describing it aloud would somehow breathe life into his troubles, and if they stayed silent, they stayed dead.

Of them, Monica had always thought that *he* was the strong one; carrying not only his own burdens, but demanding hers whenever she had one, too. No matter what was troubling him, he always made Monica feel like she had no reason to worry. So, to see him not only scared, but admitting it, meant this was serious. And if he was asking for help, it meant that he'd lost hope of solving this on his own.

It was Monica's turn to be the strong one, to be the fixer, to be the protector. She wasn't sure she knew how to be *any* of those things, but maybe figuring it out would be the first step in atoning for costing Monroe his life in the first place.

Blinking away the mist that began to cloud her eyes, Monica peered up at Monroe and laid an open palm on his large forearm in a gesture of comfort.

"Tell me what happened, Monster," she started gently, hoping that the forgiveness in her tone didn't sound as forced and unnatural as it felt. It had been too long since she'd had to comfort anyone. "It's okay for you to be scared."

His gaze fixed on the spot of white ash between the gap where his boots were planted. His jaw clenched in silent protest, making the veins in his temples pulse twice before it released for him to speak. When his words finally came, they were halting and tenuous, as if he couldn't quite find the right way to say what he was feeling, in addition to fighting the obvious pain that laced each syllable.

"You and I, we faced a lot in Vhenra, *and* Vhalta, but this…" he lifted his eyes briefly to the sky before his gaze flitted to Monica's face for reassurance. "This was nothing like any of that. Perhaps it was worse because I had nothing to prepare me, nothing and no one to rely on except my own instinct. Every time I thought I'd gotten my bearings, new and countless terrors of this realm revealed themselves to me.

"It's torture having to watch everyone else getting devoured, one by one; knowing I'm helpless to do anything about it, and worse still, knowing the inevitability of sharing that fate."

"You won't get eaten, Monroe. I won't let—"

"Shh." Monroe nodded, his eyes glassy with gratitude despite the cold mask of stoicism he still wore. When he continued, his words had become more rigid and detached. His gaze went distant with the effort of trying to get through everything he knew he needed to say. "Just when I'd lost all hope, I met this girl. She was so young… near the same age we were when everything changed. She'd been here awhile. She knew exactly what she needed to do to survive, and she made *me* look like a lost little puppy in the shadow of a wolf."

Monica barely registered the chuckle as it grew in her throat, trying to picture Monroe as anything less than a wolf himself.

There was reverence in his words as he said, "I don't know how it was even possible, but it was like she wasn't afraid of anything. She looked out for me and taught me how to survive, too. She reminded me so much of you…" he paused. His eyes fell, and his voice turned cold. "Her name was Lizzie."

The way he said it, was like the girl's name was somehow the most important part of the story. Instantly, Monica understood.

"What happened?"

"A magpie got her." Monroe paused, his breath now wavering with tears, despite his eyes remaining stoically distant and clear. "And even though she was the one protecting me, it made all of my fears about you being alone come flooding back."

"That's why you reached out? To make sure I was okay?"

"Mostly," he sniffled, followed by a clearing of his throat in an attempt to disguise it. "But it'd be a lie to not acknowledge that I'm also scared of dying, for good. I'm scared of what would happen to you if all of me was gone, forever. I can't stand the thought of you feeling anywhere near as alone as I felt when I came here.

"It came of desperation, my call. I thought that if I could let you know that I was still out there somewhere, even just knowing that could help you."

Despite the lingering softness in her expression, Monica's eyes narrowed in skeptical judgment.

"You liar. You *didn't* lose hope. You knew that if I knew you weren't gone, I'd never settle for merely *knowing* it."

Monroe's mouth curled with a small smile of acknowledgement as he whispered, "I wouldn't have admitted it then, but you're right. Against even the most unforgiving odds, somewhere in the back of my mind, I *did* hope that you might find some miraculous way to bring me back." His smile faded, and in a brief pause, his expression turned remorseful. "It's probably unfair to hope such a thing of you, but I know that if anyone can figure out how to achieve the impossible, it's my stubborn sister."

A half-hearted chuckle bubbled up from Monroe's chest, garnering an echo of the sound from Monica.

"I don't think it's unfair. You know I would've done the same. It's not in my nature to give up, nor yours, even when all the odds are against us."

"Thank you." Monroe shifted to brace his elbows against his thighs as he turned to look at her more fully. "And I'm sorry."

"Sorry?" Monica's brow furrowed in confusion and Monroe lifted his shame-filled eyes to meet her questioning gaze.

"Remember when I said you weren't thinking things through? Well, neither was I. I was desperate, and I didn't wanna lose you, especially for good. But it was also wrong of me to put you in danger by calling you to that island. Just because I had faith that you could get out of it, wasn't an excuse."

"Don't talk like that. I would've done the same."

"I know. We're both too stubborn for our own good."

"Damn right," Monica attempted a small smile.

Monroe's chest collapsed to expel a sigh of what sounded like relief. His head lifted, his eyes floating to the dark, void-like sky overhead. Monica followed his gaze, saying nothing even when it lingered. After a long, quiet moment, she finally dared, "What am I gonna do?"

"We," Monroe reminded without breaking his distant stare.

"We," Monica echoed softly, turning to study his face with such intensity, as if trying to convince herself that he was really real— that, even though he was dead, he wasn't gone, and she wasn't alone.

In studying his face, Monica was forced to see the dark purple semi-circles that had sunken the skin below his pale eyes, eyes whose sparkle of life had dulled dramatically. Though something about them seemed muted, weary, and maybe even a little desperate, Monica gleaned some small, brief comfort in finding that his eyes were the same crystal blue that she remembered.

But that was the only thing about him that looked like she remembered. His cheeks were thin and gaunt, making his features look more angular and mature than when he was alive, It was like everything he'd seen had worn on him. Even his posture was tired. His shoulders, despite their strong, toned appearance, sagged as if loaded with an invisible weight. But she found herself going back to his eyes, which shone with the same cool blue of the cloudless sky that had so often hung over the field in which they'd played in the days before they ever knew that magic existed. At least *something* about him was the same.

Finally, recognizing the changes, Monica knew better than to believe his promises. Even though Monroe wanted to be there for her, wanted to help, his "we" rang hollow. It was just *her*. She had to be the strong one. She had to fix this. But the funny thing was, that didn't make her feel as scared as she should have been. She *wanted* to be strong for him. And more often than not, Monica found that being strong for someone else was a lot easier than being strong for herself.

Feeling Monica studying him, Monroe peered back at her, meeting her troubled gaze with a newly relieved expression. Hope. Even though they had nothing near a solution, his expression told her just how much he believed in her, how much he trusted her. That should have terrified her even more so, but it didn't. Her mind was tempted by the dread of what would happen if she wasn't strong enough, if she couldn't save him, but she couldn't hear any of those dark thoughts beyond the hope in his eyes. Fear was no longer an option, nor was failure.

Suddenly, a word pulled her mind, urging her to speak. It was a word that had once made her horrified of her own uncertainty, but in the same breath, promised how much the person that had spoken it and believed in her. Even more than she had believed in herself. Just like Monroe did now. And that was why she had to be strong.

Their eyes locked and Monica's brow flattened in determination.

"Overcome," she promised softly. "That's what I'm gonna do. I'm gonna find a way to bring you back, no matter what."

Chapter 34

As they walked, the silence beneath Finn and Dahvi's footsteps was stiff and uncomfortable. Or… was it only uncomfortable to Finn? After the first few blocks, he gathered enough courage to sneak a glimpse towards Dahvi, who appeared at ease. His shoulders weren't tight, and his lips wore the tiniest suggestion of a smile. His eyes were distant with thought, only until he caught Finn looking at him.

When their eyes met, the shifter's smile widened slightly, as if in encouragement. Finn's lips parted, eyelids fluttering as he dared to speak, but no sound came.

When Finn remained silent, Dahvi finally asked with a softly playful lilt, "What's wrong? Is this still weird?"

"Weird?" Finn cleared his throat after he choked on the word, turning away to hide the heat now rising in his cheeks. "No?"

The questioning tone of his timid response earned a chuckle from Dahvi.

"You know, it's okay."

"Is it?" Finn dared quietly, letting his shoulders fall to unobscure his face as he peered back in question.

Dahvi's eyebrows rose and he gave a small nod. "I'm not mad. I'm not hurt. But I'm also not buying that you're not interested."

Finn flushed a little too quickly to hide it, prompting Dahvi's grin to widen even further. Finn began to stutter unintelligibly as he reached for a response, but before one could form, the shifter reassured, "You don't have to worry. I'm not going to push anything. But I'm not going to pretend that I don't also enjoy seeing you flustered."

Finn gave an awkward laugh. He rubbed his neck with a nervous hand, trying to will the color to leave his cheeks before he finally squeaked, "Can you blame me? It's not like I've ever had to remain friends before with someone who I *know* likes me…" he paused, his lingering gaze falling noticeably to Dahvi's lips, before he added, "like *that.*"

"Do you?" Dahvi asked, trying to look as innocent as possible, despite the wry twist that remained at the corner of his mouth.

Finn faltered. "Do I what?"

"Like me like that?" Dahvi finished the question so coolly that Finn almost thought he had imagined it. "Because, I'd understand if you didn't. But this reaction," Dahvi paused, his gray-green eyes falling to take in a quick scan of Finn's presence, "makes it seem like this is more about you, than it is about *remaining friends with someone who likes you.*"

Finn swallowed audibly, trying not to sound shaken as he drew in a breath.

The quiet washed back over them as Finn searched wordlessly for a response.

He couldn't deny the way he felt around Dahvi. He knew better than to brush it off as mere friendship, but it was as if processing anything beyond that fact evaded him. Was it because this was his first kiss? Because he'd had so little experience and opportunity to explore all the possibilities of what he liked, what he wanted? Was it the initial guilt of making Dahvi feel the need to change for him? Or was it something else entirely?

Finn's lower lip trembled at the influence of each shallow breath passing through the small part in his lips. Deciding to be merciful, Dahvi finally spoke, freeing Finn from the silent struggle.

"It's okay," he cooed softly, his pace slowing as he turned to look at Finn. "You don't have to answer. I just want you to be as honest with yourself as you were with me last night."

Finn's dark eyes fell with the weight of a new shame. When he spoke again, his voice was no longer afraid, merely soft with apology.

"I'm sorry."

"Why?" Dahvi asked, seeming genuinely curious. "Because you don't like me? Or because you don't want to?"

"Neither," Finn sighed decisively. "I'm sorry for ignoring the obvious. Because you're right. This isn't about you. It's about Monica."

"Monica?" Though there was little surprise revealed in his voice, Dahvi's stride halted so abruptly that Finn tripped over his own feet to avoid absently outpacing him. The question burned bright in the shifter's jade eyes as their gazes aligned, and for the first time today, Finn felt brave again.

He nodded, his chin rising with an instinctual pride that announced he would not apologize for that particular reservation. "I don't want to hurt her."

Dahvi's head tipped quizzically to one side, his brow twisting in perplexity as he considered this.

"I figured that. But why would this," he gestured between them with a single, elegant finger, "hurt her?"

Finn paused to consider this. Maybe he was afraid that finding happiness with someone else would make Monica feel alone again. Maybe it was his desire to help her, and being afraid that *any* distraction would get in the way of that goal.

Either way, the last thing he wanted to do was make her feel like he didn't care.

"Oh." Dahvi's realization of the situation shook Finn from his distant musings with another cautious question. "Does *she* like you?"

Finn shook his head before turning with a slow invitation for Dahvi to join in resuming their pace. "It's not like that. She's very protective of me. She has it in her head that if I get hurt for *any* reason, that it's her fault, because it wouldn't have happened if she had never accidentally brought me here."

"Oh." Dahvi murmured, his eyes lifting with an honest sadness that quickly narrowed into concern. "She thinks I'm going to hurt you?"

"She might. That's the problem because I haven't had the chance to tell her."

"Tell her what?"

Finn's focus lifted, allowing Dahvi to peer into the vulnerable depths of his forcibly open expression. "That *I* don't. I don't think you'll hurt me."

Dahvi's eyes widened with passing surprise before the expression softened and he offered a small smile. Even in the silence, Finn didn't look away. Dahvi's gaze broke from him, lifting towards something off in the distance as they walked.

"You know," he pondered aloud, thoughtfully folding his hands behind him in the small of his back. "I understand her apprehension. After all, you barely know me."

Finn let out a scoff. "As if nightly training for several weeks doesn't count? I've gotten to know you a lot during those. And I mean, I've only known her for a few days longer than I've known you."

"But you've spent a *lot* more time with her. Time enough to get close, for her to feel like she has something to lose if you get hurt." Dahvi paused just long enough for that to sink in before he added, "You're sweet to be mindful of her fears, but they're not your responsibility."

"I know..." Finn gave a reluctant sigh. "I just don't want to hurt her. I don't want to hurt *anybody.*"

"Such a goal is admirable." Dahvi's mouth pressed into a thin line, and something akin to sadness emerged in his eyes. "But at the end of the day, you have to live for *you.* That doesn't mean you should live recklessly or with total disregard for the feelings and wishes of others, but you also shouldn't put off what you want for fear of hurting them. Otherwise, you'll never get to live your own life. So... what *do* you want?"

"What do *I* want?" Finn repeated, the sound of the mere question startling a nervous laugh from within him. His cheeks bloomed with color, and one eyebrow lifted in suggestion as he asked, "You're not just saying that so I'll—"

"No," Dahvi interjected firmly. "I mean, if you decide to take a chance on me, I certainly won't stop you, but... is it really so hard to imagine that *I* want to see you happy, too? Just like you said that *I* shouldn't have to change for anyone, neither should you. Your heart is strong, honest; you should honor what it tells you to do."

"Hmm..." Finn breathed a thoughtful hum of consideration. He barely noticed when his apartment building came into view. His pace slowed, and, without acknowledgement, Dahvi's stalled to match it.

Instead of answering the question, Finn turned back with an apology in his eyes.

"Man, it's like this walk keeps getting shorter and shorter. I can't believe we're here already."

"It's almost like magic, huh?" Dahvi joked, letting his head fall to one side as he studied Finn's reaction. "See how much fun it is, talking with me? Time flies."

Finn forced a breathy laugh, but a subtle, creeping concern still loomed on his brow as the humor abated. The two were quiet as they approached the door of the apartment building. Finn's hand rose to rest on the handle and their eyes met once more.

"Well, good night, I guess," Finn said, his words still laced with something akin to regret.

"Wait." Dahvi called softly, and before Finn could respond, Dahvi's warm hand was cupping the one still hanging at his side. The urgency in his tone softened when their gazes locked again. "Please."

Finn's breath caught, making his face pulse briefly hot against the cool night air before Dahvi released his hand and drew back.

"I'm sorry," Dahvi said, still sounding miraculously cool against the innate alarm of the phrase. "It's not—"

Finn shook his head, peering down at Dahvi's hand as the temptation to retake the hold popped through his mind like fireworks before it sizzled away into demure uncertainty.

"It's okay," he stammered in response, hoping he didn't sound as shaken as even such a simple touch had made him feel. "What's—"

"I just needed to ask…" Dahvi interjected, suddenly sounding just as nervous himself. It wasn't like Dahvi for the cool, charming, unconcerned shifter that he was to falter at the suggestion of attraction, but Finn found it endearing.

Everything about Dahvi's current expression was endearing, from the tremble of his lower lip to the anticipation in his curious, seeking eyes, and even the faintest hue of pink Finn almost missed, that danced across his cheeks.

"What?" Finn encouraged softly.

Dahvi looked away, cleared his throat, and straightened himself. And, when he looked back again, he was as cool as ever, his question sounding more detached than the true meaning it held within.

"You never responded when I said that you should honor what your heart is telling you to do… so, what *is* your heart telling you to do?"

Finn's gaze fell, and his eyes darkened as his thoughts retreated inwardly. The curve dissolved from his mouth, and for a moment, Dahvi worried that Finn had found the question upsetting.

When Finn hesitated, Dahvi added, "You don't *have* to tell me. I'm only curious."

Finn's head lifted, and he forced a flat smile. "It's just that… my heart's telling me to do something… really stupid. Actually, it's been telling me to do several stupid things lately."

Dahvi's expression was quizzical, but his response was hesitant to avoid seeming too persistent.

"Like what?" He finally asked, inching towards Finn with movements so slight that he almost didn't notice the distance closing between them.

Finn's dark eyes sparkled with a mix of emotions that was too muddy to discern, that gave his face a strange air of guardedness when he peered up at Dahvi. But then, just as quickly, his features softened when he whispered, "Well, for one, it's been telling me, all night, how much I want to try again."

Finn winced shyly, bracing for Dahvi's surprise, which passed far more quickly than he anticipated, shifting only into something that looked to be akin to relief.

"Try again? You mean, the kiss?" When Finn forced an embarrassed nod, Dahvi added gently, "I thought you didn't like guys."

“I thought I didn’t either. But I like you.” Finn’s chin dipped as he succumbed to a sudden sadness with his own reply. “I just don’t think now’s the right time.”

Dahvi paused, his brow furrowing as he sensed the weight of something more. “And… you don’t think there will *ever* be a right time, is that it?”

Finn sighed and gave a half-hearted shrug. “Maybe. If I take your advice to live my own life and listen to what my heart is telling me, I’m afraid there won’t be.”

“Why not?”

“That’s… The other stupid thing.”

“What is it?”

Finn’s jaw clenched. His hand tightened around the doorknob and he turned his back to Dahvi.

“You can’t say. That’s okay. Everybody’s allowed to have their secrets.”

“Thank you…” Finn murmured into his shoulder as he only half glanced back towards Dahvi. “...for understanding.”

Before he could turn away to slip inside, Dahvi’s clear call cut through the chilled night air.

“Wait,” Finn’s attention lifted to take in the newly serious expression that had crossed Dahvi’s facade. “Can I come in for a bit?”

For a moment, Finn's whole body tensed. He didn't realize how his grip now strangled the handle of the door as he turned back to look over his shoulder.

"Why?" He almost couldn't hear the softness of his own voice above the sudden and intense drumming of his heart.

But as Dahvi's lips parted to answer, he paused. His brow caved, as if in concern, and something about his expression suddenly looked so serious. Startlingly serious. In fact, not even a fraction of the flirtatious sparkle that usually permeated his features remained.

It wasn't like Dahvi to be speechless.

Something about this silence was different… less thoughtful, or even awkwardly charming. Instead, it seemed grave, and almost unnerved.

Finn’s ears piqued at the sound when the tiniest breath hitched in Dahvi's throat. Dahvi lowered his head, looking almost as if he was trying to peer up at Finn, despite the impossibility created by the vast difference in height. His eyes turned pleading; something about them seemed almost afraid.

"It’s not what you think. To be honest," Dahvi began softly, looking almost ashamed of his words. "I need your help. Can we talk, in private?"

In a moment of pause, Finn lifted his dark eyes to scan the quiet neighborhood, seeing not a soul around them.

“Is this not private enough?”

“Please?” Dahvi asked again, shaking his head. Just from the tone of that one word, Finn saw the seriousness of what was on Dahvi’s mind.

Finn's answer came as a tentative, wordless nod. He pushed open the door of the apartment building with his back, pressing himself up against the glass so that Dahvi could sidle in past him.

He hoped his agreement would bring Dahvi *some* relief, but all he saw when his eyes skimmed past was worry. He hoped that, whatever was troubling Dahvi, he could help. After all, that's all Finn had ever wanted to do was help.

Chapter 35

It was far harder for Monica to leave Monroe this time, even though she knew she had to. Perhaps she had taken the magpie's "help" in chasing her out for granted. At least, it was a challenge that was eased by the new swell of determination that rose in her chest. It sparked in her brain, the sensation of new ideas, dangling just out of reach. There had to be *something*, some obvious solution she was overlooking. And she *would* find it. This time would be different. This time, she wasn't alone.

Hours had passed easily in her absence. What had only felt like one in Enderfel had proven to be several in Vhalta. Arkynesta was quiet, glittering against a screen of silken nightfall. Monica was grateful to be back under a familiar sky. Despite its midnight black, this expanse was soothing rather than haunting, its faint light so different from the flat void of Enderfel's sky that it seemed to shimmer like a tapestry of velvet overlaid with glittering tulle.

Monica shook herself from the grateful trance to survey the buildings around her. Gulfport. She was getting better at using the multiple realm keys in tandem, because this return had managed to bring her less than a block from her apartment building.

Barely aware of the shift, her mind pivoted to thoughts of Finn.

Dismayed realization fueled her haste when she remembered her promise to him. They were supposed to talk. Something had happened. She'd been too wrapped up in her own problems to even give him a shred of her attention. Her throat burned with guilt as she ran, letting her feet carry her as her mind fixed on him.

It was suddenly easy to focus on him, now that worries of Monroe had been cleared from the forefront of her mind. Though her brother still lingered in a dangerous space, she felt better having seen him again, not to mention, better after gaining the understanding of his uncharacteristically rash reactions. Things made sense again.

The chill of night air dissolved from around Monica as she slipped into the apartment building. Mere heartbeats later, she was unlatching the door, unaware that she was holding her breath as she tried to remain quiet.

It was dark inside, with no signs of life as there had been last night. A small pang of sadness squeezed her heart in realizing that Finn hadn't waited for her tonight. Maybe it was selfish to have hoped he would, especially after bailing on him again, with no explanation. Only this time, she'd broken his trust by not keeping her promise to talk. She'd been numb to his insistence this morning but looking back on the memory only made her hyper-aware of the sparkle of desperation in his pleading eyes. Was he mad? Or had something happened?

Without warning, her mind flooded with worry. She pushed it aside, certain that it was merely an overreaction triggered by guilt. He was just asleep, that's all. She tried to convince herself that whatever had been on his mind before was nothing serious, but now, she couldn't fully shake a sinking feeling that warned her otherwise. She knew better than to ignore her instincts. Even if the denial was comforting, at least subconsciously, she knew what those instincts were telling her.

The door closed softly behind her in the darkness, and the light flicked on just in time to catch a large, slender figure springing up off the couch.

In a split second of instinct, Monica's dagger was drawn and her shoulders had inflated with defensive tension as she pivoted to face the intruder.

Mid-lunge, Monica was stopped by a familiar voice crying, "Wait!"

"Dahvi?" His name came out as barely more than a gasp beneath the weight of Monica's surprise. She drew back, blinking as she tried to process his unexpected presence. Her arm cautiously fell, but she still gripped her dagger with suspicious anticipation.

His expression was steeped in a symphony of emotion that sang with far more notes than simple fear and surprise. It was the kind of look of someone tormented, mulling over their fears and regrets at length. Despite trying to steel herself against the urge to read into it, the look made Monica's throat tighten with ominous certainty.

"What are you doing here?" Her voice fell, teeth remaining unconsciously clenched as she tried to relax her posture. Her hand throbbed from the tightness of its grip around her dagger, refusing to return it to its sheath until she had answers.

"I can explain," Dahvi insisted, his palms lifted towards her in a pleading gesture.

"Then explain."

When Dahvi said nothing, Monica's scowl sharpened at the expectant silence. Dahvi wasn't one she would've expected to see so unnerved, especially after his cool interactions with Maal, who was likely the most intimidating being she knew. This made her even more viscerally suspicious that something was wrong.

Dahvi swallowed nervously as he shifted on his feet. Monica glanced down. *Feet.* Not hooves. Dahvi's current iteration was fully human, which she could justify as either respect for or necessity of the relatively small apartment.

After her eyes returned to stare fixedly at his face again, he finally spoke, spitting the words out as if he was now desperate to be rid of them.

"We need to talk."

Monica wasn't about to let him, *an intruder*, control the conversation. No. She needed to feel in charge. This was her space, after all. Whatever he wanted to say, it would wait until the questions *she* chose were answered.

"Why are you in my apartment?" She began, the accusation of her words growing sharper with each additional question. "Alone? In the dark? How did you even get in here?"

He almost didn't react. But Monica saw a glint of softness in his eyes that sparked the start of a revelation in her mind. A pulse of clammy dread traveled through Monica's limbs in a sudden throb as she realized the answer to her question.

"Finn." They both said, Dahvi in gentle confirmation and her, in realization.

Suddenly, without effort, things made sense. Things that she had been too preoccupied and self-absorbed to see. Her mind laid it all out in front of her like a spread of artifacts for inspection. Her mind's eye flitted quickly across a slideshow of events from the last few weeks, stringing together the clues. Even after Dahvi's suggestive banter upon their first meeting had made Finn so uncomfortable, he had warmed up to Dahvi in a way that Monica hadn't —not that she had wanted to.

But it was more than just that. Finn and Dahvi were *friends* now. She'd seen it in Finn's reaction upon seeing Dahvi waiting for them at Maal's tower. Excitement. Fondness. It made her gut knot with an unexpected twinge of jealousy.

Finn was allowed to have other friends. It was stupid to think otherwise, especially since she'd only known him for a few weeks. But then again, Finn *had* admitted that he hadn't had another close friend since his *best* friend died. Neither had she, since losing her brother. She hadn't wanted to acknowledge it before, but now it was clear as day. All of her feelings, her uncertainty, thinking that she *liked* him; it was because *she* wanted to be Finn's best friend. And all she had done in the last few days was push him away. *Stupid.* Had she lost that chance?

This thought was the springboard for another, one she would've rather ignored, but it was too late for that. Dahvi had been there when she had run off. When she had left Finn alone, probably angry, or at least hurt, Dahvi was there. The realization not only hurt her but made her angry. It was making too much sense why he was here now, and she hated that. She hated the guilt it made her feel, for not being there, for not being good enough, for wanting to be his friend so badly that it scared her back into her old ways of guarded evasion and self-absorption.

Monica was forced to see this when she looked up and saw the melancholy care in Dahvi's eyes. And, beyond that, it forced her to see that his presence here meant that something was wrong.

Even now that it was staring her in the face, she didn't want to believe it. Monica's head first swiveled around in obvious search.

"Where *is* Finn?" She asked, her voice tight and level as she choked down the panic that was already roiling in her gut.

"He's not here," Dahvi responded with equal rigidity.

"What?" Monica questioned, her focus snapping back to his face with such severe intensity, her eyes seemed to hold a flicker of destructive magic. "Then why are you?"

"*We* need to talk." He repeated, this time, his tone dark with warning.

Monica held her breath, her eyes glassy as she held her stare against the sting that rose behind them.

"Where is he?" she demanded, each word punctuated with the confrontation of quiet wrath.

After a long silence, Dahvi swallowed softly and gathered his words. His eyes never broke from hers, bearing the excruciating weight of her death-glare as he finally admitted, "I needed his help."

His voice was level, but his eyes were teary beneath a brow sinking with shame.

"Where is he?" she repeated, her voice rising with rage. She barely noticed her dagger arm floating upwards until the flat of her blade cast a silver glint in her periphery.

"Put the knife down, so that I can speak." Dahvi bargained, only to be cut off by another bark from Monica.

"No! Tell me where he is, *now!* And then *I* decide if you can speak."

A muscle in Dahvi's jaw feathered as he grit his teeth, an expression that revealed he was all too aware of how Monica was going to take his answer.

"He's… on his way to a ship off the coast of Arkynesta."

"What?" Monica barked. "What in the seven realms did you do?"

"*He* did it, to help me." Dahvi deflected, trying his best to sound calm in the shadow of Monica's growing fury.

"Did what? And how does that help you?"

"It was a trade. Finn for my family."

Monica's stomach dropped. Her vision blurred, eyes stinging as they filled with what might as well have been acid instead of tears. She drew in a sharp breath through bared teeth, trying to steady herself enough to at least get the information needed to help him before she let her rage take over.

“Tell me you’re lying.”

“I wish I could.”

"Who—?" Before Dahvi could even answer, the look in his eyes told Monica all she needed to know, and a cannonball of understanding struck Monica squarely in the stomach. She felt immediately sick, wanting so badly to ignore the inevitable next question, but she couldn't. "The Enclave?"

Dahvi barely nodded, fear bright in his eyes that cut through his remorse as he focused on Monica's still-poised dagger.

"How could you do this?" Monica trembled, her voice barely more than a whisper.

"I didn't have a choice," Dahvi said shamefully. "Wouldn't you have done the same, if it meant saving your family’s lives?"

For a moment, Monica paused to consider this. As she did, she let her arm slowly begin to fall, flexing her fingers around its hilt to relieve some of the tension of her grip. Would she have done the same? It didn’t matter now because she’d never have that choice. It was *not* the same.

“You can’t trust them!” She finally shot back, fists clenched at her sides. Despite the venom returning to her tone, Dahvi relaxed after a brief acknowledgement that her aggressive stance had eased, even slightly. “You really believe that The Enclave will keep their word and let your family go just because you did what they wanted?"

"No." Dahvi scoffed. "Of course not. That's why I went to Maal. I knew that with his power, there'd still be a chance to get them back alive. So, in exchange for working with him, for working with *you*, Maal promised me he'd make sure that The Enclave kept their end of the bargain, since I had no choice but to keep mine."

"Maal knew?" The realization bloomed from deep with Monica's chest, a growl of something wild and wounded.

Immediately, Dahvi's eyes widened, realizing his misstep. He began shaking his head, glancing around in desperate pursuit of the thought that would get him out of this, but they all evaded him.

"Maal *knew?"* Monica demanded again, the power of her voice rising to a near scream, fueled by tears of welling betrayal. "He *knew* that you were going to give Finn to The Enclave?!"

"Only temporarily—"

"It doesn't matter!" Monica fumed, blinking rapidly to clear her vision as the tears began to spill down her face, streaking her pale porcelain cheeks with the bright crimson of agony. "*You've* put him in danger. And Maal allowed it, didn't he? Answer me!"

Faced with defeat, Dahvi gave a shallow, tremulous exhale, followed by an apologetic, "Yes."

Dahvi's muscles tensed, his eyes squeezing closed as he braced for an attack that never came. Instead, when he lifted his eyes to Monica, he only saw her clenching and unclenching her fingers from around the hilt of her dagger, making it twist in her hand with each cycle of the movement.

Monica gave a bitter scoff and a dismissive shake of her head. She smeared the tears from her cheeks with the backs of her still-clenched fists, letting them fall to reveal an expression of pure contempt. Her eyes lowered to the floor as she processed the information. She didn't look surprised by this new development. Disgusted, enraged, but not surprised. After all, she knew. It was only a matter of time until Maal betrayed her, too. Everyone always did. She hated that her fears had been right, and more so that she had let Celene almost talk her out of them. Was Celene in on all of this too? She wouldn't put it past Maal. After all, he was the one that brought the siren here.

He was *always* the one in control. Of course he knew that this was going to happen. Then, in fleeting wonder, Monica realized why he was suddenly so unconcerned by her inability to use the eye to locate Rowan. *Other options*, he had said. The eye may have been the original plan, but how easily plans can change.

Her stomach churned at how much sense this was all making— *too much.*

Maal was forcing her to find Rowan by playing into the wielder's hand. When he realized that Rowan wanted *her*, Maal saw an opportunity. Because if Rowan knew as much about Monica as he claimed to know, Rowan would have also known that taking Finn would force her to come straight to him.

And Maal knew that, too. He knew that there was no way Monica would have agreed to this willingly. He *knew* that she cared for Finn, and still, he did this anyway. In fact, wasn't it Maal who had convinced her that maybe keeping Finn around would be useful so that she would have something to protect? Maal *knew* that after what happened to her brother, she would do anything not to go through that again. She would do anything to protect Finn, including throwing herself into enemy territory to save him.

So he and Dahvi went behind her back to make it happen. Was there no one left she could trust?

Chapter 36

"Did Finn know?" Monica growled, her tone more controlled now despite the lingering edge of bitterness.

Dahvi's eyes widened, his head tilting in clear indication that, of all the turns he had expected this confrontation to take, this question wasn't among those he'd prepared answers for.

"Know what?" He began cautiously, the question measured as he strove to match Monica's newly guarded demeanor.

"That he was being traded to The Enclave?"

It was unsettling to hear such a question spoken so coldly and without pause. It was suddenly like Monica was deaf to the content of her own words, so driven by her goal that she wasn't allowing herself to focus on the reality of the implications. It was almost like, to her, this interaction itself could be a trap.

Dahvi understood her caution. After all, she barely trusted him before. What reason did she have to believe anything he could say other than the mere promise of getting her friend back?

Dahvi finally shook his head. "No. All he knew was that I needed help in order to save my family. He consented without much explanation. Then, when he finally *did* ask for specifics, the magic took hold."

"Magic?" Monica repeated, panic returning to her question. "What magic?"

"Just a sleeping potion, so he couldn't struggle or see where he was being taken. He'll be fine."

"Will he? Because if he's with The Enclave, he's with Rowan now, too, and you *must* know what that evil snake is capable of!"

"He'll be fine," Dahvi repeated, and his calm certainty made Monica draw back.

Her brow furrowed. And then, she remembered.

"He's not the one Rowan wants." Dahvi hummed a wordless confirmation that earned an equally angry glare from Monica.

"That doesn't mean they won't still hurt him."

Dahvi paled, looking dismayed at the thought, or perhaps, the fact that he agreed with her. He didn't dispute it. In fact, that's when he said, "That's part of why I want to help you."

"What?" Monica's glare narrowed into a squint as she studied the shifter's face even more closely, as if scrutinizing for fault or falsehood. "After what you did, you want to help?"

"Why else would I have stayed? I didn't have to, you know. My trade never involved you. Just Finn. They knew he wouldn't be hard to convince, with the right circumstances. In fact, they wanted me to leave after they took him, and let you stew, not knowing what happened to him until you figured it out on your own."

Monica's head cocked to one side and her squint intensified. "But that doesn't make any sense. Rowan wants *me*."

Dahvi shrugged, a movement that claimed ignorance. “Would you really put it past him to want to torture you in the process?”

“I mean… no.” Monica shook off her surprise, stiffening as she demanded, “But it’s not like him to be patient. In fact, I don’t understand why he even waited *this* long. You've been here the whole time. Why wouldn't The Enclave just have you drug me and kidnap me at the first opportunity?"

At this, Dahvi’s expression darkened with the smallest tinge of offense, before seeming to think better of his right to be offended after his recent crime.

“I want you to know,” Dahvi began, “I haven’t been blackmailed this whole time. When I first met you and Finn, I had no idea who you were or what you were involved in. It was only after I’d been spotted with him the first week of training that a member of The Enclave approached me with the threat. The reason I had to wait was because, in Arkynesta, you're still under Maal's protection, both of you. Because of that, you’d have to go willingly. That was limiting to Rowan’s opinions."

"So he made you get close to Finn and take advantage of him in order to get him to agree blindly, because he thought he was helping out a friend?"

“Don’t say it like that.”

“But it’s true, isn’t it?” Monica shot back furiously, making Dahvi shrink back when she followed with, “Are you his friend at all?”

"Yes," Dahvi answered emphatically with tears in his eyes. "I am. I didn't want to do this. Even with Maal's help, I truly saw no other way. I care about Finn. I don't want to see him get hurt."

"Cut the crap," Monica snapped. “If you *really* cared, you would *not* have done this. You would have told me what was going on first, and then we would've found a way around it."

"Oh, really? And what would you have done? You would have said it was too dangerous to go in by yourself, without a plan. You would have stayed as far away from Rowan as you could have, for as long as you could have."

"I could have gone to Maal, told him where Rowan is."

"You think Rowan would be stupid enough to tell *me* that? It's not like I know *where* he is. I only give the signal."

"The signal? For what? For us to be put to sleep and whisked away to this *mysterious ship*?" Dahvi nodded, and Monica turned away in clear derision. "That's ridiculous."

"I know. But that doesn't make it any less true. I was sent to do a job. He knew there was no way I could trick you into going with me. It had to be Finn. You would only go willingly as long as they already had him because you would do anything for him. Like I wish I could…"

"You wish? Then why didn't you?"

Dahvi's tone sharpened. "Sacrifice my family for him? That's the one thing I couldn't do. And I thought that you, of all people, would understand that."

"Don't you *dare* pretend to know me. This is *nothing* like what I've been through."

"You're right," Dahvi sniffed. "This *isn't* like what you went through because *I* actually have a chance to save mine. Even though you weren't offered such a mercy, you cannot tell me that you'd be so quick to reject it if you had, no matter how much the exchange would have cost."

Monica's gaze turned glassy and distant as she paused to consider Dahvi's plea. In the silence, her lower lip began to quiver, and sympathy shone from within the cracks of her stoic mask. Her eyes evaded the shifter's as he sought her focus, as if looking at him would force her to admit that he was right.

After a moment, she bit her lip and her expression sobered with the pain. She drew in a staggered breath, and when her eyes lifted again, they were cold once more.

"I don't care anymore," she declared, crossing her arms. "You messed up. I don't trust you. But, if you want to help me, I'm not in any place to turn that down. What can you do for me?"

"I can get you to where Finn is, the same way he went. With this."

Dahvi's chin fell as he produced a thin, glass vial, barely the length of his palm, from inside the small leather satchel that hung at his waist. Inside, it shimmered with a transparent gray-blue liquid that swirled with glitter, making it look like a tiny tube of dusky nightfall.

His fingers uncurled, offering the vial to Monica on a flat hand.

"A sleeping potion?"

Dahvi nodded, and Monica reached for it without thinking, only stopping seconds before her fingertips would have touched the glass. Instead, she drew back, crossing her arms. Her nostrils flared as she drew in a long, irritated breath. She rolled her eyes inwardly, apparently annoyed with herself for the initial, and dangerously hasty impulse.

Monica cleared her throat, and her body language shifted to that of a seasoned negotiator. Her voice was rigid with practiced care as she began, as if the questions would grant her a coveted advantage over the countless unknowns of her impending mission.

"How long does it take to go into effect?"

"Based on Finn's experience, about fifteen minutes."

"And how long does it last?"

"Well, I'm no potions expert, but I was warned not to delay the signal once it has been administered. So, I'd guess not more than an hour or two."

Monica's eyes narrowed, and she grit her teeth at Dahvi's attempt at encouragement.

"I still don't like it. Giving myself over to The Enclave, unconscious and vulnerable, especially with all of my artifacts on my person, may be one of the worst ideas I've ever heard. Besides, if they were only planning for you to use this on Finn, how can you be sure they'll even come if you call again?"

"Trust me, Monica. If I call them to come get *you*, do you really think Rowan's men are going to even question it, let alone turn me down?"

"No, you're right." She sighed in irritation, her fingers now itching to reach for the vial and get this over with. So instead, she pulled her arms even tighter to her chest, biding her patience as she dug for a few last questions. "I suppose that *this* is exactly what they wanted from the beginning, even if they didn't tell you that."

Dahvi looked away in wordless agreement, guilty that he either hadn't thought this through, or had wanted to remain dumb to the thought entirely.

Monica said nothing, but there was a clear and sudden shift in her posture that communicated a new reassurance with the emergence of another option.

Intrigued, Dahvi cautiously lifted his head. Looking her up and down, he ventured, "You have an idea, don't you?"

Though her response was coy, the glint in her eye confirmed it. "Perhaps."

"What are you thinking?"

Without warning, Monica snatched the tiny tube of glittering liquid from Dahvi's outstretched hand, raising it between pinched fingers for closer inspection.

"I'm thinking that you're going to help me give Rowan *exactly* what he wants. How long does it take for them to get here after you give the signal?"

"With Finn, they were here within twenty minutes."

"Then they're close." Monica sighed, her focus narrowing to the vial pinched between her fingers. She drew in a sharp breath, as if to steady herself. "And we'll have to be fast."

"Are you really going to—" Dahvi began, stopping to watch in disbelief as Monica uncorked the vial, tossed the stopper aside and emptied its shimmering contents into her mouth.

Even though Monica hadn't revealed her new idea aloud, Dahvi certainly wouldn't have planned on her being so willing to simply accept the path that fate had handed her, especially not one that was so vulnerable and likely damning as this one.

In a blur of movement, Monica lunged at Dahvi, so swiftly and without warning, that he didn't have time to react before her mouth was on his. Her eyes, now cold with determination, never broke from his as a warm burst of citrusy-sweet liquid gushed through the narrow part in his lips.

The mouthful of potion involuntarily seeped down Dahvi's throat upon trying to breathe. He pulled away, coughing and gasping, and it took him several seconds before he was able to speak again.

"Monica, what in the *seven realms* did you just do?" He sputtered, wiping his mouth on his sleeve.

"Now you *have* to help me." She smirked, taking vindictive pleasure in what she'd just done.

"I was already going to!"

"But now you have to do it my way."

"You couldn't have just told me what the plan was first?"

"And waste precious time listening to you go through all the reasons why it might not work? No. We do this now, and we do it my way, got it?"

Dahvi nodded with uncertainty, still trying to gather himself against the shock of her uncharacteristic advance.

“You know, if you wanted to kiss me that badly, you could’ve just said so.”

Monica shot Dahvi a thoroughly unamused glare. “Now’s not the time.”

A twinge of humor tickled Dahvi’s brain, but, seeing the absolute coldness in Monica’s facade made the next quip he had prepared, *If not now, then when,* melt away into a more serious response.

But it wasn’t the response Monica had been expecting.

“What about Celene?”

Monica’s eyes widened in a level of shock that betrayed her. She hadn’t told anyone about her recent… *closeness* with Celene, and it certainly wasn’t anyone else’s business. Her surprise flared into indignation. She wouldn’t have expected Celene to tell, but there was no other way for Dahvi to know that.

Monica managed to school her features before she growled, “What *about* Celene?”

The last thing Monica was in the mood for was a lecture from this shifter that she barely knew, or worse, for him to attach meaning to Monica’s actions where there were none and use it to gloat beyond his initial joke.

But she got neither of these things. Instead, looking genuinely perplexed and a little concerned, Dahvi asked, “Don’t you think we should include her in *whatever* it is we’re about to do?”

The tension immediately left Monica's body, which she was sure was obvious by the sudden slump of her shoulders, but she didn't care. Returning to her state of practiced aloofness, Monica hissed, "No. There's no time."

Dahvi looked unconvinced but didn't argue. He was silent for a long moment before he dared to ask, "What is it that we're going to do, exactly?"

"You're gonna call Rowan's goons to come get me."

"But you didn't—" Dahvi's objection was interrupted as Monica grabbed his left hand and jammed her tiger's eye ring onto his thumb with a swift and forceful gesture. Dahvi cried out as the silver band bit into the width of his finger, which involuntarily shifted to accommodate a more dainty circumference. "What are you—"

"Shut up!" Monica commanded, stripping both her cardigan and shirt over her head with a hasty shrug before she threw the wadded ball of fabric at his face. "Put this on. And don't look at me till I say so."

"Why do I—"

"Just do it." Monica said, just before her boots landed on the floor between them with two heavy thumps.

Dahvi turned one shoulder towards Monica, trying to ignore the movement of her undressing in his periphery while he replaced his own shirt with hers. The fabric pulled snug around his shoulders, forcing his body to shift into a more slender form to accommodate the garment, which then slipped easily down over a newly narrow, boyish chest. No sooner was this done, and he stooped forwards to find Monica's jeans in a rumpled pile at his feet.

His lips parted with a second dissent, only to notice that Monica's presence had disappeared from beside him.

Sighing, Dahvi let his own pants fall easily from his body, stepping out with a pair of gracefully petite changed legs. He shimmied into the jeans, letting his form meld to perfectly accommodate their shapely seams. The bite of the zipper coming together momentarily broke the silence.

"The boots too!" Monica's voice called distantly from down the hall.

"You know, I can mimic clothing just fine with my abilities. I don't need to wear yours."

"Just do it!" Monica repeated, her tone even more annoyed.

Resigned to his fate, Dahvi fought off a yawn as he stepped into each boot with a *clonk.*

Monica reemerged, wearing a strikingly similar black t-shirt and jeans to those she had just made Dahvi change into, paired with a semi-worn pair of dark ankle boots and a button-down sweater with a navy to cerulean gradient knit. Seeing this, Dahvi's expression twisted with irritation as he gestured at her, before motioning at the clothes that now adorned his shifted body.

"This wasn't necessary, you know," he hissed, gesturing at his new outfit. "You could have just used your words to tell me that you wanted me to shift into you. I would've been able to copy the clothes, too."

"Oh really?" Monica challenged, an eyebrow raised as if she knew something that Dahvi didn't. "What about this?"

She lunged at him with hands outstretched, pulling a leather strap tight around his right thigh before he could pull away.

Dahvi had stopped fighting once the dagger was holstered snuggly in place, stammering a reluctant, "N-no. I can only conjure the appearance of fabrics, but not jewelry or accessories."

"Uh-huh." Monica scoffed sarcastically, her brows jumping as if to say, *that's what I thought,* even though there was no way she could've known such a thing about Dahvi's abilities. It's not like she'd ever known another shapeshifter before.

Then, Monica's expression sobered with a solemn reverence and she bowed her head, removing the two amulets that hung around her neck. "So not these either, then?"

Dahvi shook his head. "Even if I could, they'd only be for show. And, even then, they'd vanish the moment they were taken off my body."

"That's what I was afraid of." Monica said knowingly before reaching up to string both amulets around Dahvi's neck. "I wish I didn't have to do this, but they *have* to believe that you're me. And, since Rowan's been watching me, I can't chance leaving any of my valuables behind. The tiniest missing detail could tip him off."

"Oh." Suddenly, Dahvi understood. "That's why you insisted on the *exact* clothes. You know he's going to take these, though, right?"

"Yes." Monica sighed heavily. "I'm counting on it. It'll be what really sells the illusion."

"Hey!" Dahvi's brows knitted in offense. "I wouldn't be here if my shapeshifting couldn't sell itself, thank you *very* much."

Monica rolled her eyes. "You know what I mean. He *has* to believe that you're me. It's our only chance. *Finn's* only chance."

Dahvi's expression immediately changed, his offense becoming awash beneath a sudden wave of shame, and he nodded his reluctant agreement.

Monica matched his sullen silence, her eyes falling as if she was suddenly pained by her thoughts. But then, she drew in a sharp breath, steeling herself before she locked eyes with Dahvi with renewed determination.

"Finish the job."

A sheen of sympathy mirrored in Dahvi's eyes as he let their green pale to icy blue, the rest of his features gradually morphing to follow. The half-crown of braids in his silvery-white hair unfurled into waves, morphing into an inky black that started at his scalp and dripped down, until every strand gleamed the color of the midnight sky.

Their gazes aligned as Dahvi's height shrank to bring him down to Monica's level. He studied her face, making small adjustments until both his features and body were a perfect reflection of hers.

Monica's jaw set as she stared, a sheen of tears welling in her eyes. They seemed to turn to steam as they hit the air, as if Monica was somehow able to refuse to let them fall. The twist of contempt that snuck onto her brow as she stared at the near perfect replica of herself was not lost on Dahvi.

"How's this?" He asked cautiously in her voice.

"Fine." She snarled, her tone cold once more. "You can hold this shape asleep?"

Dahvi nodded, making ebony waves dance around his newly delicate jawline. "The effort is all in the shift itself. Once the form is solid, maintaining it is easy. Does everything look… correct?"

Monica's stare didn't shift to look him over. Instead, she remained frozen for a long moment, seeming to meditate on her anger. Then, nodding, it eased. She exhaled sharply through her nose before one hand rose to gather her hair off of her neck. She turned her back briefly to Dahvi to show Maal's star, inked at the base of her neck.

"Don't forget this." She paused, giving him a moment to memorize the design before she turned back. "Or this."

Her middle finger swiped down along the right side of her face, pulling back the loose wave that usually framed her forehead, before tucking it behind her ear. Between her temple and her hairline sat a small scar that would've been unnoticeable if Dahvi hadn't been actively looking for it. The scar was made up of three, thin white lines, only a few shades lighter than her ivory skin. The lines were raised in the shape of an upended triangle, the shape no larger than the nail of her little finger.

Dahvi's heart almost stopped. Though he'd only encountered the mark once before, he knew what it meant with unshakable certainty.

"Monica…" he murmured softly, his voice tinged with a concern that only made her pull back. "What is that?"

"None of your business," she tugged at the tucked hair to make it fall again to cover the mark. "Just copy it, okay?"

Dahvi swallowed, his breaths suddenly shallow with sadness in realizing that she didn't understand. He did as she said, pulling back the equivalent strand of hair so that she could watch the scar shifting into existence. She seemed to ease a little once it was done. But, knowing what he did, Dahvi felt the new weight of responsibility tugging at his conscience, and knew he couldn't let her ignore it.

"Do you know what that is?" He asked again, pointing at the scar's replica and struggling to make her believe that his concern was genuine. She was quiet, her eyes dark with mistrust. When she didn't answer, he continued solemnly, "Because I do."

She flinched in surprise, only allowing a flash of emotion to cross her face before her skilled composure returned.

"No, you don't." Contempt dripped from Monica's almost *command.*

"I do." His whisper made the pale reflection of her eyes sparkle as he studied her from behind her own face. "Memory magic. Someone tampered with your mind. I only know because the same was once done to my little sister.

They… made her forget the terrible things she once saw when a battle broke out in our village, because no little girl should have to grow up seeing so much blood so early. But you…" He paused, gingerly reaching towards Monica's brow with the tip of an extended index finger, but stopped when she cowered away, before ever touching her. "What did they take from you?"

Monica stiffened, realizing her weak and frightened posture. The corners of her mouth sagged into a scowl and she inclined her chin with stubborn pride. Though her reaction was austere and angry, a flicker of fear sparked in her eyes.

"We don't have time for this now. Send the signal and tell me where to wait."

Dahvi nodded, fighting against eyelids now drooping with the increasing weight of onset slumber.

Chapter 37

Disorientation pounced the second Finn opened his eyes. His head spun as he tried to focus, allowing him only brief glimpses of the small, unfamiliar room that now encircled him. The illusion of motion made his fingers claw at the bed beneath him as he grappled for his bearings. After what felt like several minutes, his swimming vision finally stilled enough to focus, but made his stomach flip when he tried to lock onto the door on the opposite wall.

Sensing the futility of it, Finn squeezed his eyes closed again, taking in a few deep breaths as the cool blackness of his eyelids stopped the spinning of the world around him. On his inhale, he noticed that the air was warm and tasted of sea spray and dust, familiar things that grounded him to that moment.

When he opened his eyes again, he let out a shallow sigh of relief to find that the room was finally stationary. This prompted him to sit up, and a little too quickly, because the motion sent a wave of pounding pressure shooting into his skull. He winced, closing his eyes again just long enough for the effects of the initial movement to pass.

The pressure remained as he glanced around, exacerbating the sick feeling that still churned in his stomach. But he was finally stable enough to process his surroundings.

The room was small with wooden walls, simple furniture, and only one window. He wouldn't have noticed the window, which was almost entirely covered by a tall, narrow bookcase, were it not for the occasional but undeniable drafts of sea air, and the needle-width stripe of cool, watery sunlight that slanted across the floor.

Simple though it was, the space was not without its comforts. Across the room sat a pair of high-backed chairs upholstered in well-worn leather that were angled around a small table, atop which sat a dimly flickering lantern.

Though the room was not unfriendly, it also wasn't the least bit familiar.

Finn's eyes went wide as the panic set in.

Where am I? He quietly wondered, suddenly finding it hard to breathe. Abandoning his study of the room, Finn instead turned his focus inwards as he tried to remember the last things that Dahvi had said to him. *I need your help. My family is in trouble. The people who took them will give them back if—*

His thought was interrupted by the click of a lock and the slight squeal of hinges as the door slowly opened.

Finn's knees drew up to his chest, and his veins pounded with adrenaline as the door peeled open to reveal the body of a tall, slender man.

The man was alone. The door closed softly with a click before he turned to face Finn with a smile. His manner was easy, not even bothering to conceal the simple brass key in his hand before he pocketed it. His shoulders were stiff with pride, but his gait was languid and unconcerned. His footsteps muffled into the thick rug that covered the floorboards as he took a step towards Finn.

Finn jerked back at the man's approach, which made his footsteps cease mid-stride. He slightly drew back, though the lack of caution in his manner suggested that the movement was merely a conciliatory gesture.

"Good, you're finally awake." The man purred in a deliberate, hypnotic whisper. His voice was smooth, as if he was trying to be charming, comforting even, but it only made Finn all the more uneasy.

His grin widened to reveal a glimmer of teeth as he looked Finn over, the only aspect of his face that was clear in the casting of the dim light. It was a sinister smile, like a fox eyeing its dinner. Finn could just make out the lines of his thin, narrow features, before they became obscured beneath a veil of shadow that had reclaimed the room when the door had closed behind him. Though searching for his identity in the dim wouldn't do any good, Finn fleetingly wondered if he should know this man. After all, who would want him in trade for Dahvi's family?

He didn't even have to *think* it. Unbidden, his mind stepped in to offer the haunting, subconscious whisper of his worst fears.

The Enclave.

Finn's eyes fell to acknowledge the swish of fabric around the man's legs and noticed a curl of green velvet. Though he hadn't previously had the misfortune of actually crossing paths with any members of The Enclave, he knew that such a garment meant that this was no longer the case, and his first fear was correct. His eyes returned to the man's face, catching a circular glint of silver displayed proudly on his chest on the way back up. A Riftrider.

Finn's hand went involuntarily to clutch his own, but found his neck bare beneath the collar of his shirt.

A brief burst of terror twisted in Finn's gut before it was sucked under by a tide of hopelessness and he let his hand fall.

Catching Finn's desperate movement, the man let his head fall to one side, a curtain of chestnut curls falling loose over his shoulder.

Fear continued to writhe in Finn's stomach, tickling the back of his throat with the need to retch at the distinct wrongness of this man's demeanor. Behind flared nostrils and gritted teeth, he forced it down, managing only a silent, seething stare that he hoped looked more angry than frightened. That's how Monica did it, right? Quiet, strong confidence to hold her ground?

The man didn't acknowledge Finn's facade for either emotion, instead, embarking on his own line of seemingly unimportant questioning.

"How do you feel? Tired? Dizzy? Perhaps even *weak?"* When Finn didn't answer, the man continued, unfazed. "You were out for more than a day. It seems that you may have been given more tonic than necessary. Either that, or being unaccustomed to potions, you may have metabolized it slower than expected."

Why is he wasting his time talking about such things? Finn wondered, desperately trying to maintain his guard against this stranger. He wasn't used to looking for the dark motive in people, but, given the sudden shift in circumstances, he had no choice.

"Who are you?" Finn began softly, trying hard to hide any tremble of uncertainty that lingered beneath his words.

The man only acknowledged the question with a small scoff before sidestepping it entirely.

"Now that you're awake, I imagine that you're starving. Do you think you could eat?"

Finn swallowed hard, shaken by the man's almost hopeful tone.

"No," he finally croaked. "I won't eat anything until you tell me who you are and where I am."

The man's lips pursed in thought and his shoulders flinched with what may have been a small shrug of acceptance.

"I understand. You're confused, disoriented, *afraid.* But you needn't fear me, at least for the time being."

"Why should I trust you? You're talking in circles. Who *are* you?"

The man's smile fell and his cold eyes filled the room with a sudden chill that Finn sensed even from beneath the shadow obscuring his face.

"Not fearing me and actually trusting me are two *very* different things." Calmly, and after several seconds of hesitation to let this sink in, the man conceded. "You know who I am. Though we have never met, I guarantee your friends consider me the villain."

A chill raced up Finn's spine, making his scalp ache as every hair stood on end.

"You're Rowan Drake?" He asked, his voice as flat as he could manage, attempting to hide both his fear and emerging anger beneath a pane of feigned indifference.

The man's scowl flexed into a brief and fleeting simper of confirmation.

"I am."

"Where am I?"

"You're on a ship far, *far* off the coast of Elandis," Rowan sang softly, with a lilt that made his explanation sound almost as if he was telling a story. "So far, in fact, I wouldn't be surprised if we've slipped by Arkynesta entirely, past Triccane, maybe even nearing Gauldor by now."

Finn had never seen a map of any part of this realm, but he didn't need to to recognize that Rowan's remark was meant to insinuate that Monica wouldn't be able to find him.

Despite Finn's previously measured control, Rowan's brazen intimidation was enough to make his next question sound desperate.

"Where's Monica?"

Rowan shrugged. "On her way, I'd imagine." He said it as though he wouldn't be bothered whether she ever did show up or not, but Finn suspected this was merely more manipulation.

"And Dahvi? He was with me last."

"Dahvi is no longer your concern."

Finn's brow furrowed in dismay. "But you gave his family back, right?"

Rowan's eyes crinkled with joy and his lips peeled back to exhale a sharp, humorous scoff.

"All in due time. As soon as he's stopped being useful to me."

Finn's chest tightened in indignation, barely aware as his hands fisted in the blanket beneath him.

"It was meant to be a trade. Me for them," Finn huffed, almost surprising himself with how much demand he threw behind his words. "Where are they?"

"They're safe," Rowan hummed, clearly unconcerned by the question. "And *they* are not your concern, either."

"But Dahvi *is*. And I wouldn't have done it if—"

"Yes, yes, you're very loyal," Rowan interrupted, and the shadows that fell across his face hinted at a sparkle in his eyes as they rolled in annoyance. "What do you want? A pat on the head?"

And then, he leaned forward as if he planned to actually offer one. Finn drew violently back, pressing his back flush against the headboard as he cried, "Stay back! Don't come any closer to me. What do you want with me?"

Rowan inclined his chin, staring down at Finn from an already menacing height. His gaze shifted, seeming to allow the passing of a few seconds in consideration before he answered.

"For now, I simply wanted to know the state of my guest's well-being. You will learn the rest in due time."

"Your guest?" Finn hissed with confusion and contempt, making Rowan stop on his heel, mid-pivot on his way back towards the door. "Don't you mean *prisoner*?"

Rowan shrugged as if he didn't see the difference, before turning back over his shoulder to add, "Do you want that food or not? It'd be wise to build your strength back up, especially since you do not know what awaits you."

Rowan waited only long enough for Finn to lapse back into obstinate silence before he left. The lock on the door clicked as it closed.

Chapter 38

Outside, the air was cool and damp, making Monica shiver as she watched "herself" get picked up by Rowan's goons from a park bench in lower Gulfport, a few blocks away from her apartment building. It's not like they probably didn't already know where she lived, but better safe than sorry, if she could help it.

Only two men came. Their builds were intimidatingly large and muscular, even from beneath the drape of rich veridian that obscured their bodies from the neck down. The men hesitated when they found Monica's unconscious body, stooped and alone, and looked to and fro for anyone watching. When the first man saw nothing, he turned to the other and gave a command that was lost on Monica's ears from her distant vantage point. Even though she was too far away to hear any of their conversation, she was also too far away to be noticed unless she was excruciatingly careless, so it was a worthy sacrifice. Even if it meant missing out on getting to hear their justification when they discussed the simple note that had been pinned to one of the upper sleeves of her dup's cardigan.

Dahvi had scrawled a simple excuse just before the sleeping potion had rendered him too incapacitated to function; something along the lines of, he couldn't bear to hang around, but he knew the men would make sure *Monica was delivered safely.*

From their body language, Monica deduced that the men found this funny. *Because of course they would.*

The first man crumpled the note into a ball and tossed it into the gutter before setting it alight with a spark flicked from his fingertips. He stomped out the burning note as the second man hoisted the limp body into his arms. The first curled his arms to cradle its dangling feet, though it didn't seem to matter much, as their size made Monica's replica look like a doll in their tree-trunk arms.

Monica fought the yawn creeping up from the back of her throat, which made her eyes water as she forced her gaze to remain fixed on the men shuffling down the block in the direction of the pier. That made sense, after all, since Dahvi had said Finn had been taken to Rowan's *ship*.

Nevertheless, this struck Monica as odd, considering that the waters beyond Arkynesta too often held magical dangers most were unwilling to confront. Even The Enclave, with their amassed abilities to harness immense amounts of flow magic, avoided it. Too much left to chance. So, what was so big, so important, that Rowan was suddenly willing to take that chance? Monica pondered the likely probability that he was no longer operating on behalf of his organization, but merely, his own interests. If that were the case, going somewhere where he could hide his activities from the rest of his wielder brethren made sense.

As soon as the men carrying Monica's body began to shrink down the street, the real Monica made a move from her current hiding place to follow them. She moved in swift bursts, sidling along buildings that would offer her enough cover should the moment suddenly call for her to duck. When the swish of ocean waves and hiss of sea breeze broke in her ears, Monica had to become even more mindful of every sound she made, as the distance between them was forced to shrink.

Within minutes, the city tore away, leaving only a stretch of open coast, scattered with a few small piers. The sparse, tiny docks of Gulfport weren't conducive to loading and unloading the cargo of large transport ships, which also meant that there was little monitoring of these areas.

Monica watched from behind the edge of one of the last buildings along the shore, timing her transition to take cover beneath a pier overhang until she knew that Rowan's men wouldn't notice her crossing the empty sand.

Their boots clunked loud and hard against the wooden stretch even after they edged out of sight. Monica darted, struggling to hold her breath once she was hidden by the overhang until she knew her panting wouldn't give her away.

From beneath the dock, she could see the ship that was waiting for them. It wasn't large by any means but had enough of a hold that she would be able to tuck herself away fairly easily. The trick was going to be in not getting caught docking it. *This couldn't be Rowan's ship, could it?* She wondered, thinking that the vessel was far too small to be holding prisoners. No, if he was using the danger of the Elandian waters to obscure anyone from looking for him, there's no way he'd bring his main ship to the coast so blatantly, even if it *was* the middle of the night.

No sooner had the two men returned with the body, the ship launched, forcing Monica to dive into the waters after it. The icy waters were unknowingly to her benefit, filling her body with an arctic shock that zapped the weariness that had been looming over her with increasing intensity, ever since she'd taken the sleeping potion into her mouth, however briefly. Most potions *did* have some amount of contact side effects, a fact she'd learned in her potions training after returning from the Isle of Reflection but had chosen to ignore in favor of the demanding circumstances. After all, it's not like she swallowed it, or *much* of it, anyway. If it *was* going to do anything at all, the side effects would be mild, and would take far more time to set in on her than they had on Dahvi.

Monica clung to the side of the little ship, hoisting herself up only when she was *sure* no one was watching. Then, she shoved her dripping-wet mass into as tight a ball as she could manage and hid behind a grouping of barrels for the time being. She didn't know how long the transport to Rowan's ship would be, but she hoped it wouldn't be long.

As the chill of her wet clothes numbed her to the discomfort of such a state, she found the heaviness of sleep returning to her eyelids. Snapping awake after nearly nodding off once, she fixed her gaze on what little she could see of the horizon from her hiding place. Its fragmented length was marked by a needle's width of dusky amber light, marking the first breaths of the encroaching dawn. Her vision blurred as she forced her focus to remain, willing herself to stay awake.

The next thing Monica knew, she was opening her eyes to the sounds of clambering and shouted commands. The crew brought the ship to a halt and then gathered to make the transfer.

The sky was now growing incredibly light overhead, the pale rose of dawn soon brightened to overtake the fading dark of the night sky. How long had she been dozing? It didn't matter. Monica had more important things to worry about.

She crept forwards, seeing one of the same two men as before, hoisting a still-limp replica of Monica from somewhere beyond her sight. A breath of relief spilled from her nostrils to see that Dahvi's shape was still the same, a likeness so similar to the real Monica that it still unsettled her to see.

They carried the body towards a plank that now extended from the near side of the ship, hanging off into what appeared to be open air. Monica drew back, cautious to avoid sight even as her curiosity pulled her towards the uncertain exit. It looked like they had docked to another ship, but where that second ship was, she couldn't see. Nevertheless, the single man now carrying the limp body, stepped out onto the plank with little pause. It didn't bow or flex under his great weight like Monica would've assumed.

When the man paused towards the center of its protruding length, he stopped and hoisted the body away from his chest, holding her out like a sacrificial offering. He seemed to be speaking, but Monica only caught the abstract tones of his voice, muddled in the breeze before any complete words could reach her.

He waited, until suddenly, a tall, thin body appeared on the far end of the plank, manifesting as if he'd stepped out of nothing. Barely a split second's glance of his face sent Monica's heart off in a gallop. Rowan.

Her stomach clenched with involuntary unease as she took in his figure. His emerald cloak swayed in the sea breeze, a satisfied smile shadowing his lips as he looked Monica's replica over. Then, he nodded, extending his hands towards the empty air beyond the plank's end. The wielder stepped through, vanishing completely with the body, as if he just stepped beyond a curtain made completely of sky.

Rowan's ship was invisible. When Monica squinted hard and focused on the empty space beyond the plank's end, she could see vague flickers of magic, rippling over the occasional glimpse of wood. A cloaking ward. He was using a cloaking ward, just like Maal did for his tower. But how? Monica knew that Rowan must be strong, and while he almost certainly wasn't the only wielder on that ship, the amount of magic that it takes to maintain a cloaking ward large enough to obscure an entire ship is truly unreasonable. But, based on how easily the wielder was able to pass through at Rowan's mere invitation meant that it likely wasn't much more than camouflage. Maal's ward had additional enchantments that actively prevented people from entering who weren't supposed to. This ward didn't seem to do that, but then again, it wouldn't really need to since the requirement of having to traverse dangerous waters and find it first would both be strong deterrents. And if it left again, Monica would lose this chance.

She knew what she had to do. Her eyes darted to scan the crew of the meager ship she was currently on. Not only did they seem unaffected by their crew mate's disappearance, but they also appeared far more eager to resume their voyage than stay and watch the interaction with The Enclave's most infamous wielder. Knowing his unpredictability, that was probably wise.

With their focus on their duties, Monica had a clear shot at escape, as long as she was quick. There was a good likelihood that someone might still see her, but if she could get to the other ship and hunker down quickly in a new hiding place, she might just get away with it.

A risky plan, but what else was new? It's not like she had the time to wait around for a better opportunity.

When she looked back over, she caught only the last ripple of green before Rowan had disappeared back into his ship as well. With Rowan gone, she needed no more convincing.

Monica drew in a breath, pulled herself to her feet, and took off running. On instinct, she leapt across the plank, careening through the ward and into the new ship. She landed, tumbling into a somersault before scuttling for the nearest cover she could find.

Catching her breath, she waited.

All was quiet.

No. There was no way she'd been lucky enough that no one had seen or *heard* her on either ship.

She was too scared to look, but her ears perked up to scan her surroundings for any other life. In the distance, she heard voices. They were soft, but this time she could actually hear what they were saying.

"A Riftrider. And an artifact ring of minor lock picking; no, she won't be needing those here. A dagger, ordinary—" Which then fell on the floorboards with the *clunk* as the search continued. "And what's this? This looks interesting."

Monica couldn't help herself. Cautiously, she gripped the lip of the crate she had dove behind and pulled her face to the edge to peer over. There was hardly as much danger as she initially feared, since Rowan and everyone with him seemed far more occupied by searching her replica for artifacts, rather than having been aware of a new stowaway.

Monica's eyes burned with a returning weariness that had clearly not been appeased by her dozing catnap on the other ship, but she fought it to get a look at the happenings at the other end of the ship.

Rowan lifted a dark orb in his hand, twisting it to and fro in his fingers as he inspected it. From the distance, the Eye of Desire looked almost entirely black in his hand, absent its normal red sparkle and gunmetal whorls that twisted along its surface. He handed it to another green clad man standing over him before stooping again to check the replica for any remaining treasures.

Monica swallowed, feeling her skin pulse with a nervous fever. She had known that going in this way meant sacrificing her precious artifacts in order to get Rowan to buy into her ploy. She was determined to only let the confiscation be temporary, but it still hurt her to see her precious things in such malevolent hands.

Biting her lip, she braced herself for what came next.

"Well, well, well... " Rowan sang smugly, lifting the second amulet that he had originally missed due to it being tucked inside her shirt. "What do we have here?"

"Looks like a realm key." One of the other wielders chimed in, earning an annoyed glare from Rowan.

"Yes," Rowan drawled, letting a sarcastic smile creep slowly back onto his face. "I can see that. I think it's best if I hang on to this one for safekeeping."

Rowan slipped the Soulseeker into a pocket inside of his cloak before turning on his heel. With a wave of his hand, he commanded, "Take her to a secure room. I will deliver some food to our other guest. He is surely hungry."

Other guest? Finn!

Monica was only dimly aware of the sudden shift when her panic and Rowan's voice began to slip away behind a bleary screen of murky gray. Her mind sent the signal to her eyelids to blink to try to clear the urge to sleep from them, but she couldn't get them to obey.

I don't have time for this. She was frustrated as she tried to force her mind to return to thoughts of finding Finn.

He must be close... she hoped, but it was her last thought before everything went from gray to black, and she finally surrendered to the side effects of the sleeping potion.

Chapter 39

Rowan returned to Finn's room carrying a metal tray, atop which was perched a bowl that appeared to contain some kind of stew, along with a couple of pieces of toast and a cup of tea. This time, Rowan said not a word as he placed the tray on the table beside Finn and quickly turned to leave with barely more than a look.

Finn briefly considered the interaction as odd but wasn't eager to make conversation with Rowan again.

Wary of the offerings, Finn put off eating despite the audible dissent of his growling stomach. Instead, he performed a thorough inspection of his quarters, confirming beyond all doubt, that all of his possessions had been confiscated; his wallet, the notebook and pen that grandad had given him as a belated birthday present, and, worst of all, the Riftrider. Beyond that, there was little in the room that he could use to escape. With little left to hold his attention, he thumbed through the books, finding several in a language he did not recognize. Elandian perhaps? The ones he *could* read were historical accounts, skewed from the perspective of The Enclave. After glimpsing just enough to feed his curiosity, he decided he didn't want to indulge the potential of empathizing with their cause.

Hours after it had gotten cold, Finn couldn't deny the food any longer. As much as he hated to admit it, Rowan was right. He needed his strength since he didn't know how long he was going to be here. The last thing he wanted was to be weak enough to become a hindrance when help actually came for him.

The food only made Finn feel better briefly. Once it had started to digest, he became dizzied by the sensation of time creeping quickly away. His mind was fuzzy, like when many days start to blur into one. Soon he only vaguely remembered sleeping and seeing someone bringing him food several times —he lost track after twenty— and each time, no matter what he did or said, no one ever acknowledged him. In fact, it was like he was trapped inside a bubble of speeding time and all he could do was watch the world outside go by in a blur. Finn could barely comprehend how long he'd remained in the blur until it somehow miraculously lifted. It was then that fear gripped Finn and he understood the mistake he'd made. Had it been two weeks? Three? More?

But he didn't have time to do the math, because the haze had only lifted when Rowan finally returned. The change hit Finn like a bowling ball to the stomach, snapping him into a reality so sharp that Rowan seemed almost more real than any of those other people he had seen. He *was* more real. Finn was sure of it, because not only did he not blur by like all the others had, but he also lingered long enough for Finn to notice things he hadn't before; actual conscious thoughts that made linear sense, as well as emotions those thoughts cultivated.

Finn was now awake enough to realize that during all the time that had passed, whether it had been an illusion or unfortunate reality, made him feel desperate and angry. While it had been happening, Finn was numb to how little there was to do except sit and stare at the ceiling.

But now, looking back, Finn re-experienced every second that had passed in a flash that somehow felt more real than they had the first time. Had it been days, or even weeks that he had been here? The frightening realization ignited an ember of hatred that burned low in his gut. Had he ever been this angry? He didn't know. All he could do now was feel, and it was like he was feeling everything all at once from the entire *however long* he'd been here.

He was mad at Rowan for taking advantage of Dahvi and not keeping his word after the trade, but more so, he was angry at himself for actually thinking that what he did would've worked. It *should* have worked! He had wanted it to work… And it wasn't his fault that it didn't, but he felt stupid and helpless all the same, like he should have known better. It made him angry and sad to see anyone hurting his friends, and his frustrations were growing into desperation. He wanted to help. He *needed* to help, before his stupid decisions ended up making everything worse. But how? What could he do, trapped in this room?

It was even worse realizing that this was pretty much the only thought he could remember having across that entire span of lost time. He wasn't sure who he was madder at; Rowan for stealing all of that time, or himself for wasting it. If it *had* been days or even weeks, he feared Monica's reaction to his absence. What if she had tried to come after him, only to get caught herself? After all, Rowan had said that Monica would be here soon, too. What if that was why he'd returned? Was Monica finally here?

Finn mustered his most venomous glare when Rowan entered with a tray of food in one hand, and the brass key in the other, acting like not so much as an hour had passed. Rowan didn't seem to notice Finn's glare. Nevertheless, Finn persisted, noticing that, in the presence of his anger, his fear was diminished upon seeing his captor for a second time. But that still didn't stop his whole body from knotting with tension as he watched Rowan turn to close and lock the door behind himself.

He pocketed the same, simple brass key as he crossed the room with a cautious gait, setting the tray on the table beside Finn's bed before withdrawing enough to make Finn's guarded cower ease slightly. Rowan then stepped back, reaching down to produce something from his pocket.

"I thought you might want these back."

Finn flinched when Rowan's hand extended the offering in his direction. Rowan waited, silent and still as Finn unfurled to cautiously investigate.

It was his notebook and pen.

Finn's gaze flicked to Rowan's face and his eyes narrowed in distrust.

"Why?"

"They seemed like they might be important to you."

"But why are you giving them back? And why do you care?"

"They're clearly not artifacts, nor do I see any harm in you having something that might help occupy your time here," Rowan said, making no effort to address the second question.

"Would've been nice, weeks ago." Finn mumbled angrily under his breath, crossing his arms to make it clear that he had no intention of taking his things from Rowan's hand.

Seeing this, Rowan instead placed them on the bedside table, next to the tray of food before he withdrew, making his way across the room to the leather armchairs in the far corner.

As soon as he sat, his relaxed posture resumed and he took up a cross-legged slouch that made his utter lack of wariness for Finn insultingly blatant. He didn't appear armed, but then again, if he was as skilled a wielder as his reputation suggested, he didn't need to be.

Rowan leaned forward, anchoring his elbows against his knees as he peered intently into Finn's face. The two held a silent stare for nearly a minute before Finn challenged him with a defiance that felt both foreign and yet liberating.

"What do you expect? Do you want me to thank you for not stealing *all* of my things?"

This earned a soft chuckle from Rowan.

"You are sounding far too like our mutual friend."

Finn's upper lip twitched, tempted by a snarl of contempt, but he held his face still, trying not to acknowledge his understanding of Rowan's comparison. He *was* acting like Monica. And he wasn't sure if that made him feel more comfortable or afraid. He wanted to be strong like Monica, but he also didn't want all of the things that had made her strong.

"You had better eat." Rowan persuaded. "The stew is far less pleasant cold."

Now more mindful of the angry edge in his tone, Finn asked, no less distrustfully, "Do you plan to just sit there and watch me eat?"

Rowan's lips pursed with a small smile, one that seemed more irritation than amusement. "I care not if you choose to starve yourself."

"Then why are you here?"

"Because *you* are here."

The cryptic answer made Finn's skin itch with indignation. Was Rowan just here to torment him? Since he was already a prisoner, Finn didn't understand what else Rowan had to gain from interacting with him.

Seeing the opportunity, the question formed on the tip of Finn's tongue finally came forth, more tentatively hopeful, as opposed to demanding, as he'd wanted.

"I've been here—" Finn paused, frustrated when he found he was unable to recount the specifics of just how much time had passed, and decided to take a shot for emphasis over accuracy. "—for *weeks!* What took you so long?"

The far corner of Rowan's mouth lifted in a satisfied grin and he purred, "I didn't think you'd be so eager to see me again."

Finn's cheeks flushed hot with resentment for the way his words were so easily twisted.

"I'm not! But after so long by myself…" Finn sighed, scowling as he decided against hoping to make Rowan understand. After all, that's probably what Rowan wanted.

"You're desperate to talk to anyone?" Rowan finally finished for him.

Finn grit his teeth. "And what is it you're hoping I'll say?"

Rowan's smile widened, and his stare grew even colder, like a man skilled in using his eyes as a weapon. It forced Finn to glance away, if only to steady himself before braving the intensity of the wielder's cruel, slate-blue stare once more.

"I think you know." Rowan began with a tone that was unsettlingly calm, almost even placating, but the phrase's lack of a questioning lilt put Finn even more on edge.

"I don't." Finn swore defiantly.

Rowan's head tilted inquisitively to one side, and he coolly commanded, "Tell me where Monica is."

Finn drew back in involuntary confusion. "What?"

"Tell me where Monica is." Rowan repeated sternly. "Why isn't she here yet?"

"You— you made it sound like *you* knew where she was." Finn squawked, trying not to sound *too* startled at the shift in Rowan's motive. "You said she'd be here soon. You thought she was coming."

"But that was so long ago." Rowan chided. "She must not care about you after all if she's not even willing to try to save you."

"She's really not here?" Finn swallowed, his gaze flickering with apprehension as Rowan's words continued on to narrate Finn's fears aloud.

"Perhaps she got into trouble somewhere along the way. What if she got hurt or lost because of you? What if she's so mad at you for leaving that she's abandoned you to figure it out, *alone?"*

"She wouldn't!" Finn protested tearfully. "She would come for me! I know it!"

"Perhaps..." Rowan offered with a hiss, steepling his fingers against the cleft in his chin as he leaned forward into his stare. "We can find her, together."

"No!" Finn snapped. "If she's not here, there's a reason. And I'm not going to do *anything* to help you."

"What if she *is* hurt? What if this is your chance to save her?"

Finn paused only briefly to consider this, struggling not to be tempted by Rowan's pretty words.

"You're trying to trick me." Finn shook his head. "You're the one she needs to be saved from."

Rowan leaned back in his chair and exhaled with a wordless hum that almost seemed to convey a hint of admiration for Finn's attempt at resistance. The wielder's gaze finally broke from his, turning to survey the state of his nails as he curved his hand towards himself.

"Maybe we should do this a different way," Rowan warned, beginning to pick at one of his cuticles with his thumbnail in an unconcerned manner, before the faintest sizzle of yellow-gold magic began to crackle at his fingertips. "Or, you can tell me what I want to know and forgo the torture, for *now*."

"All those days alone weren't enough? That's what that was, wasn't it? Torture?"

Rowan's expression steeled, his eyelids heavy with disinterested impatience.

"Where. Is. Monica?" Rowan asked in a sharp growl.

"I don't know where she is," Finn admitted honestly, sounding almost more ashamed than afraid.

He wasn't afraid, not for himself, not like he should've been. He would be terrified out of his mind as soon as the realization of the true weight of the situation fully unfolded for him, but now, having just been taken, he wasn't convinced that this wasn't somehow a dream, or some kind of illusion. *What if it was like the island?* He asked himself, believing that there was somehow less danger from within an illusion.

Even though his hope couldn't *be* more misguided, it was what he needed right now. Hope. Hope that wherever Monica was right now, she was safe, and not in a place where Rowan could easily find and take her. Hope that someone would come to his rescue soon, or better, that he could take down Rowan himself, even with as unlikely as that seemed. Hope that Monica would *not* do what was in her nature to do and put herself in danger by trying to come after him. Hope had been Finn's parachute during a time that had looked like an otherwise fatal descent, and even though the landing had been painful, that hope had made the crucial difference.

But Rowan wasn't buying it. The sparks that eddied around the wielder's fingertips crackled louder as he leaned forwards with a menacing glare. A single lock of spiraling chestnut hair fell across his forehead, but he paid it no mind as he channeled his intent into that increasingly uncomfortable stare.

"You don't know? Or you don't want *me* to know?"

Finn surrendered a passing glance towards the magic before he swallowed nervously. But neither his voice nor his focus broke when he repeated, “I don’t know.”

A haze of irritation clouded Rowan’s otherwise guarded expression, but the magic gathering at his fingertips died suddenly as he let his hand fall into his lap. He believed Finn. Why?

A cold pinch of confusion rose in Finn’s chest as he tried to rationalize it. This was a man who had tried to kill Monica, a man who belonged to a group known for their merciless and barbaric treatment of others with little motive beyond satisfying their own vicious desires. Finn knew that Rowan didn’t have to be lenient with him. Hell, he didn't even have to be gentle. He could do anything he wanted as long as Finn stayed alive long enough to be used as bait to lure Monica here. So why was he? What was his angle?

Then, a low growl rose from within Rowan’s throat, forming into words that Finn had not expected to hear.

“You would do *anything* to protect her, wouldn’t you?”

“Of course I would,” Finn hissed defiantly. “She’s my friend.”

"Would you suffer for her?"

Finn swallowed, averting his gaze. His response, when it finally came, was timid but honest.

"Haven’t I proved that already?"

"What would you give to keep her safe?"

"Anything," Finn squeaked, terrified at the truth of his own confession. He wasn't just saying what he knew Rowan wanted to hear. He said the truth. He believed it.

“Anything?” Rowan repeated, the word suddenly sounding more like a question.

Understanding smoothed the wrinkles of confusion in Finn’s brow, making his head shake in vehement rejection as he said, “But I won’t bargain with *you*. After all, you’ve already proven that *your* word means nothing.”

At this, Rowan gave a quiet scoff, leaning back in his chair as he regarded Finn with a new respect.

"Why?" Rowan asked contemplatively, but as Finn lifted his head, the question changed into something unexpected. "Why do you love Monica so much? You know that she hasn't done anything but hurt you."

"That's not true."

"But it is. If it weren't for her, you wouldn't even be here."

"I *chose* to be here. And I love Monica because she's changed my life. More than I could have ever hoped. She helped me see what I truly wanted out of life, and she showed me how to fight for it. She showed me how to be strong when I'm afraid, and how it's worth it to do anything to protect what you love. She has done nothing but try to protect me, even at the expense of her own feelings."

Rowan's chin dipped and a shadow flitted over his face as his expression went contemplative and solemn. For several long seconds, he was still, letting the sounds of his slow breaths fill the air between them.

And then, lifting his hand to brace his head against his knuckles, he let his head fall to the side as he looked at Finn again. Only now, his eyes were surprisingly soft, almost melancholic.

“You… are not what I thought you were.” He began, the fingers of his other hand giving a curl of movement to accompany his words as he spoke. “You are far more loyal, your admiration sincere, and though you’re weak, your love for Monica makes you dangerous.”

“Dangerous?” Finn dared to question, his voice falling to a whisper. “I don’t know what you mean.”

"She has suffered a great loss —many great losses— throughout her life. They have made her strong. Healing from them will return her to a state of weakness. I need her strength, her desire to shield herself from any more losses that may occur. One more loss may finally make her strong enough for what I need."

One more loss. The words rang hollow in Finn's ears, making heat sting his eyes. A sinking feeling of dread welled in his stomach, heavy and cold like a glacier.

"What do you want with her?" Finn asked, revealing the beginnings of a tremble in his voice. "What did Monica *ever* do to you?"

"It's not about *what* she has *done*, but what she *can do,* for me."

Finn exhaled a scoff of disgust. "Hasn't she suffered enough? If anything, *you* should be looking to see what *you* can do for her."

Rowan blinked in surprise as a contemptuous laugh escaped his lips. "W- what *I* can do *for her*? And why would I want to do that?"

"Well, for one, you tried to kill her."

"She must trust you an awful lot to tell you about the dark nightmares that occurred only as mental illusions on that island."

"And how do *you* know about it, if it was only an illusion?" Finn interrupted, making Rowan's scowl tighten.

"I can do a lot with my magic, including creating a copy of my presence on that island, without chancing the same risks that you did by going there physically. But since someone like you wouldn't know anything about magic, I'm hardly going to waste my time explaining it to you. I'm more interested in what Monica has shared with you. She may have told you about what happened on the island, but did she also tell you how *she* killed *me*? Your precious Monica is a murderer."

"You don't look very dead to me." Finn challenged. "But even if you were, it wouldn't change my opinion of her. You deserve far worse than a quick death for your crimes, anyway. You took her family away. You killed her brother. You left her with no one, and it hurts me every day to see that I can't do anything to take that pain away from her."

"Well, then." Rowan hissed, standing from his seat. "Perhaps you should figure out how to stop being so damn useless."

The jab, however cheap, sent a javelin of pain rippling through Finn's heart and stole the retort from Finn's lips. All he could do was muster what ineffectual glare remained to watch as Rowan turned to leave. The wielder unlocked the door, pausing with his hand on the knob before he slipped out.

"You should have stayed home when you had the chance. Now, that damn djinn's got you *too* involved. You'd better be careful, because something unfortunate is likely to happen to you if you get in the way."

Without awaiting a response, Rowan slipped out of the room, securing the door with a single click after he left.

Finn's mind reeled at the interaction. His heart and eyes stung with the lasting bitterness of Rowan's words. His head spun with so many questions, so many things that didn't make sense. How was Rowan so calm, and yet so twisted, all at once? He threatened torture with not even a blink. Even more so, the glimpses of humanity that he had seen in the wielder's gaze frightened him. But then again, he must have been human once too before The Enclave got him. What kind of horrors had to befall someone before they turned into a monster like that?

A tiny flash of light caught Finn's attention. He looked up, seeing that there was something now laying on the floor in front of the door, sparkling in the thin thread of sunlight that crept in through the sliver of exposed window.

That wasn't there before. Unless his mind was playing tricks on him, too. But as he stared, the sparkle didn't change. Whatever it was, was real, and this made him curious; curious enough to get up off the bed to investigate.

Finn crossed the room, elated to find a Soulseeker amulet resting on the floorboard in front of the door. He hadn't even heard it fall. His heart shot into his throat in disbelief as he snatched it, desperately shoving it into his pocket before anyone could discover it and take it away. He only paused for a second to wonder if this was a trap, too. He couldn't trust anything in this place. He couldn't trust anything but himself…

And then, a second wave of fear gripped him as he realized what the Soulseeker meant. Monica *was* here. Was Rowan testing Finn's loyalty to her? Or maybe, he had only been trying to convince Finn that she *wasn't* here, so he wouldn't want to try to get out and look for her. But, then why give him this? Was it an accident?

Finn glanced over his shoulder at the pen and notebook that had been returned to him with an idea blooming in his mind. He suddenly knew how he could be useful in this impossible situation.

His interaction with Rowan had taught Finn two monumentally important things: one, Rowan didn't think much of Finn, and was therefore likely to vastly underestimate his capabilities, and two, his room was merely locked, not warded. Which meant that the time had come for his thus far innocuous lock picking ability to be put to better use than simply breaking into customers' houses to put away their perishable groceries.

Finn was going to make Rowan regret returning his "harmless" tactical pen.

Chapter 40

Dahvi awoke still wearing Monica's form. His head pounded as his eyes peeled open to peer around the small room now encircling him.

This place held no fear for Dahvi. After all, even if it *was* an Enclave ship, normal walls wouldn't hold him. Now that he was here, he could get out whenever he wanted; make himself look like whomever he wanted. He could rescue Finn, make sure Monica, the *real* Monica, had made it safely, or take down Rowan himself. That last idea appealed the most to Dahvi, probably more than it should have, especially since the only edge his shapeshifting abilities really gave him was the element of surprise, which would only go so far against such powerful magic.

Disregarding his limited chances of success, Dahvi indulged the fantasy, since there wasn't much more that he wanted at that moment than to end the man responsible for so many of his recent fears. He would've liked to claim a selflessness to the urge, to be able to help end the agony and suffering for others that would continue for as long as Rowan was alive, but he knew better than to deny that the temptation was more borne from his own desire for retribution and lasting safety than anything else.

Davhi's head ached with a pang of swelling resentment, making him wince as he remembered the horrendous potion hangover that currently plagued him. A fleeting temptation crossed his mind, wondering if shifting to another form would also let him shake it. But the risk of shifting without it being explicitly an escape attempt was unwise, even if he was alone. Not only would he risk being seen if a visitor came unannounced, but there also wasn't much sense in diminishing his energy to allay a potentially temporary discomfort. No, Dahvi decided that for now, his best use was to stay put and buy the *real* Monica time. Especially, because if Dahvi slipped out and Rowan discovered his absence, the first thing the whole crew would do was start looking for Monica.

The decision didn't make the waiting any less awful, though. Thankfully, he didn't have to wait long. The click of the door's lock made him flinch, sitting up on the bed to watch as the subject of his contempt entered the small room.

Rowan was dressed in his standard green cloak and wielder's attire, down to a Riftrider that hung blatantly on display atop his chest. Dahvi found this a little odd, since The Enclave's trademark veridian cloak was typically only worn for ceremonies, or for dealing with those unaware of a wielder's status or identity, like a badge. Sure, it had made sense at their first meeting, to negotiate Rowan's commands in exchange for Dahvi's family. But now, on a ship away from the rest of The Enclave, on which he was holding prisoners who all knew his identity, who was he trying to inform or intimidate?

The lock clicked behind him and Rowan turned, revealing a tray balanced on one hand.

"Good morning, anomaly," Rowan purred. His slate-blue eyes met Dahvi's, which still shimmered the color of ice from behind a perfect likeness of Monica. "I *had* hoped you'd be awake. Less chance for your food to get cold."

Dahvi watched him distrustfully, his entire body tensing with defensive instinct as Rowan neared just long enough to place the tray on the table beside the bed before withdrawing to a respectful distance.

It wasn't hard for Dahvi to put on Monica's mask of petulant, hateful defiance. After all, this vile man had wronged Dahvi, too. Admittedly, not as much as killing his entire family, but things could still head in that direction if this all went poorly. With that thought, Dahvi noticed the warmth of rage beginning to simmer deep in his chest. He stared at Rowan with a judgmental calm, his eyes cold with venomous contempt as they fixed the wielder in a steady gaze.

"How do you like your new room?" Rowan asked with a sweeping gesture, showing off the meager accommodations as if they were lavish and impressive. "I want to make sure you're comfortable. After all, you'll be staying here for a long, *long* time."

Gathering Monica's voice in his throat, Dahvi focused to make the words come out smooth and stern, with just enough trepidation to be convincing.

"Where's Finn?"

Rowan ignored the question, continuing with his own separate train of thought.

"Because, you see, this ship is warded. It's quite a clever one, if I do say so myself. I've been experimenting with using artifacts as conduits for other spells in order to evolve their effects into new hybrids. For this, I combined a cloaking artifact with a one way ward, making the ship entirely invisible from the outside. Anyone can pass into the ward, but out… out is another story entirely."

Dahvi paused to consider his response, remembering Monica's persistence when she had asked this same question of him, not six hours ago. She wouldn't have given in to Rowan's clumsy, though concerning, redirect.

"Where. Is. Finn?" Dahvi demanded again, each word punctuated with the confrontation of quiet wrath. He felt his own anger rising beyond that which had been gathered for the demonstration, mixing with his own feelings of fear and guilt for what he'd been forced to do. Dahvi owed it to Finn to make sure he got out of this all right. And, even though he knew Finn was meant to be bait, Rowan's evasions didn't bring him any comfort that Finn was safe and unharmed.

Dahvi gathered himself up on the bed, rising from his knees to his feet, so that even from Monica's diminutive five foot height, he could mimic the effect of looking down at Rowan. He made his fists clench, surprised by how much strength he felt in her tiny palms.

Rowan only smiled, leaning his back against the door as his head tilted to play into the illusion of their opposite difference in height, clearly unfazed by the attempted intimidation. When he spoke again, the wielder disregarded the repeated inquiry, cracking a grin as he reveled in how angry it would make Monica to be ignored.

"Do you know why?" Rowan challenged with a clever twinge of his thick eyebrows. "Because, unlike most prolonged but impermanent wards, which must be cast and recast by several different wielders to maintain a stable patchwork of magic to cover a large area like this one, my ward is singular and continuous. Not to mention, now that it's feeding off the supplementary power of an artifact, it's strong enough that it cannot be broken or manipulated except by its original caster. Me."

Dahvi's upper lip rolled back in a sneer to cover the twinge of uncertainty that Rowan's threat had involuntarily prompted. While Rowan's claims were certainly lofty and intimidating, Dahvi had never heard of such a thing. No one was strong enough to keep up such a large ward on their own, indefinitely; especially a supposedly unbreakable one. But, if he was telling the truth, Dahvi shuddered to think of the challenges such a thing would impose on their chances of escape.

Gritting his teeth, Dahvi turned his focus back to Rowan.

"I will not ask again," he threatened in Monica's low, frighteningly composed growl that often signaled the calm before an outburst. "Where is Finn?"

At this, Rowan's expression darkened as he picked himself up off the door with a slow rise. He turned, now only resting one shoulder against its surface so that he could face Dahvi fully.

"My, you *are* persistent, aren't you?"

"You have my friend. I want him back."

"Yes, yes. Well, I want immortality, but we can't all have what we want, at least not immediately, can we?"

Dahvi paused, noticeably taking note of Rowan's choice of words. *Immortality? Even with magic no one is immortal, except for the few immortal angels who balance the flow of the universe.* Dahvi puzzled at this, wondering, hoping, that maybe this was just an expression he'd never heard before.

Choosing to ignore it, Dahvi finally decided that, since Rowan was also ignoring Dahvi's first question, perhaps it was time to move on to other questions.

"Why am I here?" Dahvi paused, recalling the brief explanation he'd gotten from Finn about Monica's first encounter with Rowan. "You wanted to kill me, right? So why the theatrics? Why bother bringing me food?"

Rowan tsked and crossed his arms. "You *clearly* weren't listening, anomaly, when I said you'd be here for a long, *long* time."

"It's to be torture, then?"

Rowan rolled his eyes and gave a sigh of annoyance.

"I *had* originally come to discuss the specifics of your stay here, but I see no use in reasoning with you in your current agitated state." Rowan relented, turning back towards the door. "I will return once you've had some food, rest, and time to think about what you could do to benefit yourself in this otherwise hopeless situation."

"Your mere presence agitates me. Nothing is going to change that."

Rowan ignored the baited comment, exiting without pause. The door softly clicked closed behind him, inspiring a spark of anticipation to rise within Dahvi's chest, only to be smothered by the sound of the lock finally engaging.

Dahvi's muscles slackened as he slipped back down onto the bed, contemplating his interaction with Rowan. Why did the wielder seem so unconcerned with killing Monica, as he had once threatened? Something had changed... Monica had something Rowan wanted. But what?

He spent several minutes pondering this, but with no success. He didn't know enough about Monica to have all the pieces for this puzzle. After all, it's not like they had talked much. Most of what he knew came from conversations with Finn, and overheard discussions between him and Celene. Dahvi understood that, as the newest addition to the group, he was far from earning her trust. But in watching Monica's dealings, he almost wondered if that would ever be possible for him. Especially after what he'd done.

Dahvi wasn't sure for how long he'd lost himself in thought, but his contemplative trance was eventually broken by a commotion outside. Somewhere in the distance, a muffled shout bellowed, *"How did she get out? Grab her!"*

A brief scuffle ended in a rhythmic marching of heavy boots, which it became immediately apparent were getting closer.

Dahvi's heart pounded with the panicked realization that the wielders had found Monica— the *real* Monica. Already?

He barely had time to register his disappointment before his instinct to shift kicked in. His body shrank and he threw himself under the bed, transforming into a rat to accommodate the shallow space. Just as his new rat-form scuttled into the shadows, the door of the cabin flew open, and Monica came stumbling fast inside. She careened forwards as if she'd been pushed, landing hard on her knees a second before the door slammed closed behind her.

From the other side of the door, the angry voice bellowed again, *"And stay in there!"*

Monica gave an angry scoff before slowly picking herself up with her scuffed palms. She winced, pushing herself to stand on knees that wobbled with evident weakness. She lifted her head to look around, and it became clear to Dahvi from the way she paused that her vision was still blurry with disorientation. After she'd gotten a look at the room and found it empty, a hushed whisper lifted from within her.

"Hello?" She called, her voice crackling from disuse, as if she'd only just awoken. "Are you here?"

At first, Dahvi remained quiet and still, watching her for a few seconds more before he made a move to reveal himself. It was only when Monica plopped down on the bed with a defeated sigh, that Dahvi took it as his cue to emerge.

Monica gasped at his rat form, disgusted but not afraid, before her glare sharpened with intimidation. She scowled a warning, crossing her arms as she snapped, "What, Rowan's got spies on me, even in here?"

Her contempt withered into revelation as Dahvi morphed back into the human version of himself, a feat that left him breathless from the effort. He couldn't remember the last time he'd had to shift so many times in such a short span. The fatigue of the task made him wonder if he should've trained for this.

"You *are* here." She greeted softly once he'd finally changed.

Monica made no move to rise from the bed, acknowledging him with barely a trace of her former surprise. How easily her guard fell into place. Despite his own talents as an actor, Dahvi briefly both envied Monica and pitied her for this skill.

"Where else would I be?" He retorted, trying not to sound as clipped as her already confrontational coldness was tempting him to be. Not to mention, the lingering irritation at her for not trusting him with her plan. How careless it was for her to force him to drink the sleeping potion and come in her place, simply expecting him to wait until she was ready. But, then again, did he really have that much room to be annoyed with her?

"I would've thought you'd shift and slip out of here the first chance you got."

"What?" Dahvi's brow crinkled in annoyed confusion. "Why?"

"Because the plan was to get me here so that I could save Finn. You had no other tasks."

Dahvi shook his head, mystified by her assumptions. "I'm here to save Finn, too. Besides, if Rowan's claims are true, I can't leave, even if I wanted to."

Monica bristled at this.

"What claims?" She asked, trying not to seem too perturbed by Dahvi's insinuation.

"Oh, just the fact that he has this ship warded in such a way that no one can leave without his help."

Monica's expression narrowed in suspicion.

"Why? I know *I'm* no wielder, but wards are hardly unbreakable if you can find the right way to manipulate them with either flow magic or an artifact. Besides, a ship this large will likely have multiple wards. If we can find a seam, we can slip out."

"No," Dahvi insisted. "While I'll admit I don't know much about wards, or even artifacts, this is different. He's using an artifact in conjunction with a single ward to make it stronger, seamless. It's a one-way cloaking ward."

Monica's expression brightened momentarily with understanding before her skepticism returned. "Well, that makes sense why I couldn't see the ship from the outside. But I've never heard of anything like that even being possible. Most wards, including Maal's, don't let anything in or out without their controller's permission. And how would *you* even know something like that?"

"Rowan told me himself. Or rather, he told you."

Monica's eyes darkened with understanding. "I'm surprised he didn't try to kill you."

"So was I. I even asked him about that."

"And?"

"And, he expressed absolutely no desire to do so, at least for the time being. Said he plans to keep you here for a long, *long* time. His words."

Monica's head slowly fell to one side, her gaze growing glassy in thought. After a long moment, Dahvi saw the last thing he ever expected to see on her face. A smile. A small smile, but still.

Though the expression urged Dahvi's curiosity to double, he knew better than to question her plan, seeing as how unwilling she had been to trust him with that information last time.

When it became obvious that Monica seemed content to enjoy whatever idea had come to her in perfect, prolonged silence, Dahvi decided it best to change the subject.

"So… what happened?" He asked, swallowing his trepidation. "Did you find Finn?"

Monica's smile faded almost instantly, and the cross of her arms seemed to tighten.

"No," she hissed. "And what does it look like? I got caught."

"How?"

"I…" She paused, looking briefly and uncharacteristically sheepish before the irritation returned to her demeanor, "I fell asleep. Turns out that even a little contact from that sleeping potion gave me side effects that were pretty persistent. I fought them for as long as I could, but—" She shrugged, letting her arms unfurl to make a defeated gesture at the room around them.

"Yeah," Dahvi agreed gravely. "It's pretty potent stuff. The Enclave doesn't mess around."

Monica's chin dipped, but the shadows that fell to cover her face were hardly enough to obscure the new wave of anger now boiling behind her expression. Dahvi fleetingly wondered what she was thinking. Was she mad at herself for getting caught? Or was that anger something more?

As if feeling his stare, Monica's head lifted and she met his gaze with a clenched jaw.

"Well," she finally said with a sigh, turning to let herself sprawl in a laying position across the bed. "I guess now that I'm here, *you* have to go find Finn."

"Really?"

She shrugged without turning to face him.

"I mean, it's not like there's much else *I* can do at this point. You can at least shift and slip out of here. You can find him and let me know that he's alright."

By the glassy sheen now rising to a shine across her distant eyes, Dahvi sensed that her instructions were more of a plea than a command.

"You trust me to do that?"

"I don't exactly have a choice now, do I? You wanted to help. So prove it. Find Finn. And then come back to me. Maybe by then I'll have a plan."

Dahvi gave a slow, solemn nod. He turned to leave, pausing for a moment to say, "Be careful, okay? Rowan plans to come back."

Monica scoffed, sounding unfazed, if not mildly perturbed by the warning. "Of course he does. If I'm to be here for a long, *long* time, I must have something he wants."

At first, Dahvi didn't acknowledge her response, despite the validation he felt for confirmation of his suspicions. The urge rose again to ask, but he greatly doubted whether Monica would oblige his curiosity, just for the sake of it. He tried to resist the question, but the more he tried, the more he failed, until he could no longer leave the question unspoken.

"What does he want from you?"

"I'll let you know when I figure it out," Monica answered dryly, making Dahvi wonder whether this was another evasion, or if she genuinely didn't know.

He hesitated, lingering to make a vain attempt to read her face, but she only stared at him, blank and cold. It wasn't worth it, he decided. Not while there were more pressing matters at hand.

In an instant, Dahvi shrank into a spider and skittered out of the room beneath the door, leaving Monica alone with her thoughts. Off to find Finn he went.

Chapter 41

Finn's heart shot into his throat when a familiar voice called to him from behind. He knew he shouldn't have stopped. After all, this too, was probably a trap. There was *no way* Dahvi should be here. But then again, knowing that Rowan had lied about setting Dahvi's family free once the trade had been made, maybe it wasn't so far-fetched to think that he would've come to take them back. If nothing else, Finn knew the lengths Dahvi would go to in order to protect the people he cared about. If he hadn't, Finn wouldn't have been here. They had that in common.

Though Finn hesitated, he was almost too afraid to look, lest the sound be merely a hiccup of his hopeful imagination.

"Finn!" His name came a second time, a hushed whisper that he could no longer deny.

"Dahvi?" Finn turned to glance down the hallway, but still saw no one.

Because of this, Finn had managed to slip out of his room unnoticed. Thankfully, there hadn't been anyone standing guard. Odd, but he hadn't stopped to question why Rowan would be so careless as to trust his security to a simple, ordinary lock. Finn didn't mind being underestimated, since he could use it to his advantage.

He hadn't gotten far yet, but he knew he had to be careful to make this attempt count. Because if someone caught him, he could be sure that picking the lock and slipping out a second time would no longer be an option.

"Finn!"

He glanced around, puzzling at where the voice could be coming from. It sounded so small, so distant, more like a voice from within his mind than a real one. Maybe his paranoia of sneaking around was making him hear things.

He turned to continue down the hallway, only to be stopped by another whispered shout.

"Finn! I'm up here."

"Where?" Finn whirled, his voice falling to match the hushed pitch of Dahvi's.

"Up here! I'm a spider!"

Finn's brow flattened with the effort of his focus as his eyes scanned the high length of walls, where they met with the ceiling. There, just below the corner, and about a yard from where he stood, Finn glimpsed a black spider the size of his thumbnail clinging to the wood.

"Dahvi?" He exhaled breathlessly, his mouth hanging open in shock. "Is that *really* you?"

"It's me!"

The hope that flickered in Finn's dark eyes was fleeting, replaced just as quickly by an uncharacteristic suspicion.

"What took you so long?"

"What?" Dahvi scoffed, "We came as soon as Monica returned. You were taken only a few hours before then."

"No…" Finn argued hesitantly, his brow twisting with confusion. Something was off. He'd been here for more than just a few hours… hadn't he? Those days… those days all blurred together, but they had felt *so* real. Finn suddenly worried that he didn't know what was real anymore. Seeking reassurance, Finn pleaded, "How do I know that *you're* real? That you're not a trap or a spell?"

"Because if I was, I wouldn't know that you're here because you took my advice to honor the thing your heart told you to do." A tentative smile tugged at the corners of Finn's mouth as Dahvi added, "You were right. It *was* stupid. But I'm so proud of you for doing it anyway."

Finn's smile crippled with a sudden realization, and an apology came spilling from his lips with a breathless urgency.

"Dahvi, I'm so sorry. I thought Rowan would—"

"I know. And I'm sorry too because *I* knew he wouldn't. But I had to do it anyway, because if I didn't, he would have killed them. He still might if he finds me here."

"What are you going to do?" Finn worried aloud. "How are you going to get your family back?"

"Maal promised to help. But first, I have to make sure that *you're* safe."

Finn's expression softened beneath a wave of gratitude, clearly oblivious to Maal's incriminating knowledge of the situation, that Monica had previously read as betrayal. Finn was more concerned about making sure his friends were safe, rather than finding fault in his potential adversaries.

"How did you get here? Did Monica send you?"

Dahvi paused, and though a spider's face hardly betrayed emotion of any kind, Finn felt Dahvi's regret in the silence.

"Yes," he finally admitted, quickly adding, "but I would've come anyway. I made a mistake."

Finn nodded a slow acknowledgement, his features sagging with sadness as he said, "I don't think you had a choice."

Dahvi said nothing, his regret making even the short silence between questions uncomfortable.

"Where's Monica?" Finn shifted. "Is she okay?"

"Yes. She's here."

"She is?" Finn asked, his question equal parts hope and fear. "Where is she? Can you take me to her?"

"I can't." Dahvi warned tersely. "They'll have her cabin guarded."

Finn's face twisted with indignance at the implication. "But not mine?"

"They think she's already gotten out once. They don't know that you have. Besides, I'm sure you've figured out that Monica is more important to Rowan than anyone else."

Finn's gaze fell as he considered this. He seemed to understand, but still asked, "Why?"

"I don't know," Dahvi answered candidly. "I think she has something he wants. So he's going to be watching her far more closely than you. It's great that you got out, but there's so much more you could do to help than risk capture by going to see her."

Finn swallowed, his exhale heavy with frustration. His gaze again lifted to where Dahvi's spider form sat near the ceiling. He was filled with so much determination that whatever thoughts Dahvi had previously about talking him out of this were gone. Finn would not be dissuaded.

"No," Finn said, clenching his fists at his sides. "I *have* to see her. I have a way to help. It's what I've wanted to do since I figured it out, but things didn't line up for that… until now."

"Finn," Dahvi warned again. "What are you saying? What have you figured out?"

Finn's right hand uncurled, hovering over the pocket of his jeans, itching with temptation to reveal his plan. But, even if he could still find it in his heart to trust Dahvi after what happened, he knew how risky revealing it to *anyone* could be. He only had one shot at this. His hand recoiled into a fist and he shook his head.

"I'm sorry, I can't. I just *have* to talk to Monica. I have to." Finn's voice trailed off and his eyes turned pleading.

"Fine," Dahvi sighed. "After all, I do owe you. I guess I can cause enough of a distraction to get you in and out, but you have to be fast. I can trick the wielders, but I can't guarantee I'd be able to do much to trick Rowan if he comes to see her while you're still there."

Finn nodded his eager ascent.

"Do you know where she is?"

"Yes," Dahvi answered, skittering away along the wall. "I'll show you. But be careful. Don't let anyone see you, okay?"

"Okay."

Chapter 42

Monica had expected Rowan's surveillance to be impatient and insistent, but it still surprised her to hear the lock of her door rattling open within the same hour that she'd traded places with Dahvi. Part of her was more annoyed than scared. After all, she'd almost managed to drift off to sleep again; a sleep she sorely needed, after her late night and lingering potion-induced weariness. They were only offset by the few, forbidden catnaps she'd surrendered to. She didn't look up, planning to play it as cool and evasive as she always did.

The rattling of the lock stopped and the door inched open the smallest crack.

"Monica?" The sound of her own whispered name was so soft that had she not seen the accompanying movement of the door, she would have convinced herself that she had imagined it.

That… didn't sound like Rowan. After all, if he'd already seen her once, what would stop him from barging into her room again? He certainly wasn't going to be respectful of her space or privacy, nor was there anything that should have made him wary in her presence, unless Dahvi had left out some aggressive and perhaps confrontational details of their first encounter. Though she still didn't trust the shifter, she decided that was unlikely.

Monica lifted her head to investigate. Her heart skipped a beat when she saw the door of her room continually inching open, a reaction she wasn't sure whether was more out of hope or panic. Even though whoever had come to see her was likely not Rowan, she couldn't see who it was, and she didn't trust her options on this ship.

She gathered herself into a ball at the foot of the bed, pushing the tension into her legs in preparation to strike at the intruder if need be. Her eyes skimmed the room around her for anything she could use as a weapon, but short of the few, small books that were afforded to her, the room was meticulously devoid of anything even remotely large or heavy enough to be used as a potential bludgeon.

"Monica?" The door peeled away to reveal a friendly, if not terrified face.

"Finn?" Monica's heart dropped into her stomach as she cautiously let her legs unfurl from their tucked position against her chest. Her breath came in shallow, barely audible pants as she eagerly looked him over. "Are you okay?"

He swallowed visibly before turning to latch the door behind him as softly as he could, looking relieved the second he had sealed their privacy. Then, he rushed to her, taking her in a shaky hug that squeezed the air out of her lungs and knocked her back onto the bed.

"Monica! I was so worried I wouldn't see you again. He tried to make me think you wouldn't come for me. But I knew that was a lie. I knew you'd come for me."

Monica stiffened, startled by the embrace, but quickly melted with Finn's desperation.

"Of course I would come for you, Finn," she answered breathlessly, unable to hug him back as his arms strapped hers to her sides. "What happened?"

"What took you so long?" He trembled, the words muffled against her shoulder, Finn still clinging to her as if he feared she'd disappear if he let go.

"I came as fast as I could." Monica pulled back, trying to glimpse anything in his expression that might soothe her confusion. "What are you talking about?"

Finn let his hold dissolve. He looked dazedly towards the floor, as if trying to decide something, before he said, "I've been here for weeks, I think." He sounded just as confused as she felt, only his was tinged with denial.

"No." Monica shook her head, looking startled as she held Finn an arm's length away. "I came as soon as I found you gone last night. Are you okay?"

Sniffling, Finn let his head drop. His shoulders suddenly tightened, and his whole stance shifted from welcoming relief to something more guarded and cold. The shift alarmed Monica.

"Yeah... I'm fine."

"Finn..." His name rose as a low growl of warning from deep in her throat. Even trying to hide it, he was too easy to read. "Don't lie. What happened?"

Finn shook his head and swallowed, careful to keep his gaze from meeting hers; not that that would make him any less predictable. Something was wrong. She could see it all over him, from the way his shoulders tensed, to the nervous tremble of his lower lip, and even in the effort he took to look brave when he finally did get up his courage to look her in the eye.

His eyes were dark, haunted with a bitter sadness that she had never seen on him. He backed away from her, creating a space between them that suddenly felt cold and empty. Monica's mouth hung agape to let a shallow exhale pass as she rose from the bed, longing to close that space. She stood, approaching him slowly with outstretched hands.

"Did Rowan hurt you?" She asked, tracing his arm with the lightest of touches, searching for any signs of physical damage.

"No!" Finn snapped, stealing his arm away from her. The gesture rattled her, especially after he'd been so desperate for physical comfort barely a moment ago. The harsh edge of his voice commanded her focus, frightening Monica into the suspicion that something about Finn was different now. "He didn't hurt me, not physically."

Monica's guard shattered to reveal the momentary sting that his brash response had conjured within her.

"What did he do to you?" She asked, sounding afraid of the question.

Finn's eyes fell and he gave a tight shake of his head as he gathered himself. Straightening, he spoke again with a forced courage that made his voice seem rigid and unfamiliar. "Well, I'm beginning to think he's messing with my mind. He did something to me to make me lose track of time, making me think that I was alone in my room for a *long* time. Then, he used that to convince me that you hadn't come, that you didn't care enough to come after me."

"Finn…" Monica swallowed hard, "you know that's not true. I'm here."

"I know. But it was enough to make me truly believe otherwise, even briefly. And if he can do all that to me, without ever laying a hand on me, I'm more afraid of what he's going to do to you."

Monica chuckled nervously, her brows still knit in concern.

"Is that all?" She mused dryly "I'm fine."

"For now," Finn warned. "But he's going to do something far more horrible to you if you stay; I just know it. He's going to kill you, or—"

"He won't." Monica tried to comfort him, her tone now startlingly serene. "He won't."

"You don't know that."

Monica shook her head. "Apparently, I have something he wants."

Finn paused, briefly placated by this, at least enough to dull the edge of his voice when he surrendered to the next natural question. "That's what Dahvi said, too. What is it?"

Monica shook her head again, this time, even more vehemently. "It doesn't matter. All that matters is that you're safe."

"We are *not* safe as long as we're prisoners here. My mind hardly feels safe! And how can you believe that, after everything you told me about The Enclave?"

Monica seized Finn's wrist, forcing his eyes to meet hers as she growled, "We're safe as long as we're more useful to him alive than dead. And I *have* to believe that. You *have* to believe that too, because it's all we have right now."

The color drained from his face, and Finn suddenly looked as if he felt ill. Monica could feel him trembling in her grasp, but he didn't fight it, nor did he fight her again.

"We're… not getting out of here, are we?" Finn dared to ask, his voice falling to barely a whisper.

"We will." Monica unfurled her fingers from around his wrist before lifting her hand to rest on one of his still shaking shoulders. "I just don't know when... Or how."

Finn's eyes dropped to the floor and he gave a shallow sigh. Biting his lip, he remained silent for a long moment, so long that Monica worried he might not have heard her. But the look on his face said that he had.

Monica's eyes remained on him, seeking any fleeting reactions of fear or sadness. Anything that she might be able to somehow fix. But he just looked uncharacteristically blank. Was he shutting down? Avoiding it? Was this situation so much that it was forcing Finn to guard himself behind a wall of denial?

Monica knew that wasn't true. No, if anything, Finn became stronger when he was scared. She had seen it on the island, when he had saved her, as well as when he'd stood up to his mother. It wasn't like him to hide from his fears.

Despite the wave of dismay that now drenched Finn's features, a sudden, brief spark of hope passed through his eyes; an idea.

"You're here, and Dahvi's here… but what about Celene? Could she—"

"Oh, Finn," Monica sighed apologetically, giving a small shake of her head that looked more like a tremble than a confirmation. Monica paused, her gut twisting with despair as she carefully weighed her next words. She hated having to crush Finn's hope, but the last thing she wanted to do was lie to him. There was no getting out of here, not that Monica could see. And, even if there was, the siren being the one to do it was the longest shot there was. "Celene doesn't know."

"Doesn't know what?"

"She doesn't know that you were taken. She doesn't know that Dahvi and I came after you. The last time I spoke to Celene was…" Monica paused, her gaze flitting briefly distant as if chasing the realization, "the last time we were at Maal's tower."

"You… you didn't call her before you came after me?" Finn asked, the disappointment clear in his voice.

"There wasn't time."

"But she'll come looking for us, right?"

Monica's heart sank like a rock in her chest at Finn's continued persistence. No, not persistence, desperation.

"She might, but she has no idea where we've gone."

"She'll figure it out." Finn insisted, though the uncertainty in his words made them turn into a question instead of the reassurance they had initially meant to be. "She will, right?"

"Even if she did, it wouldn't matter." Monica's answer came out sharper than she'd meant.

"Why not?"

"Because." Monica drew in a sharp breath, before trying to explain what she knew as gently as she could. "Rowan warded the ship with a magic so strong that it can't be broken without his command. The ward he described would mean that no one can leave the ship as long as the spell is intact. So, even if Celene *did* somehow figure out where we went and manage to make it to us, she'd be just as trapped as we are. Although, that won't happen, since Rowan magically veiled the ship from view, so even if Celene *did* come looking, she wouldn't be able find us."

Finn hesitated for a moment, his eyes darting about the room as he searched for his next question.

"How do you know all this?"

"Rowan told me. Well, he told Dahvi, while he was shifted to look like me."

"Why?"

Monica shrugged, looking more dejected than she usually did when things went wrong. That wasn't like her... Monica got angry or even sad, but she always fought back. So to see her just laying down and accepting her fate made Finn's stomach drop with a growing fear that fought to sink his persistent balloon of hope. What if... Rowan had tortured Monica, too?

"Does he even *need* a reason? The situation is hopeless, and Rowan wants us to know that he's got the upper hand. There's no way off this ship unless we can defeat him, not to mention an *entire* ship of magic wielders. Which, if the three of us could do, we could've solved this problem a long time ago. But now... Now it's too late."

Finn drew back, shaking his head. A spark of hope still brightened his voice, though he had to fight to keep it alive beneath the wet blanket of Monica's despair.

"No. Rowan's gotta be bluffing. He just wants us to *think* that it's hopeless."

"With his reputation, he wouldn't need to be bluffing. He's one of the strongest wielders I know. There's nothing we can do."

Finn swallowed, his voice dropping to a disappointed whisper. "So, you're just gonna give up? The Monica I know doesn't give up. You always have a plan."

"The plan was to not get caught and look how that turned out." Monica shrugged angrily as she looked at the cabin around them. "And even if I did, what in the seven realms am I supposed to do from inside this cell?"

"I got out of mine and into yours. There has to be a way!" Finn insisted, only to be cut off by Monica's adamant denial.

"Mine is guarded by *wielders*, Finn. They think I already got out once. I have no chance of getting out again, and even if I did, the chances of us overtaking them would be next to impossible, even if Rowan *hadn't* taken my weapons and artifacts. If he warded the ship like he said, our only hope would be to overtake him *and* the ship, and being three against who knows how many, I don't know what we can actually do without magic, ourselves."

"He… he took your artifacts?" Finn asked, voice trembling as he finally realized the weight of the situation. "Even the Riftrider?"

"Of course he did! He took everything, my dagger, the ring, the Riftrider, even—" Monica laughed bitterly, the sound catching in her throat before turning into a strangled sob. "—even the Soulseeker."

The way Monica's cadence leaned into the word made it obvious that of all the things that she was upset about, that was the most troubling to her. She was trapped with a man who wanted her dead, the man who'd killed her family and sold her into slavery. If she truly believed she was never getting out, why was she so concerned about the Soulseeker of all things? Finn knew it was rare, but with everything else going on, that was the thing Finn just didn't understand. Or maybe he did, he just didn't want it to be true.

Monica was getting desperate, and seeing it made Finn fear for her, for what she might do when she believed that she was truly out of options. He needed to hear it from her.

"What would you do with the Soulseeker?" Finn asked.

Monica shook her head. "I can't…" She started softly and her focus suddenly dissolved from his face when she started to struggle with the words. "I can't get my brother back without it."

Finn paused. That was the truth of all this, wasn't it? Monica feeling trapped and out of options wasn't just because of that moment, but because she couldn't see how to move forward to fix *anything*: not how to stop the Enclave, not how to save her brother, not even how to keep Finn safe.

And in the silence, she didn't have to say any of it out loud. She felt Finn's somber, wordless understanding. But just when Monica thought Finn might not say anything else, he cleared his throat and spoke again with a tone so gentle with empathy that it made Monica's chest spasm painfully around her quivering heart.

"You can't get your brother back anyway if you're trapped here. Don't you think he'd want you to get out of here? Then, you can continue looking for someone to trade places with him so that he can come back."

Though Finn's tentative lilt made the phrase sound like a question, Monica had been sure that Finn understood the situation, even though he'd only overheard Monica telling Celene, rather than him directly. Sure, he was oblivious a lot of the time, but he *had* to know this, didn't he? He had to know what she wanted to do. He *had* to understand how hopeless everything felt, not only this situation, but the one her brother was in, too.

Monica regarded Finn with glassy eyes, no longer trying to hide her desperation behind a wall of stoicism. Even trapped here, as Rowan's prisoner, all Monica could think about was how she'd left things with Monroe. It had been agonizing to leave him without a plan, without knowing how she was going to save him, and without knowing how much time he had left.

It seemed to her like if Monroe were here, it'd fix both problems. And there was only one way to achieve that

The pity in Finn's eyes shook her from her moment of vulnerability. She hated anyone seeing her like this, most of all, the one she wanted to protect.

She cleared her throat, straightening to bring any amount of strength back to her posture.

"Monroe is a wielder, and a powerful one," She explained. "He could break the ward with his magic. He could get you out. It wouldn't be permanent, I could just stay in Enderfel until—"

"No." Finn drew in a sharp, angry breath. His face reddened, and Monica caught the brief glint of tears dwelling in his eyes before he turned away. Before Monica could decipher his reaction, Finn's demeanor changed, darkened, and he dropped his head. "Monica, we need to talk about... some stuff."

"About what?"

“We never talked earlier, after the first time you came back from Enderfel."

"But…" She wrung her hands. "You heard what happened, right?"

"Yes, but this isn't about what happened to you. This is about what happened to me… between me and Dahvi. I have to tell you the truth.”

“The truth?” Monica cleared her throat as she reigned in the burst of volume triggered by a new wave of panic. “Finn, it’s fine that you have other friends, but now’s not the time—”

“It doesn’t sound fine,” Finn snapped, revealing that the harshness of his tone surprised even him with a slight widening of his eyes. "You've been distant since then, like you've been avoiding me. I've been terrified that I hurt you somehow."

"I haven't been avoiding you." The sharpness of her voice made restraining her tears nearly impossible. "I've been trying to figure out how to fix everything."

"Fix everything?" Finn sniffed. "Do you really think that *you* trading places with your brother is going to fix *anything*?"

Monica froze, suddenly understanding the anger she had seen on his face before. As she peered into his crushingly hurt eyes, she could no longer feel her heartbeat, whether it was pounding so fast it was no longer distinctive beat, or whether it had stopped completely.

Monica swallowed.

She couldn't deny that she had seriously considered Finn's accusation as an option, especially now, since few others existed.

Wavering, she pleaded, "I don't know what else to do. I don't have any other way to bring him back. And that's all

I've ever wanted, for as long as I remember. He could help bring down The Enclave. He deserves to be a part of that."

"Don't you deserve that as well?"

Their eyes met from behind trembling domes of tears. Finn's question stung her heart like a poisoned dagger, with an ache that would far outlast the initial blow. The pleading in his eyes stole her breath away.

Only once she finally caught it again did she whisper, "Sometimes, we have to pick what's most important to us."

A tear spilled down Monica's cheek.

Finn's anger flushed into sorrow. He nodded, reaching forward to hug her. Monica welcomed it, hugging him back just as tightly. She felt so small in Finn's arms. He was so warm, and, for a second she almost let herself forget where she was because of how safe his embrace felt. Did he feel how much she was shaking? For the first time, she actually didn't care. Being so strong all the time was exhausting. But, in his arms, she found the comfort to let that forced strength go, even for just a moment. She wasn't sure what this hug meant. Was he agreeing with her? Telling her that it was all right to trade places with Monroe? For some reason, no matter how sweet and selfless Finn was, she couldn't quite let herself believe that he'd really be okay with that. She was reading too much into it. It was for comfort, that's all. After all, trapped as a prisoner on this ship, what could she do without her Soulseeker?

Monica pulled away, wiping her cheeks with her hands before there was enough distance between them to reveal any tears that had fallen. But Finn wasn't ready to let go, squeezing to keep her body pressed to his.

"I understand." He whispered, breath warm as it stirred her hair. "I get it. And you *will* have your brother back."

When Finn's embrace loosened, Monica pulled away, sniffling and nodding, and trying not to cry at his reassurance. How did he know exactly what she needed to hear? Even though he couldn't do anything to help, for a moment, she believed him.

"Thank you."

Finn sniffled, and Monica realized that his cheeks were wet and streaked with his own tears.

"Finn, why are you crying? I know everything feels hopeless now, but we'll be okay."

"Yeah," Finn agreed, forcing a small smile that ended up jagged with hesitation. "It *will* be okay."

He looked like there was more he wanted to say, much more, but Monica didn't want to press anything. Even if this whole situation had shaken him and terrified him to tears, she was just relieved to have seen him. As long as he was okay, she could make herself believe that they would both be able to get out of this alive.

Sighing, Monica steadied herself. She laid a hand on Finn's shoulder, calling his gaze to meet hers with the gesture.

"Just give me some time, okay?"

Finn bit his lip, looking hesitant. His eyes darted away and he whispered, "You won't need it."

This earned a dry chuckle from Monica. "Thanks for believing in me." As her voice trailed off, Monica found herself still unsettled by the worry that twisted Finn's mouth. It wasn't like him… Deciding to lay on another reassurance, she added, "You *do* believe we'll get out of here, right? Together?"

Finn said nothing. He shrugged out of her grasp, forcing her to see something she had worked hard to avoid, until now.

"We won't, Monica." A muscle feathered in his jaw as he admitted his hesitation with clenched teeth. His eyes were suddenly so cold and his dour expression was so severe that it aged him. When he continued, his voice was so steady, it was like he wasn't even him anymore. "Like you said, the ward can only be broken with magic, which neither of us have. We can't stay here forever, whether that forever is real or just an illusion. I won't let you."

Her brow furrowed at the switch in his demeanor. "You won't *let* me?" She repeated, in a way that made her unsure if she was merely echoing his question or clarifying his ominous statement.

He shook his head.

"I won't let you go through what I did… those terrible weeks alone. When you get out of here, I will be somewhere else."

"Where?" Monica began, shaking her head as she struggled to understand. "Look, I'm so sorry. You're right to want to go home after all of this, and when I get you out, you can—"

"No. Monica, will you just listen to me?" She bristled at the demand in his voice, relaxing only when she met his eyes, which were now glassy with tears. "Please. I need to tell you the truth. I almost couldn't, but I can't do this if you don't know."

"Know what?"

When their gazes met, Finn's were soft again, warm with the same youthful innocence he wore when they had first met.

"That I don't want to hurt you. I've never wanted to hurt you. But I have to, in order to save you."

"Finn?" Monica gasped, her eyes widening in clear panic. "What are you talking about? I came to save *you*, not the other way around."

He shook his head.

"I see it now. It was always meant to be this way."

The threat of finality in his phrasing forced Monica to fall silent. Fear made her throat too dry to speak, and it hurt to breathe. She reached for his hand, but he pulled away, instead using his fingers to retrieve something from within his pocket. Letting it dangle between them, the object glittered and refracted a spray of sunlight that momentarily obstructed Monica's recognition.

"How did you get that?"

"It doesn't matter."

"Give it to me." Monica swiped at the Soulseeker, only for Finn to flick it away just as deftly, denying her fingers even a fleeting graze of contact.

"I can't," Finn said, his eyes sad as he held the amulet high enough that it was no longer within her grasp.

She briefly considered leaping for it, but she didn't want to take it from Finn by force, nor did she believe she could, in seeing the determination rising in his posture. She froze, peering up at him from a perspective that made her feel physically small in comparison. Not only did the amulet glitter in the light, he seemed to, too. His silhouette was unusually strong, noble, and statuesque. It was… almost like he wasn't even real.

As the growing sheen of light strobed across his pale skin, Monica realized what was happening. The surface of her eyes swam under a new sheen of tears as she looked up into his face.

"No," she pleaded, the word swallowed beneath a staggered gasp. "No, Finn! Please. You can't."

"I have to." His fingers already pinched the ivory coin, which had flicked up into his hand when he'd pulled it away from Monica.

Monica reached for him, and Finn's entire being flashed in an ethereal blaze. Monica fell back onto the bed, shielding her eyes from the boy who now flared before her like a human star.

"Finn, don't!" She squinted against the rapidly increasing light. "I can fix this! You don't know what you're doing!"

"I do." His voice rang softly through the air, like the clear peal of a distant bell. "I want you to be happy, as happy as I've been since I came here. I'm picking what's most important to me: *you*."

The light flashed so brilliantly that the room was now awash in a white so thick that it blinded Monica, making her unable to see for almost a whole minute after Finn finally vanished.

Chapter 43

Two days had passed since Monica watched Finn cross into Enderfel. Denial, as stupid as it was, was the only thing that kept her balanced atop the precarious edge between determination and despair. She couldn't lose him. Not after everything she'd done to keep him safe. This was just one of Rowan's spells, an illusion made to torment her. And she certainly couldn't do anything to save him if she let herself spiral. No. He was still here. He *had* to be. She *had* to find a way to get out and find him and get off this damned ship!

The first day, she'd spent a few hours searching for a way out of her cabin, but to no avail. Unlike the perfunctory watch that her cabin had been kept under before, her door was now consistently guarded by at least two large wielders with more in the near vicinity. And there was no way she'd get out of the small window that had been blocked off by a large bookshelf, without making too much noise that the watch would figure out what she was doing. So, she spent the rest of that day angrily pacing the length of her small cabin until she was finally exhausted enough to sleep. She didn't even wake when someone brought her food, only finding it cold on the table beside her when she finally woke.

The second day filled Monica with an exhausted numbness that kept her from overthinking the situation to the point of angry, desperate denial. Instead, this tranquil apathy helped her transition to another state of vague hopefulness and curiosity. She wondered where Dahvi was since he hadn't come back to her with news of finding Finn. Either, he hadn't found him yet, or… She killed the thought before it transitioned into fear, deciding to leave it with the hope that the shifter was finding a way to make himself useful, somehow.

During that second day, her hollow coping was interrupted by an emotional flare that brought everything back to the surface.

The lock of her door clattered briefly before it clicked open. She looked up, chiding herself for the hope the sound had conjured in knowing that, if Finn was still here, he wouldn't be able to see her for the guard standing watch at her door. She knew who was at her door. Rowan.

Monica's nostrils flared and a hot, bitter rage flicked up the back of her throat the moment her eyes landed on his contemptuous, smirking face.

Rowan's eyebrows rose in pleasant greeting as he observed her body gathering in a tensed, defensive crouch atop one of the arms of the chairs in the far corner of the room.

"Well," he mused, "you seem to be settling in nicely. Nightmares treating you okay?"

"Where's Finn?" Monica snarled.

Rowan sauntered farther into the room, unfazed. "That again? I'd hoped your respite between visits would have made you realize that he's not here."

"He is. I *know* he is. *You* know he is. After all, that's why I'm here, isn't it?"

"Oh," Rowan pursed his lips in mocking pity. "If only it were that simple. You're here because I need you here."

Rowan *needed* her? Monica wasn't sure whether to be flattered, mortified, or disgusted. But, at least, hearing him say that out loud confirmed her hope of gaining an upper hand. If she could learn *why* he needed her, she could use that to her advantage. But, at the moment, she was too mad to pursue that course, yet.

Instead, she shouted, "So you kidnapped my friend to make it happen?"

Rowan shrugged, leaning his weight against Monica's empty bed until the mattress sagged. Her bed was so tidy that it looked like she'd barely even slept in it. Even as a prisoner, her habits of leaving everything just as she found it from her days of "visiting" empty houses followed her.

"Really, don't act like you would've come if I'd asked nicely. And technically, it's not kidnapping since he came willingly."

"After everything you've done, including blackmailing, stealing, and *murder*, you wanna argue about the semantics of kidnapping?"

Rowan's grin rippled wide. "At least it's got you talking, now."

Realizing that he was right, Monica's jaw clenched and she shrugged down into her tightly crossed arms, wishing that she could shrink more and disappear. After everything, she was hardly in the mood for a confrontation, much less a negotiation. And, if he knew her, that's what Rowan would expect, wouldn't he? A negotiation?

As if he'd ever come to a compromise with her, especially since he was holding all the cards in the current situation. Still, it wouldn't hurt to try. Maybe she could get *him* talking, too.

Monica straightened, uncrossing her arms to facilitate a challenge of pride arching across her shoulders. It had been so long since she had to consciously remind herself of the steps in facilitating a successful negotiation, but then again, when was the last time she had to make such a high stakes deal under such sweltering pressure? She caught her breath, holding it until she found enough courage to stare Rowan in the eye, intent on projecting that she wasn't afraid of him.

"What do you want with me?" Monica asked firmly.

Rowan's expression was impassive behind his lasting grin, which, paired with his cold, calculating eyes, served its purpose to make Monica feel unsettled, to say the least. She shifted as he looked her over, trying not to betray more discomfort than she already had. A spark of satisfaction danced across Rowan's eyes, yet he maintained a respectful distance.

"I want your help with something." Rowan purred, his voice suddenly becoming sickeningly sweet. "A favor."

"Favor?" Monica's eyes narrowed. "You wanted me dead. You said so yourself. What changed?"

"Nothing." Rowan sighed, letting his head tilt this way and that, making his chestnut curls dance around the collar of his cloak. "I never wanted you dead, not truly. I merely wanted you to value your own life more. And what better way to do that than to remind you of how quickly you can lose it?"

Monica scoffed to hide a small catch in her throat. "That's ridiculous. Why should you care?"

"Do you deny that your life means little to you?"

"I don't think that's any of your business."

"Bold of you to say that when you display your disregard so openly for all to see. It wasn't hard to ascertain. From your dealings with a djinn who treats you as disposable, to risking your life on a constant basis to do his bidding, to saving the skin of a mortal you've just met, over and over, with no regard to what personal cost it may carry?" Rowan tsked. "If that's not *asking* for death, you have me fooled."

"That's enough!" Monica bit back. "You have no right to judge who I chose to do business with, and even less for whom I chose to protect."

"Perhaps I'm trying to understand. Before, you seemed to *want* death… yet, you did everything to fight it when I came to offer it to you on The Isle of Reflection. Why?"

Monica sniffed, her stare cold and unblinking. She wasn't about to explain herself to this monster—for empathy, personal comfort, or anything else that may come of it. He didn't care. Someone like him; he *couldn't* care. This was just an act to figure out what was tied to her heartstrings so that he could decide which ones to pluck in order to make her dance like the puppet he craved.

With eyes that seemed to reach into the depths of her soul, Rowan observed, "Is it because you finally feel like you have something to lose?"

Despite the jolt of anxiety that flooded her veins at his lucky guess —or maybe it was just observation— Monica's defiant silence remained.

When she said nothing, Rowan relaxed, his posture pushing back to recline even further. He laced his fingers behind his head, looking up as if the sky overhead was unobstructed by the low cabin ceiling.

"You know," he began with a sigh, "I know what that's like. Everything I've done has been a means to prevent losing the things that are dear to me."

Monica felt a tiny twinge of contempt tugging at her upper lip, a response not to his words, but to the innate softening she felt in her chest at the sentimentality. It all seemed more human than she liked. He was a monster. He wasn't allowed to make her want to understand his cruel actions, let alone sympathize with him. *It's just an act,* she told herself, but seeing the too familiar wistfulness in his distant gaze making him look vulnerable, made her doubt, even slightly.

"I had a family once, too. And, like you, I lost them. Since then, I patched together a new family, gathered people who could be just as influential. And, wouldn't you know it, I lost them too. In the end, there's always something that takes them away. Death, greed, betrayal." Rowan sighed. "So, I got to thinking, wouldn't it be nice if there wasn't anything that could cause that anymore? What would happen if I took away all the things that facilitate loss?"

With the tightness of a new fear coiling around her lungs, Monica managed a tight-lipped, "It's not possible."

This brought Rowan back to reality. His gaze fell from the obstructed sky to Monica, his face soft with a smile that was equal parts wistful with bittersweet longing, and hungry in an unnerving sort of way. Cocking his head to one side, Rowan pondered, "Wouldn't you like that, too? If no one could ever be taken from you again? No death to separate you. No lies to twist their minds away or betrayal to blacken their hearts against loving you? Wouldn't you love a world without fear of pain or loss?"

Breathless, all Monica could say was, "It's not possible."

Her words were tight with fear, the phrase trembling with denial, and worse, longing. She knew it couldn't be, that something like that wasn't possible, but Rowan *did* know how to spin a pretty lie. And, what if it was? What if she could have such a world? How could something like that be bad?

Sensing her hesitation, Rowan's tone darkened.

"It is. And I could make it happen, with your help. You simply have to want it as badly as I do."

This broke Monica from the spell. Drawing back, she gave her head a quick shake.

"No. What I want is for my friend to have his freedom."

Rowan's expression muddied, twisting into something pieced together from bafflement, amusement, and perhaps even a hint of annoyance.

"You would sacrifice all that, as well as yourself for *him?* Why?"

"He's my friend. And if I have to justify that to you, you mustn't have anyone important enough to make you understand."

"Hmm..." The wielder steepled his fingers briefly against his chin in consideration. "Having someone like that is trouble, you know?"

Monica bristled, trying to protect herself against the jab she should've seen coming. His pretty words had lulled her into a lowered guard, and now, realizing that he was trying to turn her against Finn and make her feel guilty for wanting and failing to protect him made her distrust sharpen. Why did he care about Finn? About using him to torture her? The sheer pleasure of it? She wouldn't put it past him. But, then again, maybe he predicted she'd be more malleable if she didn't have anything left to lose. Rowan *was* a two-faced snake of contradictions. She held her tongue. She wasn't about to feed the fire that sought to burn her.

When Monica said nothing, Rowan continued, "He's going to get you killed. After all, you've already risked yourself for him, what, twice? Three times? In a few short weeks, you've gone and gotten yourself a weakness. You know that's part of what I was waiting for, right? You were so strong when you had nothing left to lose, but you... you get desperate and you lose all sense of rational thought when you want to keep from losing something that's important to you. There's a difference between wanting to protect something you care about and being so desperate to do so that you let it put you at risk. How often has that backfired on you? Like when your brother smuggled you out of Vhalta and back into Vhenra. You were so scared you were going to lose him again. You were terrified that it was only a matter of time before The Enclave found him that you took matters into your own hands. Your selfish attempt to buy his freedom led us right to your door. *You* were the reason you lost him. And what about when—"

"Stop!" Monica demanded, her voice small but firm, unwavering despite the tears welling in her eyes. "Don't pretend to know me."

"Really? I know that you were prepared to sacrifice yourself to save that boy, otherwise, you wouldn't have come here."

"He has a name. Finn."

Rowan shrugged, unconcerned.

"This *Finn*…" He said, lifting himself up from against the bed to stand. "He's important to you. You don't want to lose him."

An expectant pause.

Monica didn't want to give Rowan the satisfaction, but she couldn't help it.

"And?" She asked, trying not to sound too curious.

"And I have things *I* don't want to lose. If you help me, I can help you."

"That sounds like a threat."

"No," Rowan chortled, a small dimple forming in one check. "Not a threat. Merely a promise."

A flare of indignance rose in Monica's chest as she remembered to whom she was talking. She couldn't trust him. She couldn't even listen to him without feeling the itch of his every lie skittering across her skin. So… why was there a small part of her that wanted to hear him out?

"And why should I trust the promise of a murderer?"

"Because this promise is what stands between you and everything you've ever wanted. And it can help you, or it can keep you from those things."

"What do you know of everything I want?" Monica fists clenched against her stomach as a spike of uneasy bile rose in her throat, making her voice hoarse.

"I know that getting everything you've ever wanted means nothing if you can't keep it. I can help you keep it, *all of it*, if you'll only help me keep mine."

Monica hesitated. Her eyelids fluttered and her mind stalled as she found herself briefly considering it. After all, he *was* one of the most powerful wielders she knew. Was he really powerful enough to help her get *everything* she's ever wanted? But at what price, considering she'd already lost her parents, her brother, and her freedom to similarly hungry wielders? What was to keep him from turning on her and falling back into those treacherous, cruel patterns? A shock of electric realization ripped through her mind, making it scream against the urge. Why was she even entertaining the thought? Magic? Or because part of her actually *did* want to hear him out? Monica wasn't sure which bothered her more.

She leapt from the arm of the chair, landing with a ship-rocking *thud* as she recoiled to stand.

"Get out!" She lifted one arm and pointed towards the door.

Rowan's lips parted with a sinister sneer that sparkled with such satisfaction that it made Monica's stomach turn.

"You don't even want to hear what the favor is?" Rowan persisted.

It was too tempting. Her eyes squeezed closed, momentarily struggling against the thought and knowing that if she gave in, she might not be able to give up his offer. And that sickened her. This man, whom she hated more than anything, whom she should want to see dead more than anything, saw her desperation and was set on using it against her. Just as The Eye of Desire had shown, she wanted Rowan dead, but not more than she wanted her brother back, and perhaps not more than protecting herself from losing anyone else that was important to her.

Her eyes snapped open, remembering why she had come here. If she gave into Rowan's persuasions, where did that leave Finn? He couldn't stay. He wouldn't be safe here, ever. So, she decided that she couldn't indulge her own desires until he was safe; hopefully somewhere far, far away. Until then, she had to stay strong.

"I *will not* help you, not for anything."

"Not even if I could guarantee you'll *never* lose anyone who's important to you, *ever again*?"

A pulse of ice radiated through Monica's synapses, making every inch of her skin rise into goosebumps. She hated that she was tempted by his words, curious, interested. No.

"Get out! Now!"

Rowan's smirk dimmed momentarily as he turned and strode towards the door, sauntering with the proud gait of an uninjured man. The doorknob clicked in his hand. He hesitated, looked back over his shoulder. His eyes locked with Monica's and he whispered, "Think about it. You know you want to."

And before she could protest or threaten him again, Rowan disappeared, the lock clicked, and his satisfied chuckle echoed behind him.

Chapter 44

Finn's skin numbed after a sharp prickle of cold that rose as soon as the light of the Soulseeker enveloped him. When he disappeared from Vhalta, it was as if the world flipped inside out, and that light collapsed into a vacuum of darkness. The darkness was so complete and suffocating, that Finn began to feel the edges of his mind fraying, smothering him in a helpless sensation not unlike the blurry flow of time that Rowan's illusion had used to stretch hours into weeks. The deeper he plunged into the darkness, the colder and emptier it grew, until he imagined himself floating, alone and forgotten in the middle of space. Finn even once considered if he was really *real* anymore. Did he exist? Had he ever existed in the first place?

Jolting awake from the icy, numb nothingness, the rift peeled away and spat Finn out onto the hard ground of a foreign realm. He tumbled to a stop, feeling dizzy as he pushed himself upright in a small drift of soft soil. *No, not soil,* he realized, staring at the powdery gray-white substance that sifted through his fingers and left a dusty residue on his fingertips. Ash.

He glanced up. The sky overhead was an inky, starless black, devoid of a moon or stars of any kind. Was it even really a sky? Or just a dome with a black tarp flung over it? It made his stomach twist with an inherent wrongness, it's cold lifelessness crushing down on him with a weight that the normal night sky did not possess.

The only illumination that misted his vision came from a thin line of pale amber, etched low along the wide, flat horizon. It didn't seem *that* bright, as to fill an entire black space with the eerie warmth of several candles, but it did. Finn squinted at it, following the band of amber around himself in a perfect circle. Everything was flat as far as he could see, creating the illusion that the featureless expanse of cool gray ash was both endless and empty.

But it wasn't empty. Despite the total lack of buildings or trees, Finn's attention suddenly leapt to the throng of people gathered around him, sprawling in every direction. Thousands, no, maybe even hundreds of thousands. He hadn't heard them when he'd fallen, and even now as he stood, this world seemed muffled, the voices of thousands no more than a whisper of wind dancing through an open meadow.

How could so many people be so quiet? Were they dead? *Stupid question.* Finn shook his head. But they weren't dead, not like the way dead people were in his world. His gaze slowly scanned the encampments around him, flicking up rows and rows of makeshift villages. Movement. It was slight, sluggish, like these people were actors moving in slow-mo, but they still moved.

As he studied them, Finn realized they weren't that quiet after all. Their voices blended into a low-level droning that was so consistently monotone that his mind had initially dismissed it as white noise. But as he focused on it, the noise became sharper, merely from awareness than actual clarity, as the conversations remained indistinct.

Distracted by a glint of light reflecting up from his hand, Finn remembered the Soulseeker, quickly followed by why he was here.

He swallowed nervously, looping the amulet around his neck so that it could hide beneath the collar of his shirt, as he'd so often seen Monica do. The action let him relax, and Finn approached the nearest group of bystanders with urgent intention.

"Um, excuse me?"

His voice was sharp against the muddled din of this world, but no one responded. He glanced around, unsure of who specifically he was addressing. His focus fixed on the nearest person, a sprawled skeletal man that looked more like a bag of bones only held together by a thin layer of gray skin than a man.

"Excuse me?"

The man stared up at Finn with hollow, black eyes that sat vacant above two deep crescents of sunken purple exhaustion. His crooked nose poked through a disheveled mass of unwashed salt and pepper hair and beard

The man barely seemed to have the energy to look Finn up and down before his chin sunk into his chest in a lull akin to sleep. Sensing the uselessness of pushing the subject, Finn dove into the crowd to find someone remotely more alive.

An insistent shoulder tap earned Finn the attention of a graying middle aged woman, whose face was soft with motherly care despite an overcast of weariness.

"Excuse me." Finn met the woman's dark eyes with his own as he gestured the details of his inquiry. "Have you seen a guy about my age…" His hand rose to indicate the area a few inches above his own head, "this tall, dark hair in a bun that's shaved on the sides and light blue eyes?"

"Light blue eyes?" The woman spluttered humorously with a waggle of her head. "Nobody here has light eyes anymore."

Finn's brow crinkled. "What do you mean?"

The woman pulled down one of her purple lower lids with a dramatic fingertip to show off one of her own coal-black irises.

"When the life leaves a person, so does the light, followed by the colors, and then the hope. It may start gradually, but if he's been here longer than a few days, his eyes won't be blue anymore."

Blinking, Finn shook his head, trying to remember any other details from his one encounter with Monroe that might help.

"Okay, what about a leather jacket?" He motioned as if pulling one on himself before pointing to the left side of his chest with two fingers. "With band pins?"

The woman stalled, and Finn wasn't sure if she was thinking, or she'd gotten lost in a distant thought.

Finn tapped her shoulder.

"No, don't recall seeing anyone like that here."

"Okay. Thanks."

After nearly a dozen similar encounters to the first, and only a few like the second, but that ended in the same answer, Finn's determination began to wane with the weight of an unusual exhaustion. He tried to shake it off, knowing that he shouldn't reasonably feel like he'd just run a marathon, but his lungs burned and his body ached in evidence.

Deciding he was getting nowhere asking around, Finn instead shifted his focus to their faces, reduced to having to rely on nothing more than his own memory. Would he even know Monroe if he saw him again? *Of course he would,* Finn told himself. After all, he looked just like Monica, albeit masculine and much, much taller. Regardless of color, they had the same eyes, the same guarded expression that was only a hard shell to protect so much more. He'd seen Monica's face too often not to recognize its likeness, even on a stranger.

Finn wasn't sure how long it took him to finally make progress, but he didn't stop to worry about the hours or maybe even days, as they passed. If he stopped, he might not be able to start again. He continued with the single thought in mind of finding Monroe and saving Monica, and that kept him going.

Scanning faces, Finn inevitably came across those he recognized: a cousin who'd drowned in a swimming pool when they were kids, his uncle, who'd he'd only seen a few times before the car fell on him in his own mechanic shop, acquaintances, people whose names he didn't know, and whose deaths he had been oblivious to before now. Even so, all of them twanged the same familiar chord of knowing and sadness. At first, Finn wondered if it was his imagination, showing him *his* ghosts in a place full of them. But, what were the chances of seeing so many he knew in a place so crowded and vast? He didn't have time to question whether any of them were real, until he came across the one he could not ignore.

His eyes locked with those of a dark-skinned boy from across the distance, and the look immediately rooted him to the spot.

Akash? In shock, the name never left his lips, but the boy in question stared back like he'd heard it, nonetheless. Akash's eyes were wide and doe-like, unblinking and reflecting the same disbelief that Finn's did. He looked *exactly* the same as when Finn had last seen him, down to the youth lingering in his still boyish features that Finn himself had only recently begun to outgrow. His hair might have been a little longer, his eyes a little more tired, but there was no denying who he was looking at.

And then, it was like everything else melted away. The crowd vanished, the distance closed, and Finn found himself stumbling into the little alcove in which Akash sat, away from everyone else.

Barely able to breathe, Finn asked softly, "Akash? Is it really you?"

Akash slowly rose from his cross-legged position in the ashes, approaching his friend with similar caution. His head gave a single shake, his stare never faltering.

"Tell me you're not here," Akash commanded, his words swaying with the same lilting affectation of his faint, native accent despite the dread flattening their emotion to a fearful monotone.

"I am." Finn's vision suddenly blurred as Akash wrapped him in a spontaneous hug.

Finn stumbled but quickly stilled, marveling at the wonder of Akash's tangibility and the pressure of his urgent embrace. He wasn't sure what he'd been expecting, but part of his mind had anticipated moving through the embrace, as if his friend was a ghost. Finn sighed in relief for a subconscious hope he hadn't acknowledged until now.

Akash held on for a long time, gripping Finn with disbelief and fear similar to Finn's own when he had embraced Monica after the illusion on Rowan's ship had half-convinced him that he'd never see her again. When Akash finally pulled away, it was with silent tears streaming down his face. He wiped his cheeks with the backs of his hands, never taking his eyes off of Finn.

"I wish you weren't," Akash finally said, so solemnly that Finn wondered if his ears were misinterpreting the greeting.

"What? Why not? I never thought I'd get to see you again."

"Nor did I, but I eventually took comfort in that. You being here means you are dead."

"I'm not." Finn shook his head and Akash's thick brow knotted.

"Then how are you here?"

"I'm—" Finn paused, holding his chin rigid against the instinctual urge to glance down at his hidden amulet. Remembering what he'd come here to do, he suddenly realized with a hollow ache in his chest that he'd have unlimited time to explain it all to Akash, later. "I'm looking for somebody."

Finn launched into his now well-rehearsed series of questions. Not even halfway through, Akash's sorrow-heavy eyes lightened with a flicker of recognition.

"You mean Monroe?"

"Yes!" Finn gasped, the sound catching in his throat as he reached forward to grip his friend's arms in eager hands. "Where is he?"

Akash lifted his eyes to look beyond Finn's shoulders, not seeming to mind how tightly his upper arms were being squeezed. Forcing a shrug against Finn's grip, he answered, "I dunno. He kinda comes and goes. But he always comes back, eventually. Sit, we will wait for him."

Finn shook his head, letting his hands fall back down to his sides.

"It's… urgent." He said tightly.

"Well, there's nothing I can really do."

And no sooner had Akash dissented, and a voice rang out from behind him.

"Finn? Is it really you? Thank the Guardians." Relief was apparent in the voice, but surprise was not.

Both of their heads lifted to see Monroe coming over a small hill, as if he'd been summoned out of nowhere at the mere mention of his name. Neither of them questioned that he was nowhere in sight a moment ago, nor did they question Monroe's visible lack of astonishment at the staggering improbability of Finn's presence. After all, there were far more important things at hand.

"Monroe," Finn ambled towards him, ripping the Soulseeker from around his neck and not even hesitating before shoving it into Monroe's hand. "You have to go back. You have to save Monica."

Monroe's mouth gaped slightly as he peered down at the small ivory coin shimmering in his palm. His face above his nose seemed to sag with tiredness, as if his features were too heavy to react to the surprise he should have felt. But, however arduous, the smallest sparkle of it flickered in his light blue eyes for just a second.

Finn noticed this with a twinge of suspicion that he pushed away in favor of the far graver situation at hand, Monica's safety. After all, with everything he'd seen, maybe this too was an illusion, an obstacle meant to make him doubt. He didn't know Monroe, nor could he afford to start questioning all of the potential possibilities for the obvious inconsistency. Monica needed him. That was enough.

The sparkle of surprise faded from Monroe's pale eyes, replaced by wariness.

"You… don't even know me. You would sacrifice yourself for me?"

"I don't have to know you. Monica needs you. That's all I need to know." When Monroe hesitated, Finn added, "I promised you I would keep her safe."

Monroe gave a small nod of gratitude, which creased his lips into the shadow of a smile.

"Thank you." He pressed the coin between his knuckles. "I can't tell you what it means to me that my sister has someone so important to her."

"She's important to me too."

Monroe's smile widened slightly with clear effort. Lifting the Soulseeker, he announced, "Well, no time to waste, right?"

Reaching for his arm before he could disappear, Finn called out, "Wait! When we first met, you asked a favor of me, and I kept it. Would you do the same for me, now?"

"Sure." Monroe looked a little caught off guard. "What do you need?"

"There's someone else who thinks Monica is important, too, and… she doesn't know what's happened. Would you please call her?"

Monroe hesitated only briefly before taking the slip of paper Finn now held out in his hand.

"That's it?" Monroe probed.

Finn's mouth wavered with an uncertain smile and he shook his head.

"I just need you to do one other thing for me when you get there."

"Of course." Monroe's easy agreement made Finn's tight expression relax with relief. "Whatever you need."

Chapter 45

Dahvi hadn't seen or heard what Finn had done, but after he never came out of Monica's cabin, Dahvi's retrospective analysis of the clues Finn had left him gave him enough to infer that Finn had done something stupid. What, he wasn't sure, but after two days of watching and still no Finn, Dahvi figured that he wasn't here anymore, especially after watching Rowan visit Monica and leave alone. If Finn *was* in there, there was no way Rowan wouldn't have noticed or been okay with the two remaining together. He was too cruel for that.

Dahvi briefly considered sneaking back into Monica's room to confirm whatever had happened, but the constant shifts back and forth were becoming too taxing, so he worried even one more might trap him there. And that wouldn't be good for anyone. He desperately wanted to be of more help but knew he couldn't do much in his current state, without sufficient enough rest to facilitate more shifts. So instead, Dahvi laid low as a spider for several days, recuperating and gathering any potentially useful information he overheard from the common areas of the ship.

At one point, he *had* followed Rowan to observe the man in charge for any weaknesses, only to be denied access by another layer of wards around his personal chambers. These were so airtight that not even a gnat could squeeze in without the key spell. But, even forced to remain outside, Dahvi had noticed some inconsistencies in hanging out around Rowan's personal quarters. He didn't imagine that, even such a large ship would have cabins or personal quarters with more than one exit, and yet, sometimes he saw Rowan coming and never going, or reemerging from the room long, *long* after he'd last entered… almost as if he was coming from somewhere else. Suspicious, Dahvi did his best to inspect the connectivity of passages in the ship, but found no clear answer for this, at least from the outside of Rowan's personal quarters.

Still, it was curious enough to prompt Dahvi to take a thorough inventory of the rest of the ship's layout. After all, he might discover something that could prove useful in an escape plan. This was how he discovered what must've been Finn's room, which was now empty. Though he'd only seen it in passing, Dahvi recognized the notebook on the nightstand. And beside it, were three pieces of paper, each folded inward on themselves and stacked in such a way that he was unable to glimpse their contents as a spider. They wouldn't have been so interesting had he not noticed his name written on one of the corners poking out of the stack.

He didn't like snooping on someone close to him, but with Finn gone and a clear indication that something here had been left for him, Dahvi knew he'd feel guilty leaving Finn's intentional messages unread. Finn *wanted* him to read this, perhaps even hoped that he would. Dahvi almost felt like he owed it to Finn to know.

Feeling relatively safe in the closed confinement of Finn's empty room, Dahvi let himself shift from spider back to man, taking a moment to stretch before turning to analyze the letters. After several days as a spider, it was gratifying to be able to stretch the muscles of a human body again. Though bigger shapes were more taxing to maintain until each was well practiced, they were far more comfortable than the small ones. Beyond that, he welcomed the safe feeling of comfort that this familiar form returned to him, even without the horse half he preferred to include when it was feasible. But hooves on a ship were *not* a great idea.

Sighing, Dahvi stooped over the table, carefully taking up the first tri-folded sheet in gentle fingertips. Turning it over, he saw that the names written in the upper left corner on its back read, *Mom and Grandad.* Obviously, this one wasn't meant for him. Laying it aside, he gave a cursory glance to the second, which was addressed to Celene, before shuffling it aside by the first. A spark flared in his chest upon seeing his name scrawled hurriedly in the same corresponding corner on the third sheet. But before he opened it, his eyes fell to the fourth and final page, still sitting on the table. It was addressed to Monica.

The paper fluttered crisply at his touch as he bent back the folds. His gaze swept down the body of text, only a few paragraphs long but littered with sentimental words with private meanings that leapt off the page to prick his eyes with tears before he'd even read it. It was a goodbye letter. Whatever he'd done, Finn hadn't intended to come back.

Dahvi swallowed, his jaw tightening in resentment as he tried to calm his blurring vision on that first line.

Dahvi, thank you for helping me find my independence, both with the ability to defend myself in combat, as well as in pursuing the dreams within my own heart.

Before he could continue, the words melted behind a screen of tears that Dahvi did his best to choke back, even if there was no one here to see him crying. They weren't sad tears, not entirely. Part of it was anger at Finn for not saying a proper goodbye or telling him the truth and giving him a chance to talk him out of it. But also, at himself, because he knew that his actions, even if forgiven since he had had no choice, made him feel like he'd built that wall that had kept Finn from trusting him with those things. He had anticipated hurting Finn in order to complete the tasks Rowan had forced on him in exchange for his family's safety, but he'd never thought *he'd* be the one who contributed to Finn's final demise. Despite what denial would've comforted him to believe, he knew he had had a hand in convincing Finn to honor what his heart had told him to do, no matter how stupid.

And now look at what's happened. He thought, trying hard not to crumple the letter in his tense fingers. *I'm the stupid one. I betrayed the most honest heart I've ever met.*

Sniffling, Dahvi tried to compose himself, lifting his eyes to the next line of the letter. Finn wouldn't want to see him crying. Even though a letter wasn't what Dahvi would've preferred, he realized that it signaled that Finn had cared enough to say goodbye at all, and that meant something. He needed to know what it meant. No matter how hard it was to read, he needed to finish it.

But before he could read so much as another word, a small click sounded behind him. A mix of hope and dread shot up his spine. His whole body tensed, and before he could shift out of sight, the door squealed open.

He began to turn around but was stopped by the thick command of a male voice he did not recognize.

"Stop. Don't move."

It wasn't Rowan's voice. Though he'd only heard it a few times, Rowan's voice wasn't the kind he would forget. It was the kind of voice that would haunt him, hanging from the corners of all of his recent nightmares to torment him with what he'd done.

The air hummed with the ominous sound of magic swelling behind him, the crackling of either lightning or of flame gathering at the man's fingertips. Dahvi's hands unfurled to show that his fingers were empty, as much as possible without dropping the letter.

"I'm unarmed," he announced.

A pause. Perhaps the man was considering whether to trust his word, or inquire whether Dahvi had any magic of his own? But, when the voice came again, there was a slight humor to it.

"I know." The voice sounded almost pleased.

"Then wh—"

"Don't move, I said." He repeated with a threatening sizzle that was definitely fire.

Dahvi did as he was told. His eyes fixed on the bookshelf beside him, lingering on the tiny glimmer of sunlight he could see between the window and its edge. He considered if he could shift fast enough into a fly to dart out of it, but then again, being that the outermost edge of the ship was warded, it was likely that even the crack in the window would deny him. Not to mention that doing so would force him to leave the rest of Finn's letter behind, *unread*, which was hardly something he wanted to do. Besides, it wouldn't take much fire to kill a fly.

"What've you got there?" The voice asked.

"What does it look like?" Dahvi asked honestly, his voice without the challenging edge of sarcasm that the answer could've held if he'd wished it. "A letter." And then, on impulse, Dahvi added, "There's one here for Monica, too."

He immediately winced, regretting having said such a thing, even if the distraction might have bought him time, or earned him any favor with this unseen adversary. Now, what if they took it away? What if Monica never saw her goodbye, or worse, they held it over her head and butchered it to make it say what *they* wanted, rather than what Finn had intended? It's not like Monica could hate Dahvi any more than she already did, could she?

But, to his surprise, the man seemed uninterested.

To be fair, Dahvi didn't know that this man was an adversary. It seemed likely, being on a ship entirely populated with prisoners and wielder guards. But the man hadn't attacked yet, which most wielders would have already done. Few underlings had the wit or the desire to ask questions before they struck. Instead, this man asked, "What are you doing in here?"

"I hid under the—"

"Don't lie," the man interrupted. "I know how you got in. I asked what you're doing."

Dahvi's shoulders tensed. He knew how Dahvi had gotten in? Surely, he hadn't been *that* careless, shifting just now, had he? And after so long of being so careful. Even when they were blackmailing him for his involvement with Finn and Monica, he'd still managed to keep his abilities secret from The Enclave. Now, knowing what he could do, they'd never let him go.

"You saw how I got in," Dahvi tested hesitantly, "and you care more about me reading some letter?"

"You're not a wielder, are you?" The man asked, sounding defensive.

"No. Are you?"

Though he knew the answer, the sound of crackling fire had quelled, and the air now smelled lightly of smoke.

"Not *his*," the man replied, the words touched with a hint of disdain.

"Then who are you?" Dahvi dared to ask, stopping as soon as the man hissed another warning for Dahvi *not* to turn around.

Okay... Even if he's not my enemy, he doesn't want me to know who he is. Dahvi reasoned before asking instead, "If you're not one of Rowan's men, what are *you* doing in here?"

"Give me that letter," he said in lieu of a clear answer. "The one for Monica."

Dahvi drew in a pensive breath but did as he was told, lifting the last letter and holding it back over one shoulder without ever turning around. Behind him, footsteps shuffled forwards, creating two muted wooden *thunks* before they muffled into the carpet underfoot. The letter swished in the air as it was snatched from his fingers, rustling for only a few seconds more. "And the others."

"This one's mine!" Dahvi protested sharply.

"The others on the table." The man clarified, pacifying Dahvi into wordless acquiescence.

He snatched the letters and drew back, falling silent. When the man made no more demands, Dahvi ventured, "So, what happens now?"

"Now, you're going to do something for me."

There it is. Dahvi let out a sigh, almost disappointed for foreseeing the consequences of his misstep. To be fair, it would've been worse if his slip had been in front of one of Rowan's men, but still, it was seeming like *this* one didn't want to let him go free and easy, either.

"What did you have in mind?" Dahvi asked, his newly compliant tone catching the man off guard for just long enough for Dahvi to leap into the air and whirl on him.

Even unarmed, Dahvi had enough years of combat training to not be entirely defenseless. And, it would've worked, too, had the man not cast a spell causing Dahvi's floating form to freeze in place before he could bring his flat hand chopping down into the man's shoulder.

Panic coursed through Dahvi as he found himself suspended, entirely unable to move. He couldn't blink. He couldn't even breathe, not that he seemed to need to, but still. His focus settled on the man before him, who was holding an outstretched hand gloved in gold illumination that was feeding into the barrier holding Dahvi aloft. The man's hair was dark and his face was young, but beyond that, his features blurred into obscurity. Dahvi wasn't sure if that, itself, was a spell, or merely a side effect of looking out through the warbling wall of magical arrest.

From inside the spell, the man on the outside seemed to move at double speed. He made a quick gesture that funneled the sphere of magic into a rippling rope that quickly fed around Dahvi's arms, tying them together before setting him gently down on the floor. Before Dahvi's gaze could lift, the rope coiled around his eyes, continuing to obstruct him from taking in the man's identity, but not muffling his sight completely. Echoes of movement ghosted across his vision, which now saw everything in the haziest tones of yellow and showed him the man coming to crouch before him.

"That wasn't very kind," the man chided with a hard tone that was surprisingly devoid of cruelty or anger. "I wasn't going to hurt you."

"I didn't know that." Dahvi protested, finding himself unable to squirm when he tried. "I *don't* know that."

"I won't hurt you," the man repeated darkly. "But since you've shown an inclination towards mistrust, I worry it would be unwise to work together without some compulsion to ensure your compliance."

"Work together?" Dahvi sputtered. "I don't even know who you are, or what it is you want from me! And I *don't* know if I can trust you. After all, why would I? If I'm found, I'm a prisoner on a warded Enclave ship."

The man tilted his head to the side, as if in agreement. "You've always been a prisoner. Being unknown only gave you the smallest of freedoms. But their magic still made you prisoner, just as it has with me."

"What do you mean?" Dahvi barely got out the last word before a rope of incandescent magic snaked into his mouth, coiling down into his throat as a gag.

He choked on it for an uncomfortable moment, swallowing hard against the lump it made in his throat. Just as quickly, it dissolved, but a heavy sensation in his stomach prickled with the fear that it wasn't gone, just misplaced.

The man remained crouched over him for a long moment before he finally stood, letting the ropes fall away from Dahvi's eyes and body with a fanning curl of his fingers. Dahvi looked up at him in perplexity, too stunned to be frightened.

"There," the man proclaimed with an unreadable expression. "Now I can trust you."

A question burbled up in Dahvi's throat, *what did you do to me?* But before he could speak it, the muscles in his neck clamped down and suffocated it. Instead, he answered with a serene obeisance that barely made his head move at all.

Even though the magic's grasp had gone from around him, Dahvi couldn't move his body. His mind screamed the commands, but none of his muscles would obey. Unbidden, his body rose to stand, leaving him stunned at the ease of the movement, confirming that he was no longer the one giving the commands for it to move. Worse still, Dahvi felt the itch of something tangled writing inside of him, something that made his mind ache and his consciousness begin to blur at the edges. Something that wasn't his.

Who are you? He thought, trying to study the man's face with traitorous eyes that could only look away. Compulsion magic was rare and incredibly difficult to master, with good reason, yet this man had exerted almost no visible effort with the implementation of a spell that wouldn't even let Dahvi *attempt* to resist.

The man lifted one of his hands, now calm without any sparks or light crackling at his fingertips and laid his palm down on one of Dahvi's shoulders. Leaning forward, he spoke in a whisper like one might use when confiding in a friend.

"I have some other business to attend to, but I trust you aren't going to get into any trouble?" The casual lilt of the phrase molded it into more of a question than a command, but Dahvi felt the tingle of compulsion just the same. He nodded.

"Good. Stay here, and I will return for you when I'm ready. In the meantime, don't fight it. The experience will be far more comfortable for you if you let it happen."

A shiver traced Dahvi's body when the sudden warmth of the hand lifted from his shoulder, and the man disappeared, his footsteps echoing only briefly down the hallway as he left. He didn't even wait to see if Dahvi would obey. To be fair, he didn't need to, but his instruction had been so vague that even though the itch to comply was rising with each second, it wasn't forceful enough to cause much urgency, yet.

Dahvi puzzled as to what to make of that interaction, knowing better than to trust a man who would use magic to bend someone to his will. But then again, Dahvi *had* tried to attack him. So, it *was* fair, since the man didn't know if he could trust Dahvi either. But still, something didn't feel right about it. How could someone unassociated with Rowan, with The Enclave, and still have magic that strong, be here? And why? Perhaps he had someone he wanted to save, just like Dahvi? If that were true, it made the comment about *working together* make a lot more sense. Dahvi still didn't trust him, but now, he didn't have a choice. Funny the way that always seemed to be his fate.

Dahvi was tired of not having a choice.

Chapter 46

Monica awoke on the morning of the third day to her door opening again. Even the soft click of the lock and the gradual, courteous inching open of the door made her flinch awake, immediately switching into a defensive alertness.

Had she been awake enough to realize, she would have seen that this arrival wasn't like Rowan's previous intrusion, which, though it hadn't been loud or forceful, also hadn't been cautious. Even when the wielders who brought her food came, it was with no reserve or hesitation.

Monica craned her neck to look, and the door fanned open, revealing a familiar figure with a wide stance standing unapologetically behind it, obviously unconcerned at the prospect of being seen by anyone outside the room.

Monica leapt from the bed in surprise, gasping against a lump rising in her throat. If her eyes hadn't felt so suddenly dry with guarded disbelief, the sight would have brought tears stinging to the surface.

"Monster?" Monica gasped, her voice nearly abandoning her in her incredulity. "It can't be you. I must still be asleep. I'm dreaming."

She lifted her arms in front of her, briefly taking her gaze from her visitor to stare at her flexing fingers. This didn't *feel* like a dream. It was sharper than the hazy edges that dreams usually carried, not to mention that the emotions were crisper too, even as her denial tried to suppress them.

This couldn't be real. If it was, it meant that what Finn had done was also real, and she wasn't sure she could bear the thought of his loss not being a cruel illusion, even with the mercy of a trade.

Monroe swallowed, greeting her with a guilty shake of his head that she didn't understand.

"No, Mo, you're not dreaming. It's really me."

Monica's hands fell to her lap and she allowed herself to take him in.

He looked just as he had in Enderfel, if perhaps less faded. The gray had gone from his pale complexion, and the weariness had lifted slightly from beneath his pale eyes. His hair was still a mess, overgrown and mostly escaping the topknot he usually wore. His chin was shadowed with more stubble than she'd ever seen on him. He *actually* looked like a man. The remains of the boyish charm she remembered were gone now and hidden beneath a brow set with somber confession.

Monroe's clothes were dusty with ash, his jeans fraying at the bottom, making her wonder what he had gone through in their time apart. On his chest glittered an ivory coin, hanging from twine braided with a scattering of tiny gold beads that authenticated his presence. The Soulseeker. He *was* real.

Her heart squeezed, mortified to find that she was anything other than purely happy at the confirmation that the one thing she had wanted most had finally come to be.

"You don't look happy to see me. I'm real. Your waiting and pain are finally over."

His chin dipped to rest against his chest, looking down at the Soulseeker as he lifted it with gentle fingers and a pleading, bittersweet smile.

That broke her. She sniffled, her vision blurring behind a hot screen of tears as she looked away.

"I don't disbelieve that now. And I *am* happy to see you," she paused, tempting just enough of an upward glance to see whether or not he looked like he believed her, because she wasn't sure if she believed the second part herself now, but she still couldn't see him through her sorrow, "but your return came at such a cost."

His jaw set, lowering in a sagely nod of respect and acknowledgment.

"I'm glad he was with you." Monroe finally said. His hand dove into his leather jacket, interrupting the solemn quiet with a brief rustling before it emerged clutching a folded sheet of lined paper. "Not that I think it will make the cost any less unavoidable, I have something to give you.

Monica lifted her head hopefully. "Wh-what is it?"

"A letter… from Finn."

Despite wanting to, when Monica's hand rose to reach for the letter, it trembled so much that she could barely keep it aloft. Seeing this, Monroe approached and placed it in her hand. Her fingers closed around it, hugging it to her chest.

"What does it say?"

Monroe only shook his head to indicate that he hadn't read it. "That isn't for me to know."

"How did Finn look when you saw him?"

"Determined. Insistent, even. He would barely tell me anything, set on not wasting any time before he commanded me to come."

"He *commanded* you?" Monica asked with a sad smile.

That sounded like Finn all right. Despite her own opinions of him, he always *did* manage to surprise her with how strong and courageous he could be when it counted most. The thought sparked a flicker of gratitude in her chest and her attention returned to the letter. It unfolded easily in spite of its stiff creases, welcoming her into lines of messy, boyish script. Each word selected made his voice leap off the page, playing out as clearly in her mind as though he was standing before her, reading it aloud.

Monica,

I want you to know that I don't regret it. I knew from the moment I overheard you telling Celene what it would take to use the Soulseeker in order to get Monroe back, that I needed to be the one to do it. And I decided then that I needed *to do it. For you. For Vhalta. But funny enough, also for me. Because even though trading places with your brother sounds like I'm giving up my life, I'm actually making a difference, and that's all I've ever wanted. Because of me, maybe you'll actually have a chance to take down The Enclave and give so many people a better life, including yourself. I hope so.*

I don't regret not telling you, because I knew that if I did, you'd only try to stop me. And I don't regret it, because it also means that this is and always was one hundred percent my choice. You didn't know, so it couldn't be your fault. And don't you dare blame yourself for my choice, especially one that I don't regret.

She paused only briefly, realizing that Finn had written this letter before he had seen her, and that he had fully planned on chickening out. Though seeing him leave using the Soulseeker had been traumatic, it would've been worse never seeing it and having Rowan able to use the state of his unknown location and well-being to torment her. At least she knew. She was grateful he had been able to tell her. She resumed reading before she lost the strength to start again.

I don't regret not telling you goodbye to your face, because even though I won't get a chance to say with words all that you mean to me, and to thank you for everything you've done for me, I know hearing those things, only for me to leave, would hurt you more. And the last thing I want to do is cause you any more pain. You've lost enough. I don't want you to feel like you're losing me, too. Because you're not. It's just a trade. And just because I'm not physically there, doesn't mean I'm not with you. Even though our time together was short, I'll always remember you, just like I know you'll remember me.

The only thing I regret is leaving you with a final favor to me. I hate to ask it of you, especially since I know how mad she'll be, but I can't go knowing that my mom and grandad are left without goodbyes. So, no matter what else happens, please promise you'll get their letter to them, too. It's fine if it's not right away, since I know you have The Enclave overthrow and a world to save first, so 'eventually' is fine. That way, once it is done, I'll have absolutely nothing to regret.

Thank you for showing me everything my life was meant to be. Thank you for helping me be courageous and strong, even when I felt lost and useless. Thank you for helping me make a difference.

I know it'll be hard, but please try to not regret meeting me. Because I know I'll never regret meeting you and doing everything we did, because it ended with me making another best friend. And together or apart, I'll always think of you that way, Monica, my best friend. Thank you.

-Finn

Numb with denial, Monica let the letter flutter to the ground. Her eyes stung as her focus lifted to Monroe standing before her, now within an arm's length. In his hand were two other folded slips of paper, one labeled *Mom and Grandad,* and the other addressed to Celene.

He offered it to her, but instead, she rushed to embrace him, burying her face into his chest before exploding into tears.

Monroe wrapped his strong arms around her, cradling her as she sobbed. She found some comfort in the lingering smell of incense on him, even though she was sure he couldn't have been performing summonings from Enderfel. She clung to the familiarity of him; something she once thought an impossibility to ever get to do again.

She should've been afraid of how loud she was wailing, of it attracting unwanted attention, but Monroe did nothing to stop her. Both of them knew that his magic was enough to protect them, and that it was only a matter of time before the inevitable confrontation to overtake the ship and its wards would come, whether they were ready or not. The tide of time would carry them swiftly in that direction soon enough. The least it could do was let her cry.

And she needed it. Losing Finn was the end of her resilience. Even though she'd gotten the one thing that she had always been holding on for, she couldn't be strong anymore. At least, that's what she thought now. If only she knew what awaited her, the limits she had yet to be pushed to, she'd know how right Maal had been when he'd said, *loss is agony, but it is also where we find our greatest strengths.*

The agony of losing Finn was only just beginning, but so was the newest strength that would come from it. Monica just didn't know it yet.

Author Bio:

Emily Lankow discovered her passion for writing in elementary school, when she entered a young authors' contest. Her short story placed tenth in the state, illustrating the power stories have to reach and affect total strangers. As an avid reader, the idea of writing stories others could escape into and fall in love with has fueled Emily's imagination ever since.

Now, Emily is a self-proclaimed Jack-of-all-trades in all things creative. When she isn't writing, she enjoys painting with acrylics and watercolors, drawing, and crafting sculptures, ball-jointed dolls, and jewelry, as well as making miniatures using whatever materials she can get her hands on.

Emily also enjoys spending time with her husband and their three cats, drinking tea, eating chocolate, doing yoga, and appreciating the many little things that brighten her life.

If you enjoyed this book or any of her work, Emily would appreciate it if you left a review on Amazon, Goodreads, or social media.

Connect with Emily Lankow at:

www.emilylankow.com
facebook.com/AuthorEmilyLankow
instagram.com/author.emilylankow

www.ingramcontent.com/pod-product-compliance
Lightning Source LLC
LaVergne TN
LVHW050914080826
845145LV00001B/80

* 9 7 8 1 9 6 1 9 5 8 0 2 9 *